FROM UKRAINE TO AMERICA:

STORIES MY FATHER NEVER TOLD ME

VOLUME 1

Barbara Grill

Paperback ISBN: 978-1-917116-49-7

Hardcover ISBN:978-1-917116-50-3

Dedication

To Simon Swaczy

Acknowledgment

Thanks to everyone and anyone who put up with me, listening to endless conversation about this book, but specially my daughter, Laura Grill.

About the Author

Barbara Grill was born and raised in Chicago. She turned down a four-year scholarship to a teacher's college and began her life's adventure traveling the United States for several years, working alongside her husband. She loved traveling the backroads and highways of the United States. After raising two daughters, she returned to school, eventually earning two Master's degrees in Urban Planning and Public Administration from Florida State University.

Table of Content

Poignancy in human suffering is eternal and ever present.

World without end.

Amen

6-1-2021

Introduction

Jack and his daughter stood motionless, gazing seaward. Fluttering birds playfully skipped across the water, swooping up against the crystal blue sky before diving downward for breakfast again. Father and daughter were silent, both immersed in their thoughts. The young girl didn't think it unusual that her father stood saying nothing as she was familiar with his quiet, reflective ways. Had she known his thoughts that day, her life may have taken a different path, most assuredly turning out differently. But, there is no going back or starting over in life, changing this or that decision, or perhaps avoiding making one. This was not about rectifying bad choices but revealing truths to those dearest to him. His children were aware of his secretiveness to the point of joking about it. From their earliest years, the joke was that someone had turned over a rock, and there was Jack.

It is inconceivable that Jack, standing quietly for a long time, wouldn't reflect on those days and times long ago in that far-off land. He was thinking about his troubled homeland, a land of milk and honey with its unimaginable contrasts between misery, relentless human suffering, and the purest, sweetest natural beauty. On that warm summer day, standing in Battery Park in New York City, it must have seemed miraculous to him that his family had escaped.

Did he think about how that place molded him, his parents, and his brothers? Did he consider taking this young girl into his confidence, throwing off his yoke of secrecy, and unburdening himself by telling her about those fearful times? Did he think for one moment that his life could be different by committing this one simple act? That day, looking out over the harbor, Jack let slip away the perfect opportunity to tell his sixteen-year-old daughter about his former life. He did not speak the truth to her – not that day or any other for the rest of his life. He carried his secrets to his grave, lashing out in violent fits of uncontrollable anger from time to time as if those outbursts were the only way to release his inner turmoil.

What about Jack's daughter? What were her thoughts staring out toward the Statue of Liberty and beyond to the horizon? She stood patiently, intuitively knowing that it was important not to hurry or interrupt her father while at the same time not concerned about him or why he was there, or what he was thinking. She didn't ask one question except perhaps about the statue itself. Perplexed by the color, she asked herself why the statue was such an odd shade of green.

That day with her father has remained in her memory all her life. She always remembered the hurried walk from the subway to the Battery along narrow sidewalks and cross streets. Crossing Church Street, he pulled her along, almost racing down the sidewalk past huge gray-colored buildings, barely checking for traffic as he crossed the narrow streets of Lower Manhattan. She recalled seeing him standing, for a long time, at the water's edge and realized many years later he had never appeared so peaceful. Oh, if she had known! Several times over the years, in conversations with family and friends, she fell woefully short trying to describe him that day. Her words never adequately described the poignancy of those precious moments. Then one day, many years later, she received a telephone call from her mother. Her father was now a very old man who had Alzheimer's disease within a few years of dying. She barely heard her mother describing a telephone conversation with her brother. A few minutes later, she hung up the phone. Dazed and in a whirl, she only remembered her mother saying her father was not born in the United States. Rather, he was Ukrainian, born in a place called Galicia. How could this be? Pa had always said that he was Austrian. After examining maps and reading the map section of the family encyclopedia, she eventually located Galicia in Eastern Europe.

She was upset and confused, realizing there would be no answers because no one could question her father, as the ravages of his illness had left him unable to comprehend and speak. Anyway, there was no time to take up a search for her father's family. Her cousin, Dorothy, ten years older than she, had known her father and his family and sent a hand-drawn pencil sketch of part of a map showing Bukaczowce and copies of a few grainy photographs. Another cousin sent a copy of a passenger ship manifest. She was confused because it seemed that the family had a different surname than her father, and the photos were taken during an era that seemed long ago strange and alien.

Looking out toward the horizon, Jack slipped back in time to a life long ago, before his travels, before he knew anything about the world outside his small village when he was about to begin his life's journey – one beyond anything that he ever could have imagined.

PART ONE

Chapter 1

April 22, 1891

On a dark, rainy, moonless morning, Szymon Swaczy and his cousin, Theo Kubida, stood shivering and bracing themselves against the cold wind as they awaited the train's arrival. "Jesus, it's so damned cold out here."

Theo scowled. "Dark, too."

Szymon began walking up the tracks as if trying to shorten the wait by meeting the southbound train en route to Czernowitz. Straining to see up the tracks, he couldn't make out train lights, so after a few minutes, he gave up and headed back. As he approached the station, Szymon heard someone yelling at him from across the road.

"Hey! Hey! Hold up."

"Who's there?"

"I thought I was going to miss the train! It's Joe Korlaszcz from Czahrow.

Are you going to Stanislau?"

"Oh, yes, you must be going there, too."

They stood under one of the kerosene lanterns lining the tracks near the station. Joe was panting heavily. Szymon was about to ask what was wrong with him when they suddenly heard a commotion from the warehouse south of the train station.

Through the mist and drizzle, they could make out flames climbing toward the top of the structure. Within seconds Szymon and Joe reached the fire. Theo, who had been inside the station, was already attempting to lead a horse, still harnessed to a cart, away from the flames. Two oil drums had fallen from the cart onto the ground. Nearby lay a man writhing in pain, his clothes and boots on fire. Szymon and Joe tried to extinguish the flames around him to no avail. The early morning crew came running from all directions and dragged the man away while attempting to beat out the flames with tarpaulins, jackets, and their gloved hands. The man's screams frightened Szymon, who stood immobilized, staring into his terrified eyes. Men began frantically rolling the man across the wet ground and through rain puddles. Joe Korlaszcz knelt beside him and began praying. As Joe recited the rosary, he pressed his rosary into the suffering man's hand. While the flames were extinguished, the injured man was slid onto a board and carried away into the warehouse. Szymon and Theo saw that the buildings were not in any real danger. The roof over a shed next to the warehouse had already collapsed but posed no danger to other structures. No one noticed a horse and cart holding a single kerosene drum.

It was Jerzy's job to hitch the mule to the cart to haul drums of kerosene around the base and to fill the kerosene lanterns which hung along the train platform before the morning crew arrived each day. But Jerzy had been drinking all night and got drunk. He stood on the back of the cart, carelessly reached for the lantern at the end of the platform, and allowed the lantern to slip through his wet hands, fall to the ground, and start the initial fire. But the previous night, Jerzy hitched a horse to the cart rather than the mule. A mule never rears up on its hind legs. At that moment, the horse reared, tilting the cart to one side. The drum fell over, and kerosene began splashing onto the ground, perilously close to the remaining fire. Szymon took the reins while Theo mounted the frightened animal. Theo guided the horse, circling the buildings and heading for the train station gates onto the hard road and back again until the horse appeared to lose fear. It took several minutes, but they were able to get the situation under control.

"What a miserable morning," Joe remarked.

"You don't live in town, do you?"

After a long pause, Joe shook his head and said, "No, I live off Czahrow Road, about three miles from here. There wasn't anyone to take me to town, so my satchel is soaked from the rain."

They rode toward the warehouse where the morning crew had joined in to clear the debris and temporarily repair the fire-damaged shed. Theo dismounted and led the horse away. Another heavy rain began to pour down upon them.

Theo called out for Szymon and Joe inside the station, "C'mon, C'mon. Get out of the rain and come back inside."

They were too upset to sit, but standing outside in the rain didn't help them either. Joe Korlaszcz went off to check on Jerzy Krawczyk while Szymon and Theo stood by the door, opening it every few minutes to check for the train. Inside the station was a waiting room with a coal stove in the middle and a few chairs scattered around in a haphazard manner. They were afraid they would miss the train if they walked away from the station. There was no sense asking the station master if he knew anything about the train's arrival, but Theo went to the window anyway.

"That train has been rescheduled to arrive fifteen minutes later than last month's schedule," remarked Mr. Raab, the homely, old, balding station manager grinning slyly at him.

Szymon thought, "Why the hell didn't he tell us sooner?"

He looked helplessly at Mr. Raab, who he realized wouldn't offer any more information. They shrugged and walked outside again.

Joe came over to them. He was somber. "Jerzy isn't going to make it."

"What do you mean?" asked Szymon.

"He had a heart attack and isn't breathing."

"Oh, Jeez!"

The clock on a shelf behind Mr. Raab read 5:45. They stood outside, not saying anything. Time seemed like it would never pass. Squinting through the small window into the dimly lit station, Szymon strained to see the clock again. "It's already 5:55." silence fell over the three young men again, each drifting away into his thoughts, until Theo cursed softly, "I'm freezing. Let's go back to the station. That God damned train is always late."

Once more, Szymon strained to see through the morning drizzle, but he thought he saw lights in the distance this time. "Wait a few more minutes."

All three stared up the tracks. Joe was the first to notice the train slowly approaching the terminal. He could feel the locomotive's vibration under his feet as it moved along the tracks. The familiar rumble of the oncoming train and the announcement of its arrival was a relief for the young men. They hurried into the station, picked up their meager belongings, waved goodbye to Agent Raab, and started out the door.

"Good luck, boys," yelled Mr. Raab. "I'll tell your parents that you got off alright." He laughed sarcastically and said, "Follow orders and keep your noses clean."

Szymon winced, smiled nervously, and filed out the door, passing the train conductor. He bristled at Mr. Raab's remark, implying he was still too young to care for himself. He didn't need Mr. Raab to report to his parents. Theo's shabby cardboard suitcase banged against the conductor. He jerked, and Szymon was immediately brought back to the present when he heard the conductor, "Watch it, son, keep that God damned filthy thing next to you." His voice was gruff, and he looked like a defeated man who was sick of life. "Wait for me next to the door of the second coach," he barked.

Once again, they stood bracing themselves against the cold wind.

"Damn! Christ, help us."

"Watch it, Theo," said Joe, crossing himself.

They stood grumbling under their breath. Theo told Joe to mind his own business; Joe ignored the remark. They continued complaining about the weather and were worried about where they would go once they arrived in Stanislau.

"This isn't starting out good, but maybe things will go better now," said Joe.

Just then, the conductor walked out the door, followed by another man wearing an Austrian Army uniform.

"What's this? Where did he come from?" Before he finished his thought, Szymon wondered if the soldier may have been in the station all along. "Probably spying on us," he thought, instantly disliking this man.

"Hurry up, boys. Let's go; we're running late," the conductor yelled.

The five boarded immediately, the train horn honked, and the three boys jerked backward as the wheels began rolling along the track away from town. Szymon took a long, final look out the train window, watching his hometown fade away ever so slowly into the distance, past familiar businesses, stables, and a blacksmith's shop. The train passed through the outskirts of town, past large structures, the chimneys of the kilns at the brickworks, the sheds where coal was stored, and the sawmill where mountains of timber were stacked, waiting to be sawed into boards for constructing buildings for various purposes. All signs of life disappeared as the train made the broad sweep to the east before heading south again. As the train made the turn, he saw new telegraph poles following the tracks, hung with wires that mysteriously carried communications between railroad stations. Then, a barren winter scene lay in all directions, a scene of rolling countryside with fields lying fallow waiting for spring planting.

He glanced at the sergeant, who told them his name was Sergeant William Schoeppler. He spoke with a heavy German accent. Szymon felt intimidated, and his stomach churned. He suspected that Theo and Joe had the same unpleasant feeling. Schoeppler, a big man, only said a little once the train was underway. The three young men sat quietly with about twenty others who had boarded before them, all of whom appeared to be scared, afraid to speak. About ten miles from Bukaczowce, the train rattled to a stop in Halych. Schoeppler left the train. He escorted eight more young men, including Szymon's cousin,

Joannes, onboard a few minutes later. Eleven miles further south, another five boarded. All but a few onboard were Ruthenian young men, sitting motionless in the coach, staring straight ahead, wearing almost identical, uneasy expressions. They were unsophisticated young men, hardly boys, but not yet men. For most, this trip to Stanislau was not their first venture alone away from home, but this time it was different. Inside the coach, the scene was almost comical, but Schoeppler sat unamused, wearing a dull expression, failing to see the humor in these young men's terrified faces. He had been at this for too long.

The train crept along, swaying from side to side. The tracks badly needed repair, so it was impossible to travel faster than the allowable minimum speed limit for fear of jumping off the tracks. As villages and towns appeared closer together, many dilapidated buildings also appeared up against the tracks. The scene broke the spell of fear that had gripped everyone in the coach except Schoeppler. Szymon glanced around and saw the boys grinning, whispering to each other, and pointing out the windows. He could see the excitement in their eyes. Then, the train rolled along faster on smoother tracks into the city but slowed again upon nearing the station. As it came to a stop, Schoeppler jumped to his feet, speaking loud with a staccato German accent.

"Gather your stuff, and file out single file down the steps, stand in rows of two. Remain at attention when you are all off the train."

A pang of fear gripped them again. Schoeppler repeated himself, in German this time, and barked orders to maintain a formation two abreast and to follow him to the training center. Some large buildings lay ahead, but arriving at a grassy field took only six to eight minutes. The sign on an old two-story building read Stanislau 58th Infantry Training Center.

"Take 10 minutes. Toilets are on your left."

The men fell into a single-file line and walked down a dimly lit hallway where they were told to undress.

"Oh, no!" One of the men groaned. Szymon suspected that the moan was meant to be a futile protest against the thought of standing bare assed naked in front of God and all these strangers. Two men, maybe a doctor and his assistant, sat watching the new recruits in a large, well-lit room. No one spoke, and there were no new orders as the line moved slowly. It was cold in this building, and the temperature outside hovered around 45 degrees. Szymon watched the two men. While his assistant measured and recorded the height and weight of each man, the doctor examined each man's ears, eyes, throat, and genitals, listened to his heart, and probed and poked different parts of his body.

Szymon figured that each examination took at most seven or eight minutes. There were still 40 ahead of him. "I'll be here all day," he thought.

Standing there, Szymon was overwhelmed by

strange, unfamiliar feelings of loneliness. How could he already miss home? He was thinking about what he would be doing if he were there. He tried to distract himself from feeling uncomfortably cold. He shook off his loneliness just as a second doctor walked in and pulled up another stool. He instructed the men at the end of the line to step forward. From there on, the line moved more quickly, and finally, he was only two men from being examined.

Szymon heard a voice saying, "Theodorus Kubida!"

As Theo stepped forward, the other man called, "Szymon Swaczy."

"Name?"

"Szymon Swaczy, sir!"

Following the medical examinations, there was a series of orders.

March to the induction center to be sworn in and receive dog tags. Be ready at 10 a.m. Pick up uniforms. March to the bathroom. Line up two abreast. Line up two abreast. Line up two abreast. And so it went; it was all a blur.

Szymon began to wonder, "Do we march everywhere?"

"After receiving assignments, prepare to begin your first full day in the Austro-Hungarian Army."

About four that afternoon, as the men lined up in formation for the ninth or tenth time that day, Sergeant Schoeppler broke the platoon into four squads of twelve men each, with Luc Slobodianyk, Theo Kubida, Joannes Hanchyk, and Stephan Katanyk as squad leaders. Luc was a tall, lanky kid nearly six feet tall who bore the appearance of a born leader. Szymon looked around and realized that all of the chosen men were about the same height – the tallest men in the platoon.

"They were about six feet," Szymon thought. "Each is blond and blue-eyed, just like me." He wondered why these four were chosen for squad leaders. Except for their height, what else did they have in common?

The men fell into formation, two abreast with Schoeppler leading. This time they marched back to their barracks. He halted the line and told them to fall into a formation of four abreast and remain at attention. Schoeppler began reading from a notebook. An hour later, with the sun descending in the western sky, Schoeppler stopped and looked around.

"Are you paying attention?" he growled. "I'm warning you, bastards, not to sleep through this because you will be asked questions," he barked in his thick German accent.

Szymon snapped out of his daydream and focused on Schoeppler's words. "What did he say?"

Then Schoeppler called out, "Swaczy! What time will bugle sound for wake up tomorrow morning?"

"At 5:30 and lights out at 8:30, sir," Szymon shouted.

Schoeppler looked irritated and more than a tad

confused. He knew that Swaczy wasn't paying attention, so he wondered, "How in hell did he answer correctly?"

Szymon's heart was pounding as he breathed a sigh of relief, silently thanking his father, who had, over the years, told him stories about his military escapades, which had been the highlight of his life. He had served in the Austro-Hungarian army and told his son about his adventures. Many times Szymon had heard how he hated to hear the wake-up call at 5:30 and had struggled many mornings to get out of bed, especially after returning from a weekend pass.

Schoeppler droned on. Everyone was dead tired, struggling to stay alert. Finally, he concluded his lecture and began moving the formation forward, stopping again at the mess hall. It had been a long day. They sat silently, eating their supper. Thank God there was plenty of good food: meat and vegetable stew, freshly baked bread, and rice pudding. Supper lasted only 30 minutes, and afterward, they marched back to the barracks. Schoeppler finished his evening orders, showed them how to make their beds, and instructed them to pick up their toilet kits from the supply Sergeant before cleaning up.

When Schoeppler left the barracks, the men were alone in their new quarters for the first time. Most of them who traveled with Szymon that day were still together. The tall kid named Luc called the men to attention and marched them to pick up their toilet kits. There was a community bathhouse. One squad at a time bathed in the order Schoeppler assigned, filing down the aisles between the beds and foot lockers to wash off the grime and dirt. Some men didn't want to bathe because they were shy and intimidated by community bathing. Still, they followed Schoeppler's instructions washing with the de-lousing soap assigned to them, making the best of the situation. Afterward, they sat on their beds, reliving the past 12 hours. Somebody said three of the recruits did not participate in the induction ceremony.

"They failed the medical," called someone across the room. "Venereal disease and open sores on their bodies. One had a fever."

Tymko Parczyk from Szymon's village left crying because the doctor told him he failed the physical examination due to bad eyesight. There was a hush in the room as each contemplated how he would feel in a similar situation.

"Poor bastard," thought Szymon.

Someone snickered as another said, "Lucky for him."

The banter trailed off until a voice in the back asked whether anyone wanted to recite the rosary. "Come back near the toilet."

One by one, the men began preparing for bed. Szymon held his new shaving supplies and thought, "I don't have to share them with Pa and Michael."

He placed the straight-edge razor, brush, and mug in the foot locker, rearranged his uniforms neatly, and checked to see if he had brought a pencil and paper.

He intended to write to his parents as soon as he could, but tonight was not the night. He lay back on the bed, thinking about them, especially his mother. Feeling his eyes well up with tears, he turned on his side. A wave of peace overcame him, and he began drifting off when he was startled awake by the sound of the whistle announcing lights out. Finally, all was quiet.

Just before dozing off, Szymon thought about Schoeppler. An imposing, intimidating man who was overweight, over six feet tall, with dirty blond hair, who he suspected had a deep mean streak. He had seen it before. Schoeppler wanted him to fail to answer the question, so he could make an example of him. He told himself he would have to be careful to pay attention and not smart off so as not to get on his wrong side. That night, Szymon slept soundly.

Awakening the next morning slowly, it took a few minutes to remember where he was. "It must be nearly 5 o'clock," he thought. He lay awake for a few minutes thinking about the previous day. He was used to awakening early – even earlier than 5:30. He, like most everyone he knew, was a farm laborer, working on a dairy farm that demanded arising each morning before four a.m. to milk dozens of cows each day. Lying here was a luxury that Szymon seldom experienced. It felt good to lie in a clean bed.

Life in Galicia was a rough struggle for Szymon and his family. His father, Roman, looked many years older than his fifty-five years. His poor, dear mother, Helena, appeared to be an old lady, although she actually was a few years younger than Pa. Both had been born in Bukaczowce before serfdom ended. Both had experienced devastating changes in their lives resulting from harsh policies favoring the noble class. In the late 1840s, in many places across the region, peasants rose up and rioted against the nobility, killing close to 2,000 and destroying manors and other property. The nobility, which was mainly Polish, soon gained the upper hand again. Although the people had won their freedom, hopes were soon dashed. They were no better off. In fact, their circumstances worsened because the nobility retaliated, forbidding peasants all access to the forest. The parliament had sided with the Polish nobility against the serfs giving them ownership of rustic lands in areas of western Galicia. Previously, villagers and townspeople alike could hunt, fish, graze cattle, and cut timber for building their homes.

They could gather wood for furniture and, more importantly, for firewood, as well as bark for weaving useful baskets, shoes, and all manner of household items. Ruthenians had almost no rights, and the nobility could pay them a paltry wage. Peasants experienced crushing poverty and desperate circumstances. Once the Polish government sided with the noble class, the people's lives took on a quality of desperation, knowing that, for now, there was no way out. Many said they looked forward to dying.

His thoughts were interrupted by the sound of the bugle announcing the start of the second day of army life. Szymon arose quickly and dressed in his new work uniform. He made his bed, meticulously following Schoeppler's instruction, hoping that he would pass inspection. Hurriedly, he used the toilet and, from a large basin in the small room, splashed water on his face. He made it out the door just as Schoeppler was rounding the corner of the building. He avoided looking into his eyes. It was still pitch dark, so he could see a few lights of Stanislau twinkling in the distance. Schoeppler called the men to attention and proceeded to call the roll prior to issuing the orders for the day.

Then, Luc Slobodianyk called cadence from his position at the left side of the first row as he marched them to the mess hall.

At breakfast, Szymon sat with his cousins, Theo and Joannes, along with several men he did not know. Half a dozen new recruits had been assigned to Schoeppler's platoon. They talked among themselves in lowered voices about the previous day. Their self-consciousness and nervousness wore off as they ate. They didn't linger because breakfast, like their other meals, lasted only 30 minutes unless otherwise ordered.

One by one, the men left the table, stopping along the way at outhouses near the training center (TC). It was exactly 6:15 when Szymon joined the others lined up at attention to greet Sergeant Schoeppler, who stood with his arms folded which made him appear like a giant authority figure—one to be feared.

Stragglers took up the rear, and Schoeppler roared at those who ran up after the whistle had sounded. He called out three names and told them that their punishment for arriving late was to clean the toilets between 10 and 11 that morning, which made an impression on Szymon. After filing inside, Schoeppler led the entire platoon to a room where they sat at long tables. There was a blackboard where he drew diagrams of the base. He showed them where the buildings were located. Later that day, they would march up the hill to see the old fortress, as well as more recently constructed fortifications. The men were genuinely interested in Schoeppler's lecture. He erased the blackboard and then drew sketches of structures and buildings on top of the hill. He described what they were expected to know in order to defend the city and military base.

Sergeant Schoeppler paused to ask if there were any questions. The men were quiet. After a minute or two, he sneered, "So, you know it all? We will see!"

He ignored the silence and went on with his talk. He covered the fortress, drawing detailed sketches of different areas, identifying the buildings, and describing the functions of infrastructure. It was nearing 10 a.m. when he abruptly halted. "We will be losing Kubida, Hanczyk, and Melnyk, who will report to Sergeant Stemmler downstairs." He called the remaining men to attention. They followed him out the door forming two columns and halted on the first floor, where they were dismissed for a short break. No one was late returning to join Schoeppler this time.

They were standing at attention as several officers entered the building. The men stared. Szymon caught sight out of the corner of his eye of someone saluting. Quickly he followed suit. The officers returned their salutes.

"Men, the Commander will address you."

Commander Swartzdorf was an old man who had made a 45-year career in the army. He was impressive in his magnificent uniform and spoke fluent Polish to the new recruits. Ruthenians and Poles understood each other's languages. He welcomed them to the base and made a few remarks of little consequence. The men cheered. Swartzdorf saluted the men. They saluted him and remained at attention until his party had left the building. All faces turned toward Schoeppler, trying to gauge his reaction to their performance. Again, Schoeppler said nothing.

At precisely 11 a.m., Kubida, Melnyk, and Hanczyk returned to the TC, rejoining the platoon as it prepared to march to the parade grounds. This time Sergeant Schoeppler directed the men to fall in rows of four abreast. He told Luc to lead the men, giving him instructions to march in formation to the end of the other two platoons already on the field.

Three sergeants stood watching as the men paraded in formation across the grounds, each calling out to the assemblage to straighten the line and calling cadence. "Left. Left. Left. Straighten up. Shoulders back, chin up, eyes forward!" One of the sergeants called a halt. "Remain at attention!" There was activity at one end of the grounds where several people had assembled.

Sergeant Schoeppler called out, "Attention! Left, left, left." Although the start was ragged, the men soon stepped in time to the cadence. "Left, left, left. Right, left. Left."

At the end of the parade grounds were several officers, including Commander Swartzdorf. Schoeppler and the two other sergeants walked up the field. Just as they approached the assembled officers, Schoeppler roared, "Halt!"

About half the men remembered to salute. Schoeppler yelled, "Salute!"

The men marched back down the field, and this time they seemed to get the hang of it. Approaching the officers, he yelled, "Salute!" There was an improvement, but everything depended on what Sergeant Schoeppler would say. All of the soldiers on the field remained at attention saluting, including Schoeppler, while commander Swartzdorf and his party left the field. One of the sergeants addressed the men. "You are part of Company A. Remember that piece of information."

After receiving their orders for afternoon assignments, each platoon marched off the field. Szymon was hungry and looking forward to dinner, but Schoeppler had other ideas. He called the men to a halt in front of the TC and then to attention. Proceeding to lecture them, he railed against their performance that day. "You bastards are the poorest examples of soldiers, unworthy of being in the Austro-Hungarian Army. You don't know when or how to salute an officer, and you act like you are on vacation. You think you know it all! Tomorrow, you will become real soldiers, or my name is not William Schoeppler. You are in the 1st platoon and part of Company A. What company is this?" he sputtered.

Most were too intimidated to respond. Szymon and a few others called, "Company A, sir!"

"Pitiful!" yelled Schoeppler. "What company is this?"

This time the entire 48 men of the first platoon responded, "Company A, sir!"

"Drop the sir," bellowed Schoeppler. "What company is this?"

"Company A!"

"Louder, you stupid bastards!"

"Company A!"

"Again!"

"Company A!"

He finally ground to a stop. No one moved. Szymon didn't know whether to be afraid or laugh. He caught Theo's eye and looked away quickly. Theo was struggling to suppress a grin or maybe worse.

After dinner, the afternoon was taken up with a short march to the top of a nearby hill. The sun shone brightly, providing an expansive view below them of

Stanislau and the surrounding rural areas. Schoeppler's classroom sketches proved to be invaluable, and he lectured them about the history of the hilltop artillery installation, which was located on the exact spot where the original fortress had been situated. "This hilltop is over 1,300 feet high." The men could see for several miles with the aid of binoculars and a telescope. Schoeppler pointed out where their barracks were located. An hour later, the platoon was on its way down the hill stopping at several locations along the way. As the afternoon sun descended in the western sky, the temperature began to drop. They marched past the barracks and turned toward the training center when one of the men fainted. It was Joe Korlaszcz.

"For Christ's sake! What the hell is wrong with him?" demanded Sergeant Schoeppler. He appeared to be annoyed and impatient, unconcerned about why one of the men was lying crumpled on the ground. "I need two men to run to the hospital for a litter." They were gone only two or three minutes when he had second thoughts and tried to find Joe's pulse. He thought he felt it and listened to Joe's chest for a heartbeat. He looked up and ordered two of the men to run double quick to get a doctor from the TC. Szymon and Theo were back almost before they were out of sight. Following them were the doctors who had performed the physical exams yesterday. One of them began to resuscitate Joe. The other doctor asked the men whether anyone had noticed anything wrong with Joe that afternoon.

They looked at each other, shaking their heads. "No sir." Then, one man spoke up, "I noticed that he seemed to be dizzy and was sweating before he fainted."

As Joe was being examined, another two medics approached bearing a litter. Szymon overheard one of them speak with Schoeppler. "We saw another recruit keel over today."

The doctor examining Joe said that his skin was cold and his face was pale.

"Did you give the men a water break this afternoon?"

Schoeppler's head jerked. "No, sir."

Seeing no canteens hanging from the men's belts they asked, "Where are their canteens? Didn't your men carry canteens?"

"No, sir." Schoeppler's expression began to change. "Dehydration? Maybe heat stroke? It's dry this afternoon, and the humidity is low."

"Sergeant, for Christ's sake, you must remember to carry water with you at all times, even on base."

"Yes, sir," said Schoeppler, for the first time appearing to be concerned.

After the doctor left carrying Joe on the litter to the hospital, Schoeppler told the men to fall in; reaching the TC took only a few minutes. That night Schoeppler cut his remarks short, telling them that they would receive orders and assignments in the morning at 6:15. With that, he ordered Luc to lead them to the mess and then return to the barracks.

That evening, they talked about Sergeant Schoeppler. All of them agreed that he was a bully, a tough guy who drove them hard. They were afraid of him.

Someone spoke up, "I don't think he forgot to issue canteens. He did it on purpose. I wonder if Joe drank water early this morning. We had a long day and only a fifteen-minute dinner. Besides marching on the parade grounds, we hiked up the hill, and the temperature was warmer today than in months." The talk stopped abruptly as Schoeppler entered the barracks. He didn't say anything to them, but went straight to his room, slamming the door behind him.

One of the guys asked about Joe Korlaszcz. There was silence. No one knew anything about Joe. Szymon cursed under his breath, "God damn it! Schoeppler could have told us something."

On day three, Szymon awakens to the sound of heavy rain on the tin roof. The light was too dim in the barracks to see the clock, but he guessed it was almost time to get up. He heard someone leaving the barracks. A minute later, the door opened, and he heard Schoeppler's room door slam shut.

"What's he doing out there in the rain?" For the next several minutes, the outside door and Schoeppler's door kept opening and slamming shut. "He's dumping something on the floor after each trip."

This went on for some time until the bugle sounded the wake-up call. When the men arose, they watched Schoeppler, accompanied by another sergeant, carrying canteens and throwing them in a pile on the floor. To the right of the door, a large stack of canteens, field packs, and boxes was piled high. Schoeppler glanced up and growled, "What the hell are you staring at?"

Szymon heard the man in the bunk below say, "That son of a bitch doesn't know when to quit."

Schoeppler and the sergeant finished their job and then went into the office. The outside door flung open again, and two men entered carrying rifles and stacked them alongside the boxes. Schoeppler yelled, "Luc, take the men to the mess and get back here by 6:30." As they left, they overheard Sergeant Schoeppler arguing in his office with the other sergeants, but they quickly forgot about him as they trotted toward the mess hall. The heaviest of the rain had let up by then, yet still, their clothes were soaked to the skin in the few minutes it took to arrive there.

As they ate their breakfast, a man from another platoon came over to the table and told them that Joe Korlaszcz was readmitted to the hospital the night before because of dehydration. "I checked on him, asking my friend who works in the hospital, but that's all the information he gave me. Joe was suffering from exhaustion, so he had to drink plenty of water. The doctor is going to dismiss him this morning with a supply of salt pills for your platoon."

Szymon asked, "When were canteens issued for your platoon?"

"On the first day."

The men looked at each other. Someone said, "Schoeppler has real problems." A few others voiced their opinion of what was wrong with him, but most thought he was an asshole.

These young men were crude farm boys, born in a time and place where life was hard. They had no use for Sergeant Schoeppler even though they were used to harsh treatment from everyone else in their young lives: parents, employers, schoolmasters, and priests.

The smallest infraction was followed by a slap across the face. Parents, including Roman Swaczy, cursed their children, beating their sons with whips, belts, switches, bare hands, and fists. Servants who worked for noble and wealthy families were whipped for spilling something or not moving quickly. Children often grew up resenting, even hating, authority figures. Sadly, when they grew up and had children of their own, they continued the practice of corporal punishment.

Until recently, men serving in the army could be punished with fifty lashes across their backs for infractions such as not following orders, insubordination, or even a lesser offense such as mumbling under their breath in barely audible voices. Szymon contemplated what kind of hell his future army life held under Sergeant Schoeppler. If he was apprehensive, he was certain the others were, too.

Szymon realized that each day Schoeppler was getting worse. It wasn't only that he was meaner, but also seemed to lose control of his temper more frequently. Szymon wondered if anyone knew the real story behind Sergeant Schoeppler.

26

Chapter 2

William Schoeppler began life as Johann Wilhelm Schmid, born in Graz, Austria, on September 16, 1824. He was the bastard son of Maria Schmid. Maria's parents were Johann Schmid and Anna Barbara Schoeppler, and they were considered better off than many living in Graz. Johann Schmid came from the rural areas around Graz, raised on a large farm. After serving in the Austrian military, he settled in Graz with his wife, Anna Barbara, and their three children, Wolfgang, Konrad, and Maria, who was the middle child. Mr. Schmid owned two butcher shops in thriving middle-class neighborhoods. Anna Barbara did not have to work but wanted her children to experience what ordinary people's lives were like.

Maria's mother spoke with Mrs. Schwalm, a good customer whose husband was a wealthy nobleman. Seventeen-year-old Maria was hired as governess and tutor for her son Phillip's only child, Valenty, whose mother died shortly after he was born. Maria often stayed at the mansion, caring for Valenty when the couple was away, or when Anna Barbara was busy with important family matters. Maria was treated as a member of the Schwalm family, and she loved them like her mother and father. One weekend, Maria was asked by Mrs. Schwalm to assist with preparations for the annual New Year's Eve party. Ignatzy, the youngest son of

Graf Josef and Anna Barbara were home, so Maria knew the weekend would be lively and fun.

Mrs. Schwalm always decorated the mansion with lavish and beautiful holiday decorations. Everything had to be perfect because many notable people were invited, and the Schwalm galas were the talk of Graz. The Christmas Eve and New Year's Eve parties were the most opulent. Sixty guests had been invited, and all were ready as the guests were announced one by one. A magnificent smorgasbord offered the most beautiful selection of fish, fowl, beef, and ham for the New Year's Eve supper. There were rare delicacies heaped on silver platters, loaves of bread, cheeses, and the most elaborate desserts. Champagne, wines, and other spirits flowed freely. The evening was filled with music provided by a formally attired orchestra. The beautifully coiffed and bejeweled ladies danced their favorite waltzes in glimmering gowns. Nothing could have been more perfect.

Maria spied on the guests while holding Valenty's hand from a niche above the ballroom floor. They were like two little kids spying on St. Nick, placing gifts for little children under the tree. They sat for a while until Valenty's eyes began to droop. Maria asked him if he wanted to go to sleep. In his sweet little voice, he told her he was ready for bed. The two of them left their perch to prepare his bed. They saw Ignatzy bouncing down the hallway. He picked up the little boy, waltzed him to his room, and shared a platter of treats he had brought from the festivities below. Ignatzy was very kind and always took the time to think about Maria and his young nephew. He wanted them to be part of the fun that the others were having. After half an hour, Valenty began to doze. "

"Well, enough for tonight. I think he had fun, Maria, don't you?"

"Oh, yes, but please join your lady friend, or she will find another beau, and you won't like that!"

"I'll just take you down there," he teased.

"In my servant's dress, dancing alongside all of those ladies stuffed into their fancy gowns," she exclaimed.

"What a sight!"

"Oh, Ignatzy, don't be silly. We had fun in our perch and could see and hear everything. I think your mother will be very happy that the ball is a grand success."

As they talked, Ignatzy helped her prepare the little boy's bed, then carried him and tucked him in, covering him with quilts. "He's such a sweet boy." Maria walked to the door, and Ignatzy gave her a peck on the cheek. Maria blushed. He said, "Thank you,

Maria, for taking care of Val. You make his life easier and even fun."

He ducked out the door as Maria's thoughts turned to Valenty, who had contracted polio two years prior. Luckily, he was not completely paralyzed, as were so many children from this epidemic. His father brought in the best doctors from Graz and Vienna to administer to the little boy. They saved his life and, last fall recommended that Graf Schwalm allow them to speak with a doctor who was perfecting braces that Valenty could wear once he was strong enough to exercise and learn to walk again. This year, the brave little boy had learned to use the braces and persevered with his exercises. Maria took him outdoors every day, as long as the weather allowed. Graf Schwalm renovated several rooms, opening them up to create one large room to continue therapy during the winter months. Valenty was always determined to walk and was cheerful and pleasant, even though he suffered severe, never-ending pain.

Maria finished tucking him in, kissed the little boy goodnight, dimmed the lights, and quietly closed the door behind her. As she walked away, her thoughts turned to the weeks of parties and galas. Oh, it had been so much fun. Hearing the music drifting up from the ballroom, she began humming along. She turned into the narrow hallway and ducked into the corridor with the staircase leading up to her room. As she rounded the corner on the fourth floor, she saw a figure in the dimly lit hallway. "Who is it?" She stood still as the figure approached. "Who is it?"

"Hello, Maria."

"Oh, it's you, Phillip. I just put little Valenty to bed. What are you doing here?"

Phillip grinned, and then suddenly, he grabbed them and began kissing her. With his right hand fondling her breasts and his left hand anchoring her shoulder against the wall, he began dancing. "You like my little brother. Don't you like me, Maria?"

As he pushed her toward her room, she realized he was drunk. These words were the last she remembered. When she came to, she slowly remembered a terrible struggle and her face hitting the bedpost. "Oh, no! My God, Phillip raped me." Her underclothing was torn from her body, and she felt bruises on her face and teeth marks on her neck. She was so ashamed. "Oh, what am I going to do?"

There was urgent tapping at her door and a voice asking if she could come in. Valenty was calling for her. "Who is it?"

"It's Mrs. Schwalm." Maria began to sob. "Maria, are you alright? "Maria, "Maria!" Mrs. Schwalm turned the handle and entered the room. "Oh, no, Maria! What has happened?" Mrs. Schwalm was stunned. Maria lay on the bed with her clothes torn, her hair disheveled, and her face scratched and bruised. An oil lamp had been knocked over onto the floor. While fixing her bed, she found a men's handkerchief with the monogram PAS sown into the fabric. It was Phillip! "Oh, Mrs. Schwalm," sobbed Maria, gulping air, her chest heaving uncontrollably.

Mrs. Schwalm moved Maria into a room near her suite and took care of her, washing and salving her bruises and scratches and combing her hair. She undressed her and gave her a nightgown and a robe from her own closet. All the while, she tried to calm her, telling her everything would be alright. Maria interrupted her thoughts, "Mrs. Schwalm, would you allow Valenty to stay with me? I would like to have him here. I know everything will be alright. I'll take good care of him, please?"

Maria tried to hold back tears. Mrs. Schwalm gazed at her for a long time and thought it might be good for her to have little Val to take her mind off her terrible situation. "Yes, dear." She then kissed the distraught girl.

"Oh, Mrs. Schwalm, would you say prayers with me?" The two women knelt and recited the rosary, and then Maria whispered, "Dear God in heaven, please give me strength to know what to do. God bless Mrs. Schwalm and Graf Schwalm. Bless them for caring for me in my hour of need. Please bless little Valenty and heal him so he can be a normal little boy. Amen."

Mrs. Schwalm strained to hear Maria's words. They clung to each other for a long time, choking back tears. She held Maria, stroking her hair, saying quietly, "Thank you, dear. Remember, I'm only three doors down the hallway."

Then she left the room and started walking to her suite, where her husband was preparing for bed. "This will be the hardest thing I have ever done," she thought. As Mrs. Schwalm walked, she began trembling, trying to think about what could be done to help this girl and remedy her situation. She realized that Maria's parents would have to be told immediately. She had to be strong in order to speak with her husband and confront Phillip. This could not wait. For Maria's and everyone's sake, she had to act now.

Maria's life changed after that night. To varying degrees, all the lives of those touched by this tragedy were altered in some way. Early the next day, Mrs. Schwalm called her personal maid and had her deliver a note to Phillip's room. She sent a message to her husband's stable man to have his coach ready by 1:00 p.m. After dressing for breakfast with her house guests, she went to her husband's dressing room, and the two descended downstairs by 8:30. No one would have guessed that anything was wrong as the couple greeted each guest at breakfast. The setting was lovely, and within an hour, her guests had eaten and were preparing to depart.

When Phillip came to their door, he was contrite and wore an expression of remorse. He confessed what had happened and vowed to take care of Maria and would do anything to make amends. It was obvious that Josef Schwalm took Phillip's indecent behavior personally. He chastised him severely, telling him that he was a disappointment to him and had diminished his standing among his peers. "Gentlemen do not conduct themselves in such a perverted and salacious manner."

"Father, I will walk to the ends of the earth to repair my standing in your eyes."

Out of concern for her husband, Anna called the meeting to an end, worried that her husband was becoming emotional. After dinner, the couple called on Johann and Anna Barbara Schmid. The strain was even greater that afternoon for Josef Schwalm as he sat explaining to them what happened the night before. The Schmids sat quietly. Their eyes wore an expression of pain and sadness, but they were gentle and kind and told them that they would pray for their family and for Phillip. Continuing their conversation about what could be done for Maria. Mr. Schmid said that he would ask her what she would like to do. She was happy and content with her position, taking care of your grandson. The visit ended cordially, and as they parted, Mr. Schmid asked them to pray for Maria.

Four months had passed when Maria discovered she was pregnant. She had no choice but to leave the Schwalms and leave behind little Valenty and Ignatzy, who she had depended upon to cheer her up during the past weeks. Valenty had not allowed her to dwell on the past and continued being his fun-loving self. They did have fun at times, and Maria knew that she had a responsibility to Valenty to be the person he had come to rely upon. But now they would have to part, most likely forever. She would be going away to wait for her baby to be born. Before leaving, she returned home for several weeks until her pregnancy became obvious.

Her father and mother had changed too. Mr. Schmid had aged in a matter of weeks. He was quiet, but still kind and loving to her, as well as to her mother and his longtime customers. Anna Barbara was also quieter, but her main concern, other than Maria, was her husband. She could not overlook his aged appearance and tired demeanor.

The Schwalms arranged for Maria to stay at a convent with a Catholic order dedicated to taking in women who were bearing out-of-wedlock babies. Mrs. Schwalm's sister was a devout Catholic and made the arrangements with her church. So, in late April, Maria bade goodbye to her parents and traveled by train to Vienna, over 200 miles away. She learned she was pregnant 16 weeks after the rape. She was at her parent's for almost two weeks and then gave birth at the convent. She gave him her father's surname and remained at the convent for another three months before returning to Graz. Her father was in worse condition than he had been before she left; he was aging quickly. It was obvious she could not stay with her parents, as she and her newborn son, Wilhelm, would be too great a burden for him to carry. Her mother called Mrs. Schwalm. After a brief conversation, she told Maria that she would be moving away again to a small house Phillip had purchased for her. The next words pained her to tell Maria that the house was located in Vienna.

Maria had no trouble finding employment with the help of Graf and Mrs. Schwalm's references. Her son was a sweet, little 12-month-old when she was offered and accepted a position with the Altshul family, who had three children; the youngest was a mildly retarded boy who was a joy to be around. Maria and her son Wilhelm lived in a small four-room house in a beautiful setting near the central part of the city. She could walk to work, to her new church and shops, and to visit friends, too. Wilhelm played with Vasily, so she was very busy with no time to brood.

Maria had no trouble finding employment, but she left the convent three months after Wilhelm was born, and now he was a year old.

About three years after moving to Vienna, she received an urgent message that her father was dying. She returned home, just in time. The apartment hung heavily with sadness. The butcher shops closed for what was supposed to be a short period of mourning, but it was obvious that her mother could not operate two of them. Wolfgang, Maria's oldest brother, handled the sale of the shops and arranged for Anna Barbara's move to be closer to Maria and their younger brother. While Maria was with her mother, she received a note from Anna Schwalm. Mr. Schwalm was desperately ill and was not expected to survive the night. Could she come? She didn't arrive in time to see the old gentleman before he died but was greeted warmly by Mrs. Schwalm and Ignatzy. She brought three-year-old Wilhelm with her; they were delighted to see the boy. Ignatzy asked if he could visit Maria, as he would be staying in Vienna next spring to oversee the opening of a new headquarters. She agreed. The visit ended, and she kissed them goodbye. Sitting in the coach bound for Vienna, she wondered if Ignatzy would visit, dreading that she may have seen the Schwalms, particularly Ignatzy, for the last time.

Life was about to change again for Maria and Willy, as she now called him. Upon her return, the Altschuls told her that they could not keep her in their employ. This was a shock to her because they gave no reason. When she used them for references, they wrote glowing comments, so she knew her job performance was not the reason she was suddenly unemployed. Shortly, Maria found another position with the Werner family. She was now 23 years old, and this was her third job. This time, the setting was not so private, nor was it so beautiful. The family was very nice, but they were not well off. Mr. Werner taught at the University, and she reasoned that his job was maintained. This began a very quiet period in Maria's life. She and her growing boy lived modestly, enjoying the different cultures of this Jewish family and their quaint neighborhood. For fifteen years, she traveled on a tram to her job, passing bearded Jews recognizable by their quaint hats.

During those years, Wilhelm completed school and was accepted at the University. He was not a scholar and struggled to maintain acceptable passing grades. His mother told him the real story of his birth and their circumstances. At about this time, Wilhelm changed his surname from Schmid to Schoeppler.

She didn't know who told him her mother's maiden name but suspected that it was one of her brothers.

Maria was puzzled but didn't object. Wilhelm was 19 years old and certainly could decide for himself what he wanted to be called. But, life did not look kindly upon Wilhelm Schoeppler. He failed his exams and wasn't accepted for the second year at University.

At about this time, Mrs. Werner suffered a slight stroke and required personal nursing services. This additional cost burden meant the family could no longer afford to keep Maria to tutor their son. So, at age 39, Maria and Wilhelm considered selling their house and moving into an apartment nearer the central city. It would be difficult for them. They had been happy in their home, but Maria was certain she would never be able to live in such a beautiful house and neighborhood again.

Will began to brood and spend his days alone in his room. He never seemed able to make close friends. One day, after his 20th birthday, and on impulse, he went to a recruiting office to sign up for military service in the Austro-Hungarian Army. He didn't know exactly why. At first, Wilhelm liked the army. He had dreams that he would someday be an officer. He also knew he wanted to make a life-long career out of military service. He received recognition for his performance and achievements while he served in Bosnia for about six months, but the highest rank he achieved after seven years was Sergeant. He felt like a cornered rat. It occurred to him that after seven years of military service, he was stuck at this rank because he did not have an education, and his family was not wealthy, well-connected, or distinguished in any way. After ten years of military service, he began thinking of almost nothing else, becoming resentful and unable to come to terms with or resign himself to his circumstances. In spite of his preference for being alone, he found no peace. He had no male friends nor any lady friends; he'd never married and seemed to drive people away from him. The years dragged on, and eventually, he received an indefinite leave. His commanding officer spoke with him about his hot temper, poor attitude, and badgering of new recruits in his platoon, warning him this behavior wouldn't be tolerated.

Returning to the garrison, he led a platoon in a newly formed company. However, his respite didn't make a difference. He picked up exactly where he left off, more and more frequently losing control in stressful situations or for any perceived slight. He brooded every day.

Chapter 3

Schoeppler was daydreaming when Hanczyk knocked on his door. "Who is it?" Hanczyk hurried him to the mess hall, filling him in about what happened on the way. Joe had collapsed again. Swaczy and Kubida rushed to Joe's side to check his pulse and heartbeat while two other men ran to locate a stretcher. After finding one, they rushed him to the hospital. Schoeppler was puzzled by this latest fainting spell. He asked the men what had happened.

"One minute he was sitting, and the next minute he was on the floor," someone said.

Schoeppler headed to the hospital and located Joe, who was listening to a doctor. "What happened, Joe?"

"I don't know what happened. One minute I was sitting, and the next thing I remembered, I woke up in the hospital."

"Did you fill your canteen this morning?" asked Schoeppler. Joe looked sheepish and admitted that he had forgotten. "Joe, damn it! You have to carry your canteen and drink water because if this keeps up, you will be going home permanently. Don't you like military life?"

Joe was quiet and said, "I like it, but I don't like the stress. I get upset and think I'm always going to screw up and cause problems."

Nodding slowly, Schoeppler fixed his gaze on this young man. "Okay, Joe. Get your ass to the exercise room after you fill your God damned canteen. I'm not your mother, and damn it, I can't remind you to fill your canteen every morning. Now, get out of here! I want to talk to the doctor."

"Yes sir," said Joe, suppressing the faint hint of a grin.

Schoeppler liked this kid because he reminded him of himself. He believed he was telling him the truth. Preoccupied with Joe, he walked back to the barracks thinking that Joe was a good person, probably the most liked and kindest young man in the platoon. He was a tall kid—a bit over six feet, broad-shouldered, heavy-boned, round-faced, with kind, brown eyes. "In fact, he's the nicest kid I've ever met," thought Schoeppler. "He is a peacemaker, not a peace breaker, a very religious man who leads the other men in prayers before supper and before retiring at night." On occasion, he watched Joe cross himself when no one was around.

Schoeppler walked back to the barracks, thinking about his conversation with the doc who examined Joe. The doctor thought Joe might have had a low stress level, but this is the army. What's going to happen to him when there's a rebellion, and these kids are brought in to quell it? There may be a place for him, but I will have to speak to someone who can make something happen.

Chapter 4

Joe, Theo and Szymon had stuck together over the past six weeks, sharing information they learned with each other. Theo and Szymon told Joe that Schoeppler was easier on him than any other recruit. "You're the only one who can get along with him, and you get special treatment around here," Theo commented. "You defend him sometimes, and the guys don't like it."

Joe realized this, and it bothered him because Sarge was still riding the other men with no let-up in sight.

A few days later, Schoeppler needed some men to go to the supply depot and bring back crates of guns and ammunition. They were on the firing range when Schoeppler said, "I need three volunteers," pointing to Swaczy, Kubida, and Korlaszcz. "You, You, and You. Double-quick! Get your God damned asses to the supply depot, find the sergeant, and tell him to load two crates of handguns and ammunition into the cart. Throw a couple of new targets on top."

Upon their return, they found Schoeppler ranting out of control, screaming at one of the men. Schoeppler didn't let up, even when the mule slowed and pulled the cart to a halt next to him. The men stood staring at him; for the moment, he ignored the cart. Szymon could see that Schoeppler was injured. Blood from his forehead and nose was running down his face. The jacket in front of his uniform was covered with mud and streaked with blood and dirt. Schoeppler finally ran out of steam and just stood there.

Joe crossed himself and called, "Are you alright, Sergeant?"

"No, God damn it."

"Do you want to ride in the cart to the hospital?"

Schoeppler did not move or say anything. Joe turned to Szymon and beckoned for him to help lift Sergeant Schoeppler onto the cart, then he flicked the reins, and the mule plodded off. Szymon looked behind and saw that a few of the men were following. Sergeant Schoeppler was bleeding profusely as the cart reached the building and was helped down to the ground. He was pale and shaky on his feet. Once inside, only Joe remained with him.

With Luc in the lead, Szymon walked with the others back toward the range, catching up with the rest of the platoon returning to their barracks. On the way, the men filled in Szymon and Theo on the incident that provoked Schoeppler's anger.

Schoeppler was walking out to inspect the targets,

carrying his gun, when he slipped and fell. The field was muddy from recent spring rains, and as he walked back, he fell face forward. His face struck a low railing near the target. His gun flipped out of his hand. He retrieved the weapon, but as he did, he slipped in the mud again, and the gun discharged. The men offered to help him, but Schoeppler didn't answer and attempted to walk by himself. It was obvious that he was injured, struggling, and mired in mud. A couple of guys held him up as he walked back. Someone laughed, and Schoeppler exploded. The rest, you know."

It was late in the afternoon when Joe Korlaszcz joined his platoon in the mess hall. "Looks like Sergeant Schoeppler has a broken nose and a wound caused by a bullet grazing his forehead. He will stay overnight in the hospital, at least tonight. He's weak from losing blood."

"Who's in charge?" asked Theo Kubida.

"I don't think there will be anyone here tonight."

No one came after they returned to the barracks, so Luc Slobodianyk took over. The men were quiet that evening. After they cleaned up and were all together in the barracks, Joe asked if the Roman Catholic boys would recite the rosary for Sergeant Schoeppler. No one protested. Joe prayed for the men in the first platoon and for Sergeant Schoeppler. His words touched the men who were deeply moved. Their mood was quiet and somber afterward. Szymon took a piece of paper and pencil from his foot locker and began a letter to his father and mother.

April 18, 1891

Dear father, Roman Swaczy, Sir, and my mother, Helena Swaczy,

Army life is good. Today, we were supposed to shoot handguns on the firing range but couldn't. We get the guns and ammunition and practice tomorrow. I feel good. All the boys with me are good. Our sergeant had an accident. He is in the hospital but will be out maybe tomorrow morning. His gun shot himself. My cousin, Theo Kubida, is doing well, too. I am friends with Joe Korlaszcz, who lives in Czahrow. He is the best soldier, and I prayed for Sergeant Schoeppler today. I will remember what he said for many days. Joe helps everyone. All the men like him.

Hello to my sister Anna, brothers Stephen and Michael, and Grandma Anna and Grandpa Jonas. If I stayed at home, Pa and I would be preparing the land to seed a garden. Is it hot yet? Do my letters come for you? Thank you. I hope you write soon.

Your son in Stanislau,

Szymon Swaczy

Chapter 5

The men began looking forward to completing basic training and their first leave. Someone put a calendar on the wall to mark off the days. Only three weeks remained until July 15.

After Sergeant Schoeppler's accident, attitudes changed on both the part of the men in the platoon and their sergeant. No, it wasn't sweetness and light, but there were plenty more good moments than bad. Joe Korlaszcz was an influence for good on both sides. Everyone liked Joe. They couldn't help it. Joe was a straight arrow who didn't have a corrupt or mean bone in his body. He acted as a mediator numerous times over the past weeks. Fear of Schoeppler faded away, and the men began to appreciate his experience and respect him for his insistence to live up to high standards. He pushed them; thus, they became well-trained soldiers.

Schoeppler told them the commander had his eye on them, and they had gained a good reputation among the new platoons in the newly formed company. Luc, Theo and Hanczyk were good squad leaders and kept them in line. Not so with Katanyk, therefore, Schoeppler rode his ass hard. Luc caught several men gambling one day, shooting dice. Katanyk was in on it. Luc told them he would have to report it. The men asked that he not go to Schoeppler. Luc told them he had no choice but would try to soften the blow. He asked them what punishment he should recommend.

Schoeppler wasn't surprised that men were gambling, but nothing could be done about it once basic training was over. In the end, Schoeppler talked to the entire platoon. He told them they just had to wait three more weeks. Then, if they continued to throw their money away, they would have to take responsibility and suffer the consequences for their behavior. All he said to the men was, "If you want to act like damned fools, no one can stop you."

His attitude toward Katanyk was different. He called him to his office, laid him out, and told him that he already had disciplinary reports in his file. "If you have one more incident, you're out," he said.

Altogether there were seven hundred and fifty men in Company A. There were eight platoons on the parade ground. By far, the first platoon led the field when it came to precision. Luc had molded them into a sharp marching unit. It was evident the 1st Platoon of Company A had spent hours drilling. Rumors circulated of a visit by Archduke Karl Salvator, Lieutenant-Field Marshal of the Imperial Common Austro-Hungarian Army. He was developing an early prototype of the Mitrailleuse machine gun and traveling around the empire demonstrating its use. On Sunday, a parade was scheduled to welcome the Archduke.

It was a perfect day with just enough wind to unfurl the regimental colors and flags. They fluttered in the breeze against a cloudless blue sky. At precisely 12:30 on Sunday, June 29, 1891, the band struck the familiar army marching song of the common army of the Austro-Hungarian Empire. The men were on the field in their dress uniforms, marching onto the broad grassy expanse toward the array of uniformed officers on horseback at the far end of the field. Soldiers lined each side standing at attention as row upon row, platoon after platoon passed. Szymon caught a glimpse out of the corner of his eye of the crowds lining the field, including many retired army personnel wearing their old uniforms, as he marched past. "My God!" he gasped, swallowing hard. Every man was focused, eyes straight ahead, rifles rested perfectly on their shoulders, including Szymon's own, as they marched in perfect step to the rat-a-tat-tat of the drum beat.

As the platoon approached the dignitaries, he heard Luc's cadence, "Left . . . Left . . . Left . . . Platoon, halt!" The men automatically thrust their hands up in a salute. Szymon could hear each platoon coming up behind him. The men stood at attention as the band played the anthem of the Austro-Hungarian Empire, *God Save Francis Joseph I.*

The pageant unfolded before Szymon's eyes. Priests blessed Emperor Franz Joseph, and prayed for the men, the Company and its horses. Commander Swartzdorf, attired in his magnificent uniform, addressed the men. He was followed by a Major whom none of the men knew who introduced another speaker, followed by Archduke Karl Salvator. The speeches went on too long and almost spoiled the day. Salvator droned on but didn't have anything memorable to say. His career evidently was undistinguished, although he made a very handsome figure in an elaborate, colorful uniform. Thankfully, after Salvator finished his remarks, the band struck the Franz Josef on March 2. Every soldier in the place exploded in cheers. Salvator thought the cheers were for him and waved to the men. It didn't matter and Szymon doubted that Salvator would ever know why the men were cheering. After several lively marches, the distinguished guests saluted the soldiers on the field and left to a hail of hoorahs and cheers. Finally, it was over.

Luc Slobodianyk shouted, "Attention!" and the first platoon fell in, saluted, and marched off the field to the roar of even louder cheers. Their heads were held higher that day, their eyes focused, shoulders back, chest thrust forward and the lines straighter. The men were proud because they knew they had distinguished themselves and their sergeant, William Schoeppler.

In sharp contrast to the day before, on Monday it rained. Despite a steady downpour, the 58th infantry assembled, fully equipped, wearing their field packs under ponchos. Their mood was as gloomy as the weather when the men of the first platoon marched to the same siding where they had detrained on their arrival at the garrison three months earlier. A train was waiting, and they wasted no time boarding.

Amid all the grumbling, Szymon heard Sergeant Schoeppler telling them to stop complaining about the weather. "You're in the army now. You can't order the weather when you are on the battlefield, and the enemy is approaching. Knock it off."

Szymon stretched his legs and hoped the train trip was a lengthy one. However, the train sat at the siding for more than an hour, waiting for the Archduke. Cursing softly under his breath, he watched as Salvator boarded his private coach. Still, the train did not move. Word passed up the aisle that there was a delay while supplies were loaded into boxcars on the end of the train. All the while, the rain continued to fall. It was nearly 12:00 before Szymon felt a jerk as the train began to roll.

The ride through the dark, damp forest should have taken only forty-five minutes, but halfway to the camp, the train stopped. Now what? Szymon overheard Schoeppler cursing as he walked up the aisle and opened the exit door. Ten minutes later, Schoeppler returned and told the men that a farmer was moving cattle across the tracks. "We'll be here for a while longer," he said. At 4:30, the train finally arrived at a clearing in the woods. Thank God no one expected the men to stand in formation saluting some horse's ass dignitaries. Evidently, the Sergeant had decided on a plan to make things hurry along more efficiently once the train arrived at its destination.

Each platoon was assigned a job, and there would be no slackers as they began grabbing tents and pounding stakes into the ground. Within 20 minutes, most were up.

Then, there was a steady parade of equipment and supplies hauled from the boxcars into what was to be the supply depot. Half the men carried boxes, the other men grabbed sleeping bags, throwing one or two into each tent. An hour and a half later, most of the heavy work was finished. The camp mess was set up, and the cooks were busy preparing a meal. It wasn't the best start to these war games but once the men ate their long-delayed dinner, they stopped complaining, then huddled around Sergeant Schoeppler who explained what would happen the next day.

He showed them a map of the area, pointing to their present location, identifying several enemy encampments, enemy artillery positions, trails, a ravine, creeks and footbridges. He pointed out the highest elevation.

"If you are separated or lost, remember to use your compasses traveling south-southwest." He pointed out several landmarks near Company A's position. A Y fork in the road, an unusual rock formation, a large stand of burned-out trees. "Our camp is located between and behind the rock formation and the burned-out trees. Questions?"

Someone called out asking whether there would be instructions in the morning, Schoeppler told them the

Sergeant would meet tonight to finalize the war games. After several questions related to the next day's games were answered, someone asked about firewood. "There should be cords of wood under canvas tarpaulins." Several men accompanied Schoeppler to look for the wood. The rain let up, and later in the evening, they sat around a huge bonfire on boxes, logs, empty containers, and anything to stay off the soaked ground. Some of the men carried musical instruments. Szymon had a harmonica with him and joined several others playing familiar Polish and Ruthenian folk songs. They sang for a while until one by one they trailed off to their tents. The men were asleep that night before 8:30 p.m.

The men of Company A were up before daylight, awakened by the aroma of coffee coming from the mess. There were four companies on the field this morning. Each Company commander gave the sergeants directions. Schoeppler groused, worrying that all the men weren't receiving the same information. Confusion is created from inaccurate instructions.

At exactly 7:30 a.m. the noise of heavy guns shook the ground, startling Szymon. It was coming from the rear, south of the regimental camp. The guns fired for half an hour. Each company commander called up the platoons under his command. Company A was instructed to conduct a flanking maneuver to the right while Company D moved to the left. Companies B and C were to conduct a frontal assault.

"Remember if you are lost, use your compasses

and travel SSW."

Little could Schoeppler have known the chaos that was about to befall them. As though a conductor had lowered his baton in front of the orchestra, the sky opened up, and it began to pour. Szymon knew nothing was going to stop these God damned so-called war games, so he resigned himself to a miserably wet day, tightening up the line, moving closer to the man in front of him.

"Close ranks. Stay together. Move up!" Szymon heard Schoeppler yelling. "Stay together." The men moved along, across the clearing, turning left onto a trail that headed into the forest.

"I sure hope he knows where the hell he is going," thought Szymon. The canopy of dense trees protected the men from the sting of the heaviest rain; nonetheless, it didn't let up much. Just as the men moved into the denser forest, they came across several fallen trees. They worked their way around the trees and came to a creek that was overflowing its bank, stopping until Schoeppler figured out where it was safe to cross. He sent Szymon and Luc to the east along the edge of the creek and Mazurek and Malenko to the west. Szymon and Luc reported that there was a spot where the creek was only 15 feet across, warning the water was running fast. The current almost swept a couple of men off their feet, but they all made it safely and worked their way back, locating the trail.

They could hear the sound of rifle fire and knew the games were on, but as they drove deeper into the forest, the sounds became muffled and then vanished. Still, Schoeppler moved forward looking for the path that turned sharply left, away from the trail, dropping directly to the south. If he found the path, it should drop down directly behind the enemy position and connect with Company D. After walking about half an hour, he halted the platoon.

"We're not finding this God damned path," Schoeppler ordered Mazurek and Malenko to scout ahead and try to find it. "We'll wait here until you return." He looked at his timepiece and told them to walk for ten minutes, then turn around and meet up with the platoon if they weren't successful.

He heard Joe Korlaszcz yelling. Joe was standing waving off to the left in a small clearing. A few guys thought the platoon should not move until Mazurek and Malenko returned but Szymon, siding with the majority, argued that there wasn't a choice.

"If this were a real war, we would have to follow the plan." The platoon made its way to Joe. There still was no sign of Mazurek and Malenko. Schoeppler ordered Joe to accompany Swaczy back to the original trail and search for the missing men. Schoeppler spoke with Swaczy telling him to keep an eye on Joe, just in case he fainted again.

"Find them and catch up with us as soon as you can. Don't forget to mark the location where Joe turned off the trail toward the path."

Even though it began raining again, Joe and Szymon had no trouble locating the trail and headed west. They watched the time and about ten minutes later the trail vanished. In front of them was a wall of dense, tall growth. "There must be a way around this," thought Szymon as he began walking north. The ground was muddy from two days of rain. He began calling for Mazurek. He knew they had to be nearby. He pushed farther into the dense growth and began to slide downward. Regaining his footing, he hollered for Joe. They both stood calling for the missing men again.

"Mazurek, it's Swaczy." He heard cries for help. "Where are you?"

"We fell in the ravine. Malenko is unconscious."

"How in the hell did you get through this growth?"

"We found a low place, and pushed through, but be careful, the edge of the ravine is right there," Mazurek warned.

Szymon and Joe probed the area and decided to try to dig their way through the thick growth. They carried small shovels on their backs and started digging through the soft, muddy, rain-soaked ground.

"Can you see us, Mazurek?"

"No, it's overgrown down here."

"Mazurek, can you stand?"

"I don't know. My foot hurts like hell," he said.

"Take off your shirt and wave it," said Joe.

Shortly, they caught sight of a bandana tied to a

small limb waving back and forth, about fifteen feet further north. A few minutes later, they were at the bottom of the ravine examining Malenko, listening for his heartbeat.

"Malenko toppled head first, hitting his head on a rock after he slid into the ravine."

"He's unconscious, not dead," said Joe, making the sign of the cross.

"I think we can get you out of here," said Szymon, but not so sure about Malenko."

It took a heroic effort on all of their parts to make it to the top of the ravine. Joe and Szymon almost carried Mazurek, who had no choice except to bear weight on his painfully injured foot.

"I wonder if we can drag Malenko up here?" asked Joe. "It's about a twenty-foot climb." They struggled, trying to lift him and realized that the incline was too steep, deciding instead to scout the area for a more favorable position.

About 150 feet to the south, they came upon a spot where the incline was less steep to the top of the ravine. There were large boulders that might help them shorten the distance even more if they could drag Malenko on top. Szymon, Joe and Mazurek rigged a harness to move Malenko using rope they carried in their field packs. Before beginning the final effort, they cleared a two-foot-wide area on the slope leading to the top of the ravine and managed to turn Malenko head first.

Slowly, Mazurek was able to drag him up the side to the top. All four men were safe. Malenko regained consciousness but was in pain, and dizzy, and he had suffered injuries that prevented him from standing. Luckily, Malenko was a small man and didn't have any injuries to his upper body except for an ugly lump on the side of his head. Joe wanted to return to the platoon as soon as possible. It was about 1 p.m. Mazurek and Malenko had rations and water. The rain had temporarily let up. They guessed they were about forty-five minutes from the platoon.

"We'll leave you here and return as soon as possible." Since there was no more that could be done for Malenko, Szymon and Joe started to retrace their steps, and to get word to the medics to come for the injured men. Joe suggested they first look for Schoeppler and the platoon. They decided to follow the path, dropping down to the enemy infantry company. They heard someone coming and stepped off the path into the bushes. Several men from their platoon were coming toward them.

"Hold up!" yelled Joe. Sergeant Schoeppler listened while Joe and Swaczy reiterated what happened to Mazurek and Malenko.

Schoeppler told them about a change in plans. Archduke Salvator was dragging his machine guns up the hill. "We're supposed to advance toward the left, southwest of the enemy nest and attack in the morning."

"We will spend the night up here." Schoeppler

ordered Szymon and Joe to scout for the enemy machine gun position, then return to base and locate the company commander.

"Give him the position and ask for further instructions." "Run double quick."

By now, Joe and Szymon were familiar with these paths, and after finding the nest to the north and west, they doubled back to inform Sergeant Schoeppler, then dropped down to find the Major directing the war games. Half an hour later, they were back in camp, telling him what the first platoon of Company A had discovered.

Two men from the second platoon approached, saying that a lost band from Company B was coming toward camp carrying two injured. Szymon and Luc intercepted the men and lifted Malenko off and carried him to the field hospital. Malenko's body was limp. "He's dizzy, exhausted, was puking, and he crapped his pants. A medic has to see him immediately."

The medic told them he needed a real doctor.

"He landed hard on his head," said Major Melnyk.

Joe told Major Melnyk that he was delivering a message from Sergeant Schoeppler. After he gave him the position of the enemy nest, he asked for the new instructions. The Major told them to grab a cup of coffee and get back to their platoons. "Tell the Sergeant to stay in place. Someone will be out there in the morning."

Along the way to rejoin their platoon, Szymon talked about the next day's war games. "Wouldn't it make sense for our squad to cut across the ravine to attack the enemy nest?" asked Szymon.

Joe agreed that it was a good idea. "If nothing else, it would be quicker and catch the enemy off guard."

They made it back to the place where Schoeppler was waiting with the first platoon. It had stopped raining, and the men were resting, some lying on the wet ground sound asleep. After listening to the message from Major Melnyk, Schoeppler cursed softly, "It's going to be a long, miserable night, he said. "Go find Luc," he said.

"Someone has to notify the second platoon from Company B of our position," said Swaczy. "Go find the sergeant."

Luc started off to locate the sergeant when Szymon ran up behind him.

"Luc, why don't you suggest to Sergeant Schoeppler that he try to get Melnyk to change the plan for knocking out the enemy nest? Our platoon can do it. All we have to do is split the platoon and move two squads up to the left side of the ravine. I can help you move two squads around to the right side cutting across near the bottom. We'll come up near the machine guns position where we would have the guns between the two squads. That's all it would take. I've been down in the ravine and know that this is all it would take, saving a hell of a lot of time and speeding up the war game."

"Szymon, I don't know if they would want to change the original plan at this late date, but I will mention it," said Luc.

"For Christ's sake, Luc," said Szymon, glancing at Joe who was crossing himself, "if we cut off a couple of hours from these damn games, we could all go home earlier. I'm getting tired of playing war!"

"Okay, okay, Szymon."

Schoeppler listened to Luc and told him that he would talk to the Sergeant later to see what they thought of Swaczy's idea. He sent Luc, Joe and Swaczy to scout the area around the ravine again, and report back to him.

That night it rained again. Everything was saturated and beginning to stink with mold. Schoeppler knew the men were undergoing a real trial. He hoped he could persuade the higher-ups to shorten the games and adopt Swaczy's plan.

About 5:30 on Wednesday morning, Schoeppler was surprised to see a cart pulled by a donkey coming up the trail. The cooks had sent canteens of coffee and water, enough for each man. That reminded Schoeppler to have someone check on Joe.

"Tell him to drink all the God damned water in his canteen. I don't want him passing out today. On top of everything else, we don't need to haul his fat ass around," he told Hanczyk, who climbed into the cart, unable to suppress his laughter.

The Sergeant from Company A and Company B met

off to the side away from the men in their platoons. Then all hell broke loose as the artillery from behind the 58ᵗʰ Regiment opened up. Schoeppler proposed Szymon Swaczy's idea to knock out the nest, telling them it would make sense and shorten the war games. He said, "I don't know about you, but I think these boys have done their job and put up with enough. It's time to take them home." The Sergeant voiced support for the plan, but Major Melnyk wasn't sure the Commander would approve.

"I've sent scouts to reconnoiter the bottom of the ravine twice, and my boys say it can be done." He took out his map and traced the outline of the ravine with his finger, pointed to the south end and stopped on the spot where Luc Slobodianyk's squad would slip down into the ravine. He pointed to where they would come up over the top near the nest. He marked the spot where Theo Kubida's squad was holding up. "Kubida will move in on the nest. Then Slobodianyk's squad will fire." Schoeppler said that was the only part of the war games that would change. "I'll take responsibility for any fallout, and for Christ's sake, the brass won't even know. They're tired of living in the woods and want to go home, anyway." In the end, Melnyk relented and gave permission to proceed.

Schoeppler breathed a sigh of relief, walking back to his position.

The new plan was to capture the enemy nest and move around the left side to rejoin Company A, heading to the north and west side behind the enemy artillery company. Company A would connect with

Company B, if everything went as planned. Company C would move into position in front of the enemy artillery position, while Company D would head up the right side to the north, and locate an east-west trail then capture a bridge to prevent the enemy's retreat. Then Company D would capture the retreating enemy artillery company, and march the prisoners into camp tonight.

Schoeppler met with his men. "Okay, boys, this is it." He pointed to several places on his map. "These are several features that would help you locate the enemy positions. Any questions?"

This morning, the men had plenty of questions. They asked about obstacles. "Bull Shit! I'm not telling you anything about them. Hell no! Do you want me to spoon-feed you?" sneered Schoeppler. "That is making it too God damned easy for you sons of bitches. This is supposed to be war! Will the enemy give you any help in a real battle?" The men looked at the map again, trying to determine where there might be trouble. "They're learning."

It began drizzling again and continued on and off the rest of the morning. Szymon and Luc left quickly and joined the platoon. Luc told the men that the new plan was a go. The men cheered. Joe stepped forward and offered a short prayer for the safety of all the men on the field this morning. Schoeppler ordered the men to fall in two abreast. They moved to the west, turning toward the north as they had yesterday morning. They had more confidence in Luc, and once deep in the forest, he led them along a well-worn trail that twisted around to the left, climbing up a steep incline. Theo took out his compass and checked due north. "We're still southwest of where I think we should make the turn." They found the path and turned into the woods to the right. Within ten minutes, they came upon the southern end of the ravine. Now, where were the machine guns?

Luc halted the platoon. "If this were a real war, the rain would help us."

The rain would muffle the sound of our approach." Luc didn't want the disaster that Mazurek and Malenko experienced two days ago. He sent Theo and Szymon out to scout the south end of the ravine again. They trudged off, and within minutes they were back saying the edge of the ravine was about one hundred and fifty feet to the east of the enemy nest and about 300 feet to the northwest of their current position. Luc split the platoon, with Theo heading to the west of the enemy machine gun nest, and Luc's squad moving to the east, dropping down into the ravine where Malenko and Mazurek were pulled out on Tuesday.

He worked his way around the ravine wall, while Theo and his men crawled northwest of the ravine, inching their way toward a position about 150 feet southwest of the machine gun nest. Hanczyk was to start firing first, drawing the enemy's attention away from the ravine and giving Luc time to climb on the rocks to fire over the top toward the nest. The maneuver was a success.

Luc sent Hanczyk and Szymon out to scout for trails and enemy positions toward the enemy artillery position. Luc drew another sketch in the muddy ground marking the old enemy infantry position taken out in yesterday's war games. Then he marked the features that Swaczy and Hanczyk reported to connect with Company B behind the artillery position, which he pointed to on the map. "Anyone remember Schoeppler's map?" Several men spoke up and described some features of the map including trails and the creek which Luc drew on the muddy sketch. He drew a big X where the enemy artillery position was located.

The platoon was hampered by the on-and-off rain showers. This was the third day of rain and everything was wet: their clothes, boots and socks. The ponchos did not offer much protection from this kind of weather. Even their field packs were soggy. There was no shelter in the woods except to huddle under the tree canopy.

"It's about 10:30, said Luc. "If you have anything in your pack to eat, I'd do it now." Most of the guys rummaged in their field packs and, pulled out a hard roll and stood gnawing on it. Just before 11:00 they were startled to see a couple of men they didn't recognize. It turned out that these were men from Company B.

"Where the hell did you come from?" asked Szymon.

While the men were explaining how they got

separated from their platoon, several more came around the south side of the ravine and headed their way.

Luc and Sergeant Panczyk stood filling each other in on their platoon's plan.

"Let's go, said Panczykn." "Let's get these damned games over."

They marched two abreast heading slightly east of north, rejoining both Companies A and B. Company D was coming in from the east. The Sergeant from Company C was ready to move his platoons into position in front of the enemy artillery. Men from Companies A and B moved south to confront the enemy, while two platoons from Company D moved eastward toward the wooden bridge. The Sergeant standing nearby looked on in horror as the bridge began to collapse.

For a few minutes, the situation looked perilous as three men had to be rescued from falls into the ravine. There were several injuries. At 1:30 on Wednesday afternoon, Major Melnyk declared that the war games had finally come to an end.

Major Melnyk conferred with the Sergeant, and ordered them to take the men back to the camp. At 4:30, two platoons were still filtering into camp. It felt good to lie down, to rest until supper. The smell of food made the wait almost unbearable. That evening the men sat around several big fires hoping their clothes and shoes would dry. Major Melnyk addressed them and said that overall, the games went well.

"There were some injuries including several sprains, two broken ankles, one broken arm, several dislocated shoulders, one concussion, plenty of bad scrapes, bruises and black eyes, and two men lost front teeth. What do you think?" he asked. "We learned a lot in three days."

Luc, Theo, Szymon and Joe stood waiting to board the train the next morning. They were still weary from the two days spent outdoors in the weather. Their bodies ached. Theo and Joe had sore throats and were beginning to cough. The Claxton honked signaling to them to board the train. Sergeant Schoeppler followed behind. Black smoke and cinders belched from the smoke stack, and then the train lurched forward. Later that afternoon, Sergeant Schoeppler told them that Dimitri Malenko was taken to the hospital in Stanislau yesterday. "He doesn't look too good," he said. They were quiet. The returning train ride was faster this morning, arriving in Stanislau at 1 p.m. Schoeppler wasted no time getting them off the train and into formation, two abreast. They marched directly to the mess for dinner. Afterward, Luc took the lead and marched them back to the barracks. The men and Sergeant Schoeppler discussed their common experiences for a long time that afternoon. They fell silent.

Sergeant Schoeppler spoke, "Every one of you did a good job. Luc and Theo performed well, and several others showed that they could think on their feet. Unfortunately, we had injuries. The most serious is Dimitri Malenko. We'll have to see how he does. It may take some time to learn how serious his injuries are. This is the army, and every soldier has to learn what real military life is like. I know that most of you came here from harsh conditions, but this can and will be harsher. That is why it is important to work as a team. You passed the first test today with flying colors. Congratulations on a job well done!"

Chapter 6

When Szymon arrived at the Stanislau military base, he had been dazzled by the array of buildings, roads and infrastructure, but after six months, he realized that the base was much smaller than he originally had envisioned. At first, he liked the neatness and order, but slowly began to see the decay behind the fresh paint. All buildings and infrastructure on the base were outdated and in need of replacement or major renovation. Gas lights had come into common usage but many of the buildings didn't have access to gas lines. As a result, fires were not uncommon due to accidents caused by upended kerosene lanterns. Funding for the military during the years following the formation, in 1867, of the common army had fallen behind, and as a result, the army languished in a state of neglect. For decades following the peasant uprisings in 1848, the Empire enjoyed a period of peace, lulling the politicians in Vienna into complacency until an incident forced them to face reality.

Bosnia Herzegovina had become a hotbed of unrest. In June of 1878, the Austro-Hungarian Empire began mobilization of a military force numbering more than 82,000 men to meet the growing crisis. In that year, a rebellion against the Ottoman Empire, and uprisings between ethnic groups and social classes in far-off Bosnia and Herzegovina erupted. Ethnic and religious resentments often, but not always, aligned along the three religious sects (Greek Catholic, Roman Catholic, and Muslim) throughout the Empire.

The rebellion prompted the Austro-Hungarian military to send troops to quell the unrest, but to no avail. In early August 1878, a battle was fought near the town of Jajce resulting in the loss of 600 Austro-Hungarian soldiers. Also, fear of an Ottoman Empire takeover and some minor skirmishes led to a major battle and the fall of the city of Sarajevo, in October 1878.

The Ottoman Empire had a 40,000-man army and another 50,000 men in local militias. Several ferocious battles took place in many cities in the region. Although the major battles were quashed in three months, over 5,000 Austro-Hungarian soldiers were killed or wounded including 57 officers. In September 1878, the Treaty of Berlin had been signed mandating an occupation force of four to five thousand men to remain in three cities. Matters did not end there and the uprisings spread. The Bosnians continued to resist the Monarchy's pacification efforts with significant uprisings in 1881 and 1882. At one point, Austro-Hungarian Army troops numbered over 80,000 in the region. Thereafter, the Austrian military budgets were increased resulting in a building program and equipment upgrades. As a result, training for the common soldier was improved, with emphasis on marksmanship.

War planners realized that better marksmanship was cost effective resulting in savings. The containment of uprisings in the Empire was Vienna's foremost goal along with better training for the common soldier. It was inevitable that Szymon's company would be deployed to far away Bosnia Herzegovina someday. But, that was far off in the future, and life in Stanislau continued at a predictable, peaceful pace.

Over the next nine months, life on the small base at Stanislau Galicia took on an expected, steady rhythm. The boys who had arrived in March became mature men, exuding a sense of pride. They took responsibility for their job performance within the platoon and in other assignments. Their physical condition improved due to better diets, sanitation, regular calisthenics, and strenuous work. There was a medic on the base and a small hospital in town for the treatment of accidents, diseases, serious infections and other conditions.

They learned to care for both their rifles and for their bodies, as well as their personal appearance. They took pride in the cleanliness and orderliness of their barracks. Their assignments varied from cutting grass, disposing of garbage, cleaning the stables, delivering coal and ice to the various facilities, or any place that a sturdy body and strong back were needed. Sergeant Schoeppler managed to have Joe Korlaszcz assigned to the Chaplaincy. Luc Slobodianyk was assigned as Schoeppler's assistant, and Szymon's job on base was, not surprisingly, no more than a common laborer—hard labor at that.

It was October 1891, the thirteenth year of the occupation, and the men in the 58th infantry realized that they would be going to Bosnia Herzegovina. Fourteen years earlier, in far-off Vienna, the prevailing belief was that Bosnia Herzegovina would be a minor campaign, prompting the common Army Foreign Minister at the time to nonchalantly quip, "It will be like a walk with a brass band." Instead, Bosnia turned into a costly 30-year occupation involving over 200,000 military men. Under the Treaty of Berlin, the participants agreed to an occupation by the Austro-Hungarians lasting from 1878 to 1908.

Schoeppler told them about the mobilization and occupation several weeks earlier. After target practice on a fall day in late October 1891, he informed the men that they had passed the proficiency requirements for their marksmanship badge with flying colors. "You will receive your Qualification Badge in a few weeks," he told them. "For the next several months we'll be in the field training for your assignment to Bosnia or Herzegovina."

Szymon spoke up. "Where is the place?"

Schoeppler took out a map on which he outlined the two small nations.

"Both Bosnia and Herzegovina are still technically administered by the Ottomans, but actually, they are part of the Austro-Hungarian Empire." He looked around at their puzzled faces. "Don't ask me how this came about, what the hell do I know? I'm just a mere soldier," said Schoeppler. "The cultures are far apart."

He traced the train route between Stanislau and Bosnia Herzegovina,

"It's about 700 miles between the cities of Stanislau and Sarajevo, the capital of Bosnia," he said. It's too complicated to get into, but the Austro-Hungarians have ruled the area since 1878. Like everything else, the most powerful Empires win in the end. The truth is that I don't know exactly where you are heading, but we will know soon."

A few days later, Szymon's company began field training and for the next several weeks were exposed to the elements, no matter if it was raining or snowing. He organized competitive games between platoons, to motivate the men.

Luc's squad crawled on their bellies, sometimes in the mud, racing against Theo's squad. They set up hurdles to jump over or under, scaled walls using hooks and ropes, and rappelling straight-up vertical walls. They forded streams and creeks, in water up to their hips, under all kinds of conditions. The Company traveled into the Carpathians near Hoverla the highest mountain in Galicia to train for warfare in mountainous terrain.

They learned to break their rifles down and put

them back together blindfolded. Schoeppler informed them that there would be a language barrier because Bosnians spoke Serbian. They would experience many differences in culture, including differences in clothing, music, religion and food. Most Ruthenians recognized the Cyrillic alphabet, although few knew how to read or write using any language other than the Latin alphabet. Schoeppler was preparing the men for culture shock.

On a Sunday afternoon, Szymon asked his cousin, "Theo, what do you think about transferring to Bosnia?" Theo didn't really care about traveling someplace else, and asked Szymon what he thought about the move. "I don't know and don't really care much one way or the other," answered Szymon.

"Why?"

"I like the idea of going somewhere I've never seen before," said Szymon. "Why in hell would you say that? Don't you like Galicia?"

"Hell, no!" said Szymon.

Theo stopped and stood watching him. He said, "You are different than the rest of us, except Luc, that is, you both go your separate ways and don't seem to mind being alone."

"Why would anyone care what I do?" asked Szymon, with mild irritation in his voice.

"I don't mean to say they don't like you, but they say you are a loner."

Szymon thought about this for a minute or two,

ultimately deciding not to respond.

They arrived at the company store. It was Sunday, and they were at rest. Earlier that morning, most men on base attended church. Afterward, they were free to go most places on base. Szymon liked to read a newspaper, or sometimes write a letter to his father. Occasionally, he played cards with some of his buddies. They liked to smoke, make small talk, tell jokes or stories, and just goof off. No alcohol was allowed on base. This Sunday, there were a couple dozen men standing around outside the store. It was a cloudy, warm day and it felt good to be outdoors. Theo and Szymon stopped to talk for a while. There were always one or two guys who tried to drag anyone they could get to agree to join a small group who had access to illegal vodka. Szymon just avoided getting involved when the conversation turned to buying into a secret plan.

One of the guys came over to Szymon and attempted to persuade him saying, "It's only harmless fun."

Szymon shook his head. Roman had warned him not to be tempted. He told them that if he were caught, he would be thrown out of the Army. The fellow persisted, and finally Szymon had enough and spoke in a raised voice, "Don't bother me. I'm not interested. Go away and don't ask me again."

Theo walked over, "Hey, what's going on?"

The other man said, "Nothing, just a friendly disagreement." Theo's eyes shifted to Szymon.

"It's nothing," said Szymon.

When they returned to their barracks, Theo said, "That guy is a pain in the ass."

"I hear he isn't much of a soldier," Szymon said. "If I want to sneak a drink, I'm not going to advertise it."

November 28, 1891

Dear Father, Roman Swaczy and dear Mother, Helena Swaczy,

I am writing to tell you about the things we are doing on base. Sergeant Schoeppler is training my squad to go to Bosnia, I think. We learned a lot and go over the same things almost every day. We learn about the Serbian language. I can read a few words and speak some sentences. I can say hello and goodbye.

Two weeks ago, we went to Mountain Hervela, about 60 miles from here. We trained there for three days. I liked it. No one got hurt this time. We don't know when we will leave for Bosnia, but I will go home before then, maybe before Christmas.

Say hello to my sister and brothers, grandma and grandpa.

I hope the vegetables were good. I missed planting in the garden. Are you well? This is all I have for now.

Your son, yours truly,

Szymon Swaczy

Szymon was sitting, on his bed, cleaning his rifle

when Sergeant Schoeppler came over and spoke to him in a lowered voice, "Go to the Company Commander's Office after dinner. He has a few questions to ask you."

Szymon stared at Schoeppler, wondering why in the hell the Commander would want to speak to him. "Szymon, I want you to speak directly to him. He will give you the details. Keep this quiet. Be there by 2 p.m."

Szymon nodded. It was difficult for him to concentrate even on a mere task such as cleaning his rifle. No matter how he tried to relive the events of the last few days, he couldn't come up with any reason why he should speak directly to Field Marshall Swartzdorf. Hell, he had never spoken to the man in his life. When Szymon looked around the barracks, he was relieved that no one was watching him. Most of the men were cleaning their guns, straightening their foot locker or performing some other routine task. "I guess I will know soon enough," he thought.

The morning dragged painfully slow. Major Melnyk showed up for inspection. As usual, a few men didn't pass. They were lazy about keeping their foot lockers orderly, or their guns clean. Sometimes, their beds were improperly made. The worst case would be when someone had items in the foot lockers that were disallowed.

"Afterward," Szymon said, "I guess the mess needs a few guys to peel potatoes today." The joke fell flat because the joke was overdone, although always true.

Schoeppler had Luc call the platoon to attention, two abreast, a few minutes earlier. "After you finish dinner, return here. I'll be going over some important information about your leave and reassignment to Bosnia Herzegovina. Get here on time, because I won't repeat any of this. Don't bother coming to my door for information that you should have gotten. Take the wax out of your ears."

No one treated Szymon differently this afternoon at dinner. "Maybe there is nothing to my meeting with Swartzdorf, but why the hell does he want to speak to me?"

Finally, there was information about the date of their furlough. It would begin on December 20th and end January 5th. Everyone should plan on leaving here before noon and returning on the 5th before 1p.m. A cheer went up. Even Szymon let go with a whoop! The information about transferring to Bosnia Herzegovina took longer, but Schoeppler told them the basics. The company would leave Stanislau on April 29th for Pljevlja.

"We will talk a lot about Pljevlja in the next few weeks. There is a lot of information to cover. We will go over the protocols that you should know about leaving Galicia and entering the borders of other nations. I will tell you what you should be prepared to leave behind or take with you on furlough later this month. Boys, there is a lot to cover, but at least you know where you will be spending the next year of your life!"

Later that day, Szymon sat speechless in Lieutenant Swartzdorf's office. He could not believe his ears. He was being accused of purchasing and sneaking illegal vodka onto the Stanislau base. His heart pounded. When he spoke, his mouth felt dry and he had a difficult time finding his words. He stuttered, "Sir, I do not know anything about illegal vodka."

"Szymon," Swartzdorf spoke sternly, "I want to help you, and if you tell me the truth, it will go easier on you. Let's go over what you do know. Do you know about the illegal alcohol coming on base?"

"Only that some men have asked me if I was interested in joining in."

"Joining in what? What did you say to the man?" asked Swartzdorf. Szymon told him what he knew which Swartzdorf agreed wasn't much.

"When was the last time you heard about alcohol being brought on base?" asked Swartzdorf. Commander Swartzdorf sat listening and taking notes while Szymon answered his questions. He asked if he could remember the date of the last time he was asked to participate.

"Only a few days ago, sir."

"Do you know of any others in on this scheme or who else knows about it?"

Szymon hesitated. "Sir, I don't want anyone to get into trouble who isn't directly involved."

The questioning went on for another fifteen

minutes. Swartzdorf abruptly stood and said, "You haven't told me anything I don't already know. I can't tell if you are telling the truth, but you are sticking to your story." Szymon was silent.

"Soldier, go back to your barracks, I'll be calling on you again."

Szymon saluted, "Yes, sir!" He left confused and worried. He knew that Stephan Katanyk and some other guy were involved, but didn't want to be the person to implicate them.

It must have been evident that something had happened to Szymon because the men in his squad kept staring at him as he joined the discussion about transferring to Bosnia. Szymon gave up trying to concentrate after a few minutes.

"This can't be happening to me!"

For the first time, since he arrived on base, he realized that he liked his military life after all, and wanted to stay.

Schoeppler spoke to him again the next morning, "Szymon, tell me the truth. Did you drink any of that booze?"

"No, sir," replied Szymon.

"Not one drink?"

"No, sir!"

"Szymon, where were you while all that was happening?"

"I was here."

"What were you doing?"

"I wrote a letter home."

"Were there any other guys with you here in the barracks?"

"I'll have to think about that. Sir, do you think they will find out who did this?"

The next two days were a living hell. It seemed that no one could back up Szymon's alibi. He didn't want to ask around to other men, but he might have to do something to save his ass. He realized that he was thinking of nothing else these days.

After supper that evening, Theo came over and asked if everything was ok. Szymon just nodded. "The guys are beginning to suspect there is something wrong with you. Oh, did you hear about Lev Sawchuk?" asked Theo.

"No," said Szymon as he began drifting away again. He thought he heard Theo say that Lev was in trouble for stealing. "Who is Lev?" asked Szymon.

"He is the guy who tried to get you to join the vodka deal," said Theo."

"What's his name?" Szymon slowly realized that Sawchuk tried to get him to buy into the booze party. "Is he still purchasing illegal booze?"

"He gets it from someone who comes onto the base, regularly."

"Are people still buying into that scheme?" asked Szymon.

"Something is up with that. The party was called off last Sunday. Some of the guys told me that they were questioned about what they knew."

"Were you questioned?"

"No, but there are plenty of rumors, and I hear that two or three guys are suspected of being ringleaders."

"Well, let me know what you find out," pleaded Szymon.

The next day, at dinner, Theo sought out Szymon and whispered:

"I hear you are being questioned." Szymon nodded. "Oh shit! For Christ's sake, Szymon, why didn't you say something? What the hell is wrong with you? You have to fend for yourself, don't you know that?" Szymon shrugged. "Szymon, I know you weren't involved in this scheme. I was with you when Lev approached you. We walked back to the barracks together.

Don't you remember? That afternoon, you wrote letters to a couple of guys, didn't you? Do they suspect it is you?" Szymon nodded. "Oh, shit! For Christ's sake, why would that son of a bitch Lev let someone he barely knows take the rap for him?"

That evening, Theo and two other guys went to speak with Schoeppler. They told him that Szymon was innocent, that he had been with Theo and later returned to the barracks where he wrote letters for two boys who don't read or write very well. The three men agreed to speak to Lieutenant Swartzdorf. Afterward, Theo told Szymon about their conversation with the commander. Szymon felt the weight of the world lift from his shoulders. That evening, while going through his foot locker, he came across the letter he had written to his father but had forgotten to mail. He had written the date November 28, 1891 on the letter. Now, the whole thing became clearer.

The base was abuzz with the story of Lev's scheme. Lev worked in the ice house receiving ice for the base six days a week. He arranged deals with someone who worked for the ice company. It was easy to smuggle bottles of vodka onto the base hidden in the straw covering the blocks of ice. Lev's job was to unload the wagon on Saturday mornings. After Lev had rounded up enough guys to buy into the booze party, he would pay for three or four bottles and have them hidden in the wagon. Since no one was working at the ice house on Sunday, Lev passed the word to meet there in the afternoons. The men would drink and shoot craps. On Sunday, November 28th, they overdid the drinking, and several guys became unruly and rowdy. A couple of them passed out and had to be carried back to their barracks. Altogether, fifteen men were identified.

Following the revelations about Lev's scheme, Szymon was notified by Sergeant Schoeppler that Lieutenant Swartzdorf wanted to speak to him in his office. "Szymon, the men told me that you were not part of the scheme to bring booze on this base. Three men backed up your story that you weren't involved.

I realize now that you told me the truth and understood from Schoeppler that you are doing a fine job. There will be no mention of this incident in your record. Your record is clear. Keep it that way."

"Thank you, sir."

"You are dismissed, soldier. As you were."

Szymon saluted and left the office dazed, weak-kneed, in great relief. He felt sick in his stomach and it had made a temporary mess of his life. The next day Szymon heard a rumor that Lev Sawchuk was going to be kicked out of the army and sent home. He went to see Sergeant Schoeppler to confirm the story, which turned out to be true.

Over the next couple of days, several of the men approached him to ask questions about the vodka deal. Szymon felt uncomfortable in the limelight until Joe Korlaszcz sat next to him at supper one evening.

"Szymon, I think you handled the situation like a mature man. But, you didn't have to face all the charges alone. You could have made it easier on yourself if you had talked to one of the guys. Don't be so hard on yourself. Don't act like a martyr, and next time come and talk to me. I'll help you whenever I can."

Szymon told Joe about his conversation with Schoeppler. He had left his office feeling foolish. Instead of seeing his point, Schoeppler blew up. "I just asked him to reconsider throwing Lev out and to give him another chance."

"Szymon, sometimes things happen to us for our own good. I think Sergeant Schoeppler meant well, but Lev needs to face up and stop trying to get away with this kind of thing. He has to stop before it's too late, or he will have a life of misery ahead of him."

"Joe, I didn't know what to do. My father would have been mad as hell if Theo hadn't spoken up and gotten me out of that jam. I don't know if I could have faced him." Szymon paused for a long time. "The guys would have thought that I snitched on Lev. I didn't know what to do."

Joe had matured, too. He was the most levelheaded and compassionate person Szymon knew. "Hey, are you going home, Szymon? Why don't we ride together?" Little did Szymon know that after that day their lives would be linked, in ways neither could ever have imagined.

On Saturday morning, December 20th, Szymon and Joe stood on the train platform waiting for the northbound train along with another thirty-five to forty soldiers. Behind Joe, he caught a glimpse of guys passing a bottle. He quickly looked away.

It was a cold day, but they were dressed warmly and were not uncomfortable. "It feels good to be out here waiting for the train to go home."

Theo laughed and reminded him of his remark last month about wanting to leave his hometown. Szymon looked sheepish and muttered a reply he hoped no one could hear. "I guess I'm looking forward to seeing Ma and Pa, but that's about it. How about you, Joe? Are you looking forward to seeing your parents?"

"They're both dead; I live with my Aunt and Uncle." Szymon began to speak, apologizing for asking the question, but Joe interrupted him. "My aunt and uncle are like my parents. Mine died in a typhus outbreak three years ago. We were living in Kolomyyja," said Joe.

"How do you stay upbeat and cheerful?"

"I have a lot to be grateful for and my Lord has helped me every day to stay positive."

"Don't you miss your parents?"

Joe spoke softly, in the sincerest manner, while looking straight into Szymon's eyes. "They are with me every day." The two friends stood silently for a few minutes. It wasn't an uncomfortable silence and neither tried to fill the void. They felt the rumble of the train under their feet as it approached from the south, and within a few minutes, they departed Stanislau.

Onboard the train, they rested for a while, and in time picked up their conversation where it had left off. Joe invited Szymon and Theo to come to visit during the holiday and handed Szymon a piece of paper with his name and directions to his house.

"I hope to find the time to ride over to see you."

When the train arrived, the three young men shook hands and said goodbye. Szymon and Theo watched

Joe walk across the train tracks toward Czahrow Road. And, with a wave, he broke into a trot. Theo watched him for a few minutes, finally saying, "Kind of an odd fellow, don't you think?"

"No, Theo, he is an honest, sincere person and a good man."

Chapter 7

Ma was in the kitchen preparing supper when Szymon arrived home.

She began to cry when she saw him, but Szymon would not allow it. "Mama, don't cry. I'm home. Let's be happy." He teased her as he twirled her around the little kitchen.

"I wish I knew you were coming today," she said, with tears in her eyes.

"Didn't you receive my letter? Oh, no! Ma, I forgot to mail that letter. I'm so sorry."

He wrote the letter on November 28th but it was still inside his locker.

"Are you mad at me, Mama?" he asked, worried. But Ma was just happy to see him again.

That evening, the family sat at the table after supper listening to the stories Szymon told about the nine months he spent in the army. They were tough, but he came home with a lot of interesting adventures he couldn't wait to share with the fam.

Roman sat quietly, smoking his pipe. Szymon's brother, Michael, and sister, Anna, bombarded him with questions. They were surprised when he told them that he only had been to Stanislau a dozen times. Most of his trips off base were traveling to training camps in the region. He went to the ice company two or three times and to the post office once or twice.

Roman broke his silence. "I bet you marched in and out of Stanislau Base almost every day." Szymon was overlooking all those times his platoon marched through the town center as part of their training.

"All armies everywhere parade around just as a reminder to the locals that a military force is nearby. Anyway, there is no need to go to town, because the base meets the basic needs of any soldier."

His brothers and Anna had planned a visit to see a neighbor that night and stood up to leave. Szymon declined their invitation to tag along with them. He was tired, but mostly wanted to stay behind to talk to Pa. It had been a while since he sat down and had a conversation with them. He could really use some time with Pa.

After they were gone, Szymon told his father the story of Lev Sawchuk and the illegal alcohol. He told him about his meetings with the company commander. But, he really wanted to talk about what Sergeant Schoeppler said.

"He bawled me out, Pa. He said Lev didn't deserve a second chance because he caused a lot of trouble at the base. I know Lev broke a bunch of rules and instigated the whole thing, including gambling. But Pa, I thought Lev could be given a second chance. I hated to be the one that had caused him to be thrown out. That pissed off Schoeppler and he told me I had a lot to learn. He blamed everything on Lev. Shouldn't he have a second chance?"

"Szymon, Schoeppler is right; you do have a lot to learn. You have to get harder. The Army doesn't put up with anyone's bullshit. Lev sounds like a guy who will keep breaking the rules no matter how many chances he gets. Schoeppler is right, rules are rules. You will learn. I couldn't have kept my mouth shut. I know I would have gone after Lev and beat the shit out of him." Roman was angry. "That bastard could have gotten away with it, and you could have been thrown out on your ass. I'm surprised that you were so patient."

Szymon fought back tears. "It wasn't easy, Pa."

His mother reached for his hand. Tears were running down her face. This brought back memories of his life as a boy. Szymon loved his mother and was extremely close to her. She had been a steadfast comfort to him during his young boyhood and often stood between him and his father. He believed he could depend upon her to fend off the trials and tribulations of the world. Szymon was the youngest of eight children, two of whom had died. Pa drank, as did most men in their family circle and he had been difficult to live with in his younger days. No one questioned the abuse of alcohol, and Roman did not catch the irony in his praise for the way his son handled his situation. It took a while but as a much older man, Roman eventually recognized the harm alcohol abuse caused families, including his own. Alcoholism just compounded the misery in the personal lives of people who were trapped in almost unbearable circumstances, not of their own making.

"It's good to have you home." Nodding slowly, he looked away, briefly staring off into space, then Roman repeated, "It's good to have you home, son."

On Sunday, they attended church where they met family and friends. He heard the same comments over and over: "Szymon, you have grown up."

"You are a man!" Out of the corner of his eye, he saw the young ladies staring at him. Szymon dated a girl before he left for the army, but it never was a serious romance, and they were very different. He was still a virgin and was embarrassed by it. Back home in Bukaczowce, he was scared to have any serious involvement with a young woman from a family who might know Ma and Pa. It would be impossible to control his sexual urges. Ma and Pa were ready to return home when a friend of Ma's ran over to their wagon.

The woman, whom Szymon didn't know, began gossiping with her. Szymon sighed, climbed down from the wagon, and led old Black off the road so others could pass. When he turned around, he caught sight of a young woman walking toward him. His interest perked up; she was pretty. He remembered her as a girl he had gone to school with years earlier.

"Hello, Kashka," calling her by her pet name.

She answered in a sweet girlish voice, "Hello, Szymon, you remembered me! I heard you are in the Army now. Are you home on furlough?" He nodded thinking that her voice sounded like music to him. "My brother is home, too."

"What's his name?" asked Szymon. He didn't recognize the name and felt foolish, not knowing what to say next.

She smiled at him and said, "There is folk dancing at the community house next week. You might want to come out.

"I might be there, if I am home." His reply felt clumsy.

On the way home, his mother asked if he remember Katarzyna Tracz.

His face reddened as he said, "Yes, she has grown up. She told me about a dance next week. I might go."

His mother abruptly changed the subject. "Did you make any friends in the army?" She was always concerned about him because he spent a lot of time alone.

"Yes. Do you know a family from Czahrow named Korlaszcz? I met Joe Korlaszcz; he lives with his aunt and uncle there. Hey, Ma, do you want to ride with me tomorrow to meet them?" His mother beamed. She couldn't pass up the opportunity to ride out to the countryside with her handsome son.

The next afternoon, Mrs. Korlaszcz was pleased to meet a friend of Joe's and his friend's mother. The two ladies chatted for a long time that day. While his mother and Joe's aunt gossiped, Szymon and Joe slipped behind the house into the woods. It was a good day to be outside, cold but sunny. They walked a long way before reaching a small secluded pond. Picking up pebbles, they threw them toward the middle of the pond, watching them skitter over the frozen surface, testing the ice to determine whether or not it was solid away from the shore.

The past three nights had been bitterly cold, the temperature falling below freezing. The ice was thick, and today there was no chance of falling through into the frigid water. Szymon had brought dough balls for bait. They stood at the edge of the pond, looking out on an expanse of snow-covered ice. They chopped into the ice about fifteen feet away from the shore and dropped fish lines into the hole. In half an hour, they caught eight carp. Szymon felt another tug on his line and jerked it back hard.

"Got him!"

Then he heard Joe. "Hey, Szymon, come here. Hurry!" The sound of urgency was in his voice. Szymon dragged the flopping carp over the ice, running to see what was causing Joe's alarm. Joe and Szymon crouched down and brushed fresh snow from the ice. They could make out a face floating under the water.

"Oh, dear Jesus," whispered Joe, crossing himself. Szymon knelt horrified. The face was disfigured, and he thought no one would be able to recognize who it was. The fish had eaten away at the flesh. Joe began praying for the dead person. He fingered his rosary, reciting the words. Softly they said the Lord's Prayer; then, recited the twenty-third Psalm.

"It's a man." They whispered as if not wanting to disturb the sleep of this dead person. It was difficult for them to speak even after they had overcome their initial shock. They tried not to look at the disfigured face. Szymon wished there was something he could do but he kept reminding himself that the person was dead. Still, it seemed that something more should be done. Finally, he whispered, in a barely audible voice, "It will be spring before the ice thaws."

They left all the fish behind, pushing them back into the hole they had chopped in the ice. They said nothing as they started walking side by side back to the house. Szymon and Joe were noticeably different in appearance. Both tall young men, Joe was broad shouldered and muscular, with dark skin, hair and eyes, while Szymon was thin, fair, blond and blue-eyed. Joe was a devout Roman Catholic while Szymon was nonchalant about attending Greek Catholic mass. Szymon drank and Joe abstained. They were different but, now they shared a life-altering experience. They would be forever bonded because of the events of that day.

Szymon was deep in thought when he realized that Joe was speaking to him.

"Szymon, he is in heaven with my father and mother." As they were nearing the house, Joe saw his Uncle Jan working in the barn. He told him what they had found.

Mr. Korlaszcz stood quietly for a few minutes, before crossing himself. "Joe, that is old man Minoryk. He's been missing."

"I hate to tell Aunt Maria. She will be very upset."

"Why don't we wait and tell her after Szymon and his mother have gone? Let's not spoil their afternoon."

Joe asked, "How long has Mr. Minoryk been missing?"

"About ten days. I guess he was not in his right mind and wandered away."

They were overwhelmed by the thought of the old man wandering lost and confused, improperly dressed for a bitterly cold night. Szymon shuddered, "Poor Mr. Minoryk."

"Somehow he fell into the water..." Joe's voice trailed off.

"Joe, don't worry, I'll tell Aunt Maria."

Szymon didn't hear the rest of the conversation. He silently gazed at the blue sky and rolling hill, before telling Joe that they had to stop to see his brother and sister on the way home. Joe didn't know Szymon's brother but knew of Swaczy's living nearby. Szymon asked if he had brothers or sisters.

"I have a brother, Wally, who is four years older than me."

"Hey, Joe, are you going to the dance on Saturday?"

"Maybe. There is a lot of drunkenness at those dances, and I don't drink."

Szymon was quiet. Joe was quiet too. Szymon didn't take offense. He simply told Joe that he had been around alcohol all of his life, that some of his uncles, even his father, had struggled with addiction. "Pa isn't drinking now, but he's gone on and off the wagon many times over the years."

"Well, Szymon, I like to dance, and don't have to drink, so I think I will meet you on Saturday night. Some of the guys from the platoon should be there, too."

On the way home, Szymon's mother chattered away, excited about her new friend. "I hope to see her at the Thursday Fair." Mrs. Korlaszcz, I mean Maria, is very nice. She told me about Joe's parents. His mother hoped that he would study for the priesthood one day."

In spite of the horrific event, he felt at peace in this cold, quiet place. The sound of his mother's sing-song chatter, the warmth the setting winter sun cast upon his face, relaxed him, lulling him to sleep. Old Black slowed down and turned into the road leading up to a neat, tiny house with a chimney above the metal roof.

The house was warm and cozy. His sister-in-law,

Tekla was home preparing supper, when the mule pulled the cart into the yard. They sat at the kitchen table, while Tekla peeled turnips for supper. They exchanged the latest rumors and news circulating among their family and friends.

Helena asked, "Do you expect Stephen home soon?

"He should have been here. I'm beginning to wonder where he is."

They couldn't stay much longer. Fifteen minutes later, Stephen still hadn't arrived. Reluctantly, Szymon told his mother that they would have to leave. Tekla was obviously embarrassed. They said their goodbyes. As they were leaving Szymon glanced back and thought he saw Stephen's horse standing under trees beyond the rear of the house, still hitched to the wagon. He didn't mention this to his mother who was still chattering away about Maria Korlaszcz.

At supper that night Szymon told his father and mother about Mr. Minoryk floating in the pond, under the ice. The family was stunned. No one spoke for a long time. Then, Helena began gathering the dishes and clearing the table. She was so visibly upset, her hands shook; she dropped two knives and broke a glass.

Szymon's sister, Anna, turned pale, and was so agitated that she had to sit for a while, too upset to wash the dishes. Her brother tried comforting her, suggesting they visit a neighbor. After they left, Roman and Szymon began talking about the remaining time that Szymon would be home, as it was passing quickly. Roman asked Szymon if he wanted to make a few dollars working at the estate.

"I hadn't thought about it."

"Don't you want to help me with repairs around here?"

They talked about a few chores they could do in the barn. Szymon had helped his father clean the attic last Saturday. He washed clothes for his mother Tuesday. They planned to go to the Fair the next day so she could sell her freshly baked pastries and breads. Mama always sold her handicraft and baked goods to earn extra money for buying shoes, warm gloves and extra things for her children.

"Tell me what is important, Pa, and I can work in your place," he insisted. That would give you a rest for a few days." His father was uncomfortable accepting the offer, so nothing was decided that evening.

Ma was not in the kitchen when Pa awakened the next morning. He arose about 4:30 to milk the cows, but didn't feel well, so went back to bed. Lately he wasn't himself. Szymon, who was lying next to him, awakened and asked, "Are you feeling alright, Pa?"

"Just a little under the weather this morning. I can't sleep." After a few more minutes, he said, "I'll be alright." Roman stood, looking out of the narrow window. The room was dark except for the dim glow of the oil-filled lantern. Dawn was breaking and it looked like Thursday would be clear. He dressed, and as he did, he turned up the light on the lantern, then he lit two more lamps in the kitchen. He heard Szymon moving around, dressing, splashing water on his face.

Ma came in carrying two pails of water. "Mama," said Szymon, taking the pails from her. "I'd like to work a few days in Pa's place to give him some rest."

Ma sat down and glanced at Roman who averted his eyes. Nothing more was said on the subject. Szymon broke the silence, "Mama, would you make a pot of coffee? Let's have warm, left-over coffee cake for breakfast." Ma arose long before daybreak each week to make dough for her pastries and breads. Today, she had 10 pans ready to put in the oven. Roman opened the oven door, fiddled to adjust the temperature, and then slid four pans onto the clay floor of the pitch.

"It's so good to have you home, Szymon," said his mother.

"What are you saving your coins for this time, Mama?" Szymon asked.

"It's a surprise."

Pa was upset about Mr. Minoryk's death. "It is a terrible way to die."

The house was warm and cozy, making it seem somehow disrespectful to go to the fair today. They fell silent again. "It's difficult to think about going, but we have to because Mama has to sell her baked goods and buy groceries," Szymon said he wanted to buy some small gifts for his family for St. Nicholas

Day. Roman planned to go to the auction to check prices on young calves. They lingered enjoying each other's company, cherishing these precious moments together.

Mama wondered aloud, "What was going on with Stephen? He is avoiding me." Roman said that no one knew what was in Stephen's head, but this wasn't the first time this had happened. "Poor Tekla," said Ma. "I worry about her, and I know she wants a baby."

"Well, what have you decided?" asked Szymon. "How about it, Pa?

If you won't tell me what you want me to do, I will just plan to work in your place next week."

"Roman, you need the rest. You have chest pains and are sometimes short of breath."

"Why don't you putter around the house, Pa? I'll work in your place. If you are up to it, you can make a few repairs."

Ma had put the last four pans in the oven and was preparing dinner while Roman and Szymon went to the barn. "Pa, I want to tell you about our visit to see Stephen and Tekla." He told his father about his suspicion concerning seeing Stephan's horse and wagon pulled off the road. "I think he purposely avoided Ma and me. What's going on with him?" asked Szymon. "The more time that passes, the more Stephen pulls away from the family. What's wrong with him?"

"Tekla has not gotten pregnant," said Roman.

"I think it is more than that, Pa, because Steve pushes other people around. Neighbors started avoiding him a year ago. He wasn't too friendly before I left for Stanislau. Maybe he is resentful because I joined the army. What does Ma have to say?"

While they talked, they made a few minor repairs, then cleared and organized the piles of stuff laying everywhere. They picked up empty chicken feed sacks, odds and ends of wood, bent nails, and even found a coin lying in the dirt. Szymon raked the floor and straightened the shelves. Roman gathered the eggs and cleaned the chicken coop. He stacked old used bricks and boards along the wall. They chased a mouse or two hiding in a pile of burlap sacks.

Michael poked his head in the door asking," Do you need help?" Szymon and Michael tightened the bolts on the wagon wheels, while Roman cleaned and repaired the ox yoke and harnesses. They cleaned the rafters and stored the garden tools on hooks and nails.

Anna peeked in the door. "Hey, it finally looks nice in here." Then she called them to dinner. "We have to hurry."

Precisely at noon, the family gathered around the table for dinner. Mama reheated the ox tail stew leftover from yesterday's supper. "There wasn't much meat on the bones this time," she lamented.

Anna brought freshly churned butter and warm bread to the table. There wasn't time to linger because the fair started early this time of year, since days were short, and everything would be gone by four o'clock. Szymon looked around, remembering how much he loved this old house. It wasn't fancy and everything showed wear and tear, but it was clean and comfortable. It was small but attractive, thanks to his mother. Only palms from last year's Palm Sunday service and a picture of Holy Mother Mary adorned the walls.

"Ma, where did you get the picture of the Statue of Liberty?"

"Don't you remember, Szymon? I got it from the fair."

He would look for another picture for her, today at the fair.

So many old friends greeted Szymon that afternoon he barely had time to look for the things he wanted. He made excuses knowing he was being rude to people who only wanted to stop to wish him luck or just say hello. But next week he would be working in Pa's place and wouldn't have time. He found some ribbons for his sister's hair, a calendar for his father, a pen, ink, and a pad of paper. He couldn't find the right gift for his mother and was asking for framed pictures, when he heard a familiar voice next to him, "Szymon, why don't you come tomorrow morning to the church? I think there are some nice pictures that your mother would like." He looked up to see father Thomas, a young priest at St Mary's Greek Catholic Church. After making arrangements to meet him in the morning, Szymon went to find his father at the cattle pens.

Bukaczowce had been known as a cattle town for hundreds of years, earning its notoriety for the auction. The cattle auction was winding down when he slipped onto the chair beside Stephen and his father. "What are young calves going for, Pa?"

"Prices are good and, might continue dropping for a few more weeks.

We have to replace Old Rosie, Szymon, so I need another milk cow."

"I hate to see her go." Rosie had been in the family for years and was treated like a pet. He was glad he wouldn't be around when the day came that she was led away.

"Your brother is drunk." Stephen, who had been drinking most of the afternoon, was slumped in the chair next to Roman. Szymon asked if Tekla mentioned that he and Ma stopped the previous day.

"Yes, she told me."

Pa was engrossed in the auction and made a bid on a year-old white face calf. "I checked her out. She looks good to me." Most of the buyers were settling up with the sellers and there were few bidders left. Roman found himself as the sole bidder on the yearling. "Holy Mary!" He had bid three dollars and there were no other bids. He heard the auctioneer exclaim," "Going, going, gone!"

Then, the gavel came down. Szymon, Stephen and Roman looked at each other.

Roman shook his head in astonishment as he got up to look for the seller. "What just happened?"

Left alone with Szymon, Stephen asked, "Are you still sucking on Mama's tit?"

"Oh, for Christ's sake, get off of that, Stephen! You're always looking for a fight. What the hell did I ever do to you?"

Stephen's slurred response mocked Szymon's words. "What the hell did I ever do you?"

"I can't talk to you without an argument."

What started out as an angry conversation, quickly escalated into an overheated confrontation. Stephen was yelling at Szymon, causing people to stop to stare. Pa had settled up with the seller and was returning to get help loading the calf into the cart when he saw his sons arguing.

"Boys, knock it off! I need some help here." Szymon turned toward his father just as Stephen took a swing and missed him. Szymon shoved him away so he couldn't swing again.

Roman's frustration showed. "Damn it, Stephen, I said stop! Get yourself home. I'll be out to see you this weekend, so don't pull your bullshit and hide from me."

Steve lay motionless, sprawled out in the dirt, as Roman and Szymon lifted the calf into the wagon.

Szymon looked pleadingly from his father to his brother. "We can't just leave him lying here. Please,

Steve, let's drop it. I'll be gone next Saturday."

Roman and Szymon helped him to his feet and into the wagon. They found Mama and Anna chatting with Joe Korlaszcz and his aunt, Maria. Szymon introduced Maria and Joe to his father. Just then they saw Tekla coming toward them. Tekla reined in the mule, and tried to put on her best face, but she was clearly embarrassed. Stephen managed to get down from the wagon.

He shook Joe's hand, but ignored Szymon.

Joe, as always, took on the role of peacemaker. "How about if Szymon and I stop by tomorrow after you have supper? We want to say goodbye. We'll be leaving next month for Bosnia and will be gone for a year. How about it? We'll bring Anna and Michael."

On the way home, the family discussed Stephen's behavior.

"I wouldn't worry too much about Steve. Remember, Mama, I used to be worse when I was young," reflected Roman. Your poor Mama, she had her hands full with me, on top of caring for all those babies. Sometimes I acted like a horse's ass." Everyone laughed but didn't dare to comment. It was always hard to judge Pa's mood. Better not to comment than to say something that would cause a ruckus later. "I'll get to the bottom of Stephen's problem on Sunday."

Szymon, Anna and Michael rode over to Stephen's house on Friday evening after supper. Surprisingly, Stephen was in a good mood, neatly shaven and dressed. Joe Korlaszcz was reining in his mule just as they were entering the house. Joe had brought his brother, Wally, whose real name was Walter. There were a few awkward moments as they introduced each other. Walter was the mystery guest and the center of attention. No one knew him because he recently relocated from Kolomyyja to Czahrow. Stephen was curious about him. "How do you like living in the country after living in the big city?"

"I like it, but it might take some time to get used to a small market town.

Kolonyyja has lots of parks, libraries, reading rooms, newspapers. I know I'll miss the coffee houses. There is a German influence that you don't have here, and there's just more to do there which makes it fun. I moved to Charow to help Uncle Jan start a dairy farm. But, it is beautiful here."

They talked for a couple of hours finding that they had more in common with each other than they had first thought. The conversation turned to Joe's and Szymon's experiences in the army.

"There isn't much to say now, but when we come home a year from now, I'll bet we'll have a lot to talk about," speculated Joe. "We're heading to a far-off place called Bosnia, where we are going to see and experience a lot of new things." Szymon had seen a picture in a book of a Muslim man and woman wearing traditional clothing. "They practice a religion there called Islam."

Szymon perked up. "Oh, yeah! I heard about that in

church."

Joe and his brother were Roman Catholics, prompting Stephen to say,

"Your church preaches against Muslims, too."

Walter countered, "Both churches' attitudes toward other religions are about the same."

As she got up to bring a tray of refreshments from her tiny kitchen, Tekla diplomatically changed the subject and said, "I have some cookies and drinks." Later that evening, they were about to say goodbye when Tekla said, "We have a surprise!" The conversation ceased as they waited for Tekla to continue.

"I think I'm going to have a baby." Anna began to cry, Szymon, Michael, Walter and Joe pounded 'Stephen's back. He grinned shyly from ear to ear.

"Well, next time I see you, Steve, you will be a father."

"And you will be an uncle."

The evening turned out to be enjoyable for everyone. New friendships were formed and old ones mended. Before leaving Joe gently offered a short prayer thanking God for healing old wounds and restoring friendships. He asked God to be with Tekla, praying for her wellbeing and that of her unborn baby, and asking God for their safe, long life. He prayed for good health and peace until they met again. When Szymon looked up, he saw tears in Stephen's eyes.

Chapter 8

The following week was a busy one for Szymon. He awakened each morning at 3:30 to dress, eat breakfast, and ride out to the estate. The farm was huge, encompassing over fifteen hundred acres. The work was hard, but not difficult for him because of his excellent physical condition. Looking around that first day at the men working, he was struck by the poor health of the average peasant. He saw that some were still drunk from the previous night. Most men were dirty and slovenly in their appearance. The place reeked of foul odors. He had not noticed any of these things a year ago. He knew there was little anyone could say or do to improve these wretched peasants' lives. His heart sank. It was a stark reminder of how awful life was in Galicia.

Some of the men who greeted him on that first day resented him. It was the same resentment he saw in his brother, Stephen. The harshness of their lives molded them into caricatures of their former selves. Immediately he awakened to the grim reality that this was the future for everyone in this place including himself, unless each person had the strength to resist the temporary pleasures found in drinking vodka. Many found solace in their religion, but church wasn't a solution to the grinding poverty. The only way for him to avoid the trap was to find a way out.

On Saturday evening, for the first time, Szymon consciously tried to moderate his drinking. Young men began drinking alcohol when they were still young teenagers. It wouldn't be easy to moderate his consumption because alcohol was part of everyday life. He watched Joe mingle, drifting from one group of young people to another. It was obvious that he was having a great time even though he didn't have a drop to drink. Even Szymon's friends seemed to like him. Ruthenian dances were lots of fun. Any get-together, for any reason, had a great deal of drinking, singing, and dancing. The party began at seven and would last until eleven. Every party or community event featured a band with traditional musical instruments playing traditional folk music. These were the songs and folk dances every little Ruthenian boy and girl learned. Most dances were enjoyed by everyone, young and old. Admission cost only a few cents. The dazzling array of colorful costumes alone was worth the price of admission. Those who wanted to drink alcohol, brought their own; nonalcoholic drinks were free. It was near freezing when they arrived that night, and the temperature was expected to continue to drop into the early morning hours. Inside, the light from the kerosene lanterns cast silhouettes of the dancers on the wall as they joined hands together in circles, singing and dancing in time to the music. Joe was having a good time, so was Szymon, as were all the guys from their platoon who came that night. He couldn't remember ever having more fun.

Szymon had blossomed into a fine specimen of manhood in the year he'd been away. Although he didn't realize it, he was a very handsome young man, especially in his army uniform, and he easily attracted both young ladies and young men to him. Szymon was unsophisticated, unassuming, shy and introverted. His aloofness only added an aura of mystery to him. The attention he received confused him; he didn't know whether or not to like it.

On the way back to drop Joe off at his home, Szymon felt self-conscious as he tried not to slur his words. In spite of attempting to moderate his consumption, he had to admit he had drunk too much. He wondered if Joe noticed.

The remaining days before returning to Stanislau, were spent visiting family and friends, helping his parents, and relaxing. He knew he wouldn't see them again for a year. This time, he wouldn't be a short train ride away from them. One evening after supper he sat with his family reminiscing about days gone by and discussing Anna's and Michael's future plans.

He suddenly was riveted to his mother's face. She appeared much older than last year; her face had taken on the appearance of a very old woman. He was stunned by the revelation that she might not be alive when he returned home from Bosnia. Szymon glanced up, saw her watching him, and wondered if she could read his mind. She smiled a little, cryptic smile.

"Mama, I'm going to miss you," he blurted out. The conversation stopped. Everyone was staring at him. He averted his eyes, startled by his own words. Regaining his composure, he said, "Mama, I have a present for you." He brought a small package from the room where he and Pa slept. "These are Saint Nicholas Day presents. I didn't have time to mail presents from the post office in Stanislau," he said.

Mama carefully opened the small package. It contained a small framed picture of Saint Paraskevi, Mama's patron saint. The family agreed it was beautiful as they passed it around the table. When it was returned to Mama, she kissed the face. "I was born on Saint Paraskevi's Feast Day," she boasted.

Szymon passed around the gifts he had bought for Anna, Michael and Pa. Michael fetched a hammer and nail and hung his calendar on the wall near the front door. Anna tied the ribbons to her hair. And, Pa stored the pen, ink and paper in the cabinet hanging on the wall, over the table where he wrote his letters.

"Don't forget to mail yours or you won't get any more mail from me!" teased Szymon.

Pa laughed, a mischievous gleam in his eyes. "Does that mean you expect a letter every time you write to us?"

Pa and Szymon had chores to do before they went to bed. They went out to the barn to milk Rosie and feed the calf which Mama named June. Roman looked

June over carefully. "I think she must be older than thirteen months." Then they brought the animals into the barn and closed the door because it was expected to freeze again that night. "It's a cold winter."

Szymon glanced at his father. "Farming is a lot of work; it's hard to make a living." The conversation drifted off as they returned to the house. Szymon felt awkward, he was beginning to feel more like a guest than a member of the family. Time was passing quickly and he would be leaving for Stanislau on Saturday.

"I was in Bosnia for a few months back in 1855, and I hated the place.

I'll walk with you to the station tomorrow, son, and tell you about it."

Joe rode over to Szymon's home late the next evening to tell him he would be leaving on Friday instead of Saturday morning. "My Uncle wants to go to Stanislau to visit family."

"That's a good idea. By the way, you haven't said anything about Mr. Minoryk anymore."

"His family believes the body under the ice is old man Minoryk, but they want to wait until the ice thaws before planning a service for him. His son, already owns the property so, there are no legal transactions needed. He told Uncle Jan that he could continue to gather wood and use the pond for fishing. Oh, I forgot to tell you, Walter met Anna today at the Fair and invited her to a dance."

"Anna didn't say anything about it."

"She was probably self-conscious."

"Your brother seems like a nice man, educated, too."

"No, Wally has only two years of high school."

On Saturday morning, Roman and Szymon walked in an awkward silence to the train station. Szymon carried only a small duffle bag slung over his shoulder, some cash, and his identification papers. He wouldn't return for a year and suspected by the time he did, his life would have changed. They had left the little house long before the southbound train was due. While his parents were saddened about his departure, Szymon was nervous—more nervous than he had been last March. His hand trembled when he showed his return ticket to Mr. Raab, who treated him with exaggerated courtesy this time.

They went outside despite the cold and found a bench where they could sit.

"Son, I have to talk to you and give you some advice." His father began to tell a story about his own experience in Bosnia. Szymon stared in disbelief. His father had never discussed any of his secrets with him. Now, he understood the reason for his awkward reticence during the walk to the station.

After listening for several minutes, Szymon interrupted, "Pa, how in the hell did you get involved with that woman?"

"It's an old story. Her name was Alia. She was very

pretty and fun to be with. She liked to talk, but most of all, she liked sex. She wasn't a good girl and probably screwed many men before she put her hooks into me. You will learn what it is like to be lonely and far away from home. You don't realize it now, but you will ache at home. No matter where a person is from, he will always have a soft spot for his family, his friends, and his hometown. It's human nature."

"What happened to Alia?"

"After Alia's family caught us in bed, her brother beat me; he threatened to castrate me."

"Oh, God, Pa!"

"Oh, God, they were screaming at her that she was going to die. I was scared to death. I am a lucky son of a bitch." Roman paused to regain his composure before continuing. "Just then, all hell broke loose. My fucking ass was saved because of a skirmish between the rebels and the military police. Her brother was killed in the fight along with four of our guys." He paused again before continuing. "Once or twice a week, I would sneak over to meet her in the Muslim section. I was trapped. I thought I was going to die." Roman's voice broke and he paused again to get his bearings. In a barely audible voice he whispered again that he was the luckiest son of a bitch in the world. He told how, after the rifle fire began, he managed to sneak back into the barracks. "There was mass confusion, and to this day I can't believe no one noticed that I was away from base. I got away with it because everyone who knew about Alia, was dead."

"What happened to her?"

"I heard that her family stoned her to death. It's called an honor killing."

He stopped abruptly. Both were silent, too upset to speak. Szymon suggested they walk along the tracks.

Roman looked at his pocket watch, "It's only 11:45; you have another half an hour." As they walked, they talked about Bosnia and Roman described two or three sights he might see. "Send Ma a couple of postcards with pictures."

They walked a little way up the tracks, but on their return, they ran out of things to talk about. If Roman hadn't become upset about his experience in Bosnia, they may have sat for hours talking. Szymon and his father had never before been so candid with each other. Suddenly, he felt closer to his father, more so than at any time in his entire life.

"It's always that way, when you know you might be cut off in the middle of a story." His father's voice trailed off. They stopped reminiscing and just reminded each other about trivial things, things that each would remember anyway. They were nearing the station when Szymon heard the whistle. They stood along the tracks feeling the ground rumble as the train grew closer, then finally slowed to a stop. The train was pulled by an old coal burning steam engine. Steam belched from underneath the carriage.

"I love trains, Pa."

Roman told him that when he went to Bosnia in

1855, the troops were transported by horse or mule-drawn wagons. "You'll have some good times, but I won't lie to you, most will be miserable. Try to enjoy the experience." For a brief moment or two, they just looked at each other.

There were two or three people boarding and half a dozen leaving. One or two men hurried to use the toilet, frantically running back before the train left. They heard the conductor up the line slamming coach doors. The whistle blew. Szymon and his father embraced, kissed, and then embraced again. For the last time, the whistle blew and the train began to move. Stepping up onto the lower stairs, Szymon stood watching his father walk down the main road turning toward the little house where he, too, had spent his childhood. He watched the scene as the train rolled farther and farther away, eventually vanishing behind him.

Chapter 9

On Monday morning, Szymon awakens before daylight. He lay thinking that it was all a dream, as if he had never been away. Oh, dear mother. He was still terribly worried about her. His mother's haggard, lined face haunted him. He kept thinking about her and wondered if she would be alive when he returned.

"Poor Mama, she looks so old."

When the men returned to the base, they learned that the war plans had changed for the transfer of Company A. Instead of being assigned to the base in Mostar, they would be going to a place called the Sanjak of Novi Pazar. Several weeks passed before Sergeant Schoeppler told them that they would be leaving Stanislau on April 16th, a month later than originally planned, because of flooding in that area. "We're going to Pljevlja (Plevlje), Bosnia." Seeing their puzzled faces, he shrugged. "I'm only a Sergeant, what do I know? You will find out, when I find out, so don't ask me any stupid questions."

For the next two months, Schoeppler continued preparing the men in the platoon for the transition to

Novi Pazar. As time went on, apprehension gripped the young, inexperienced soldiers. Schoeppler told them what he knew about the area, pounding away trying to prepare them for real battle. He told them about past uprisings, describing how they began and ended, and the numbers of casualties. Then, he got around to talking about weekend passes. He said that there would be occasional one-day passes and warned them about what they should and should not do and where they should not go. "Don't think you can befriend just any of the population—especially women—it's risky business. You can never be certain where the next fight will erupt. Sometimes they go after each other, and sometimes they turn against the army. You will learn quickly, once you experience some of this for yourselves."

On the day before they were to depart, Szymon wrote a letter to his father and mother. In his letter, he gave them a new address and promised to write immediately after arriving in Pljevlja. He was sitting on his bed with Joe next to him writing to his aunt and uncle. "I feel that life is about to change."

"I wonder what my life will be like, in three or four years," Joe wondered aloud.

"Yeah, me too."

Joe and Szymon talked about their trip home at Christmas, and the changes they had seen in Galicia.

"Mostly, I'm worried about my mother."

Joe crossed himself before speaking, "I know it's difficult for you to see your mother and father grow old, Szymon. I wish I'd had the opportunity to see mine reach old age."

"That's right! Your mother and father died before they got old. I know I should be grateful that mine are still alive." Szymon briefly hesitated before continuing in a soft, lowered voice. "They look so old that I think they are going to die. I'm so afraid that she is dying."

"Just pray for them, Szymon. Remember everything is in God's hands."

As they walked to the base post office, their thoughts were interrupted when Szymon pondered aloud, "I wonder how long it will take to receive mail?" At the post office, he asked the clerk about the length of time it took for letters to go between his hometown and Novi Pazar.

The clerk had never heard of the place but said, "It's complicated because the letter is sent to Stanislau first and then to the base. It will seem like forever for mail to get into your hands."

One night shortly after they had returned to Stanislau, Schoeppler told them he had bad news. Malenko's father had notified the base that Dimitri Malenko had died. "Who's dead?" someone yelled. "Who's Dimitri?"

No one seemed to remember Malenko's first name. Another guy asked, "How did it happen?"

Schoeppler explained that Dimitri never recovered from falling fifteen feet into a ravine during the war games. "He never improved and wasn't able to rejoin his platoon. Dimitri had been hospitalized for three weeks when the doctor decided that he should go home. Shortly after he returned home, he experienced convulsions. Each episode left him less able to cope, and his condition deteriorated rapidly. He slipped deeper into despondency, until the army issued a medical discharge. His father was making arrangements to put him in a sanatorium when he found him hanging from a tree in the rear of their house." The room grew silent.

Szymon shuddered. Schoeppler continued. "The Greek Catholic Church right here in Stanislau operates a rest home for people with mental conditions like Malenko's. Maybe it could have helped, but everything else that could have been done for Dimitri was done. His fate was out of our hands." Joe volunteered to lead the men in prayers for Dimitri that night before bedtime.

For the time remaining, training continued for the three platoons going off to join the occupation force. The first, second, and third platoons from the 58th infantry were scheduled to leave Stanislau on Monday, April 16, 1892. Activity on base picked up as supplies and equipment were loaded into a boxcar sitting on the same siding where the men had detrained in March of last year. Men from Company B were waiting in Sarajevo, to return to Stanislau. The old locomotive, which was nicknamed Edelweiss, had been taken to the roundhouse for routine maintenance and needed repairs three weeks earlier.

The antiquated steam locomotive, built in 1852 was scheduled to retire in another year. Coal tenders were loaded; the coaches were scrubbed and repainted inside and out. The work had been going on for a week and was almost complete. Company A was scheduled to leave in three days.

On Monday morning, the wake-up call sounded at 5:30. No time was wasted as the men arose, dressed, and ate breakfast. By 6 a.m., they assembled, carrying full field packs and rifles. They marched to the rail siding to board the train. In a matter of minutes, the train began moving, heading south toward the border with Slovakia.

Dawn had not yet broken. Onboard, most of the men slept. The train rocked and swayed moving along the uneven tracks in the dark, early morning hours. As the train picked up speed, the swaying motion had a mesmerizing effect on Szymon. They passed through mostly small villages and occasionally a larger town, but no big cities. Dawn was breaking as the train rolled through one of the larger towns. Szymon could see a few lights, probably kerosene lanterns, hanging on a shed near the station. Only a few phantom-like figures were seen traversing the cobblestone streets as Edelweiss again picked up speed, leaving another nameless town, with forlorn-looking buildings barely visible in the ghostly, early morning mist. It looked like it would be a dull, overcast day. He watched herds of cattle standing in barren fields. Outside the small train window, the whole world seemed like one big barren winter scene.

Szymon closed his eyes. He was dreaming about being a little boy in his hometown, when the coach jerked violently to the left.

"Damn!" Szymon heard several boys cursing.

"What happened?" he wondered.

"What time is it?" a sleepy voice asked.

"About ten," someone mumbled.

Their grumbling continued.

Schoeppler, who had been asleep in the next coach, walked up the aisle telling them that the track was bad and to get used to it.

"When do we eat?"

Schoeppler told them to stop whining and get something from their backpacks. The grumbling started up again. "Knock it off," barked Schoeppler. This time it worked. They gnawed on their hard biscuits and said nothing more.

It was close to one o'clock in the afternoon when Schoeppler announced that there would be a water and coal stop in Uzhorod for about an hour. He told them that this location was about thirty-five miles from the border with Slovakia, and the first village over the border would be Čierna and Tisou. While the tender was being filled in Uzhorod they could leave the train. "Use the outhouses behind the station. A quick dinner of sausages and cheese is available. If you want soda or something other than water or juice, you can buy it at a store next to the train station."

The train pulled into Uzhorod alongside a water tank with a long pipe and a large spigot-like contraption which hung partially over the tracks. Alongside the tank, was a shed covering what appeared to be a mountain of coal. When Szymon left the train, his knees almost buckled. He was unsteady on his feet and felt like he was still swaying on the train. He walked with Theo and Joe to the outhouses.

Joe's eyes gleamed with excitement. "What a ride! I like riding the train, don't you?" he asked, looking from one to the other with childlike enthusiasm.

They stood a few minutes looking around at the buildings along the tracks. The station sign read Uzhhorod, population 12,054, elevation 550 feet. This was Szymon's and Theo's first long train ride and, they had opposite opinions on train travel. Theo said he would like to be doing something else.

The three ate their sandwiches in the railroad station, then returned to watch the water and coal being loaded onto the tender. The faces of the firemen were black. Joe went to explore while Szymon and Theo walked to a small store to buy something to drink. "Kind of a rundown place," Theo observed. "Almost makes Bukaczowce look good." The building was old and needed more than a coat of paint. Outside, there wasn't anything attractive about the place. An enormous gravel lot made the little station and small store appear even smaller and more desolate. The trees abutting the property were barren as it still was winter. They watched as two men removed a dead animal from the cowcatcher at the front of the locomotive.

Joe rejoined them, appearing disappointed. "There's not much here." Theo and Szymon nodded in agreement.

"Hey Joe, did you fill your canteen?" They walked together back to the store where Szymon bought two postcards for his mother, and after paying for drinks, looked for the place where they would refill their canteens.

They heard Schoeppler's whistle and saw a crowd waiting to board the train.

"Time to go," observed Szymon. Once the train was underway, Szymon could see a pretty town nestled in low-lying hills ringing the town. There were small industries lying along the tracks, similar to those in Bukaczowce. Uzhhorod was a larger town than he first thought.

Three church spires were visible as the train rounded a curve. The locomotive slowed as the elevation increased. The Carpathian Mountains were to the west. "Sarge was right." (The guys had begun calling Schoeppler "Sarge" behind his back.) "The track is worse on this side of the border."

Joe, Szymon and his cousin, Joannes Swaczy from Halicz were sitting together. They had been underway for almost two hours, and the sky was growing increasingly darker. In another fifteen minutes it would be completely dark, but there wasn't much to see in this part of Slovakia. Slovakia was a possession of the Austro-Hungarian Empire, as were all the nations through which the train would traverse.

Szymon was looking forward to seeing Budapest, but since they were about 125 miles away, it would be completely dark by the time they arrived. Szymon wondered when they would reach the next water stop. Luc Slobodianyk passed through the coach and Szymon learned the next water stop would be somewhere north of Budapest in about five hours.

It was after ten that evening, when the train pulled into another small town. The men left the train to use the outhouses and get free coffee from the station. It was pitch dark except for the station lights and two or three kerosene lanterns hanging alongside a shed near the tracks where water and coal were being loaded onto the train. Szymon went to see how long it would take to load the tender. Two firemen were shoveling coal into the firebox, while another two or three were loading the coal. The water tank was full, so the train would be departing shortly. Other than the activity around the coal tender and the station, there was no sign of life. He thought about asking the name of the town, but decided it wasn't worth the effort.

Once they were underway again, Sergeant Schoeppler came through the coaches telling the men that Budapest was four hours ahead. He told them that there was flooding south of Budapest, so a decision would be made tonight about rerouting the train. Later that evening, as the train neared Budapest, almost everyone onboard was asleep; everyone, Szymon thought, except himself. He wanted to see the bridge across the Danube. He walked through the coaches hoping to find a place to stand near a door or a window to have a good view of the river and bridge. As he passed through the third coach, he heard someone calling to him.

"Over here." It was Major Melnyk. He wanted to know where Szymon was going. Szymon saluted. Major Melnyk said to follow him. They walked through the coach, through a door in the rear of the train, onto an observation platform. Major Melnyk said that he liked bridges and always stood outside to take in the entire panorama. They stood in the freezing cold night air, but Szymon's desire to see the river overcame the sting of the frigid cold on his face. The moon had not yet risen, but the lights of Budapest were visible in the clear night sky. Major Melnyk was silent, only saying that the north main bridge was completed in 1876. The city was the largest place Szymon had been in his life, with buildings that looked like towers to him.

They passed huge churches and enormous government buildings. The streets in front of the buildings were illuminated with gas lights. Every window in those buildings was brightly lit. Ahead there was a complex of more lights, some soaring up into the night sky. The train rolled along toward the lights and within a few minutes it was on top of the bridge. Szymon looked across the water and saw the moon rising in the east. The clickity clack of the wheels rolling along the track and the specks of light on the shore brought a lump in his throat.

Major Melnyk stood silently next to Szymon for several minutes after the train had reached the mainland. As quickly as it began, the spell was broken. He ordered Szymon to return to his coach. There was such an abrupt change in Major Melnyk's demeanor that Szymon was taken aback. He saluted without hesitation. "Yes, sir."

Major Melnyk responded, saluting, "As you were, Swaczy."

Szymon fell into a sound sleep after returning from the observation platform. He still could not believe his good fortune to join Major Melnyk on the observation platform to see the panoramic view of Budapest.

The next morning, Szymon awakened later than usual. The stirring of the men around him interrupted his sleep. He sat back in the seat thinking about the night before. "If I saw nothing more, the entire military venture would have been worth the effort just having seen Budapest at night. It is a magical city of lights."

Luc came through the coach announcing that there would be no further stops until reaching the Bosnian border. During the night, the progress of old Edelweiss had slowed because of a mechanical problem with the locomotive hauling a train ahead of them. The train was on a rail bridge and it took three hours before the tracks were cleared. As a result, they were a few hours behind schedule. "We'll eat in the Gradiska train station," Luc informed them. It was after nine o'clock and they had slept through most of the delay. There was nothing but farmland outside the train window, so Szymon again closed his eyes. By the time the train reached Stara Gradiska, the men were grumbling about food again, they hadn't eaten since early the previous evening. The train rolled across the border, and within ten minutes it pulled into their final destination, Bodanska Gradiska, in Bosnia Herzegovina.

Luc gave the order to assemble two abreast, and once the three platoons had fallen in, they marched to the station. Major Melnyk had contacted the station from Stara Gradiska, so a dinner of ox tail stew, boiled potatoes, freshly baked bread, coffee, and strudel for dessert awaited them.

It felt good to be on a surface that wasn't moving, although there still was the strange sensation of rocking back and forth. Before they finished eating, Major Melnyk stood to address them. He told them that because of the flooding, there was a change in the route. "This is a well-equipped port, with a rail siding where the train can pull off making it easier to unload the boxcar and reload the equipment and supplies into wagons for the last leg of the journey to Pljevlja. Here in Gradiska, two paddle wheel barges are waiting for us a short walk from the station.

They will take us on a 150-mile voyage to Brcko, a city on the Sava River. Half of you will be on the Stella and the other half on the Luna. He added, "I won't try to paper over the conditions that you will experience on this voyage. Your quarters will be filthy, overcrowded, and cramped, so don't complain, but try to make the most of the situation. It's a short voyage which should take only a day and a half. At least, no one will be shooting at us!"

After dinner, they unloaded a boxcar packed full of equipment into wagons and then onto the barges. It took many hours and they finished just before sunset. Most of the guys spent the last minutes before heading to the steamboats, cleaning up and filling their canteens. The weather was warm that day, about 65 degrees. After loading pallets to be transported to the steamships, they were exhausted and wet with perspiration.

Szymon and Joe talked about what they had witnessed in the town. The local people going about their everyday business wore clothing that they had seen only in pictures. They were particularly curious about the men's hats, or fez, and the women's headscarves called hijab. They overheard people conversing but couldn't understand a word they said. Joe told Szymon he saw signs in shop windows, written in the Cyrillic alphabet, and although he was familiar with the alphabet, he couldn't understand their language. Even the buildings had facades that were different than those in Galicia and his hometown.

Chapter 10

Sergeant Schoeppler was grim-faced when he returned to address the three platoons. "Major Melnyk has decided to stay in port tonight. We'll leave at eight-thirty in the morning. The steamboats are filthy and full of roaches and rats, but I believe they will get us to Brcko, the largest port on the Sava River."

He explained that the barges were cargo and passenger carriers, 75 feet in length, and were named Bright Stella and Rising Luna. Just after dawn, the next morning, Schoeppler had Luc organize the men into squads to tackle the cleanup detail, before addressing them. "Let's get this job done. I hate rats! Boys, we have to scrub this boat, it's filthy. I don't know about you, but I can't live in filth."

Schoeppler ordered Luc to split the men into several crews, each crew responsible for cleaning different areas of the ship. Within minutes, there was a commotion heard from the galley. "Sarge, there are roaches and rats running everywhere!" The scrubbing ceased as they chased rats which were scurrying for their very lives.

"I want every rat on this ship killed and thrown overboard. I hate those sons of bitches," exclaimed Schoeppler.

There were dead rats lying around the deck in piles. The galley, heads, cabins, cabinets, floorboards, benches, chairs, and tables were scrubbed with lye. The men picked up and organized piles of junk which had been haphazardly strewn about, they coiled lines, then stored the boat fenders and all sorts of tools and equipment in lockers. They scrubbed the decks and washed windows.

Schoeppler asked the captain what was stored down below in the hold. "If we can't clean it, we have to put out poison or the ship will be infested with rats again." In the blink of an eye, the captain reached into a hatch in the wheelhouse, and handed him two unopened cans of rat poison. At last, the two paddle-wheelers were able to get underway.

Typical of watercraft of that time, the paddle boats were built flat-bottomed and drew very little water, allowing them to ply shallow waters on rivers full of snags. With the Luna taking the lead, they kept a steady six knots.

Toward evening Schoeppler addressed the men telling them that they were making slow, steady progress. "I doubt we will go through the night and I'd bet that the captain will drop anchor soon."

As he turned to leave, the men began shouting questions.

"What time does the sun set?"

Another guy yelled, "Can we take a cigarette break before it gets dark?"

Schoeppler nodded at Luc to take over. Luc allowed only four or five men out on the deck at one time, allotting ten minutes for each person to stretch. It was a peaceful night as the two boats plied the calm waters of the Sava. The sun was dipping behind the trees on shore, casting long shadows across the wide river, losing them in the vastness of the landscape. Spring was just beginning to burst free and already some varieties of trees were covered with new growth. Some seabirds were diving, while others nervously pecked the mud along the shore. Just before dark, the birds flew inland, disappearing into their rookeries.

Joe took in the scene around him. "Oh, how peaceful it is." Then, he asked the men around him if he could offer a prayer of thanksgiving for their good fortune to be on this boat under such a glorious sky. Joe, in his simple farmboy manner, thanked God and praised Him for the beauty and tranquility of this place, then recited the rosary and led the men in the Lord's Prayer. He prayed that each man would forever remember the time spent with friends and comrades and cherish the memories of this blessed day.

When it was Szymon's turn to take a short break, he left the cabin and peed under the rail. The sun had just dipped below the horizon, so he guessed it was about 6:30. Already there was barely enough light to walk around the boat to the stern. He listened to the paddles beating the water, barely able to see the foamy wake behind her.

It might have been cramped inside the cabin, but at least it was clean, so the men slept soundly that night. Sergeant Schoeppler stayed up late, sitting on top of the cabin reminiscing. The scene brought back memories of his childhood, when his mother worked as a governess for a family named Werner. The Werners lived in Vienna, but every summer the family would vacation at a hotel along the River. The family had a little boy named Richart who was retarded. When they were young boys, they played together along the shore of the river. As the boys grew into teenagers, Mr. Werner took the family on riverboat excursions to nearby villages.

Young Willy and little Ricky spent many afternoons playing in the cabin, and sometimes the jolly German steamboat captain took them up to the wheelhouse, where he allowed them to sit in the pilot's seat and instructed them how to operate the boat. These adventures began a life-long love affair with steamboats. Schoeppler would spend many furloughs traveling the rivers of Austria and Germany.

His thoughts turned to his mother. He knew that she would have loved this river cruise. Maria was retired on a modest income from a small pension and her limited savings. She lived in Vienna on her pension, savings, and the money that her son sent. He visited her on his long leaves. Tonight, the steady, familiar rhythm of the engines and the sound of splashing water lulled him into an almost hypnotic trance. He promised himself that he would discuss another short cruise with his mother on his next trip to Vienna. Catching himself dozing, Schoeppler went down below, found his place among the men in the platoon, and fell into a sound sleep.

Szymon awakened the next morning as dawn was breaking. He listened, but didn't hear the sound of the engines. "Where are we?" he wondered. This morning, he was stiff and it took extra effort to straighten his back so he could stand. He looked around and saw no one else awake. Sergeant Schoeppler wasn't in his bunk, so Szymon thought he might be in the wheelhouse. He decided to explore. It was then that he realized that the boat wasn't moving.

Szymon walked up the ramp leading to the deck. In the dim light of early morning, he could see that the boat was tied up at a dock. A small group of men were gathered near the shore. The crew was already busy preparing for the day's voyage. The men greeted Sergeant Schoeppler. Captain Hosmer, of the steamboat Luna, approached with a hearty greeting, "Hello, Bill. Did you sleep well?"

Szymon could hear their conversation drifting across the water, as the morning was still and quiet. Even the birds, flying overhead, were silent as they returned to the water's edge to fish for their breakfast.

"This is a different world," thought Szymon. Back home, those poor souls are milking hundreds of cows, stuck in a world of stifling, routine farm life." Out here on the water's edge, he felt free.

Sergeant Schoeppler and his friend talked about this day's leg of the journey. As Schoeppler turned back to the boat, Szymon overheard Captain Hosmer promising to look into a cruise down the Rhine. "You have time, it's not for another year."

Smelling coffee, Symon returned to the boat where he peeked into the galley to see two cooks preparing breakfast. One of them looked up and saw Szymon watching them, "It isn't ready. We'll call you when it is. Get lost, soldier."

The cooks turned out to be firemen from the ship's crew. Could they be the same men stoking the firebox? Their faces had been barely recognizable since they were blackened by coal soot, giving them a ghoulish appearance. Szymon plopped down next to Theo and his cousin telling them what he had observed. Luc took charge, allowing the men to go on shore. It was close to eight o'clock when the sound of a bell ringing brought them all to attention. Luc told them that they had half an hour to eat and take care of their personal business. There was plenty of food— mountains of sausages and bread, along with two kettles of mush and pots of coffee. "Eat quickly. We will shove off at eight-thirty sharp."

As the men shoveled food into their mouths, they heard the sound of the boilers firing up. Schoeppler told them, it would be a longer day than the previous one. "We have to cover over a hundred miles today. Eat seconds, eat all you want, because both dinner and supper will be skimpy. I need volunteers to wash the dirty dishes and pots and pans. Pointing at Joe and Szymon, Schoeppler said, "You and you." Before the others were finished with breakfast, Szymon went topside to watch the crew preparing to cast off. They had just finished loading coal into the bins on the deck.

"Hey you," yelled one of the crew, pointing to Szymon, and asking him to pull the line onboard as they shoved off from the dock. Within minutes, Stella was underway, following Luna. Only a few miles out of port, Luna appeared to be having problems. She slowed and began turning, as men aboard the Stella watched in silent anticipation. As Luna passed by, the men and crew pointed toward the docks they had just left. When they were back in port, Schoeppler hurried over to where Luna was tied onto the dock. The captain told Schoeppler that several of the men were complaining about pains in the abdomen. "It looks like it could be food poisoning." The Luna's co-pilot called down to Captain Hosmer telling him that several men had diarrhea and were vomiting. "Are any of your men sick?" asked Captain Hosmer.

Schoeppler told him that no one had complained yet. Captain Hosmer explained that he decided to turn around because they were so close to the docks that it was the reasonable thing to do. He didn't want to err on the side of continuing only to get stuck on the river. Although they had lost a couple of hours, by 11:30 that morning, they were underway again.

The day's weather was a repeat of the previous

one, although slightly warmer. The view of the flora and fauna along the banks on this part of the river had grown monotonous, even though an occasional bear visited the water's edge to drink and to fish for breakfast. Most of the soldiers came out on deck to watch the bears. Sometime during the early afternoon, the sound of singing from the Luna, wafted downstream. Spirits perked up as Stella's passengers joined in singing hymns and folk songs. Szymon and three or four of the guys took out harmonicas, fifes, fiddles, and Jew's harps. The soldiers danced to the old, familiar folk tunes.

Szymon heard a familiar voice. It was Joe singing a lovely song. When he finished, every one stamped their feet and clapped. During a lull between songs, someone asked if anyone had been in the galley. A couple of guys went to ask about dinner and returned saying that there were boxes with chunks of cheese and stale bread on the shelves. The men turned to Luc to decide whether or not to eat the bread and cheese. Luc said, "I'll check, but that's probably all we will get." The rest of the afternoon was spent talking or taking an occasional break to smoke.

Later in the afternoon, an upbeat Schoeppler walked into the cabin. According to the captain, they had gone approximately eighty miles.

"At this speed, we'll never get there," complained Theo.

The expression on Sergeant Schoeppler's negated the need for words, Schoeppler was disgusted. "Don't whine!" He called for Luc. "Luc, get these God damned babies outside, they need to take a shit. Smoke until it blows out your asses! Can't please you bastards, so just shut up, damn it, and stop your whining!"

After Schoeppler stomped out, Joe spoke, "He's right! Maybe time would pass more quickly if we found things to do." There was some grumbling but, the majority of men sheepishly agreed.

That evening, Luc gave the men another report from the captain. "Captain Hosmer has calculated that we have gone one hundred miles, and as of now, he plans to continue throughout the night, but at a reduced rate of speed. The co-pilot will take over at nine o'clock.

Sometime after dark, the men settled down and conversations ceased. Szymon concluded there wasn't any more that could be done, and tried to sleep.

Dawn was breaking as Sergeant Schoeppler awakened. He struggled to shake off drowsiness and to determine what had disturbed his sleep. "Can it be the boat is hitting against something?" he wondered. He walked up the ramp and was stunned to see the Stella up against a lighthouse. Schoeppler, who had studied the pilot's chart, knew where they were. This was the lighthouse near the channel leading to the Brcko port. The lighthouse was tilted sharply to one side, its base nearly split in two. The paddle wheeler was too close to shore, Schoeppler noted, and wondered if it was hung up. He looked on both sides of the barge, but saw no anchor lines.

"What the hell is going on?" He raced up the steps to the wheelhouse. In a matter of seconds, he summed up the situation. Both the captain and co-pilot were dead drunk. He spotted an empty bottle on a ledge between them. He looked down below in the cabin where he found no one awake. He yelled for Luc then turned back to the wheelhouse.

Luc's stunned face told the story. "What are you going to do?" Luc inquired.

"This, for starters!" spat an angry Schoeppler, as he flung the two drunken pilots from the captain's seat.

Hearing the commotion, Szymon came running up the ramp, "What do you need, Sarge?"

As Schoeppler wiped condensation from the inside of the windows, he told Swaczy to go topside and clean the dew from the other side. "Get these drunks out of here, lock them in their bunks." Luc went to Major Melnyk's cabin and quickly informed him of the situation, and then he summoned several men to report topside, before returning to the wheelhouse. Half a dozen men stood wide-eyed on the deck watching Luc and Szymon drag the captain and co-pilot to their cabin under the stairs. The men stood at attention saluting as a worried Major Melnyk ran up the ramp.

Sergeant Schoeppler quickly told him what he had found and said, "We're not in immediate danger, there's no wind, thank God! A fifteen-knot wind could cause a lot of damage. It looks like Stella was drifting sideways with the current when she got hung up on the lighthouse. I know that I can figure out the safest way to dislodge Stella and get her into port."

Jo Hanczyk spoke up, "Major Melnyk, sir, we, I mean a bunch of us boys, examined the paddles and there is damage back there." They heard the Luna signaling in response to the Stella's horn.

"Lower two stern anchors and one bow anchor," ordered Schoeppler, shifting the throttle to idle as the anchors were lowered. He scanned the river for the Luna and saw her approaching. She was on-site in ten minutes, maintaining a distance of 75 feet from the anchored Stella. "Get a couple of firemen up here and make sure they're sober," ordered Schoeppler. That was difficult as more than half of Stella's crew was drunk. Pointing to wading birds only thirty-five feet away from the shore, the men cautioned that the water was shallow. Schoeppler sounded for the depth before maneuvering Luna into position to tow her. The men overheard Schoeppler talking to himself. "How in the hell are the men going to eat this morning? We could be tied up all day."

The men were ordered to fill their canteens. Sergeant Schoeppler ordered Luc, Syzmon and Joe to row to the Luna to bring back a couple of lines. Schoeppler checked the anchors and determined that, if all else failed, he could use winches to free the Stella. Feeling the wind pick up, he glanced toward the horizon. The sky was overcast, and rain appeared imminent, so he knew they must work quickly. He ordered the firemen to lower two-row boats. "Don't waste any time, the weather is about to change." Luc,

Szymon and Joe climbed into one of the row boats and they were lowered into the frigid waters of the river.

While rowing against the current to the Luna, they heard a commotion onboard. The men were pointing to shore where two boats were leaving the docks and heading toward the lighthouse. Sergeant Schoeppler scanned the shore with binoculars. Luc, Szymon and Joe returned with three heavy ropes, each with one end tied onto the Luna. Maneuvering around the vessel, they shoved each coil of rope into a cradle which was then hauled onboard the Stella.

By the time the tow lines were securely tied, the wind was blowing steadily at fifteen knots. Two boats from the coaling station circled, yelling to Schoeppler that they would lead him into the docks. Things moved quickly after that. Sergeant Schoeppler ordered the forward anchor to be lifted. Luc was still struggling to get the rowboat around the stern and into position so it could be hauled aboard. The current was pulling them toward the bow. A line was lowered and tied onto the bow of the rowboat.

Sergeant Schoeppler bellowed, "What the hell were you doing, Luc?"

"We checked the damaged paddles."

Schoeppler yelled, "For Christ's sake, get your asses onboard! Tell me about it later."

He ran up the stairs to the wheelhouse, turned the big wheel hard toward the port side, ordered the anchors raised, and yelled to Luna's Captain. Captain

Hosmer reversed the paddles. The towline tightened and the front of the Stella slid sideways away from the lighthouse. The anchor was once again lowered. In a series of maneuvers, all three anchors were lifted, and as the anchors were lifted, she moved free from the lighthouse structure. All the lines were untied and the anchors raised.

Schoeppler shoved the throttle forward and the Stella slowly moved under her own power. A cheer went up. Schoeppler moved slowly away from the flotilla of boats idling around the lighthouse, he pushed the throttle between forward and reverse several times while increasing and decreasing her speed. The Luna followed, the small boats with the Stella fell in behind, all heading for shore. Once all the boats were moored to the dock, a mighty cheer rose up from all the men on shore and around the lighthouse, as a grinning Major Melnyk shook Sergeant Schoeppler's hand to congratulate him on a job well done. "Let's eat," roared a smiling Sergeant Schoeppler. An even louder cheer went up.

The men rushed toward him, hoisting him onto their shoulders. They took out their harmonicas as they made their way into the dining room, but there was little time to celebrate. As the men ate, the storm blew with greater ferocity due to a cold front moving through the area. Captain Hosmer, Melnyk, and Schoeppler discussed delivery of the two steamboats to their owners, along with the drunken captain, co-pilot, and crew.

The dockmaster came over and they asked about

the ownership of the paddle wheelers. Major Melnyk was relieved to learn that an office of the riverboats' shipping company was located in Brcko. "We have some things to sort out. They have to figure out who's in charge of these drunks."

The storm hit hard with heavy winds, rumbles of thunder, and torrents of rain. It took a couple of hours to contact Gradiska. Because of the bad weather, the telephone connection was lost several times. In the meantime, Major Melnyk was able to speak with Commander Swartzdorf back at the base in Stanislau.

Swartzdorf, with his years of experience, was familiar with the paperwork that the army required. They agreed to talk again after the men were in Pljevlja. Major Melnyk was finally able to speak with the owners, when they unexpectedly appeared at the port. More telephone calls were made between Gradiska and Brcko. Major Melnyk didn't want to get involved with the company that owned Luna and Stella, so he referred the owners to someone in the procurement division in Vienna.

Melnyk completed the incident report that evening while those involved were available. It was very late that night before all reports were completed and alternate travel arrangements had been made.

"Tomorrow we have to contact the base at Tuzla. They probably wonder where the hell we are." Company A was long overdue at the Tuzla garrison due to the flooding south of Budapest and delays on the river. Still there were more delays. They stayed in port for the next two nights, sleeping aboard the paddle wheelers.

Chapter 11

On a gray, breezy day, a convoy of canvas covered wagons, unmistakably the property of the Austro-Hungarian Army, departed from the Brcko shipping docks. Eight wagons pulled by teams of four horses each transported forty men per wagon, along with the supplies and equipment from the riverboats' decks and holds. Three days later, the convoy entered the gates of the Ottoman Empire's Tuzla garrison. The soldiers' faces indicated how exhausted they were, although there had been no further mishaps during their journey. They had been traveling for almost two weeks without a change of clothes, sleeping in bed rolls on the bare ground, and eating cold meals with only water to drink. The Major reminded them that there had been no injuries on this leg of the expedition.

During the occupation, Tuzla was the staging area for Austro-Hungarian troops on the way into the rugged mountains lying to the east. The Tuzla Garrison was under the administration of the Ottoman Empire. The base commander, not surprisingly, gave them a cool reception. He probably disagreed with the Austro-Hungarian occupation of the Sanjak of Bosnia Herzegovina after 1878. Nevertheless, he was a professional who understood the agreement that the two powers signed, a treaty of cooperation mandating the governing of the region. Over time, the Austro-Hungarian troops increasingly worked together with the Ottoman troops. Soldiers from both armies assembled food and supplies from the garrison to make the long, arduous trip through the rugged mountains between Sarajevo and Pljevlja. Beginning with the task of loading equipment and supplies on the wagons, the journey was always considered to be time-consuming and difficult, if not dangerous.

For the first time in two weeks, the soldiers slept stretched out, albeit on the ground. The convoy had started in Brcko at an altitude of 240 feet. Tuzla lay forty miles away from Brcko at an altitude of 800 feet, in the foothills of the Majevica mountain range, on the Jala River. Their next destination was Sarajevo, 96 miles away, rising to an elevation of 1640 feet. Upon leaving Sarajevo, the road traversing the rugged mountains and valleys was rough and fraught with hazardous, deep holes and gullies but, there was no other route. The road followed the ancient trade and migration route to the Sanjak. Sarajevo was the capital of Bosnia, with a military base where the Austro-Hungarian occupation armies could obtain another good meal and night's sleep on their way to the Sanjak.

Tension gripped the young, bedraggled soldiers,

most of whom had never been more than fifty miles away from home. This promised to be a truly memorable adventure into a mysterious, spectacularly picturesque land, but that was for tomorrow. Today, the men could clean up and rest after many days of traveling aboard trains, steamships and wagons. None of them were able to track the exact number of days since they left Stanislau; it was 21. At eleven o'clock in the morning, they entered the gates of the Sarajevo base. There would be no sleeping on the ground here. Large tents were clustered at one end of the base. There was a mess hall and a bath house. As they moved into the barracks, they began to relax. Their field packs and bed rolls were filthy, but harsh conditions were part of a soldier's life. Many days remained until their journey would end. Before lights out that night, the men sat on their cots discussing their experiences and the sights they had seen. In their voices one could hear confidence and self-assurance that only hardship, failure and ultimately success, teaches young soldiers. The shared experiences had forged a true bond between them.

Szymon pulled a pencil and piece of paper from his field pack and wrote to his parents.

Dear father and mother,

I am in Sarajevo tonight. We had a good trip so far. In Gradiska, we boarded a ship on the Sava River. The captain and co-pilot of the barge got drunk, so Sergeant Schoeppler took the steering wheel away from them and had to pilot the ship. All the men helped to get us to port. The ship broke down. We got on wagons in Brcko and now we are in Bosnia, Sarajevo. We rode in wagons to Tuzla and Sarajevo. We will leave tomorrow for Pljevlja. It will take a week. That is what Major Melnyk says. Did you plant your garden? I hope it is good. Tell Mama that I miss her. I hope you write to me.

Your son,

Szymon Swaczy

Szymon and Joe joined a group of guys at breakfast the next morning. Theo remarked, "The food is good here." This time, everyone agreed with him.

"There are seconds," offered Jo Hanczyk, and, as if a starting whistle had sounded, they refilled their plates.

Joe chimed in, "This is so good, and there is plenty of coffee, too. The best part is we don't have to rush."

There was no sarcasm that morning as the men discussed their voyage up the Sava River. Each man praised Sergeant Schoeppler, perhaps Szymon most of all.

"He deserves a special medal. Did you see how he steered the steamboat? He sure knows a lot about riverboats. And he's a good man."

They all agreed that without Schoeppler they wouldn't have made it into Brcko port so quickly.

"He knows a lot about everything," praised Joe.

Szymon needed to mail the letter he had written to

his parents. "Hey, does anyone want to walk to the base post office with me?"

The bell rang and Joe smiled. "Let's go, soon there will be no time left to go anywhere."

The men assembled for roll call and orders. Afterward they were given forty-five minutes to take care of any personal business before loading the wagon with food and supplies for the week-long trip to Pljevlja. They stepped it up and, by eleven thirty they were climbing into the wagons. Their destination lay at a distance of eighty-four miles from Sarajevo and rose to an elevation of 2530 feet, easily the most difficult leg of their journey. Eight teams of eight horses began the journey on a crisp, cool morning in early May. The men awakened to the bugle sounding on the last morning of their long journey.

It was four-thirty and there remained twenty miles to cover. The cooks were busy preparing breakfast; the aroma of coffee drifted toward Szymon. Joe and Theo joined the other men breaking camp. They slung their field packs, bedrolls and rifles on their shoulders, and then joined the end of the line awaiting breakfast. On this morning, the line moved quickly, each man was handed a cup of coffee and a piece of bread.

Theo, who complained about everything, remarked, "If we ever get there, I'll be happy to sleep on a real cot and eat a real meal," No one commented, they simply ignored him.

The half-moon cast little light as they kicked the

stakes out of the ground and folded tents. There was a sense of purpose and determination as they silently worked; they knew what was expected of each man.

Today everyone pitched in, wasting no time. While the horses were bridled, men piled tents and equipment onto the wagons while the camp kitchen was hitched to the rear. The fires were extinguished, and the men assembled for roll call just as dawn was breaking. Major Melnyk greeted them and gave them the day's schedule.

The Sergeant gave orders to the platoons and, Joe, in his cheerful, reassuring way, led the men in prayer. At the end of his short prayer, he reminded the men to look around them and appreciate the magnificence of the Creator's gift.

They had left Sarajevo five days earlier feeling more than a bit apprehensive about the last leg of the journey. During the previous four days, there had been numerous mishaps: a fall from a horse, a half dozen thrown shoes, two broken axles and a broken wheel. Sometime during the early afternoon, of the fifth day, the convoy hit a patch of particularly rough road.

One of the men had fallen asleep in the back of the wagon and fell four feet to the ground, chipping his right elbow, when the team of horses got too close to the edge of the road, causing the wagon to lurch violently sideways.

The teamster acted quickly, braking, and bringing the team to a halt, but not before the horse in the front, far right position stumbled, losing its footing and dropping almost a foot from the road. The horse's leg was badly injured and he had to be put down. Fortunately, the wagon remained on the road, but tilted sharply to the side. A pall came over the men who had begun to doubt they would arrive at Pljevlja before afternoon storm clouds gathered.

Everyone was overtired and wanted only to get into the Pljevlja Garrison, for a few days' rest. The garrison was still ten miles away, and it was already after three in the afternoon.

A local villager stopped to ask about the dead horse. Major Melnyk promptly gave the man the horse, and the farmer went away grinning happily, presumably to find a few strong men to help haul away the dead animal.

There was another hour-long delay as the teamster rearranged the horses and hitched them to the wagon. Sergeant Schoeppler and the sergeants from the second and third platoons, discussed whether to continue to Pljevlja. They decided to make a recommendation to Major Melnyk.

It began to rain, pouring down on the convoy, now a speck on the vast, desolate landscape. The road was deserted, the local villagers having taken shelter from the storm. The mood of the men darkened as the rain lashed the horses and seeped through cracks and tears in the canvas covering the wagons. They tried wearing their ponchos, but most gave up because they found their ponchos offered little protection.

It was now half past four o'clock in the evening. There was no choice except to remain in place for the night. The farmer returned with three young boys. Major Melnyk and his interpreter spoke with them about camping in place for the night. The Major offered the assistance of his men to help move the dead horse because the young boys who came with the farmer would be of little help moving a 900-pound animal. That pleased the farmer.

In the end, staying in place was the best decision. The young soldiers were very tired but calm. They had gone through many mishaps and difficult situations during the past 21 days, and learned that army life in the field was unpredictable. One more night in transit wouldn't matter. Safety was the number one concern of the Sergeant when they made the recommendation to pitch the tents and set up the camp mess.

"Tell the cooks to give the men a hearty meal tonight, and plenty of it," ordered Schoeppler. And so it was. They enjoyed a dinner of sauerkraut with sausage and boiled potatoes. Although the bread was stale, it tasted especially good that night, and no one complained, not even Theo, about the fresh coffee or the stale bread.

There was no bonfire that night because the forest was saturated from an overabundance of spring rain. Just as well, because the soldiers wanted to sleep. There were no speeches, no orders, no singing, not even prayers. The men just slept.

Chapter 12

They had gone about four miles, when Joe noticed more houses scattered across the hills. The rain ceased as quickly as it had begun. Although the weather was overcast on the road to Pljevlja, fifty miles ahead the peaks of the mountains were bathed in brilliant sunlight, as the sun rose in the east. Joe began to sing a beloved Ruthenian folk song, the Shadrack, in his lyrical tenor voice. It was the perfect song at the perfect moment. The men could not help but join in.

The convoy traveled along the beautiful highland valley of the Cehotina River, as the men played their crude, mostly homemade, musical instruments. The music lifted their spirits and helped to pass the time as the miles ticked down until they were only one mile from town.

In the gray, overcast morning light, they could see that Pljevlja was a town whose inhabitants took pride in their surroundings. Even though they were on the outskirts of town, neat rows of street lights lined the roads. The first thing that caught Szymon's attention was the orderliness of Pljevlja.

Smiling faces greeted the guards as the convoy rode through the gates of the sprawling garrison, where more than 2,000 soldiers and officers were stationed.

Major Melnyk rode his massive brown stallion at the front of the convoy. He had visited this base twice over the past five years, but told the men yesterday evening that there had never been a trip quite like this one. The guard at the main gate greeted Melnyk, speaking in German and saluting briskly. The wagons remained still until Major Melnyk received orders; then he motioned for the convoy to proceed. They rode along wide boulevards, lined with neat European-style brick buildings, similar to a few modern buildings back in Stanislau.

In front of the buildings, lawns were mown and edged. Each building boasted immaculately clean doors and windows framed by identically painted ledges and trim.

The soldiers moved into their barracks that afternoon, after unloading the wagons at the supply depot and camp mess. They ate dinner late prompting the mess Sergeant to voice a few caustic remarks to Luc. No one wanted an argument, so the comments were ignored. Afterward, they went to the supply depot to pick up clean uniforms, soap and shaving supplies. Arriving back at the barracks, they found sheets and towels on their beds. All the men wanted was to bathe and settle down for the evening, but to their surprise Sergeant Schoeppler had other ideas. Luc called them to assembly. They stood at attention in rows, listening to Sergeant Schoeppler giving them orders for the rest of the day. There were groans when he ordered that the barracks be scrubbed. He had found fleas and lice. "Don't complain about being tired. You boys won't be sleeping until these foot lockers and mattresses are cleaned with lye. We didn't put up with it on the Stella and won't put up with it here, not for one night."

There was nothing more to do except to get busy and scrub the building from one end to the other. It was late when they were finished. After Schoeppler inspected their work, he told Luc to march the men to the mess for supper.

It had been a long day; the men were exhausted. They ate in silence, and half an hour later, returned to the barracks.

Schoeppler addressed the men. "Good job, boys. We'll take up where we left off in the morning. Luc, take over and lead them to the bathhouse. Everyone must bathe tonight. That's an order!"

Szymon was startled awake by the bugle sounding the wake-up call. It took him a few seconds to figure out what it meant. In Stanislau, sometimes a bell sounded announcing a wake-up call. He felt surprisingly rested, and hungry.

"Hurry along, boys, and we'll eat a big breakfast," said Luc.

As they ate they relived their almost four-week

adventure. A couple of guys came over to talk to them, asking where their platoon was from. One of them said that there would be a beer party after church on Sunday. Szymon couldn't believe his ears. The men from the 58th Infantry looked at each other.

A bell sounded, Luc called them to assembly, and they returned to the barracks where Major Melnyk was waiting for them. He inspected their foot lockers and beds. Many failed inspections that morning. Sergeant Schoeppler assigned penalties. After Melnyk and Schoeppler gave orders, they asked the men whether they had any questions. They had many, including this one: "Where's the beer party?"

Major Melnyk told them they had Sunday off and were allowed to do whatever they wanted to do on base, but they weren't allowed off base without a pass. "Alcohol is not allowed on base, and you don't have a pass."

"Forget that party for now, if you want to avoid trouble," added Sergeant Schoeppler."

Szymon glanced at Joe and thought it was amazing how quickly they all had fallen into their old routine. "Sergeant Schoeppler sure slipped fast into some of his old ways. I hope he doesn't permanently change back to his old ways. He was a real son of a bitch."

"Maybe he's doing this for our own good. Things got pretty lax during the last couple of weeks of that trip."

Three or four guys were listening and one challenged Joe, "You always try to see this crap from the other person's point of view."

Theo seemed to agree. "Maybe Schoeppler is just an SOB." No one responded to Theo.

Life on base took on a familiar, predictable rhythm. Schoeppler settled down and the men began to accept more responsibility.

During their time off, until they were able to get a pass, Szymon and Joe explored the base. The store was well stocked and they discovered a reading room that had Polish language newspapers from Stanislau. Szymon inquired whether they ever got a newspaper from Bukaczowce. No one had ever heard of the place.

He began going to church, just for something to do. At mealtime, the men talked about the boredom on base. It was inescapable. Joe and Szymon talked about going fishing on their first 12-hour pass, but couldn't figure out what they would do with the fish.

A few days later, Joe told Szymon that Luc was holding a letter for him.

May 17, 1892

Dear Son,

I'm sorry to write that Ma has been ill. She has the flu. She has high fever and chills. She can't eat anything. It all comes up.

We haven't had a doctor out here yet. There are other people in town sick with the flu. I hope she gets better soon. Some young children and three old people have died of the flu. The good news is that Anna and

Walter Korlascz are talking about getting married. They just met. This talk is too soon. Since Ma has been sick, Anna hasn't gone to work. Anna is a good nurse.

The garden was planted and now beans and tomatoes need stakes. There is a lot of rain this year, so the garden won't need to be watered. We saw Joe Korlaszcz's aunt and uncle at the fair before Ma got sick. They are nice people. I know of two more people leaving for the United States. Well, I hope hear from you soon.

Your father,

Roman Swaczy

Szymon walked to the post office to mail a letter to Roman. Joe, always kind and concerned for others, walked with him. "I know you are worried about your mother."

"I know God is with her, which is comforting to Ma, but I am worried," said Szymon. Joe told Szymon that he understood how he felt, and that he would pray for his mother. "Oh, Joe, I'm sorry. I'm so upset about Ma, I forgot to tell you. Pa wrote that your brother and Anna might get married.

Joe was elated to hear the news. "We will be brothers-in-law." The two friends shook hands, slapping each other's back.

"You are a good man, Joe." smiled Szymon.

The following week, a letter arrived from Joe's

aunt. She, too, was very excited that Anna and Walter were almost engaged.

They had been in the garrison for more than two and a half months. The men were becoming restless. Arguments and an occasional fight would break out, because they had little done and too much time on their hands. The platoons marched into town daily and honed their marksmanship skills on the rifle range. Sergeant Schoeppler, aside from drilling them on their German language skills, taught them basic phrases in both the Bosnian and Serbian languages. Several times a week, they were required to go to the gym and engage in team sports.

Nonetheless, the men were confined the garrison. Sergeant Schoeppler realized that he had to issue more passes. Worried about them going off base, he stressed against getting involved with the local people, especially women.

Szymon was assigned to the grounds maintenance department. He mowed grass, trimmed bushes and shrubs, weeded and edged walkways, and from time to time, he was attached to a crew that maintained trees, by cutting limbs that were rotten or weakened by age. Once again, Joe was assigned to the chapel at the Roman Catholic Church. Szymon wanted to change jobs, but he really wasn't sure what he wanted to do. He was thinking about speaking to Sergeant Schoeppler, when one afternoon the First Sergeant responsible for the Grounds Maintenance Department approached him. He was reassigned to a crew that would be working in town maintaining gardens and trees around the city's administrative offices. It was the perfect job, at the perfect time. There was more freedom and flexibility on this job, and he looked forward to going into the city each week. He liked to watch the people. There were several ethnic groups living in the region at that time. Approximately half were Greek Orthodox; the other half were Muslim. Villagers from the surrounding countryside, easily recognizable because of their homespun clothing, came to shop occasionally.

There were clean and neatly dressed office workers, wearing fashionable, yet modest clothing and footwear. Wealthy people rode in their immaculate carriages drawn by beautifully groomed horses, on their way an afternoon outing or fancy dinner.

But what most interested Szymon were the Muslims. Their headdress was different than seen at home. Men wore the fez and women wore the hijab head scarf. Muslim dress, especially for women, differed markedly from European styles. Szymon always stopped to watch the Austrians and Germans, trying not to stare. He thought the women were beautiful, that they stood apart in many ways. He admired their physical appearance, their bearing and stature, self-confidence and social graces.

Szymon had been in his new job for only two and a half weeks, when a co-worker, named Johann Weiler, struck up a conversation. Jon, as Johan preferred to be called, was a German who had lived in Hungary and attended the University in Budapest. They hit it off and arranged to meet for dinner in a small German restaurant. Szymon had no prior knowledge of the downtown area around the government buildings, but while walking the few short blocks to meet Jon, he was impressed with what he saw.

He passed a German coffee house, a pharmacy, a post office, a music shop, a photographer, and several restaurants, including one featuring Ruthenian cooking. He made a mental note to tell Joe about his discoveries. Szymon and his new friend ordered ham sandwiches, potato salad, and coffee. He thought Joe would like this place.

On the way back to their work site, Jon told Szymon about an upcoming soccer game. "The games are fast and exciting."

Soccer was popular in Germany, but Szymon had never seen a soccer game. "How much is admission?" It turned out that some games were free, including the eleven o'clock games on Saturday mornings. "Maybe I can get a pass," thought Szymon.

That evening, at supper, Szymon told a group of guys about the soccer games. Another fellow was a big fan and made the games sound very appealing.

"How about it, Joe, want to go?"

Joe had a rehearsal for the barbershop quartet at the church. "Aren't you going to the performance on Saturday?"

Szymon glanced away. He was already looking forward to next Saturday's game. For an instant, he saw disappointment cross Joe's face. Joe knew that Szymon wanted to go to the soccer games more than to listen to a men's quartet.

"Joe, you will have to come with me sometime. We should go to dinner near the administrative buildings. There's a Ruthenian café nearby." Szymon had stuck his foot in it again. Joe was Polish.

The soccer field was located in a part of Pljevlja unfamiliar to Szymon. He spotted Jon Weiler outside one of the gates. The game was between the Huns and the Teutons, both German teams. Surprisingly, at eleven o'clock on Saturday morning, there was a large, boisterous crowd. Jon had two tickets for seats in the Teuton's section of the bleachers. He introduced Szymon to eight or ten young men, all wearing blue shirts, most speaking with a thick German accent. The Teutons wore blue uniforms; the Huns wore red.

"How many Germans live in Pljevlja?"

"Almost forty-five hundred," Jon proudly answered.

Szymon whistled in surprise, "Where the hell are they?"

The boisterous crowd began drinking beer at noon. Szymon was having a lot of fun cheering on the Teuton Titans. Jon bought Szymon a beer, but he had not had a beer since long before arriving at the Pljevlja Garrison, so it quickly went to his head. After a few more beers, the game became a blur. Szymon, sensing something was wrong, glanced around him and noticed one or two young guys watching him. Intuitively, he suspected there was going to be trouble ahead.

Szymon sat back, no longer watching the game, and tried to focus on how to get out of there without calling attention to himself. His head spun, as he realized that he wasn't going to be able to sneak away. Jon was standing, yelling; the crowd was wild. Fans around him were protesting and cursing the referee who ruled in favor of the Huns' goal, tying the game.

He heard Jon yelling to him something about the disputed call. Szymon told him that he didn't understand the rules of the game yet, when a disturbance started in back of him. As he turned to see what was happening, he saw the same two young guys still watching him. Szymon tried to sober up, sensing there was going to be trouble that he would have to fight his way out of.

Jon yelled so Szymon could hear him, "It's the second half. Only 5 minutes to go."

Szymon looked at the scoreboard, the Teutons were ahead four to three. Play resumed, but three minutes later, the Huns scored another goal. It seemed that the game went on forever. There were more penalties which Szymon didn't understand, and Jon was too drunk and excited to explain them to him.

With thirty seconds remaining on the clock, the crowd was on its feet. Szymon couldn't hear himself think. Suddenly, the game was over, but he had failed to notice that the Huns had scored another goal. The Teuton Titans had lost. The crowd was on its feet jeering the players and the referees, when Szymon felt someone pushing him, sweeping down the bleachers toward the exit. Jon stumbled falling sideways into an older man knocking him to the ground.

The crowd around them thought Jon had done it on purpose and began pummeling him with their fists. Szymon tried to help the older man but was attacked by a group of teenagers. In the pandemonium, he again noticed the two guys behind him. They would have to get out now. Jon and Szymon managed to breakaway. Szymon yelled at him to run, but Jon was too drunk. Szymon hesitated and stumbled, but decided he had to flee. He began running, but he couldn't run fast enough, and realized that the two guys were closing the gap. They caught up with him and while one held his arms behind him, the other punched him hard in the face, and then his assailant punched him in the stomach, knocking him to the ground. He put' up a struggle, but couldn't prevent one of them from grabbing his money.

The fight ended as quickly as it had begun. Szymon had been running toward the garrison, but looking back he realized that he wasn't any longer being followed, so he slowed his pace. Limping into the barracks, he was confronted by Sergeant Schoeppler who was on the way out. It was then he suddenly remembered Schoeppler saying, "Be careful who you befriend." Sergeant Schoeppler looked at him coolly, "Well, what happened to you?" Szymon just shrugged.

The next morning, when Szymon awakened, he decided he needed to go to church. He slowly got out of bed, his body aching as he straightened his back. He heard Joe ask, "What does the other guy look like?"

Szymon stared blankly into space, "I'll tell you about it at breakfast."

After cleaning up and dressing, they went to the mess hall. Szymon related the post-game attack to Joe. "At least they didn't check my shoes. I keep most of my money there. That's something Pa told me to do."

"It's a miracle they didn't beat you harder when they didn't get much money."

It was early, too early to leave for church, so they were still talking when Hanczyk and several more guys joined them. After hearing about the brawl, someone said, "I heard about it last night. Many people were injured yesterday, and an old man is in the hospital in bad shape."

"Oh, no, not again!" Szymon told them that he had seen an old man fall trying to get out. "I wonder if I will be questioned about what I saw? I'm not going to keep my mouth shut this time. If the police ask me questions about what happened at the game, I will tell them." They spent a quiet afternoon to allow Szymon to recuperate. He was grateful for a friend like Joe, his soon to be his brother-in-law.

On the following Saturday morning, Luc called them to assemble outside the barracks. They marched into town, where the streets were crowded with shoppers who stood along the curb watching as the platoons marched by. Little boys saluted, old men removed their hats, and young girls and old women waved their handkerchiefs as the soldiers passed. At the end of the march, they proceeded to the parade grounds, where the band struck up the Austrian and Hungarian anthems. Afterward, a visiting dignitary from Budapest, who was staying at the garrison, stood and saluted the men. As usual, there were speeches, but within an hour, it was all over, so they were able to rest for the remainder of the day.

Between Szymon's job in town and the familiar routines of every military base, life slipped into a predictable rut. He and Jon Weiler kept up their friendship, attending soccer games or going to a beer hall in the German section of town whenever Szymon could get a pass to leave the garrison. Szymon enjoyed German music and dancing, but especially the beer and food. He met many of Jon's friends, and it was here that he lost his virginity.

Many prostitutes and young girls looking for fun hung around the beer hall. Szymon never revealed that he was a virgin at twenty-three but knew that he hadn't fooled the young girl that afternoon. He felt embarrassed afterward, even though he was very drunk when they went to a room over the top of the beer hall. Thankfully, Szymon couldn't remember much about what happened that afternoon, except the girl teased him whenever he returned with Jon, so he was relieved when she disappeared.

Szymon and Joe finally received two-day passes at the same time. They wanted to see the mountains and a small gorge that was a several-hours hike away from the garrison. Joe mentioned the excursion to a couple of other guys. Theo and Thomas Mazurek overheard their conversation. Jo Hanczyk approached Szymon as he and Joe walked back to the barracks.

Jo asked, "How about it, if a couple of us boys join you on the mountain hike?"

During the following week, Hanczyk became ill and decided not to go. Szymon invited Jon Weiler to take Hanczyk's place. Jon didn't know the streams and lakes around Pljevlja, so said he would ask a fishing guide. Thomas Mazurek made arrangements with a local travel guide, and the group of five men would chip in to pay for a guide to take them into the mountains where they would fish in a stream and camp for the night. They planned to depart the following Saturday.

Szymon realized that none of them knew anything about what fishing equipment they would need, so a few days before their excursion, Szymon asked Mazurek, Theo, and Joe what fishing equipment and baits they used in mountain streams. Then they asked Mazurek to buy whatever they would need. In the end, the travel guide said he would take care of everything including food for breakfast and dinner.

It was the last weekend in September, barely warm

enough to camp outdoors.

Fortunately, the weather was clear and crisp when the friends began their hike up Ljubisnja Mountain. It took a while before they got into the rhythm of walking uphill on the narrow, mountainside path. They bantered good-naturedly as they climbed steadily along the trail for nearly three hours before stopping to rest. The guide told them they still were two hours from their campsite. Thomas Mazurek pulled out a bundle of candies which he offered to the men. Theo had crackers and Szymon had brought pretzels to share. While they were resting they saw a deer come out of the woods. After a brief rest, they resumed their ascent, arriving at an overlook where saw a flock of mountain sheep below.

Arriving at the campsite they took in the breathtaking view. From this vantage point they could look out across a mountain valley with pastures and meadows, to Dernećište, the highest peak on Ljubisnja.

Their guide wasted no time giving them their handlines and demonstrating how to use them in the fast-running stream. While they fished, their guide set up a primitive camp kitchen. Joe Korlaszcz was the first to catch a brook trout. Before he could land his fish, Theo had a hooked one, then Szymon, and then Tom. They all caught plenty of fish, which their guide released into the stream once they had caught enough for supper. There was more than enough to eat. Their guide had carried potatoes in his backpack, and after cleaning up, he made a pot of coffee, while the friends gathered wood and started a bonfire. They sat for a long time around the campfire reminiscing until, one by one, they began to nod off.

The next day, they had more coffee and bread for breakfast. They hadn't had enough of the great fishing and wanted to waste no time. The guide cautioned that it would be difficult to take the fish back to the garrison, so they decided to release any they caught back to the stream. About ten o'clock in the morning, they broke camp and began the trek back to the garrison. Although it was downhill all the way, Szymon noticed that Joe was short of breath and unsteady on his feet. He called to the guide and helped get Joe seated next to a tree. "Joe, did you drink enough water yesterday and today?" Joe nodded yes.

The guide took Joe's pulse, remarking to no one in particular, "His heart is racing Do you have palpitations, Joe?" Joe nodded yes. They decided to take a break. The guide laid Joe flat on the ground, covering him with his bedroll. "Let him rest for a while." The men stood off to the side out of earshot from Joe as the guide continued speaking. "Joe ate a hearty breakfast, so he must have been feeling well earlier, but some people don't do well in the higher altitudes."

If Joe wasn't able to walk on his own, two men would help him – one on either side. Szymon and Mazurek were the tallest men in the group. Although Joe was a bit taller, they were tall enough to support him as long as he could take steps.

"The trip downhill is faster than uphill, by about forty-five minutes," the guide informed them.

The group had filled their canteens before leaving the campsite, because the guide had cautioned them to drink plenty, but when Szymon shook Joe's canteen, he could tell it was still full. But Joe was sitting up, and told the group that he felt better. Once again, the guide advised them. "Drink plenty before we go."

Tom Mazurek, who still had several pieces of candy, gave them to Joe. "Suck on these, the sugar will give you pep."

Having done all, they could, the group headed out again. They were only half an hour from the barracks, and things were going well, until Joe again turned pale, began stumbling, and experienced shortness of breath. "We'll have to rig up a litter," suggested the guide.

The men found some sturdy pieces of wood off the trail and fashioned a litter using the flattened bed rolls and rope they carried in their backpacks. It took a team effort to get Joe down the mountain. He protested saying he was feeling better and could make it on his own, but the guide didn't want to chance Joe getting injured. As a result, the descent took longer than it otherwise would have. It was nearing dusk when they arrived at the garrison. Joe was now able to stand with no difficulty, but Szymon walked with him to the hospital, where they remained together in the waiting area until the doctor came to take Joe into an examination room.

The doctor checked Joe's vital signs—which now, were normal – and listened as Joe recounted the prior episodes he had experienced. "Do you have a history of heart and pulse racing, or take any medication for your heart condition? The next time this happens, you need to come here immediately."

As Joe and Szymon were leaving the hospital, Sergeant Schoeppler was hurrying up the street towards them. "What happened, Joe?" Szymon and Joe filled him in on the last two days leading up to today's episode. "What did the doctor say?"

"He couldn't find a reason for the incident, and wants me to go to see him if it happens again."

"Did you mention that you fainted before because you were dehydrated?"

"I did, but I also told him that dehydration was not the reason for the palpitations today. I drank plenty of water on the mountain."

"Well, keep an eye on it. You'd better head for the mess hall before it closes."

The weeks passed with only a handful of serious problems on base. Luckily, the 58th infantry experienced only minor incidents and none of the problems of theft and drunkenness that occurred in other units. There was a fist-fight between a couple of guys in the second platoon and another soldier didn't return to base on time after a twenty-four-hour pass. He had been found with a prostitute. Nothing ever came out of the melee at the Teutons Huns soccer game, so Szymon came to the realization that brawls were fairly commonplace. From time to time, he went with Jon Weiler to a game, learning to enjoy the spectacle without being drawn into the fights. It was good entertainment. Occasionally, he attended musical performances when Joe was singing. This quiet term was about to change.

The 58th Infantry had been at Pljevlja for about six months when Szymon, Joe and Jo Hanczyk were in the bleachers at a Teuton Huns soccer game. It seemed like the typical, rowdy fans packed the stadium. As the crowd poured down from the stands and out into the street, there were fist-fights, as well as, thieves and thugs harassing fans. But Szymon and his buddies witnessed a post-game incident away from the disorderly crowd that disturbed them.

An older man was being beaten with clubs by two rough-looking characters yelling obscenities. This incident appeared more serious than the type of harassment they typically witnessed on any given Saturday. The beating was particularly savage. They ran to assist the old man who was cut and bleeding, and as they pulled the thugs off of him Szymon recognized one of the man's assailants as one of those who had robbed him three months earlier.

The hoodlums were in a frenzy, yelling, "Imposter. Juden. Swine. Kill the Jew. Bloodsucking Christ killer." Several other young men joined in yelling, "Kill the Jew. Jew lover." Clearly, this had nothing to do with robbing an old man of his money. Szymon and Jo

Hanczyk helped the old man to his feet while Joe confronted the dozen or so assailants. Bowing his head, he made the sign of the cross. Then he raised his hand, looking into the eyes of a man still holding a club.

Joe prayed for them to have understanding and offered a benediction for Christ to be with them in peace and love that day. Although Joe was a gentle man, he presented an imposing figure. His stature threw the group of rowdies off guard and they slinked away having lost their swagger.

Back in the garrison, the soldiers told Sergeant Schoeppler about the incident.

Schoeppler sent them to Major Melnyk's office, where they were questioned as the Major filled out an incident report. Afterward, Szymon and his friends went to the Ruthenian restaurant which was just down the street from where Szymon worked. Szymon wondered why such a brutal incident would happen in this beautiful town.

That evening, at supper, Szymon, Joe and Jo Hanczyk sat together discussing the day's events. Szymon wondered aloud why the beating had been especially severe. There were several others listening to their conversation. One of the others told him that there were Jews who had converted to the Roman Catholic faith living all over Europe, and speculated that some lived surreptitiously in Pljevlja.

"How would anyone discover that they were Jews," asked Szymon.

"Jews are circumcised, that's how," came the response.

The men fell silent.

Szymon had witnessed Jews being harassed in Bukaczowce, but thought nothing of it. "Usually, obscenities were scrawled on the walls of their homes, synagogues, schools, and other buildings. No one does anything about it and no one is ever punished."

"Jews put up with a lot of bullshit,'" Theo commented.

"Churches often encourage the harassment," added Joe.

The men all turned to Joe. "What the hell do you mean?"

"The priests tell their congregations that Jews were Christ's killers, turning Christians against them."

Shortly after witnessing the brutal beating at the soccer stadium, Szymon and his platoon were put on alert. They hadn't had to quell unrest during their nearly six months at the garrison. Military police generally controlled any disturbances, but mainly they picked up soldiers who overstayed their twenty-four-hour passes.

Major Melnyk addressed the men in the auditorium, informing them that several incidents had occurred between German youths and Muslim youths over the past month. The unrest started because of gang violence and spread to the Orthodox and Muslim communities. He briefly recounted several incidents involving young men from both communities.

"We've managed to control the rowdy gangs who attend the soccer games," said major Melnyk. Our objective is to stop this unrest before it spirals out of control."

Szymon's platoon returned to the barracks where they received orders from Sergeant Schoeppler. Beginning that day, the 58th infantry would march into neighborhoods several times a week and remain on alert until the disturbances ended. The Austro-Hungarian presence consisted of nearly two thousand soldiers, of which half were Muslim and half were Orthodox. Mainly, the mission of the Austro-Hungarian troops was to improve living conditions and quality of life by building streets and maintaining a reliable water supply.

In the year eighteen ninety-two, Pljevlja was relatively peaceful, with more soldiers dying from floods, diseases and accidents, than from the hostile actions of dissatisfied citizens. Both ethnic groups had benefitted from troop presence, and they appeared satisfied with the peace and orderliness that the occupation forces had brought. But the slightest provocation could bring back centuries old racial and ethnic hatreds which simmered just beneath the surface. Few seemed to care when young thugs began harassing Jews; their apathy emboldened gang members.

Sergeant Schoeppler finished his orders and answered several questions. He told the men to clean up and shave, to comb their hair and to wear their dress uniforms for the march into the neighborhoods. "Look sharp. I know you can do it."

The men were quiet during dinner, not engaging in the usual banter and gossip that characterized meal times. After the bugle sounded, the roll was called, and they marched with Luc calling cadence.

Close to five hundred soldiers entered the Orthodox and Muslim sections that afternoon. A small band accompanied them, playing well-known Austrian and Hungarian marching songs. The populace had not expected this and stopped whatever they were doing to line the streets and view the well-disciplined units passing by. Little boys ran to join the end of the line, making a game of it. Their mothers watched closely, taking their little boys in tow before the soldiers left the neighborhood boundaries.

Sergeant Schoeppler had told them they would be marching through these Pljevlja neighborhoods more frequently over the next few months. "Maybe we can quell the unrest with no bloodshed."

However, incidents persisted, resulting in a shootout with some injuries in the Orthodox section. No one knew how it had started, but one early evening in late November, the sound of sporadic gunfire was heard coming from a residential building. The military police responded and found themselves trapped with bullets flying overhead. The 58th Infantry was sent in to quell the disturbance and rescue them.

Szymon's heart pounded. The faces of soldiers around him were grim, although their platoon had been training for this kind of street fighting. Sergeant Schoeppler led the men into alleys from which they thought the gunfire was coming. They huddled against the rear of the buildings, listening. It was quiet. Schoeppler beckoned for Szymon and Luc to move toward him. They crouched, whispering, when Szymon happened to look up. "Sarge!" Szymon yelled. "Look up!" A sniper was on the roof. Schoeppler and Luc got off two shots.

The Sergeant from the second platoon crawled over to Schoeppler. They worked out tactics, splitting platoons to cover the front, back and sides of several buildings. Soon, the buildings were surrounded by one hundred fifty Austro-Hungarian soldiers. Someone was firing from the roof where two men crouched. At the same time, Luc's squad entered the building, yelling, "Drop your guns! Raise your hands!"

A man holding a rifle surrendered and Szymon bound his hands behind his back while the rest of the soldiers fanned out searching the first floor. A dozen more soldiers stormed through the entry door and started up the staircase to search every inch of the building, including the roof, attics, and cellars. Sergeants from other platoons oversaw searches of all other buildings. They were heading away when shots rang out, striking two men. The soldiers ducked for cover. Although buildings along the street had been searched, no sniper had been found. The shootings resulted in superficial wounds. One man was shot in his thumb, while the other was grazed by a bullet hitting his head.

That night, an uneasy quiet settled over the neighborhoods, but during the next month there was even more unrest. None of it rose to the level of a full-blown rebellion, but it was unnerving to see grown men willing to take chances by participating in firefights which could end in their being shot or killed.

The unrest gradually subsided, but not before three Muslims had been wounded and one killed. The fatal shooting incident had been provoked by a misunderstanding between a Muslim family and two military police. The police had been sent to check out some gun fire which turned out to be a false alarm. When the military police showed up at an apartment in the Muslim section, they encountered two men who would not unlock their door, and neighbors who wouldn't cooperate. After an hour-long standoff, an interpreter warned the residents that the door would be kicked in if they didn't open it. When the door was broken down, they found two old men cowering in a darkened room. As the police searched, they heard a disturbance in a closet, they flung open the door and a woman appeared to be holding a gun. One shot was fired. The wound was fatal. Later, they discovered that the woman was holding the handle of a mop which was mistaken for a rifle stock.

Back at the base, the men of Szymon's platoon were shaken and grim-faced. Some of the men had tears in their eyes, when Sergeant Schoeppler what had happened. After the shooting incident, the young soldiers found it increasingly difficult to march into the neighborhoods each week. An undercurrent of mistrust and hostility permeated relations between the citizens and the army. Sergeant Schoeppler cautioned his men to be alert whenever they entered Muslim areas. The stress was almost unbearable for the young soldiers who were experiencing, for the first time, what army life was really like. Schoeppler knew he had to be tough. He couldn't coddle these boys because they needed to harden for real combat should the Muslim population reach a boiling point. Troublemakers were rounded up which only exacerbated the fragile peace that had existed prior to the shooting. Troop morale was worsening. The only bright spot was the thought that Christmas was just around the corner.

With the arrival of the Christmas season the mood among the troops lightened. Austrians and Germans loved Christmas, decorating their storefronts, restaurants, and homes with holiday ornaments, candles, pine cones, ribbons, bows, and strands of candy. Special foods and desserts were prepared, and the sounds of music were everywhere from churches to street corners. Carolers went house to house singing Christmas songs. It was here that Szymon heard Silent Night for the first time. Then, about a week before Christmas day, it was as if someone had blown a whistle at the start of a race.

The boys from Stanislau were homesick, as they

recalled past Christmas celebrations with family and friends. Christmas on the Orthodox calendar was celebrated about two weeks later than on the Julian calendar. Szymon remembered small family traditions, special foods his mother baked, church services and gifts exchanged on St. Nicholas Day. He thought about his aunts, uncles and cousins. When he was a little boy and his grandmother was still alive, there were large family gatherings with all of his cousins in attendance. In those days, he could not count the many relatives who gathered in the homes of his aunts and uncles.

Jon Weiler was excited about Christmas, too. He talked about his family celebrations and especially the food. He raved about the holiday meals his mother made and told Szymon and Joe to come for a special dinner at one of the German restaurants in town. Half a dozen buddies from the first platoon decided they would also go for this special meal that John raved about. He told them that it would cost a bit more, but that the food was very special. This was the first fancy restaurant that Szymon had ever visited. Jon told the group they had a reservation for the following Sunday.

"What's a reservation?" Joe Korlaszcz inquired.

Jon looked amused, but he told them it meant that they had to arrive at the restaurant by precisely twelve o'clock on Sunday afternoon, and dress tunics over their dress uniforms were required. Szymon wasn't so sure he wanted to go after all. He was intimidated by the prospect of eating at a fancy restaurant.

That Sunday, they walked out the front gate of the garrison and into the town center. The streets were filled with well-dressed people rushing about everywhere. Near the door of the restaurant stood a man greeting patrons and making arrangements with young lads in uniform to park their carriages. When Jon reached the front of the line, the maître d' spoke to him and he responded, in German. People were staring at the group of Austro-Hungarian soldiers. As they walked into the dining room, they were greeted with smiles, well wishes, and expressions of gratitude for their service. Although he didn't feel entirely comfortable in this setting, Szymon began to relax and enjoy himself.

Jon had paid for two bottles of wine and after drinking a glass Szymon and his friends chatted away about the beautiful dining room. It was lavishly decorated with bows and garlands of greenery, wreaths decorated with pine cones, ribbons, and bows, red and gold bows hung on the walls. Vases of flowers, and lighted candles adorned each table. In a hushed voice, Jon pointed to the table setting and whispered which fork and spoon was used for entree, salad, soup, dessert and coffee.

The special meal that Jon had raved about was everything he promised and more. Several rounds of drinks were sent to their table by patrons seated nearby. While they were finishing their dessert and coffee, Joe suggested that they go to a beer hall before returning to the barracks. They had just enough time before the curfew.

The music was lively, people were dancing, and the beers were good. A young lady came over to their table and said she had been in the restaurant when their party left. She told them that she was with a group of young ladies and had guessed the soldiers would head for the beer hall. She asked Szymon to dance with her; he was more than happy to oblige. Then, he saw Joe Korlaszcz and Jon Weiler with their pretty, young partners dancing the polka. They danced for nearly an hour, and when they said their goodbyes to the young ladies the men were invited to come back on a Saturday night. And then it was over; the fun had ended too soon.

The men rushed up the street, through the garrison gate, and hurried past as Sergeant Schoeppler watched them bound into the barracks. "Where have you been?"

"It was a helluva lot of fun, Sarge," Theo enthusiastically responded.

Szymon and Joe Korlaszcz reflected on the year which was about to end. The next day was New Year's Eve. So much had happened, including the engagement of Szymon's sister Anna to Walter Korlaszcz. Pa had written three letters to him and told him that his brother Stephen had slipped off the wagon for a few weeks, but was back on. Tekla had given birth to a baby boy and both were well. His mother's health improved but she was unable to do as much work as she once had. He wrote that Szymon's letters meant a lot to her and asked him to keep the letters coming. Szymon had been putting it off, but a few days later he wrote to his father telling him about the restaurant with its beautiful holiday decorations and flowers.

He mentioned that the 58th infantry company would be returning to Stanislau in a few months. Szymon enclosed a pretty card for his mother he had bought in a specialty shop in the downtown area. Before closing, he asked his father how the medication was working, and whether he had experienced any more episodes with his heart.

Szymon was brought back to the present when he heard Joe's voice. "We'll be leaving Pljevlja in four months. Holy cow, Szymon! I'm getting homesick."

From time to time, Szymon and a group of his buddies would visit the beer halls, but a curfew was still in place, so they couldn't stay out after dark. One Sunday afternoon, Joe, Theo and Szymon went to the same beer hall they had gone to after Christmas dinner. Here they encountered the same young ladies who had followed them from the fancy restaurant.

"Where have you been," asked Elise. The friends told the girls about the curfew. The girls were surprised and appeared disappointed. "Oh, we didn't know. We would have liked for you to come out, but had no way to contact you."

"Well, we're here now, so why don't we dance?" Joe suggested.

They danced polkas until the band took a break, at

which point they ordered cold beers. Szymon could tell that something was bothering Elise. She appeared a little tipsy when she asked him if he had had sex with anyone in Pljevlja. Szymon was taken by surprise, and not knowing what to say, he told the truth. He led Elise to a quiet table, where she asked, "Do you want to have sex?"

He cautiously stared at her, shocked by her forwardness and wondering if this beautiful, innocent-looking young lady was a prostitute. But he realized that she didn't want money for sex, she just wanted sex. He was curious if all women were like this. In the back of his mind, he could hear Sergeant Schoeppler's and his father's words cautioning him, "Don't get involved!" This wasn't exactly the same situation they had warned against, since she was not a Muslim woman, but it made him cautious.

Szymon observed Elise for a long time, listening intently as she spoke. She told him that she hadn't thought of anything but him since they met. He questioned if she might be in love with him. Then he told her that only three months remained in his Company's assignment in Pljevlja; afterward they would return home. She looked as though she would cry. "Where's home?" She had never heard of Bukaczowce. "Aren't you from Vienna?"

Szymon chuckled. "No, I'm from Bukaczowce, which is in the middle of nowhere, it's not even in Austria."

Her face fell. "You're not from Vienna?"

It was then he realized that she was a rather unsophisticated young girl.

"Where are you from, Elise?"

"Oh, I'm from a little village in a German settlement near Budapest."

Joe interrupted to tell Szymon that the curfew was fast approaching.

"Is there time to dance another polka?"

They danced once more, and when the music stopped he walked her back to the table. Elise thought aloud, "I wish we could get out of here and go someplace exciting."

Szymon stooped to kiss her cheek. "You will find someone who will take you away one day, Elise." Of that, he was certain.

Chapter 13

To the soldiers from Stanislau it felt as if time was standing still. The dark, cold, snowy weeks dragged by. The 58th infantry continued to march into the neighborhoods but the number of people lining the streets had dwindled. Hardly a soul stood alongside the streets to watch them—even on Saturdays. No mothers with children had been seen since Christmas. The world was frozen in winter's grip. Yet still the Company Commander ordered the men to march wearing full field packs. Even Szymon's job took on different characteristics. He no longer tended to the trees and shrubs in town. Instead, he remained indoors straightening the storage facilities. He shuttled back and forth to the forge or repair shops where the handles of tools were replaced or blades sharpened. He pushed carts to the stables where wheels were repaired. The German mentality was different than that of Ruthenians, he thought. Here everything is well maintained, organized and orderly, whereas back home storage buildings were cluttered with unusable junk.

The 58th infantry was scheduled to leave the garrison in six weeks, on Monday, March nineteenth, 1892. Szymon and his buddies began to wonder whether they might be delayed by harsh weather, like the flooding of the prior year. Three weeks later, the 58th infantry was targeting a new departure date of Monday, April 18th. Sergeant Schoeppler had the men on the firing range honing their marksmanship skills.

As the weather began to warm, the troops noticed many more people out and about, when they patrolled the city. The men were put to work scraping and painting everything from the handles on tools to wooden sheds and buildings. Spring had finally arrived, and preparations for 58th infantry's departure were underway.

Szymon and his buddies should have been excited about going home, but they were subdued, as they recalled encountering delays the previous year. Surprisingly, there were none this time. The men worked efficiently loading boxcars, disposing of the accumulation of junk from the barracks, emptying their foot lockers, and pitching in to help wherever something needed to be done. On the evening of April 18th, there was nothing left to do except to get a good night's sleep, and in the morning, to ensure they took all their personal items.

It was a pretty spring day as the convoy pulled away from the Pljevlja garrison. Quietly, each man congratulated himself, feeling grown up, confident, and ready to take on whatever they might encounter. The scenery was spectacular and as the miles ticked off, the black mountains of the Dinaric range receded far into the distance. Szymon loved the mountains and wished that he had had time to explore them.

On the fourth day away from the garrison, early in the morning, there was an accident involving a soldier from another platoon. A wheel bolt had come loose, and while the wagon was being raised onto supports so it could be repaired, the weight inside the wagon shifted and a man was seriously injured. Three fingers on his hand were crushed. The men's faces blanched as they heard his screams of pain. They were only one day away from Sarajevo, so after Major Melnyk consulted with the Sergeant, it was decided they would travel throughout the night.

Major Melnyk told the soldiers they would travel straight through to Sarajevo where the injured man could be treated in a large, modern hospital. Sergeant Schoeppler asked Joe Korlaszcz to stay with the injured man, and instructed the others on the preparations to be completed before beginning this part of their journey back to Stanislau. It was now two o'clock in the afternoon, the worst of the trek down the mountainside was behind them. The convoy was twenty miles south of Sarajevo and the road was good. Sandwiches were passed around with a warning that there would be no breakfast and only one stop for dinner, if needed, the following day. "Make sure your canteens are full."

Sergeant Schoeppler told them that they would likely be spending the next night in Sarajevo. They stopped once to rest and feed the horses. Periodically, information about the injured man filtered up from the wagon where he was being tended, but Szymon didn't want to hear the gruesome details.

The rest of the journey was easy, but monotonous. Although only a few had slept the night before, everyone had rested. The convoy traveled through many small towns and villages. No one wanted to stop, so they passed word to Major Melnyk that they preferred to keep going. Just after one o'clock, they reached the gates of the Sarajevo base. Even though there was a feeling of relief at reaching their destination, the condition of the injured man weighed heavily on their minds.

Major Melnyk told the guard at the gate about the man's injuries. Within moments, he was eased down from the wagon onto a litter and escorted away from the convoy. Joe Korlaszcz followed behind on foot. When Major Melnyk returned, they quickly moved into the same large tents they had previously occupied on their way to Pljevlja. After the bugle sounded assembly and rollcall were taken, they marched to the mess hall where the men of the first platoon sat silently eating their dinner, contemplating all they had learned in the preceding eleven months.

After dinner, Szymon bathed, shaved, and changed clothes. Returning to the tent, he saw Joe, who had tears in his eyes. "Szymon, it was very tough. I didn't know what to do. I felt inadequate, unable to help him. The poor fellow was in terrible pain, but all I could do was pray and hold his other hand." Joe began to weep.

"Joe, if I were in his shoes, I would want you to pray for me and stay by my side, too. You always seem to find the right words, such as, "It's in God's hands or only God can make things happen.""

The next morning, Joe asked Szymon to go with him to speak with Sergeant Schoeppler, who thanked Joe for staying with the injured man. "I know it was hard to do, and that I would have had trouble doing for him what you did, Joe."

Joe requested a pass to go to the hospital. "I want to check on him and say goodbye. Could we have a pass for Szymon, too, so he can go with me? Schoeppler nodded and told him to return before eight thirty. When they arrived at the hospital, they headed straight to the man's room. On the way, they encountered a nurse in the hallway who recognized Joe from the previous day, and told him his friend was improving.

"We're leaving in a few hours, so I want to say goodbye."

"I know he would like to see you." Turning to a closed door, the nurse tapped lightly. "Good morning," she said cheerily. "How are you this morning?

"I have two friends of yours who want to see you," the nurse told him while beckoning for Joe and Szymon to enter. As Joe introduced Szymon to Michael, Szymon smiled broadly, taking the man's outstretched hand. His injured hand lay at his side, swaddled in a large bundle of bandages. Szymon wondered which was his writing hand.

"How are you?" Joe inquired. They stood next to Michael's bed talking to him. He answered in hoarse whispers. They had only a few minutes to spend with him, so Joe asked him if he wanted to pray. Joe reached into the pocket of Michael's hospital shirt and handed him his rosary. Making the sign of the cross, he prayed. Szymon stood alongside Joe as all three men recited the rosary and the Our Father.

When they finished, Szymon caught sight of the nurse standing with her head bowed, praying along with them. After they said goodbye to Michael, she escorted them down the hallway and upon reaching the staircase, she said, "God bless you, Joe. You are a blessing for all of us."

The journey back to Stanislau was uneventful. There had been so much drama packed into the previous eleven months that the trip between Sarajevo and Budapest seemed anticlimactic. Not that the boys were looking for trouble, or wanted anything problematic to happen, rather, they were on edge because they had learned to be on alert at all times. They left Sarajevo at eleven o'clock on Thursday, April twenty-seventh and reached Budapest by six o'clock the following morning.

The train was rerouted into an area where coal and water were loaded into the tender. The train remained in the maintenance area while the men ventured into the nearby neighborhood for breakfast. Szymon whistled to himself, looking around at the railyard and facilities. "This is huge," he thought.

Szymon was able to see the Danube River as the train retraced its route, this time in daylight. Even better, he stood alone outside on the platform at the back of the last car, viewing the beautiful city of Budapest. Szymon had eaten a large breakfast before they boarded the train. The sun shone into the windows of the swaying coaches as the train rolled along. It was warm in Szymon's coach and, on a full stomach, he fell into a hypnotic stupor dozing through half the night. When he awakened everyone else was sound asleep. He guessed it was after midnight. Needing to pee, he sought an exit door, then stood on the train steps relieving himself in the cool, moonless night. There were no lights to be seen anywhere. It was a strange feeling not having any idea where he was. He heard a voice behind him. It was Major Melnyk. Szymon quickly saluted. "As you were," was all he said.

The train made a water and coal stop on the border between Hungary and Slovakia. A hot meal awaited them. In a tiny general store Szymon saw a postcard, "Do you have stamps?"

"Where is it going?" inquired the clerk.

"Sarajevo."

The clerk nodded. Szymon paid for the card and stamp, then went to look for Joe. "What's Michael Marcin's address"?" he asked Joe. Szymon wrote a note on the card then handed it to Joe who addressed it and pasted the stamp in the corner.

Hello Michael,

It's Szymon Swaczy and Joe Korlaszcz, We hope you are doing alright. We are almost home in Stanislau. Please send me your home address, and we will visit you when you return to your home. Good luck! Joe said he will continue to pray for you.

Yours truly, your friends,

Szymon Swaczy and Joe Korlaszcz

They crossed into the Ivano Frankivsk oblast, late on Sunday afternoon. Surprisingly, Szymon was tired despite all the sleep he'd had during their trip home. Outside the train's windows, the unfolding landscape was familiar to him. It was May first, so both flowers and weeds were in bloom, and much of the countryside had turned green. No longer were goats and sheep grazing on the rolling hills. Rather, there were fields of newly planted alfalfa and barley as far as he could see. Grazing cattle stood behind wire fencing along the train tracks.

After dusk, the light faded quickly. Szymon was fully awake now. The reality of leaving behind the past year hit him. He knew he would never return to any of those places with the strange-sounding names. He would read news about Budapest and Sarajevo, but it was unlikely he would hear any news about Pljevlja. He thought about Elise, about how desperately she wanted to leave Pljevlja, to run away with no destination in mind. He felt a momentary pang of sadness. He felt he was missing something, but wasn't sure what it was, and that made him feel tired again, so he closed his eyes again.

The train reached Stanislau at four-thirty on the morning on May second. Joe Korlaszcz shook Szymon awake. "Wake up. We're home."

Life on the base in Stanislau seemed to pick up where it left off, as though they had never been away. Szymon's platoon received new assignments, but other than that, nothing had changed in the year they had been away. They were awaiting orders from the base commander for their two-week furlough, and Szymon was looking forward to seeing his family, friends, and hometown. They were allowed passes to go off base, so Szymon took advantage of this privilege the next weekend. He patronized a German restaurant in Stanislau where he enjoyed a good meal, and visited the reading rooms in search of newspapers from Budapest. The weekly paper from Bukaczowce was available and although he didn't like to admit it, he eagerly read the news, often finding an article about someone or something of interest to him.

The following Saturday he went to town alone where he again made his usual rounds – first the reading room, then the German restaurant and then a German-style beer hall.

A pretty young lady came over to him. It was Katarzyna Tracz. "What are you doing here, he asked?"

Katarzyna had changed. She had grown up and now was a beautiful, young stylishly dressed woman.

"I'm with friends, she "said. "Would you like to join us?" Szymon was surprised to see two more former classmates, a couple from Bukaczowce who were living together in Stanislau. He felt a little awkward. They stayed for a while, but it was too loud to talk so, they suggested going back to their apartment. They wanted to hear more about Szymon's travels and army life. It was eleven thirty when Szymon said goodbye. Katarzyna walked with him outside the front door. "I had a nice evening, said Szymon. Why don't we meet again?" They arranged to meet, but on Monday morning when the platoon assembled to greet Sergeant Schoeppler, Szymon learned that he would be going home the next Saturday morning. He would be unable to meet Katarzyna, and there wasn't time for a letter to reach his father before he arrived in Bukaczowce.

On Monday morning when the platoon assembled to greet Sergeant Schoeppler, they learned that they would be going home the following Saturday. The mood on base changed immediately upon hearing the news. The men became upbeat and full of energy. When Schoeppler bellowed, "Clean this God damned pig sty," they didn't object. Rather, they cleaned up, ensuring that they and the barracks were clean, their clothes unwrinkled, and their shoes polished. Szymon's new job on base with the Grounds Maintenance department required no supervision given all the experience he had gained in Pljevlja. He planted flower beds, and enjoyed weeding and watering the small beds scattered around the base.

On the Saturday morning of their scheduled departure, Sergeant Schoeppler spoke to them in the barracks. "You boys did extremely well," he began. "You measured up to the task and Major Melnyk has sent a positive report to Commander Swartzdorf. Also, we heard from Michael Marcin; he lost two fingers on his right hand and his left middle finger is a stub. If you can call it good luck, he is left-handed. He is back home and the Army will discharge him next month." He finished by telling them to clean out their foot lockers after supper, "The building is scheduled to be painted while we are gone."

The men groaned. "What will we do with our stuff?"

"How the hell do I know? I've got more important things to think about. You figure it out." Somebody protested prompting Schoeppler to bellow, "Shove it up your ass!"

Once they had been dismissed, Theo remarked, "Same old Schoeppler."

Chapter 14

Ma, Pa, his sister Anna, and brother Michael were all home when Szymon came bounding up the road, across the front yard, and into the house. There were surprised cries of welcome. Mama wept, as usual. He looked around and thought how good it was to be home, and how much he would enjoy their company. Pa wanted to know why Szymon hadn't written to tell them he would be returning that day. "Pa, you know how the army operates."

He asked Ma what she was cooking for dinner. "We ate, but I have leftovers," she replied. As Szymon ate, the others filled him in on the local news. The big news was that Walter and Anna had officially set a wedding date.

"If you wait until Christmas, I'll be home," Szymon remarked hopefully.

They talked about their plans, Anna and Wally hoping for a happy life together and lots of children. Someone asked about Joe. Szymon responded, "Joe is remarkable!" Then, he told them of the many thoughtful and loving things Joe did for his buddies. He described the terrible incident on the road to Sarajevo, and how Joe had comforted Michael Marcin on the long trip to Sarajevo. Mama and Anna held back their tears as the story unfolded.

"It sounds horrible. Michael must have been in awful pain," Anna commented.

"Everywhere Joe goes, he makes friends and touches lives," Michael added.

"There is only one Joe," Szymon acknowledged.

Anna smiled. "I want to get to know him better,"

"Speak of the devil," said Pa. "Here he comes now."

They watched as Joe bounced up the road, vaulted over the hedge in the front yard, and sprang through the front door. After Joe and the family had enjoyed a nice visit, Szymon walked with him to take Old Black to a pasture, where the two friends talked.

"Joe, I want you to go to the pharmacy with me. Maybe there is something that can be done for your heart condition."

"I don't know if there is any medication, because the army doctors haven't said anything about it to me, but it can't hurt. When should we go?"

The next day, they walked into town and met at the pharmacy. It was as Joe suspected, there wasn't any medication that could help, but they were told many people believe in the powers of certain teas and herbs. Joe, as usual, was kind when he saw his friend's downcast face.

"Please, don't worry, Szymon. I think I know how to rest and get plenty of sleep. Also, I don't think I get stressed about things."

Szymon laughed, "You are right about that. I wish I could remain calm like you in difficult situations."

May 17, 1892

On Sunday morning, while Szymon's parents were drinking coffee, his Mama inquired, "Are you going to church?" He was quiet, avoiding saying that he would prefer to stay home, but she guessed the truth. "What time did you come home?"

Above all else, he resented her probing, and didn't want her asking questions about what had happened at the dance the prior night. He knew that in her sly but clumsy way, she would ask who he was with. Although he wasn't certain why, he didn't want her to know. He just wanted to stay at home while the family was away. That Sunday was another turning point in Szymon's life.

Szymon had matured during the more than two years he'd been in the army, so he no longer felt he had to answer his mother's questions about his personal life. She looked hurt when he abruptly changed the subject. He felt a momentary pang of guilt, but quickly moved on.

"Pa, how did those repairs to the barn hold up? Is there anything you would like me to do while I'm home?"

Pa glanced at Ma, "I can find a few things."

"How are you feeling, Pa?" Roman's health had improved, mostly because he wasn't drinking.

They were momentarily distracted by the sound of a horse and buggy turning into the front yard which sent them bounding out the door. Uncle Max and Aunt Katarzyna had come to visit. Szymon's mood changed as he joined in the family conversation. He liked his Uncle Max and there was no doubt that they were uncle and nephew. They sat at the kitchen table talking and drinking coffee, Szymon smoking cigarettes, Pa smoking his pipe.

"Do you want to hitch up old Black and run over to see the Korlaszcz family? We can stop to visit with Stephen, Tekla and the new baby," suggested Uncle Max."

Szymon sighed. He would have preferred to stay home and rest. But, after the three men went out to the barn to make a few necessary repairs, and they ate dinner, Szymon hitched old Black to the wagon. The family, including Uncle Max and Aunt Katarzyna, rode along the Czahrow road into the countryside to visit Joe's aunt and uncle. The ladies visited while the men disappeared into the barn to examine Mr. Korlaszcz's new milking equipment. Roman was saying goodbye to Mr. and Mrs. Korlaszcz, when another buggy pulled up to the house. Mr. Korlaszcz explained that farmers in the area had a great interest in the milking equipment because more than a few families were considering starting up dairy operations. Szymon liked the Korlaszcz family. They were a lot like Joe, religious and generous. He was happy that his sister was going to be part of this loving family. Later, they visited Stephen and Tekla. Their baby, Joannes, was a healthy little boy who had definitely made a difference in their lives. Stephen was a proud father, but on the trip back home, Ma told Szymon that Stephen still fell into bouts of heavy drinking.

Szymon wanted to go out that night but he felt trapped because he knew his mother would be upset. It came as no surprise when, later that evening, he told her he was going out to meet up with some of the friends he'd met in Stanislau, and she, indeed, looked hurt. "You don't want to stay home with me anymore?"

Szymon took a deep breath. "Mama, I'm not a little boy anymore."

"I know."

"That doesn't mean I don't love you, but I'm old enough to have a life of my own."

"I know." Her voice was barely audible.

"You aren't mad at me, are you, Ma?"

Their conversation went on for a while with Szymon's constant reassurances that he would try to always be a good son, but that he also wanted to start his own life. "I hope to move around and won't be living in Bukaczowce."

His mother seemed to accept his declaration of

independence, but he had not convinced himself, because he had no prospects for anything beyond returning to Stanislau. But his relationship with his father had definitely improved, perhaps because they were men with more in common now that he was in the army.

On the last Thursday of Szymon's leave, he went with his parents to the market fair. As usual, Mama had baked breads and pastries, this time with Szymon's help, selling enough to make more than five kroner. Mama was very happy with herself, and he could tell that she was no longer upset with him.

The fair was one of the best places to meet old friends and, on this particular Thursday, he watched as Joe approached pulling along a very shy, young woman, of about Szymon's age. The pretty woman turned out to be another former classmate of Szymon's, Marya Barasco. Marya had recognized Szymon, at the dance last Saturday night and wanted to be introduced. She was very shy and equally pretty. When Joe introduced her to Szymon, she looked down at the ground, her cheeks flushed bright red. Szymon looked quizzically at Joe. He couldn't figure out why Joe would want to bring Marya to say hello. An awkward silence ensued.

Mama, who had been standing off to one side, broke the silence. "Hello, Joe. Where is your Aunt?" Joe left Szymon with Marya and went to chat with Mama. The long, painful silence persisted. This young lady was struggling to find words to carry on a conversation. To help relieve the awkwardness,

Szymon asked if she was thirsty.

Her reply was soft and simple. "Yes."

They walked through the crowd to a popular stand that sold cold fruit drinks. It took a few minutes, but eventually, they found enough in common to carry on a conversation. Szymon found that, despite her shyness, she had a delightful sense of humor, and the more comfortable she became with him, the more she chattered away. She asked him to describe places where he had served in the army. He was telling her about Pljevlja when he saw Joe approaching. They agreed to meet at the dance the next night.

Looking around the dance hall, Szymon was about to ask Joe if Marya Barasco was there when he saw her chatting with another young lady at one end of the building. He wasted no time walking over to ask Marya to dance with him. Many at the dance engaged in excessive drinking, but that night Szymon moderated his consumption, and found he was having just as much fun as he had the Saturday night he'd been taken home drunk. It wasn't that he abstained, rather, that Marya was so much fun to be with that he lacked the desire to drink.

Szymon asked Marya to go with him after church on Sunday. To his surprise, she told him that she was not a member of his church.

"How do you know what church I attend?"

"Joe told me."

"Would your family be upset, if they knew you

were dating me?"

"I'm not sure."

"I don't mind that you aren't Greek Catholic."

"I'm not certain how I feel, but, I would like to marry a Roman Catholic boy."

"Marriage! Who's thinking of marriage?"

On the train back to Stanislau, Szymon mulled over the events of the past two weeks. The time had passed quickly, and he had resolved some problems in his relationships. He thought about the hurt in his mother's eyes when he tried to explain to her that he needed some time to himself. He didn't want her to know everything he did, concerned that she would disapprove of the choices he made and his philosophy of life.

Szymon had shed some of his tendency to be a loner, and found he enjoyed the company of both his male and female friends. When he thought about his girlfriends, he concluded that he wanted to remain unattached as long as he could. Szymon decided to date girls from town without concern for what his parents or friends thought. He still was insecure and had a lot to learn about women, but he knew he was a romantic at heart who would marry for love, sharing his life with one woman. His thoughts turned to Marya. Was she suggesting she wanted to marry him? He certainly didn't want to marry her.

It wasn't because she was Roman Catholic, although, admittedly, he preferred to marry someone who would go to church with him, rather that he wasn't ready to settle down. His mind was a tangled web of thoughts when Joe rescued him from his confusion by asking him how he liked Marya.

"She is a nice girl, but I think she wants to get married. And I'm too young to get married. I've just started dating, and I don't consider whores girlfriend-worthy."

"You need to find a good woman, Szymon."

Szymon nodded, laughing. "Someone to keep me straight you mean. For now, I have you to be my conscience, Joe."

Chapter 15

It was the end of June 1893, and they were due to complete their three-year stint at the end of March or April 1894. The two friends reminisced about the past few months wondering aloud what would happen during the rest of their time in Stanislau. Szymon resigned himself to many months of boredom, working at monotonous assignments, daily drills, practicing marksmanship, endless marching, repetitious calisthenics, self-defense strategies, and more. Then, rumors began to circulate about transferring to another base. No one knew where the rumor began, or who was responsible for it, but it persisted.

One evening, after Sergeant Schoeppler had given orders for the following day and left to take care of other business, Theo Kubida told Luc that he wanted to have a meeting of the men in the first platoon without Schoeppler present. "What's this rumor about transferring out of Stanislau? Does anyone have any credible information?"

Luc was silent for considerably longer than usual

before stating, "There is something to it, but nothing is finalized yet. What I hear is that we might replace a platoon stationed at the garrison in Lwow."

"So, there is some truth in the rumor," Joe Hanczyck offered.

"When are the top brass planning to make the move?" asked Thomas Mazurek.

"Maybe the first of September, after the war games," Luc responded.

Szymon's spirits perked up immediately. This would be a fresh start. He liked the idea, although not everyone agreed. Most of the men in the first platoon came from towns located within a twenty-five to fifty-mile radius of Stanislau, which enabled some to go home on weekends whenever they had the opportunity. Bukaczowce lay only thirty-five miles away, but Szymon chose not to go home often. His father never pressured him to come home, and he guessed that his mother didn't realize that he could travel wherever he wanted so long as he returned to the base on time.

The most exciting activity they faced was the annual war games in August. These games would be the last for Szymon and his buddies before their tour of duty ended. One morning, Sergeant Schoeppler ordered the men to attend a class concerning tentative plans for the games. There was an audible groan.

Approximately twelve hundred men – both regular enlisted and elite riflemen—would participate together for the first time, over three days. The prior year's games had been successful, so Schoeppler expected the same this year.

Szymon was curious about the games. "Anything special planned this year, Sarge?"

"Nobody coming to visit us with a newfangled cannon?" Theo's remark carried more than a bit of sarcasm.

"No, but these will be the biggest games you have been part of."

"Just more chance to screw up," Jo Hanczyk chided.

For his part, Szymon wasn't enthused about living in the woods for three or four days.

Due to fair weather, the games were able to start as scheduled in mid-August. The Company traveled into the Carpathians near Hoverla the highest mountain in Galicia. Sergeant Schoeppler had trained them well for the rugged terrain, so they were prepared to meet any conditions they might encounter, from fording mountain streams up to their hips in icy water, to scaling walls using hooks and ropes. Luc's squad was sometimes required to crawl on their bellies through mud, to jump over fallen timber or climb over boulders, alert for dangerously steep dropoffs. The seasoned men were able to avoid serious accidents, although there were numerous minor injuries. Nevertheless, they had performed well. Working as a unified team, they made these the smoothest exercises the twelve hundred men had participated in during their army careers.

Shortly after the war games ended, their reassignment to a new garrison in Lwow was made official. On the second of September the men of the first platoon detrained near the center of the city. They fell in, marching through the city to the big garrison located at the foot of the hill. Lwow was not nearly as large as Budapest, but it bustled with people and traffic, and boasted many buildings of German architecture. Not only was the city impressive, it was beautiful as well.

Szymon looked forward to having time to explore this city. Joe wanted to visit the cathedrals and churches in the old town. Some guys laughed at them, wanting only to visit the beer halls and look for whores. But Szymon knew what he most wanted to find: a German coffee shop. There were newspapers, reading rooms, two universities, theaters, and parks, including a botanical garden. The Germans loved fresh flowers. Szymon already sensed that he would enjoy living in Lwow. His intuition told him that the ability to travel to and experience new and different places offered him the opportunity to learn and grow, so he wanted to take full advantage of this opportunity.

Military routines are essentially the same no matter where the garrison, post or base is located. The next morning, Szymon was awakened by the sound of the bugle after a good night's sleep. After breakfast, the platoon returned to the barracks where Sergeant Schoeppler awaited them. He was all business as he called out their assignments for the day. "Your permanent job has yet to be determined."

Szymon listened to the conversations around him. Some guys were very pleased to be in Lwow and some would have liked to stay in Stanislau. Others liked the adventure of going to Bosnia. "Does anyone know the reason we were transferred here?" They knew that another platoon had either gone home or been assigned to some far-off place.

Theo Kubida spoke up. "I don't know why, but I'm glad to be at this base because we will have plenty of everything,"

The men cleaned up after completing the day's assignment. Szymon realized that everyone on base seemed to know what was expected of him, and that half the men were coming and going without being marched around in formation. The first chance he got, he mentioned this to Luc Slobodianyk. Luc told him he hadn't paid attention to that, but wondered whether the relaxing of rules was only at this base. There were many officers stationed at the Lwow Garrison which may have accounted for the flexibility of some rules. If the base commander identified any problems, he could simply switch back to having the soldiers march everywhere under supervision.

Szymon's new job on base was working as a bricklayer's helper on a building site. Since the Austrian government had poured more money into the military budget following the rebellions in Bosnia Herzegovina in 1878, the War Department had undertaken a major building spree, which accounted for the new buildings being erected at the Lwow garrison in 1893. True to the German and Austrian desire for orderliness, the structures were simple, sturdy, brick buildings, but nonetheless handsome.

In many ways, life at the Lwow Garrison resembled non-military life. Although some of Szymon's buddies nitpicked about small inconveniences, there wasn't much to complain about, and overall, Szymon was satisfied.

Whenever he was issued a pass, Szymon would explore the clean, well-maintained city of Lwow. He often left the garrison on his own, but sometimes teamed up with Joe or other friends. Although several churches had been razed decades earlier to build the modern garrison, he and Joe would go into the old section of the city to explore the old churches, and to enjoy the many restaurants and cafes, some serving authentic Polish and Ruthenian cooking. It wasn't unusual to strike up a conversation with someone originally from Bukaczowce or a nearby town or village. On Sunday mornings, Szymon attended services at one of the Greek Catholic Churches.

Szymon and Joe had gone sightseeing together, and were now sitting in a coffee house. "It's so beautiful here, Joe, and there appears to be plenty of work. I'd like to stay here after our stint in the army is over. Do you like it here, too?"

"I'm not sure I like it well enough to stay. And remember that I have to think about my aunt and uncle, too."

There was a pause in the conversation, while they reflected on their respective prospects. "Are you still considering going into the seminary, Joe?"

"I'm encouraged by the brothers in one of the Roman Catholic Churches in town. I can go at any time; it's up to me to determine when the time is right. Perhaps we could live in town at the same time, Szymon, but I'm not sure yet."

Szymon decided to change the subject. "We'll be going home at Christmastime. I'm hoping Wally and Anna will get married while we're home. We had better find out, so we can make plans, after all, it's only a few months away.

That night Szymon wrote a letter home.

October 13, 1893

Dear Pa and Ma,

I haven't heard from you for a while so I am writing. Is Mama doing well? Are tomatoes and peppers in the garden? Was the wheat harvest good this year? Joe Korlaszcz and I were talking about going home at Christmastime. We thought about the wedding, and wondered when will it be? I hope everything is alright with the wedding plans. We hope to leave here around the same time we did last year, but Sergeant Schoeppler hasn't told us anything yet.

Life is good in Lwow and I like it a lot. I visit the churches in the old city. There is a lot to see, and it is beautiful. The boys are all good, and so is Joe

Korlaszcz. When I come home, I will bring some coffee. Don't forget to write about Wally and Anna. Tell Mama that I think about her, and hope she is in good health.

Your son,

Szymon Swaczy

The following Monday morning, Sergeant Schoeppler told the men to be prepared to go out on patrol in the Old Town section of Lwow where trouble was brewing. "I'm not exactly sure what it is all about, but the military police need backup, because the situation isn't calming down. To Szymon's surprise, he discovered that the trouble in Old Town was related to unruly factions of Poles and Ruthenians. Agitators from the university were spreading political propaganda to foment discontent. His rational mind told him to stay out of it, but his curiosity got the best of him, so he decided to patronize a small coffee and sandwich shop in the Ruthenian section of Old Town. When Szymon entered the shop conversation ceased.

He realized he was in uniform, and people may have felt they couldn't speak freely when a soldier was present. Szymon ordered a dinner of kielbasa and sauerkraut with a cup of coffee. He read his newspaper as he ate his dinner, but he could still hear parts of whispered conversations around him. It sounded as though their conversations concerned the unrest of the past several nights. He thought he heard someone say there was something planned for that night.

As the conversations trailed off, Szymon decided to pay his bill and leave before trouble broke out. On the way out, he saw a pretty young woman behind the counter. "Do you own this shop? The food is good, just like my mother makes."

The young woman, pleased by the compliment, could not suppress her smile. "Where are you from?"

"Bukaczowce."

"Oh! I lived there for a while with my aunt and uncle. I came to Lwow to try to find a better job."

Szymon thought about her as he walked back to the base. He shouldn't have been yet being surprised by her response, as he had not thought about how many other people—including ladies—would be attracted to a big city for jobs. But it wasn't only the prospect of a good job that interested him, he also believed Lwow would be a good place to live.

Szymon returned to the little coffee shop in Old Town several more times before the liberal issuance of passes ended. He felt as though he had made a friend of the young lady. He wanted to ask her out for dinner, but wasn't able to obtain a pass for two weeks. By the time he returned to the restaurant, the young woman was gone. The girl who had replaced her said that she had found another job, but she didn't know where.

On base many things had changed since the unrest began. The situation wasn't serious enough to issue a curfew, but the more relaxed regimen had been replaced by an order for the men to again march in formation on base.

In late November, during morning orders, Schoeppler told the men to wear their dress uniforms and assemble in front of the barracks after dinner. Several companies lined up in formation to march into the city center. People stood quietly on the streets watching as the soldiers passed. As they entered Old Town, marching up Zamarstynowska Street, onlookers appeared wary.

Clearly, something had changed here. But the dissidents settled down quickly after the ringleaders were brought in for questioning about their activities.

With the crisis calmed, life on base relaxed once again. Soldiers stationed at the Lwow garrison were relieved to learn that one-day passes would resume, as Christmas was on the minds of many. Students at the university would be going home, as would the men in Szymon's platoon.

Word had begun to circulate that Sergeant Schoeppler was up for another stripe. If the rumors were true, he would begin the New Year as a Sergeant Major, but the men wondered who would replace him. Speculation about a promotion was only one rumor about Sergeant Schoeppler. The other was that he'd been seen on several occasions with a woman. No one had the courage to ask if it was true, however, something noticeable in Schoeppler's demeanor had changed. Although he treated the men as roughly as ever, his remarks weren't as personal or mean-spirited.

Sitting in a classroom listening to a lecture on venereal disease, the men were, basically, advised to abstain. There were illustrations and descriptions of the manifestations of various diseases, how they spread, and what few treatments existed. These lectures were given frequently, more frequently it seemed, when the men were going on furloughs around the holidays. As Sergeant Schoeppler wound up the presentation, a voice in the back of the room called out. "Hey, Sarge, who is going to replace you when you are bumped up?"

Schoeppler stopped and the men held their collective breath. They had come to expect one of several reactions, from an explosion to a curt remark telling them it wasn't any of their business. They only had to wait a moment. "It's a new man who is coming from another base, Czernowitz."

"Where will you be stationed?"

"Here."

No one mustered the courage to ask him about his mysterious girlfriend.

The next three weeks were uneventful, except for one incident that could have derailed the planned furloughs. A prominent political figure in the Old Town area was murdered. Fortunately, because of their quick action, the police were able to determine who committed the crime. Even though the murder wasn't politically motivated, tensions rose, and uncertainty persisted for several days until newspaper reporting clarified who had committed the crime and their motive. Not many believed the entire story, but it was plausible enough to defuse the situation and prevent it from exploding into a bigger incident. No one wanted chaos to overtake the joyous spirit of the holiday.

Stories persisted about Schoeppler and his girlfriend. Someone heard that he was seen shopping with her and another rumored that the couple had been seen together in a restaurant. The men wanted to know who this woman was. One day, just before the start of their furloughs, Joe Korlaszcz was at his job in the chapel in the Roman Catholic mission church when he caught a glimpse of Sergeant Schoeppler and his lady friend going into the priest's office. "Now, this is interesting," thought Joe. Assigned to carry some records to the parish office that day, Joe waited until Sergeant Schoeppler had left to cross the lawn to the sidewalk and carry the bundle of folders to the administration building where he had friends in every department. He delivered the folders to a secretary. "I saw Sergeant Schoeppler over here. I'm trying to catch up with him. Could I speak with someone who might know where he was heading?"

An acolyte in the parish office told him that Sergeant Schoeppler and his lady friend, Magdalena, had come to the rectory to speak to the priest about marrying. Joe was stunned. He couldn't wait to take the good news to the men in his platoon. After the Sergeant had left the barracks that evening, Joe led the men in prayers, before sharing his news. "I believe that Sergeant Schoeppler is getting married." One could have heard a pin drop.

"How do you know that, Joe?"

"Who would marry him?" wisecracked another.

As the men laughed, Joe grew concerned that he had done something sinful. "I shouldn't have snooped. I don't know what got into me."

They laughed all the more. "What did you find out?" They pressed him, wanting to know who told him the news. Joe stuttered and stumbled over his words until the boys began laughing at him hysterically. "Joe, you didn't do anything wrong, you weren't trying to hurt Sergeant Schoeppler."

"I know, still I feel like I did something bad, but I can't figure out why it's wrong."

They were teasing Joe mercilessly, acting like fools, when the door to the barracks flung open. Sergeant Schoeppler stood at the threshold yelling. "Has anyone seen Swaczy? Where the hell is Swaczy?" There was dead silence. No one knew where he had gone. Szymon often went alone into town or to the reading room on base, so no one thought anything was amiss when he was away for hours at a time. Sergeant Schoeppler said that he hadn't been issued a 24-hour pass, and hadn't returned to the garrison on time. "Do you know where he is, Joe?"

"He sometimes goes to Old Town, to the Polish restaurants for dinner."

Sergeant Schoeppler acknowledged, "We're looking there now."

"There was a hell of a storm earlier today," Theo offered. "He had to get indoors somewhere."

After Schoeppler left, the men were subdued, concerned about where Swaczy might be. Joe said nothing, although he knew that Szymon was interested in the political activity in Old Town. Szymon told Joe that he had attended two meetings of an organization promoting an independence movement. Joe racked his brain to think where else his friend might go. He remembered that Szymon went to the Prosvida, a culture center promoting Ukrainian language and culture, and to a library and reading room in one of the palaces on the east side of Rynok Square. Joe wondered whether he should share this information with Schoeppler.

Two hours later, when there still was no news of Swaczy's whereabouts, Joe led the men in prayers for Szymon. Afterward, he decided to talk to Sarge, just as Luc entered the barracks. "They found him! They found him!" Szymon was in a small hospital run by a Catholic church near the downtown area. Joe followed Luc into Schoeppler's office where the three compared the fragments of information each had learned about Swaczy's whereabouts.

Sergeant Schoeppler took Joe with him to the hospital, while Luc filled in the men about what was known. They arrived at the hospital, and went directly to Szymon's room. His head was wrapped in bandages, his shoulder was dislocated, his foot was set in a splint, and he had defensive lacerations, scrapes and bruises on his arms and hands.

A doctor followed them into the room. Szymon had been unconscious since being admitted that afternoon. The doctor, Schoeppler, and Joe stood at the end of the bed, discussing what was known about Szymon's injuries.

He had been found near a construction site where a building was being renovated. At first, it appeared a scaffold had collapsed, resulting in a debris field of bricks and mortar covering the area where Szymon lay. Part of the building was damaged, but a thorough investigation would have to wait until daylight. They discussed the severe storm that ripped through the city only minutes before Szymon was discovered lying unconscious in the mud and mortar. Joe asked if he could stay with Szymon overnight. Schoeppler agreed and left with the doctor.

Szymon didn't awaken during the night even though the hospital staff came and went frequently to check on him. Joe was worried but relieved that Szymon had been found alive and was in the care of doctors. He had faith that they would bring him through this ordeal, and prayed for Szymon throughout the night. Joe dozed on and off, feeling Szymon's chest and listening for a heartbeat each time he awakened.

He knew Szymon's breathing was slow, but didn't know what that meant. Joe asked a male orderly who came into the room if Szymon had been given any medicine. The man told him that he hadn't had anything except water. Although exhausted, Joe didn't want to abandon watching over his friend, but weariness soon overcame him and he fell asleep on the bed next to Szymon.

The rising sun was filtering through the curtains when Joe awakened. He went to the window and pushed aside a curtain so he could see Szymon's injuries. It was a horrible sight. Szymon's face was a deep purplish color; his features were swollen and distorted. No one could have guessed it was Szymon.

Joe saw numerous lacerations on his face, arms and hands. For the first time, he began to worry about whether Szymon would ever come out of the coma. He returned to the window, peering out over the city, when the door opened. It was the doctor who had spoken with him the evening before. The doctor ignored Joe and immediately strode to the bedside, examined Szymon's battered body, felt for a pulse, and listened to his heartbeat. "Well, everything seems to be normal. Young man, did your friend say anything in his sleep during the night?"

"No sir."

"Just let him rest for a while. He'll probably awaken shortly. I've seen many patients injured in accidents like this, and usually the person snaps out of this deep sleep after a day or so."

"Is there a place I can buy breakfast or just some coffee?"

"We'll send up a tray for you. If your friend awakens, call me immediately."

Dr. Schneider left the room, and Joe sat in a chair

next to the bed thinking that the doctor's words sounded encouraging. This was a difficult time, but he didn't want to lose faith, so Joe took out his rosary and began to pray. "Holy Mary, pray for us. Holy Mother of God. Holy Virgin of virgins. Mother of Christ." A breakfast tray arrived. After Joe consumed the meal, he prayed again for Szymon's recovery, but there was still no change.

The hours dragged by even though hospital staff checked on Szymon throughout the afternoon, and later in the day Sergeant Schoeppler stopped in. "What a hell of a mess."

"There has been no change, Sergeant. The doctor said to be patient."

Schoeppler gazed at Szymon, sadly shaking his head. "Well, that's all we've got. Do you want to continue to stay at your friend's side? It's your choice, Joe."

Joe stood by the window, feeling lonely as he watched Sergeant Schoeppler walk down the street and turn toward the garrison.

Thinking he had heard a moan, Joe turned to see Szymon trying to move his arm. "Szymon, can you hear me?" He did not respond, but opened his eyes. Joe returned to Szymon's side reciting the Our Father, as Szymon mumbled coherently. Tears streamed down Joe's face as he took Szymon's hand. "Don't die." Szymon squeezed back, ever so slightly.

Behind him, he heard the door open. Dr. Schneider entered, followed by a young woman dressed in a white blouse and dark blue skirt, carrying a tray with a plate of food and a cup of coffee. The doctor could see there was a change in his patient and rushed to his side. "Can you hear me, young man?"

Szymon tried to move his head but could only mutter, "Ouch," in a faint voice.

"Can you tell me your name?" Szymon merely stared at the doctor. "Szymon, are you hungry?" He replied with only a grunt. Turning to the young patient assistant, Dr. Schneider told her to go to the kitchen and ask them to prepare a special meal of pureed foods. Then, he told Joe to take a seat at the table in the corner and eat his dinner. The doctor picked up his black bag, drew the curtain around Szymon's bed and examined him further. When the assistant returned with a covered meal tray, the doctor drew back the curtain, and asked her name.

Her voice was soft. "Barbara Podosek, sir." He asked if she knew how to feed a patient with a syringe. She nodded. "Yes sir."

"Miss Podosek, please give him as much as he can eat, and use the cup or syringe to give him plenty of water. Also, get a container of juice from the kitchen." With that done, he left the room.

The three were huddled in a small group. Joe assisted the young lady setting up the tray on a movable table next to the bed; then he pushed his chair and his small table to the opposite side so he could stay close to his friend. He watched her feed Szymon cereal by spooning some into a syringe, then moving the syringe to his lips.

"What is your name?"

The young woman glanced at him quickly. "Miss Podosek."

"My name is Joe, and this is Szymon."

Szymon's recovery was slow. His days were spent sleeping, as though he could not get enough rest. After the first few days, he began to speak with considerable effort, often in incoherent sentences. Mumbling, he would begin a sentence, but could not complete his thought. She spent hours trying to encourage him to speak. About a week after he had been found lying in the debris and was admitted to the hospital, having made progress, he sat in bed, propped up on several pillows.

He could greet the hospital staff by name, and even smile at their cheery greetings when they came into his room to clean or clear the tray of dirty dishes. When the young assistant, Miss Podosek, came into his room, he was able to call her by name. "Szymon, do you remember telling me about your mother's sauerkraut and kielbasa, and the delicious pastries she baked?" He just stared at her in response, but she could see that he remembered her.

"It's you, oh yes, you remember. Do you know what day it is?" He looked confused. "It's Christmas."

Often when Szymon spoke, the syntax was mixed up. "Restaurant Old Town." She saw a spark of recognition in his eyes. "Where go you? No one knew where you go." As they chatted that afternoon, she told him that she often wondered about him.

The platoon had left on their two-week furlough about 10 days after Szymon's accident. Reluctantly, Joe left, too. Joe and Theo visited Szymon upon their return from Christmas furlough, bringing Szymon small gifts from his family.

Theo was excited to tell Szymon about their visit. "We visited your Pa. I thought your Mama would never stop crying!"

Joe told Szymon he had a letter from his father, adding, "You look much better."

"What the hell did he look like before today?"

"He looked like he had been in a war."

The three friends chatted, catching up on the news from home. Joe went first. "Your brothers and sister are okay. Wally and Anna are getting married after we muster out of the army."

Theo spoke next. "Stephen got himself into trouble again. He'd been drinking, fell from the roof of his house, and broke his arm. Now, he can't work, so no one knows what's going to happen to them. Your father is disgusted with him. Steve's going to cause a lot of suffering in your family, if he doesn't cut out this crap." Szymon didn't know what to say.

"Don't give up on him yet. I'll pray for a miracle." Szymon and Theo suppressed a chuckle.

The door opened and one of the hospital staff

came in to clear the breakfast dishes. Miss Podosek poked her head into the room, as well. "How are you feeling, Szymon?"

"Better each day. Hey, Joe, I finally figured out that Miss Podosek is the young lady I met in the Ruthenian restaurant in Old Town." She blushed. Joe's eyes glanced from her to Szymon and back again. His face took on a mischievous expression, but he remained tactfully silent. She closed the door behind her, leaving the three friends alone.

Theo picked up the conversation. "Well, you missed your two-week leave.

Do you know how much longer you will be here?"

"I'd like to go home, but doubt the doctor will allow me to travel yet. He says that the bones in my foot are bonding, but it's only been a little over three weeks since the accident, so I don't think I'll be leaving here for another two weeks."

Szymon told Joe and Theo everything he knew about how long it would take to heal. "Sarge has been here a few times and doesn't seem to be concerned about how long I stay, but I'm surprised I haven't been moved to the Garrison hospital."

Over the next two weeks, several of Szymon's friends visited him. They all remarked on the discoloration of his face. He still had some scabs on his arms and hands and suffered sharp pains under his rib cage, but every day he noticed an improvement. Toward the middle of the sixth week, Sergeant Schoeppler visited Szymon. "Glad to see you have improved. How is that foot?"

"I think I will be ready to return to the unit soon. But I was wondering if I could go home for two or three days first?"

"How could you travel home by yourself?"

"That's a problem. I'll have to figure that out."

"I'll get you a two-day pass if you can come up with someone to go with you, but we can't allow you to take anyone from the platoon."

When the doctor visited Szymon that evening, Szymon told him about his desire to visit his family in Bukaczowce. The doctor thought it was an excellent idea, but asked, "Who will go with you?"

"That's the problem. Everybody I know in Lwow is in the army.

"What about Miss Podosek? Could you ask her?"

Szymon was surprised. "I hadn't thought of her and didn't know her very well, sir. If she agreed, would the hospital give her the time off?"

"I don't see why not, if you go on a weekend. It's a sixty-five-mile train ride to Bukaczowce. Could you pay her train fare?"

Szymon was nervous when he saw Miss Podosek the next morning. She knew he wanted to ask her something and finally inquired, "Szymon, what is it?"

"I don't want to offend you, but would you go home with me?"

She was clearly puzzled. "Szymon, are you feeling alright?"

"Yes, I mean no," he stammered. Then he flushed bright red. "I mean, I have a question to ask."

"Well, what is it?"

"I don't know how to begin. Dr. Schneider told me I can go home for a day or two, but someone has to accompany me."

She looked at him, studying his face as he lay on the bed. "Szymon, you have to give me more details."

He explained that he wanted to go home, but Dr. Schneider told him he couldn't leave unless he had a capable person accompany him to Bukaczowce. "I would pay for your train ticket." It took time for Szymon to give her all the details of his plan because he kept forgetting important information, so he went back and forth, filling in the details. "Dr. Schneider will send a note to the nursing office requesting permission for you to travel with me."

Miss Podosek asked whose idea it was for her to travel with Szymon. When he told her that Dr. Schneider suggested it, she smiled. "In that case, I would like to accompany you, Szymon."

Sergeant Schoeppler visited Szymon the next day, and they finalized their plan. Szymon would send Joe to buy tickets for Ms. Podosek and himself, to leave Lwow for Bukaczowce on February 2nd, Szymon's birthday.

"Do you want to write to tell your family you will

be coming home, Syzmon?" asked Joe.

"Maybe it should be a surprise."

The week prior to Szymon's departure, Dr. Schneider ordered Miss Podosek to help Szymon learn to use his crutches, making it clear he wouldn't give permission unless he was able to use them properly. Once Szymon was up and about, his stamina increased. His sores were healing although his aches and pains did not alleviate.

The southbound train reached Bukaczowce in the late afternoon of Friday, February 2, 1894. The day was cold and overcast. Szymon had practiced walking with his crutches on the streets of Lwow during snowy weather, but was grateful that the snow had melted in Bukaczowce. He was stronger since he had learned to use them and was confident he could walk the distance between the train depot and his parent's house. They reached the house without being seen by neighbors, and no one was outside. His father opened the front door. "Szymon, what happened to you? Helena, Helena! Look who's here!" Mama stopped what she was doing, and both of them stared back and forth between Szymon and Miss Podosek.

Mama made coffee and warmed a sweet roll she had baked the day before. Then they sat at the table as Szymon recounted the accident and six-week stay in the hospital. His parents knew about the accident and had heard some details from Joe Korlaszcz and Theo Kubida, but nothing could have prepared them to see their son in such a battered and bruised condition. Szymon assured them that he was on the mend and was well past the worst of his injuries. Anyway, he didn't want to upset his mother nor relive the memories of that day. "Mama, I don't remember anything about the actual incident, and when I came to, two days later, I couldn't remember my name."

Miss Podosek sat quietly, engaging in the conversation only when asked to provide information about Szymon's care during the past six weeks. Szymon's mother glanced at her from time to time. Miss Podosek was dressed in a starched white shirt, blue skirt and jacket topped off by a little cap perched on her head. She bore a neat, professional appearance. Szymon was certain his mother had no idea of what to ask Miss Podosek concerning his nursing care. So she directed her questions to Szymon. "How long are you staying with us?"

"I have only a two-day pass, so I will leave late in the evening on Sunday." Szymon felt tired, so asked his mother if he could take a nap. Miss Podosek took the suitcase into the west room. When she returned Szymon told her that he wasn't feeling well. "What's wrong?"

"I'm sick in the stomach and dizzy."

"I think you had too much excitement for one day." She returned to the main room to tell Szymon's mother that he had to rest. "He's nauseated and dizzy."

Szymon's mother was worried. "Oh, God, do you think he will be alright?"

Miss Podosek explained that it is common for a person to have reactions to even normal exertions after staying in bed for so long and assured her that Szymon would be fine after he rested. But, he continued to experience nausea.

"You didn't eat much today. Maybe your mother will fix you something to eat, to settle your stomach before you lie down." Mama told Miss Podosek that she was preparing chicken soup for supper. "That's perfect." Mama was proud to do whatever she could to help her son. After eating, Szymon immediately dozed off.

"It's almost 1:30. I think he will sleep until supper is ready."

So, while Szymon slept, Mama and Miss Podosek prepared dinner. Mama asked where she had been born. Miss Podosek replied that she was from a little village in Poland, about three hundred miles away. While she didn't know much about her early life and childhood, she suspected that the woman who raised her was not her birth mother. All she knew about her father was that he was an older man when she was born, and many years older than her real mother. Miss Podosek added that she had moved to Bukaczowce with an aunt and uncle a few years ago, but stayed only for a short time.

Helena put the kettle of soup on the stove along with a huge kettle of water to boil noodles. The two women were now comfortable with each other, and found many things to talk about as they prepared the evening meal in the quiet of the late afternoon.

Pa awakened from a nap, and pulling a chair away from the table, asked if there was any coffee. Usually a quiet man, he was satisfied to let others do the talking. This afternoon was no exception. As the two women talked about this and that, Pa seemed content to smoke his pipe and drink coffee.

Miss Podosek said that she had better try to awaken Szymon and dress him before supper was ready. When she left the room to tend to Szymon, Mama confided to Roman. "I like her, Pa; she seems like a nice, down-to-earth girl."

Pa nodded. "Yes, she does."

Anna came home in the early evening from her job as a maid for a German family who lived in a wealthier section of town. She was ecstatic that Szymon was home, and immediately took a liking to Miss Podosek, who brought Szymon into the room and pulled up a chair next to the cooking stove where it was warm. Addressing her brother, Anna remarked, "It is cold outside. How are you feeling?"

"Better. Earlier I thought I was going to throw up."

The family sat around the table while Miss Podosek helped Helena bring bowls of soup, warm bread and butter. "Don't overdo it," warned Miss Podosek, after Szymon had taken two extra servings of the soup. She also stopped him from accepting the glass of vodka Mr. Swaczy offered to Szymon. "It's doctor's orders."

Pa started to protest, but the women stood firm.

Szymon knew he could do without the alcohol, but would have liked a snort or two. Father and son exchanged annoyed glances.

After dinner, Szymon asked Miss Podosek if he could go to the barn to help his father milk the cow. She agreed but told him not to stay in the cold night air too long. "Dr. Schneider's orders," she said with a grin. Szymon looked at his mother, thinking she would protest, but she agreed with the young nurse. Szymon grumbled and left with his father complaining that women always try to run men's lives.

Roman agreed. "They always stick together, too."

It was too cold to remain outside very long, so father and son milked the cow, gathered eggs, and hurried back inside. It was then they heard a voice calling, "Pa!" It was Michael. The three men walked into the small house. Szymon introduced Miss Podosek to his brother. They conversed, and while Michael ate supper. Afterward, Mama served coffee and warm bread pudding. The evening was pleasant, filled with storytelling about events of the past year and a half.

While Miss Podosek was making more coffee, Szymon carried several cups and placed them on the board next to her, then he whispered, "I almost forgot my gifts. Would you get them for me? They are under your chair"

Roman was surprised and pleased with his new pen. Anna, Michael and Ma had birthday gifts, too.

Szymon thanked his father for writing to him during his time away. "It's been over two years since I left home, for Stanislau."

The night grew late. Anna said she had to go to bed, and invited Miss Podosek to sleep with her.

"I am sleeping on the settee in the room where Szymon sleeps. I don't mind. He should have someone with him at all times."

"Do you want to visit Steve?" asked Pa as they were eating breakfast the next morning. "What do you say, Szymon?" Szymon shrugged; he wasn't enthused.

Mama interceded. "You should visit with him, son. It's time to turn the other cheek. Your brother is not doing very well. He is suffering, and his entire family along with him."

So, after breakfast, Pa hitched Old Black to the wagon, and they rode out old Czahrow Road to the tiny house where Steve, Tekla and little Joannes lived. The brothers embraced and Mama comforted Tekla who began to weep. Joannes, a happy, little two-year-old, played on the floor with a hand-carved wooden horse. Steve was having a difficult time since he broke his arm, but it was Steve who was shocked seeing Szymon's condition.

"I am a lot better now than I was six weeks ago."

"You must have been banged up seriously."

"I'm a lucky man. I could have been killed. I'm still weak, but I know I'll be alright soon."

"What are your plans, Szymon?"

"I would like to live in Lwow. There is a lot of work there."

After taking a stroll, they walked together back to Steve's house, sincerely concerned about each other—more than they had ever been. "It's been rough for both of us," Stephen lamented.

When they reached the house, Ma and Pa were getting ready to leave.

"Would you like to come with us to visit Mr. and Mrs. Korlaszcz?" They rode the short distance to Joe's Aunt and Uncle's house. Joe's Uncle Jan Korlaszcz was working in the barn when they arrived. The men headed to the back of the property to see his new milking equipment while the ladies visited with Joe's Aunt Maria. When the men returned to the house, Mama could tell by the tone of the conversation that Mr. Korlaszcz and Steve had been talking about Steve working for him beginning on Monday morning.

On the way home, Pa and Szymon told Mama that Jan offered to hire Steve temporarily to help Wally install new equipment and to tide Steve over until he found a permanent job. Mama fought back tears. "I've prayed for Stephen and his family. This is an answer to my prayers."

Arriving back at Ma and Pa's home, Miss Podosek asked Szymon if he wanted to rest for a while. Mama and Miss Podosek prepared a light dinner of bread and cheese, and before Szymon laid down to rest, Miss Podosek asked Szymon if he could take her into town to the Roman Catholic Church. "I'd like to give my confession."

On the way to the old Roman Catholic Church, he asked her whether she remembered much about Bukaczowce. "Yes, I remember everything. It's a nice little town. And I remember this church; it was my church." For no apparent reason, she added, wistfully, "Your mother and father love you, Szymon. You are lucky. I don't have parents to love me." There was an expression of longing in her voice. "You have a family Szymon, don't forget it. No matter how they anger or disappoint you, remember that they love you. I can tell."

Sitting next to each other on the teamster's seat of the wagon, he looked down at her and she felt that he fully understood the meaning of what she had said to him. They rode in silence for a few minutes. "I won't forget." There was no need for further conversation.

Accompanying her inside the old church, Szymon sat in a pew while she stood in the line for confession, with only a few people ahead of her in the queue. On the trip home, Szymon felt awkward with Miss Podosek for the first time, as they rode along in silence. He wanted to continue their conversation, but wasn't sure how to begin. They had no trouble chatting when the conversations were in the context of his care. Both of them were shy, timid and not sure how to act in a boy-girl relationship.

"We leave tomorrow, late afternoon," Szymon stated.

"Are you feeling better today?"

"Yes, and I think I will be able to rejoin my platoon soon after returning to Lwow."

The next day, Szymon went with his family to the Greek Catholic Church, then spent most of the day resting. Miss Podosek suggested that they walk after dinner, promising it would be a very short walk. "You won't exert yourself."

The sky was a deep blue that day as they walked along a secluded, wooded trail. All signs of snow had disappeared.

Szymon told her that he played in the woods along this trail when he was a little boy. "Pa wanted us to fish, but a law forbade it. There is a pond ahead where we would sneak to fish anyway. Pa showed us how to make dough balls to use for bait."

They chatted away and she didn't want to interrupt Szymon, but knew they should head back to the house. "We have to return. The air is cooler now that the sun is starting to descend. It will be a lovely, but cold, night."

Szymon tripped when the tip of his crutch stuck in a rotting tree limb lying on the ground as he turned to go back to the house. She steadied him.

"If you are tired, let's slow down."

"Maybe we should."

When they reached the house, Pa was still napping and Mama was just removing a pie from the oven.

"Weren't you cold out there?"

"No, it wasn't that cold, Ma."

His mother prepared a wonderful supper that afternoon consisting of beef roast, potatoes, rutabagas and carrots, pumpkin pie with whipped cream, and coffee. As the family gathered around the table that evening, Helena couldn't have been happier. She delighted in having her family surround her. She asked Miss Podosek if she planned to remain in Lwow.

"I'm not certain. My aunt and uncle live in a village outside Lwow, and work on an estate owned by the Greek Catholic Church. They are satisfied, so will remain there for a while. I live in the Old City with friends."

Mama told her to visit anytime she pleased. "Do you remember any families living here?"

Miss Podosek had lived in Bukaczowce for only a few months and said she didn't feel close enough with the people she had met there to make a special effort to see them. "I think it would be uncomfortable for all of us."

Pa and Szymon went outside to milk the cow while the ladies were clearing the table. After coffee and pie, it was time for Szymon and Miss Podosek to begin gathering their personal items and packing their small suitcases. The train to Lwow would be arriving in Bukaczowce within an hour or so. Szymon told his parents that he had a wonderful visit with them and would probably return in a few months after completing his three years in the army. "I'll be on inactive duty for a number of years."

Roman nodded. "That brings back memories. I was in the military for over ten years, but there were no serious uprisings, so I didn't have to leave my family to go off to fight a war."

Roman and Helena accompanied Miss Podosek and Szymon to the station. They chattered away during their last few minutes together. At 9:00p.m., the train from Kolomea arrived, right on schedule. Roman thanked Miss Podosek for accompanying Szymon home. They heard the train whistle, embraced, and before they could complete their conversation, the conductor was assisting Szymon up the steps onto the train platform.

The door slammed shut, the whistle blew again, and the train began to roll slowly away from the station. They waved at Szymon's happy parents. It had been a short but enjoyable visit home.

The conductor helped them to their seats and collected the tickets in a cheerful, courteous manner. It was as though all the stars were aligned that night.

Szymon and Miss Podosek chattered away.

"My father has changed. Maybe it's old age. He wasn't so cheerful years ago. Maybe he is happier if he doesn't drink so much."

Her voice was soft in reply, "I like your mother, Szymon. She is a very nice person."

"Yes, Mama is nice and she deserves better than

what she has gotten from life. I wouldn't want my wife to have a life as hard as she has had."

Meanwhile, in Bukaczowce, Roman and Helena were preparing for bed.

"I like that little nurse," offered Helena.

"She is a pretty woman. I wonder how old she is?" mused Roman.

Helena told Roman about her conversation with Miss Podosek while he was napping. "She comes from a poor family and lost both her parents as a little child, so she doesn't know much about them."

"Well, whoever raised her did a good job. And I suspect that Szymon likes her, too.

When Szymon and Miss Podosek arrived in Lwow, they walked the few blocks to the hospital. "You must be feeling better. You are doing a very good job walking with crutches. I think the visit with your parents has been very good for you." Reaching the hospital, they walked up the steps into the building where they were greeted by a stern-faced nun who looked at the couple with suspicion.

"Oh, sister, we went to Bukaczowce to visit Mr. Swaczy's parents. Doctor Schneider gave permission for me to accompany Mr. Swaczy, because he is still recuperating from the accident." Miss Podosek was wearing her nurse assistant uniform and Szymon, standing on crutches, wore his army uniform. Nevertheless, the nun wouldn't allow them to go to Szymon's room.

Miss Podosek rummaged through her suitcase to retrieve a letter addressed to the nursing administrator and written by Dr. Schneider seeking approval for Miss Podosek's travel with Mr. Swaczy to visit his parents. The nun, who was not in a kindly mood, wouldn't relent. Fortunately, one of the staff doctors entered the building, immediately recognizing both Miss Podosek and Szymon. "How was your visit with your parents, Szymon?"

Before Szymon could answer, the nun posed a question to the doctor, "Was this approved by Mother Superior?"

"Now, now, Sister Agnes, let this rest until tomorrow morning, and please let Miss Podosek assist Mr. Swaczy back to his room."

Sister Agnes glared at the doctor over the top of her glasses, rose from her seat, and sputtered curtly, "Follow me." The doctor nodded approvingly. Sister Agnes was mortified, but didn't protest. Szymon and Miss Podosek were finally rescued. They ascended the stairs to the second floor, entered the safety of Szymon's room, closed the door, and began laughing.

They laughed so hard that they fell into each other's arms. Szymon gave her a big hug and she hugged him back. Breaking away, she patted him fondly, "It was a beautiful trip, Szymon and I thank you for a lovely time."

Szymon lay awake that night. He, too, had a lovely time, as Miss Podosek had described their visit. His parents seemed to be genuinely happy to see him, and surprisingly, so did Stephen. "What got into them?" He thought about how concerned they were about his accident, and he remembered what Miss Podosek said to him, 'Your parents love you, Szymon.' He repeated over and over those words to himself, as he slowly fell asleep and drifted in and out of random dreams.

The next morning, Szymon was awakened by a doctor that he didn't recognize. He learned that his condition was being evaluated to determine whether he was strong enough to return to his platoon. The doctor examined the scabs and scars from the wounds on his body, his broken foot, and dislocated shoulder.

"How have you been walking?"

In response, Szymon showed the doctor his crutches.

"How far can you walk?"

Szymon told him that, over the weekend, he had done pretty well, except for the bout of nausea. But the doctor curtly brushed off Szymon's concerns. "That isn't unusual." Then, he told Szymon to clean up, dress and eat breakfast. "Someone will come for you sometime this morning."

He ate his breakfast after having a sponge bath. A new nursing assistant came to help him, so he wondered where Miss Podosek was this morning. As the doctor stated would happen, a thin, wiry man came to evaluate his ability to walk without the crutches. His foot didn't hurt, but he was off balance and his gait was unsteady. The doctor removed the splint and asked Szymon to walk barefoot using the crutch. "You look good, Szymon. I'll wrap your foot without the splint, then, you can try walking on it using the crutch. Or maybe we could find a cane around here."

Joe Korlaszcz visited Szymon the day after he arrived back at the hospital in Lwow. Szymon sensed that Joe was surprised to see so much improvement in his facial color and healing of the ugly wounds that had covered much of his body.

"You healed rapidly, once you got going."

Szymon told him about his visit home and told Joe that his aunt and uncle were fine. "Anna and Wally are very happy, too." He also told Joe about Stephen's change in attitude toward him, and, sheepishly admitted that he, too, had had a change of heart.

Joe beamed. "I'm so happy for all of you! Oh, where is Miss Podosek? Did you run her off?"

Szymon told Joe the story of Sister Agnes' behavior toward him and Miss Podosek, and said he hadn't seen the young aide since that night. "Sister Agnes treated us like we were sinners."

"Maybe she was jealous, because you and Miss Podosek are young and were having a good time."

Whatever the reasons, Szymon's outlook on life greatly improved. However, the next day he slipped and fell getting out of the bathtub, reinjuring his foot. The new nursing aide had not been helpful. Dr. Schneider was upset about Szymon's setback. "Where did Miss Podosek go? You were doing very well when she was taking care of you." Dr. Schneider abruptly left the room, returning with Miss Podosek. "You are assigned to this room until Mr. Swaczy leaves. I'll see that this happens."

That evening, Miss Podosek was confronted by Sister Agnes, who asked who had assigned her to Mr. Swaczy's room. Miss Podosek told her she wasn't sure. Sister Agnes left her desk and returned with Mother Superior. Miss Podosek crossed herself as she saw them approaching. "Dr. Schneider told me to go to Szymon's room." They were soon joined by the hospital administrator and Dr. Schneider. When Dr. Schneider left the room, Szymon and Miss Podosek looked at each other. "What is happening?"

Miss Podosek continued with Szymon's patient care. During the afternoon, she took him outdoors to walk around the gardens. They chatted; mostly speculating about how much longer Szymon would remain in the hospital. Dr. Schneider came to see Szymon later in the day to tell him that arrangements were being made to send him back to the garrison hospital in the morning. It seemed Sister Agnes had triumphed. Miss Podosek smiled bravely when she brought Szymon's supper tray that evening. She propped him up on his pillows and arranged the tray so he could eat comfortably, but neither mentioned Sister Agnes until Miss Podosek returned for the tray.

"There is one good thing to come out of Sister Agnes' insistence that I return to the garrison." Miss Podosek waited for him to tell her what good came out of this debacle. "I won't have to call you Miss Podosek anymore."

She smiled, "Szymon, please call me Barbara. Sometimes my friends call me Basia."

"I'm going to call you Barbara. It fits you."

Chapter 16

It was early morning when Szymon returned to the barracks. Sargeant Schoeppler was in his office when Szymon knocked on the door. Schoeppler opened the door and gaped.

"Hello, Sarge!"

"You're looking better, Szymon."

"What can I do around here? I'd want to be with the guys, but my foot was reinjured when I fell taking a bath yesterday."

"How in the hell did that happen?"

Szymon explained that the young lady assisting him with his bath was not a well trained nurse aide, the floor was wet and slick with soap, and she wasn't paying attention. Also, the doctor substituted a cane for crutches, and I wasn't accustomed to using the cane. But nothing is broken. It's just a sprain, so I can walk on the foot. Sarge, I don't want to go into the hospital, I want to go back to the barracks. I'm willing to put up with the pain, even though it hurts like hell."

Schoeppler said he would see what he could do. "The boys are at the mess. Get the hell out of here!"

Using his cane, Szymon walked to the mess hall with no trouble and found his buddies still drinking coffee. Noticing him, several of his friends called out.

"Hey, look, it's Swaczy."

"Here comes the train wreck."

"You are skin and bones!"

Some of the men returned to their conversation about mustering out and returning home. It was early April, and the men were counting down the days. Others continued to focus their attention on Szymon. Theo was one.

"Does your foot still hurt?"

"I can walk on it, Theo, but it is painful from a fall I had yesterday, not from the original accident. I was able to do almost everything until that happened."

Someone yelled, "That's a bunch of bullshit!"

"How in the hell do you know how much my foot hurts, asshole?" It was apparent that some of the men didn't believe his story about falling, and suspected he had become used to lying on his ass. Szymon shrugged, determined to keep up no matter how his foot hurt.

Every evening when he removed his shoes, his foot was swollen, but he didn't complain and only Joe

Korlaszcz knew the truth. That evening, Joe accompanied Szymon to the bathhouse, noticing his swollen foot. "My dear Lord, Szymon, that injury looks terrible! How can you stand on it?"

"It's tough, but I won't give in. The guys don't believe me now and I don't want any more breaks." Szymon couldn't disguise a slight limp, but even so, some of the guys thought he was making his injury seem worse than it was.

The weather the following Saturday morning was typical for the time of year -- cool, dull and overcast. Instead of marching into the city center, the platoons turned onto Zamarstynowska Street in Old Town. The street was familiar to Szymon, who had spent many hours exploring these neighborhoods. His sprained foot was so painful he wondered how he was going to make it back to the garrison. That is when he saw her standing along the curb, in front of the Roman Catholic Church, wearing her nursing assistant uniform. He was at the head of the formation near the end of the row. As the platoon passed, she waved at him and called out to meet her Sunday at the church. Immediately, he forgot about his painful foot.

When he arrived at church the next day, she was sitting in the last pew wearing a pretty green dress. Her light brown hair was long and flowing, not tied in a knot on top of her head. He smiled as he sat down next to her. They silently listened to the priest's homily together, but when the service was over they were the first to leave, exchanging greetings with the priest as they walked down the church steps.

"It's still early, have you had breakfast?"

"I don't know where we could find an open restaurant nearby in Old Town, do you think you can walk as far as downtown?"

Familiar with the local restaurants, Szymon suggested a small café where he had eaten before and knew it was close by. It was a German restaurant that served delicious pancakes and waffles and good coffee. They had known each other for almost three and a half months, so they chatted comfortably, relishing this time together. Although outside it was gray and chilly, the restaurant was so cozy they wanted to linger. Szymon checked his pocket watch. "There is a free concert at eleven thirty. Why don't we walk to the park and listen for a while?" They arrived at the park just as the musicians were tuning their instruments.

A small crowd was gathering as Szymon guided Barbara to a bench. She noticed that he was beginning to limp. "This probably has been too much walking for one day."

"My foot will heal someday, so let's enjoy the music today."

Although the concert was short, they lingered for a long time afterward, sharing stories about their youth, their families, and friends. The crowd had dwindled to only a few as they sat huddled together, speaking in voices just above a whisper. It felt too soon when Szymon had to say, "We should return to your residence because I have to be back on the base in another half hour."

They walked back to Old Town and turned up Zamarstynowska Street, stopping in front of a small apartment building. "This is where I live."

"Would you like to meet again in two weeks? Maybe my foot will improve enough that we can explore the area." He took her hand and kissed it, looking up to see tears welling up in her eyes. "Please don't cry, Barbara. We will do this again soon, I promise."

Szymon thought about her often in the following days. He had a real girlfriend for the first time in his life. He liked her very much and knew she was someone he could trust, someone with whom he could share his most private thoughts, someone who would listen to understand him, not to criticize or mock him.

When Barbara returned to her apartment that day, her roommates were at work. They wouldn't return until after she had gone to bed for the night, which suited her because it gave her time to relive her day with Szymon. She thought about the lovely breakfast, their conversation, the music, and Szymon's promise that they would see each other again soon. Two weeks seemed like forever to her, but she felt happy and content. Admitting to herself that she liked Szymon very much, she was hesitant to believe he shared the same feelings for her, although he did seem kind and sincere. As the two weeks slowly passed, she missed him and anxiously awaited the next time they would meet. Since last attending mass together, the weather had warmed and flowers had begun to blossom. It was spring and Barbara was in love.

Szymon's foot felt almost normal. He was able to fulfill his daily chores on base and at his job. The platoon had marched into the city on Saturday. The crowds were not only larger than they had been in months, but the people were in a different mood than they had been at the end of last year. The social unrest had subsided and life was back to normal.

On Sunday morning, Barbara and Szymon saw each other as they approached the church from opposite directions. "Are you able to walk without your cane?" Szymon told her that the pain had subsided and he walked without a limp as they ascended the steps. The sanctuary was filled with the sound of beautiful, sacred, organ music. Additional music was provided by a choir accompanied by a small ensemble. The sun coming through the stained glass windows warmed the sanctuary as the soaring music lifted their spirits.

As they left the church, Szymon commented that his family was musical. "My brothers, my sister, and nearly all my cousins either play an instrument or sing." They briskly walked from the church to another small restaurant Szymon had found and entered its cozy, bright dining room. They ordered breakfast and sat drinking coffee. Their conversation seemed to pick up exactly where it had left off two weeks earlier. Barbara looked at Szymon while he was speaking. It was as if she was seeing him for the first time. She watched his blue eyes as he expressed joy or sadness. Sometimes, it was as if he were seeing her anew, too.

She was a pretty, petite young woman with lovely features and grayish blue eyes. When she smiled, his eyes reflected an expression of tenderness. After they had eaten their breakfast, he asked if she would like to explore the downtown area. "Why don't we just walk around for an hour or so?"

Szymon was familiar with some of the side streets and they walked along looking at the shops, restaurants, hotels and hostels, the government buildings and the railroad station. On this early spring afternoon, with flowers blooming in planters everywhere, the city was especially lovely. On the return to the Old Town, they passed a small park where a puppet show and merry-go-round for children were main attractions. They stood among the children for a while, enjoying the antics of clowns and the acrobatics of tumblers and jugglers, before settling on a bench in a quiet area of the park. "Oh, Szymon, this has been fun,"

He didn't respond to her remark but blurted out that his three-year hitch was ending soon. Her face fell. Szymon took her hand. "Don't be sad. Why don't we try to think about how we can stay together?"

"Szymon, I'm not sure how that would work out."

They talked about their options, and how Szymon had been thinking about settling in Lwow. "Have you given any thought to what you would like to do in your future, Barbara?"

She shook her head. "I've never given that any thought. It never occurred to me to plan ahead because life has been unpredictable for me. Other than my aunts and uncles, I've been alone for most of my life."

"Where does your uncle live? Do you ever visit him?" She explained that her aunt and uncle lived in a farming community outside of the city in a small village. "Would you like to visit them?"

"Szymon, I doubt that they would help me because they struggle to make ends meet. There was no work for me where they live, so I stayed in Lwow when they moved. And they are happy where they are."

They sat for a long time trying to think of something that would guide them in making a plan, before coming to the realization that they were on their own. "I'm sorry if I ruined our beautiful day. I don't want you to worry, Barbara." They decided that, for now, Barbara would remain at her job in Lwow, and Szymon would return to Bukaczowce to live with his parents. He had no money saved because of the accident and would immediately need to look for a job. Szymon realized they would have no privacy until he was able to rent an apartment or a room.

At the end of April, Sargeant Schoeppler told them that they would remain on inactive duty for the next five years and could be called back, if the need arose. No one was concerned for there had been a very long period of peace in the Empire. Szymon and Barbara saw each other one last time before he returned home. He was holding a single flower when he knocked on her door that Sunday morning. She was glad that she had something to do as she poured water into a glass and placed the flower into it. She put the glass with the bright pink carnation in the middle of the table.

Szymon broke the silence. "Well, let's find a place for breakfast." They returned to the German restaurant where they had eaten that first Sunday several weeks earlier. Szymon was reaching for her hand when he saw Joe Korlaszcz walking toward the restaurant. "Join us. We attended mass at Barbara's church." Joe pulled up a chair.

The three friends discussed what they would do after the platoon went on inactive duty. Joe seemed surprised when Barbara said that she was remaining in Lwow because of her job. "What are you going to do, Joe?

"I'm going home for a while, but I still plan to return to Lwow to enter the seminary. Szymon, what kind of work are you going to do?"

Szymon laughed, "What kind of work is there in Bukaczowce? I need money to rent an apartment here in Lwow, and I guess it will take a few months to make enough." Although Szymon had not told Joe about his relationship with Barbara, he suspected that Joe knew they had been dating each other.

"Is Stephen still working for your Uncle Jan?"

"Yes, and he's doing well."

"It's hard to make much working on a farm, but

that's all there is. At least, I can live at home and save my money, but not for long because Ma and Pa can't afford to keep me there. I wonder whether there would be any construction work?"

"If I hear of anything, I'll ride over to see you." As Joe got up to leave he bent over and kissed Barbara on the cheek. "And I'll pray for you both for a happy solution to your problems." Then, Joe asked Szymon if he wanted to ride back to Bukaczowce with him, and the friends agreed to meet on Monday at the train station.

After Joe left, Szymon took her hand. "I will miss you, Barbara." He didn't know exactly why he felt the way he did toward her, but he knew that he couldn't resist the force that was drawing them together. Saying goodbye at the door to her apartment building, Szymon bent over and kissed her lightly on her lips. She couldn't speak; tears welled up in her eyes and spilled slowly down her cheeks. "Don't cry, Barbara. I'll return as soon as I make enough money to rent an apartment." An old lady opened the door, smiling quizzically when she saw them. Her eyes darted from the weeping young woman to the handsome soldier. She wondered if perhaps they had a lover's quarrel, and then bustled past them.

"I'll miss you, Barbara." She watched him walk up Zamarstynowska Street toward the garrison. When he was almost out of sight, he turned, jumped high, clicking his heels, and waved to her. Crossing herself, in that moment Barbara knew she would see him again, and one day, everything would be alright.

When Szymon returned home, he told his mother and father that he wanted to return to Lwow to find work there. He asked if he could stay home for a few months, suggesting he could sleep in the attic. His parents exchanged glances. "Where will you be working?"

"I will go back to the estate to ask for a job, and Joe Korlaszcz is going to ask around if there is any work available in construction."

Roman laughed bitterly. "Szymon, you know that nothing is ever built in Bukaczowce. Nothing ever changes around here." Szymon dropped the subject.

His mother asked him about Miss Podosek. "She is working in Lwow and plans to stay there. She can't give up her job."

The next day, he rode out to visit Joe and told him that it appeared his parents didn't want him at home. He guessed that they expected him to pay something. But he wouldn't be able to save if he paid for room and board. Joe and Szymon walked along the path toward the pond where old Mr. Minorek had been found three years ago. They threw stones into the water, watching the undulating ripples slowly recede as they moved farther from the center. Szymon again asked whether Stephen was working for Joe's Uncle Jan. It appeared that Stephen had made a remarkable turnaround in his behavior. Steve was still working at the dairy farm maintaining the equipment, as well as, milking the one hundred and twenty cows on the expanding dairy operation.

"I wish I could stay home with Ma and Pa, but where will I get enough money to pay them and save, too? The only one in the family who is successful is my Uncle Max."

They were talking about job possibilities Szymon might have, when Joe interrupted. "Why don't you speak to your Uncle Max? He's successful in business and could give you good advice."

The following day, Szymon rode out to his Uncle Max's house. From its appearance, a person would never know that Max was prospering. The house was just like every other home in the Ruthenian section of Bukaczowce with one exception: it was properly maintained. The house had a chimney, its windows and doors were new, the roof was metal instead of thatch, and everything was well-maintained. Uncle Max came out to greet Szymon as he dismounted Old Black and tied him to a railing. Szymon and his Uncle hugged and kissed before entering the tidy house. Aunt Katarzyna was not at home that morning, but there was a pot of coffee on the stovetop. Max brought a pitcher of cream to the table, along with two warm rolls and butter. Max placed a cup in front of Szymon. "Are you staying with your Ma and Pa?"

"Yes, temporarily."

"Where do you plan to look for a job?"

Szymon told his uncle about his dilemma of locating a temporary job somewhere in Bukaczowce, so he could save enough money to rent a place in Lwow. "I think I could use you for a couple of months." Szymon almost fell off his chair. He stared incredulously at his Uncle, unable to believe what he had just heard. In his youth, Uncle Max had worked as a lumberjack in camps along the Dnieper River. The work was hard and dangerous, but paid better than almost any other job in the region. Max was a saver who had accumulated enough money to start up a small construction company in Bukaczowce. Business wasn't plentiful, but Max lived within his means, avoiding debt, so over time he had managed to expand into nearby Burstyn, a town about 11 miles northeast of Bukaczowce. "Szymon, is your heart set on staying with your parents until you make the money you need?"

"No..."

Max then proposed that Szymon live onsite for the duration of a construction job that was about to start in Burstyn. Szymon could not believe his good fortune, and wished he could tell Barbara about it right then. He would write her a letter and she could locate someone to read it to her.

At supper that evening, Szymon told his parents about the job offer. Roman was caught by surprise. He put down his fork, looking hard at Szymon. "Are you going to take it?"

"Hell yes!"

Roman didn't comment, but Szymon knew that his father resented Max because he was prosperous.

Szymon's mother looked sad. "I was looking forward to having you here, son."

"Pa, it's a chance for me to make a few dollars, to get a start in Lwow."

Roman didn't answer. His mother attempted to change the subject.

"Did you see Miss Podosek before you left Lwow?"

Very briefly Szymon raised his defenses, thinking his mother was intruding on his privacy again, but thought the better of it.

"Ma, I call her Barbara. I have been seeing her over the past two months. We have known each other for five months now and I like her."

"I like her, too, Szymon." That comment about Miss Podosek eased the tension, lowering the defenses of both parents, as well.

Roman's expression softened. "We both like her, Szymon. She seems like a very good girl."

They sat talking about anything and everything, with none of the guarded conversations that had marred their relationship yesterday.

Uncle Max and Szymon rode out to Burstyn the following Monday morning, to a parcel of land in the Jewish section of town. Szymon's heart jumped into his mouth. "What the hell are you building here?"

They got down from the wagon and walked around the property as Uncle Max explained that he would be building an expansion to the school. An old man with a long beard, wearing a hat and the garb that identified him as a Jew, approached. "Shalom, Mr.

Swaczy."

Max introduced Szymon to Rabbi Zukor. The two men examined drawings that Max carried with him, while Szymon looked on. Then the old man directed them over to a small building at one end of the property. Here was located a small office with two rooms. The room in back would be Szymon's. Max planned to have him stay on the property twenty-four hours a day, six days a week.

On the return to Bukaczowce, Uncle Max told Szymon that he would be staying at the property for five or six months, or until the land was cleared, a wall could be built around the perimeter, and the construction equipment and crew were brought in. Szymon would be the only person on the property. "Do you think you want the job?" Max sensed Szymon's misgivings. "Let's talk about it, Szymon. You are the only person I know who can take on this responsibility. You are a single man, recently mustered out of the Austrian Army. You know how to handle firearms and have had training in marksmanship. Do you have any bad marks on your military record?" Szymon nodded no. "You don't want a permanent job and I need you for six months at the most." In the end, Szymon agreed to take on the job. They returned to Max's home where he gave Szymon a pistol and a box of ammunition, cautioning, "Don't hesitate to use it."

The next morning, Roman and Szymon rode out to the Jewish section of town where Uncle Max was waiting for them, and subsequently unlocked the door to the small building at the rear of the property. "Welcome to your new home, Szymon."

After his father and Uncle had departed, Szymon went to the back room noting that on a counter there were boxes containing supplies for a few weeks. In one corner of the twelve-by-twelve-foot room, next to the rear door, were a small kerosene stove and an ice box. Opposite the kitchen area, on a bed, Max had piled high blankets, towels and other items Szymon would need for the duration of his stay. Next to the bed, a small stand held a wash basin and pitcher filled with water. A chamber pot was in the corner next to the washstand. The only other items in the small room were a table, two chairs, a foot locker, and two cabinets. A kerosene lantern hung on the wall next to the door. It was still and Szymon told himself that he had better get used to it.

When Uncle Max returned the next morning, Szymon told him that he had slept well and asked if he would bring some things to read, such as writing paper and pens. Max told him that someone would come every other day to bring ice, bread, milk and anything that Szymon wanted, within reason. While they were talking, a wagon turned onto the property carrying two men and more supplies. Then came another wagon with saws, axes, shovels, scythes, wheelbarrows, and two additional men who immediately began clearing the perimeter of the property.

Max was true to his word. Every other day someone came with food, newspapers, water, and ice. Szymon didn't require much variety in his diet, so he was satisfied with eating sausage and cheese sandwiches most of the time. One day, Aunt Katarzyna rode out with Max to bring a kettle of beef stew. "Szymon, you need to eat something besides sausage and cheese." After that visit, she continued to send a meal to Szymon from time to time.

Periods of rainy weather held up progress in the early stages of the project, but Uncle Max indicated that this was normal. Rainy days were hardest for Szymon because he was confined to a small building with nothing to do but try to think of ways to pass the time. He wrote letters to Barbara but hadn't received a reply in return, causing him to wonder if she had been able to find someone to read the letters to her. It was then that he asked his uncle, if he would permit Joe Korlaszcz to come out to visit him. "Szymon, normally, I wouldn't allow anyone but you on the property, but I can make an exception for Joe. If you can't trust a future priest, who can you trust?" They both laughed.

Uncle Max visited every Sunday to take on the role of watchman while Szymon attended church. The two men embraced and entered the small building. Uncle Max looked around the room in amazement. Szymon had made the small space into a neat, clean, functional, yet inviting home away from home. He had asked his Aunt Katarzyna for curtains she could spare. On one of her visits she brought a small quilt that Szymon pulled atop the bedsheets each day. He hung an illustrated calendar and two pictures he'd cut from magazines his uncle had brought to him. A tablet of writing paper, a pen, and a bottle of ink sat on the table nearby the oil lamp. The water basin, shaving mug, razor, and soap were on the wash stand, alongside a folded towel. The room was clean, and everything was in its place. Szymon had also planted some flower and vegetable seeds in a sunny area alongside the small building.

On this Sunday, Max planned to stay overnight in order to meet a wagon delivering construction materials in the morning. He brought a meal Aunt Katarzyna had prepared for Sunday dinner to share with Szymon. She thought of everything, even dessert. They finished their dinner outdoors around a fire that Szymon had built in a raised stone pit. Most days he cooked his meals outside because there wasn't a fireplace -- only the small kerosene stove -- in the little building. As it began to drizzle, they carried the coffee pot, their cups of coffee, and bread pudding inside, where they talked while sitting at the small table until they turned in that night.

The two men had spoken about many things during the weeks Szymon worked for his uncle. That evening, Uncle Max was curious about his nephew's personal life. "Do you have a girlfriend?"

Szymon told him about Barbara and that he hadn't heard from her since he left Lwow. "She doesn't read or write, so probably needs to find someone to read my letters and respond to them. She is shy and wouldn't want to ask someone to read her personal letters."

"Doesn't she have a family living in Lwow?"

"Her parents died when she was young, so she doesn't know much about them. She was raised by an aunt and uncle. She lived with them in Bukaczowce for a short time several years ago.

"What is her last name?"

Before his nephew could answer, Max asked what her uncle's name was. He thought a minute or two before saying that he wasn't sure if he had known anyone by that name.

"Originally, they were from Radgoszcz, Poland." That additional information wasn't helpful in jogging his memory, so Max told Szymon that he would let him know if he remembered anyone with the Podoseck name.

In the middle of the night, Szymon awakened. He sat up, listening, and thought he heard voices and the sounds of a scuffle near the building. Quickly, he arose, and pulled on his pants and boots. As he walked through the little house to the front door, he realized that Max was not in his bed. Szymon, who always carried his gun, withdrew it from its holster as he reached the door. With his ear pressed to the door, he again heard the sounds of a fight coming from behind the building. Quickly, he opened the door and stepped outside. There was no one in the front, so he quietly made his way around to the rear of the building, hugging the wall as he went. Peering around the side wall towards the back, he saw three men beating and kicking a man who was sprawled on the ground. The man being beaten was yelling and groaning. It was Uncle Max.

One of the men caught a glimpse of Szymon and began running toward him. The other two men joined him, leaving Max lying motionless. Szymon, who was in excellent physical condition, tossed the first assailant over his shoulder. The man came down hard, injuring his arm. Szymon kicked another man in his groin and put the third in a headlock, but as a result he lost control of his gun. The man wrestled free and there was a brief scuffle. Szymon recovered, got to his feet and stomped on the man's hand. It was all over. Two of the men ran off into a field across the road. Szymon fired a single shot after them. When he turned around to tend to his uncle, the third assailant rose to his hands and knees pleading with Szymon to let him go. Szymon cursed him. "If you want more trouble, come back again tomorrow. Now, get the hell out of here!"

Max rose early the following morning. He said that he looked worse than he felt. After a quick breakfast of bread and coffee, he washed up, and just as he finished shaving, two wagons loaded with building materials pulled into the yard.

Uncle Max told Szymon how grateful he was for coming to his aid the previous night, but wondered how his nephew now felt about his assignment. "Do you feel safe out here by yourself?"

"There are troublemakers and dangerous Jew-baiters around."

"No, Szymon, it's worse than that. These are Jew haters."

The next week or two were uneventful. The only people who came out to the building site were Uncle Max, Aunt Katarzyna, and a couple of employees who brought Szymon's supplies, along with building materials and tools. Max increased his pay for helping to clear the property. Each Sunday they would throw kerosene on a huge pile of underbrush and tree limbs that had been cleared, and set it afire. In just a few weeks, the land was cleared, so construction on the wall could begin.

As was Szymon's evening routine, he walked around the property and out to the road surveying the area for any unusual noises, signs, or movements. Everything seemed normal until he spotted birds fluttering in the distance. He stepped off the road into a field that was awaiting spring planting. Someone was approaching. Szymon unholstered his pistol.

"Szymon!"

He heard the voice calling to him, but the sun in his eyes hampered his vision. "Who is it?"

"It's Joe!"

Szymon, who hadn't realized how fast his heart was beating, felt an instant sense of relief. Sheepishly, he holstered the gun. "What are you doing out here?"

Joe ran up to Szymon, and offered his hand. "I came to stay overnight with you. Max said I could." The two friends walked to the secluded building, on the edge of the property. Szymon pointed out the small room where Joe would sleep as they walked through to Szymon's room.

"Do you like it out here?"

"I like the peace and quiet, but it isn't always easy to pass time."

Szymon explained that there wasn't much to do except take walks around the property, talk to the workers, and read and write letters.

Joe told Szymon how grateful his uncle was to have a reliable person staying on the property. "Have any more hoodlums been around? Has there been any stealing?"

"The only serious incident was the three guys who attacked Max."

"Do you mind being alone so much?"

"It hasn't gotten to me yet. And I don't anticipate any more trouble out here."

The two friends went outside where Szymon showed Joe his garden. It was summer and his garden had produced an abundance of vegetables.

"Maybe you should go into farming." Joe was barely able to suppress a belly laugh.

"Hell no! Farming is too confining. I like having a garden, but I want my freedom, not being confined week after week to a small farm. Besides, I couldn't make much money."

After picking a cabbage and a couple of onions, the two friends walked back to the small building to prepare supper. Szymon boiled water in a big pot over his outdoor fireplace, adding the cabbage, onions, and sausage. He peeled a couple of potatoes to add to the sausage and kraut. Aunt Katarzyna always supplied Szymon with bread and something for dessert.

As they ate, Joe told Szymon about going to Lwow to visit the seminary where he planned to study for the priesthood. "While I was in the city, I also visited the hospital where you recuperated from your injuries, and spoke with Sister Agnes about Barbara. She told me that Barbara left and no one knows where she went."

As I was leaving, Dr. Schneider walked up the stairs and pulled me aside so Sister Agnes couldn't hear our conversation. He told me that Sister Agnes asked the administrator to let Barbara go. Dr. Schneider also told me that he saw an unopened letter you had written to Barbara on Sister Agnes' desk. "Something is wrong. Maybe when you are done working for your Uncle, we can travel to Lwow and try to find her."

Szymon admitted to Joe that he really missed her. "I wonder if I will ever see her again."

Joe told Szymon that he, too, felt helpless. "But I'll pray for you and Barbara. God answers prayer."

Szymon murmured, in a barely audible voice, "Yes, when this job is done, I'll travel to Lwow to try to find her." If only I knew something...

The next morning, Max stopped by and told Szymon that his six-month employment would end in four weeks. Summer was almost over and as the days became shorter, the weather turned more autumn-like.

It was early on the following Saturday morning, as Szymon was drinking his second cup of coffee, immersed in thought about how to search for Barbara, that there was a knock at the door. Szymon wondered who in the world it could be? "Who is it?" There was no answer. He hesitated. Thinking that was strange, he walked to the door, took out his gun and opened the door slowly.

"Hey, it's you!" Standing before him was Barbara, smiling shyly, her face tilted up at him. It was then he saw his Uncle Max smiling broadly. "How did you do this?" Barbara explained that she had found his mother at the Thursday Fair. It was she who told Barbara how to find Max and in turn, Szymon. Max told them that he would be at the construction site for a few hours, and slipped out the door. After the door closed, Szymon and Barbara embraced for a long time. He stepped back, his expression a mixture of anguish and relief. "I thought I'd lost you again."

He built a fire in the outdoor pit and brewed coffee, as the young couple talked about the months since they had last seen each other. They were sitting, speaking softly when Uncle Max approached. He asked if they would like to ride to Bukaczowce together. "I'll stay here while you take Barbara to see her Aunt and Uncle."

They protested but Max wouldn't be swayed. After a quick bite to eat, they climbed up onto the teamster seat and Szymon flicked the reins. The horse plodded out the construction entrance onto the hard road. Time passed quickly as they chattered away. Shortly after, Szymon turned off the road and went out to a secluded opening where there was a small lake surrounded by trees. They dismounted and ran down to the lake's edge. She removed her shoes and waded in the water. "It's still warm." She stripped off her dress and gave it to Szymon to put on the shore. Szymon returned in his underclothes, and they swam in the sun-dappled water. Neither of them wanted to miss a moment of this precious afternoon. Szymon picked her up and carried her to a grassy patch nestled in a secluded garden-like haven under a tree. He knelt, and then lay back beside her. The world seemed a far-off place; this spot was paradise. The two lovers embraced and kissed, an innocent kiss, not the hungry open-mouthed kiss of more sophisticated lovers. Gently caressing each other, Szymon told her for the first time that he loved her.

It was a rare, peaceful afternoon. They were locked in an embrace of passion and desire. "Tell me if I'm hurting you." They promised themselves to each other forever. As Barbara lay in Szymon's arms, she tilted her face upward. Concern furrowed his brow. "What's wrong? Why are you crying? I am so happy."

"I'm happy, too, but I'm also afraid it won't last."

Szymon promised that he would take care of her forever. He folded her in his arms, gently stroking her hair, as she wept.

Barbara choked back a sob. "You can't imagine how lonely my life has been."

"Barbara, will you marry me?" She stopped crying and lay quietly in his arms, but she did not answer him.

It took about half an hour to reach the little house where Szymon had spent his childhood. Late afternoon was approaching when he knocked on the door. His mother answered, flinging her arms around him. His father walked over to the door to join them. "What brings you here?"

Szymon told his parents that Uncle Max asked him to take Barbara home. "After supper, we'll leave for her Uncle's place."

Ma was just putting supper on the table when they arrived. She asked Barbara to help her bring two extra plates and rummaged through the ice box to pull out leftovers. In a matter of minutes, all four were sitting at the table listening to Szymon talk about life at the construction site over the past several months.

Barbara sat quietly, letting Szymon do most of the talking. Then, Helena asked why her Uncle and Aunt decided to move back to Bukaczowce. "I'm not sure. They don't always take me into their confidence, but I suspect that there wasn't enough work, so they were let go. Besides, I think my Aunt and Uncle liked Bukaczowce and just wanted to move back. They probably have friends here."

Mama told Barbara that she wanted to invite them to supper. Barbara hesitated; an awkward silence followed.

"Why don't we wait until I move back home, Ma?"

On the way to Barbara's uncle and aunt's place, they talked more about their future. Szymon told her that he would have enough money to afford a nice apartment in Lwow when Max paid him. "I took very little of my pay over the past six months. Uncle Max agreed to keep it for me."

The young lovers, like lovers everywhere, dreamed of their lives together. Everything was perfect that day and they couldn't imagine anything but a bright future ahead.

Szymon pulled the cart into a small yard in front of a tiny house. An elderly woman greeted him when he knocked on the door. Barbara heard a voice inside and called out, "It's me, Uncle Paul." Barbara introduced Szymon to her Aunt Agatha and Uncle Paul. The elderly gentleman eyed Szymon suspiciously, warily shaking his hand. "This is my friend, Szymon. Remember, I told you about him. He is the soldier I cared for when I worked in the hospital."

"We were beginning to worry about you, Basia,"

"I'm sorry, Aunt Agatha. Szymon's uncle suggested that he bring me home. Since Szymon hasn't been home for months, we stopped to see his parents and had supper with them."

Sensing that her aunt and uncle were not receptive

to meeting him, Szymon didn't want Barbara to be left alone before putting them at ease. He began an awkward conversation. "I hope you didn't worry too much. I'll take good care of Barbara. She is a very good person. And when I return to Bukaczowce, I would like to introduce you to my parents."

"Aunt Agatha, Szymon's mother, sells freshly baked loaves of bread and pastries at the Thursday Fair." You may have stopped to chat with her.

There was a glimmer of recognition, in her Aunt's eyes. "Oh, yes, I know who she is! I believe I have met her."

It turned out that Barbara's Aunt Agatha and Szymon's mother had met and talked about Helena's baked goods. "Your mother seems like a very nice person, Szymon."

Szymon chatted for a while longer and believed he had managed to assure Barbara's Aunt and Uncle that she was in safe hands. When there was a pause in the conversation Szymon took an opportunity to tell them that he wanted to start back to Burstyn before it got too late. "I would like to stop to see Barbara when I return in a few weeks."

When Szymon reached the construction site in Burstyn, it was approaching nine-thirty. He apologized for being so late returning. Max reassured him that it was not a problem for him to be away for so long. "How were your mother and father?"

"We had a nice visit with them, and afterward, we went to Barbara's aunt and uncle's house, so I could meet them."

Max turned the conversation to the work schedule for the next few weeks. He told Szymon that the construction project was a little ahead of schedule, that he could use him until the middle of November, and then described the work he would be doing. Szymon caught on easily for he was eager to learn the construction trade. "It's good experience for your future, and I'll give you a reference when you need one."

The next three weeks were interesting. Szymon learned how one part of a big job like this had to be completed before going on to the next phase. Szymon was a strong, willing worker who easily transitioned from digging ditches to forming footers to laying bricks to laying pipes for water, sewer gas and electricity.

Max explained that this building would be state-of-the-art, with all the modern conveniences: electricity for lighting, gas for heating and cooking, and indoor plumbing for drinking water, bathing, and toilets. Szymon couldn't help but compare the architect's drawings to buildings in Bukaczowce. This school was being built for the 20th century, which made Szymon even more determined to move to Lwow. He believed that Bukaczowce would languish years behind the times, because the only reason Bukaczowce had been pulled into the modern era was its location on the train route between Lwow and Czernowitz. When the train came to town in 1865, telephone, telegraph, and electricity were installed in the station and adjacent buildings in town. Most homes on the outskirts of town had none of these improvements. Nor did people seek to bring them into their homes. Instead, they accessed water with hand pumps and cooked over wood-burning stoves that were also used to heat the two-room homes common to the region. In a place like Bukaczowce, there were few incentives to modernize because there were few businesses and no industry. People worked the land, operated dairy farms, or were engaged in small enterprises such as honey production.

Chapter 17

Szymon stayed with his parents for a week, mainly because his mother pressed him to. It was November 1894, and Barbara suspected she was two months pregnant. She was living with her Uncle Paul and Aunt Agatha. Szymon's mother invited Barbara's aunt and uncle to supper one evening. Although the meal was delicious, and they seemed to have a nice visit, the conversation was guarded and somewhat awkward. It was obvious Uncle Paul avoided discussing the marriage between Szymon and Barbara. The next morning, while Szymon and his parents were at breakfast, Helena asked Szymon why Barbara's uncle did not want them to marry. Szymon said he didn't know but that he sensed the same thing. He thought the only possible explanation was that he wanted her to remain with them because she helped in the home and shared household expenses whenever she had managed to find work.

It had been a week since Szymon's job ended. He saw Barbara several times that week, but she always appeared upset. They met again at the Thursday fair, where Szymon had helped his mother sell her baked goods. Barbara insisted that Helena go for a walk while she and Szymon tended her tables. Barbara proceeded to tell Szymon about her uncle's demeanor around the house.

"Szymon, he won't permit me to go with you," she blurted out.

He stared at her. "What the hell does that mean? What are we going to do? It sounds like Sister Agnes and Mother Superior all over again. They hid my letters from you, you know."

This came as a surprise to Barbara because he hadn't previously told her.

"Sister Agnes and my uncle have put me through hell. What did I ever do to deserve this?"

"There is only one way out of this. We are leaving this weekend for Lwow."

"Oh, Szymon, I feel terrible."

"I don't want to hurt anyone, but I don't think we can convince them to give us their blessing. This is bullshit, Barbara; we are going." His ears were turning red, a sign he was becoming quite agitated. "I won't allow anyone to stand in the way of our happiness." He cursed while clenching and unclenching his fists. Szymon asked who had brought her to the fair; he stopped to look sternly at her. "Do you want to come with me to Lwow?"

Barbara began to tremble; her face turned pale, she lowered her head, and her voice was a barely audible whisper. "Yes."

"Barbara, I'll meet you outside the church after mass on Sunday. Bring your suitcase."

After Szymon dropped his mother at home, he visited Joe Korlaszcz. Coincidentally, Joe was turning onto the road on his way to see Szymon. They met on the road just past the Korlaszcz's house.

"What's with you, Szymon?"

"Let's turn off at the Mynorek property."

The two friends stood by the water's edge, tossing pebbles into the pond as Szymon told Joe about Barbara's dilemma. "I don't know why the old man is being so damned mean. He's a jackass."

"It's a mystery to me, too, Szymon. The thing is that I can't understand why she has such a complicated life."

"I blew up at Barbara. But I have to devise a plan by Sunday because I told her we were leaving for Lwow after church."

Joe was silent, thinking. Szymon picked up a rock and flung it hard out toward the middle of the lake, causing a loud splash. "Do you have the money Max paid you?" Szymon had almost all of the money and thought it would be more than enough to get a start in Lwow.

"Hey Joe, How's your ticker these days?"

"I'm okay, but every now and then, I get palpitations and skipped beats. The doctor didn't seem worried but told me not to get too upset about things or look for trouble. I'm following his advice." Joe was still thinking about Szymon and Barbara's dilemma. "When are you planning to leave?"

"After church on Sunday."

"Do you have any idea where you will be living?"

"No, but there are many apartments in Old Town."

"How do you think you'd like living there?"

Speaking haltingly, Szymon told Joe that he liked the neighborhoods around the downtown and near the Garrison and reminded him that Barbara had lived in Old Town. "We're both familiar with the city, and I won't have any problem getting a job, Joe. I think." It appeared that the decision was made.

In the morning, Szymon rode out to see his Uncle Max tell him his plan. Max listened intently, silent for a while, before asking Szymon whether he intended to tell his parents about his plans. Szymon said he would talk to them but had not decided whether to inform Barbara's aunt and uncle. Uncle Max was hesitant but eventually suggested that Szymon let Barbara decide. "Does Barbara have any identification?"

"Her Uncle Paul has them. Why? Will she need her papers?"

"She will need identification, especially when traveling."

That evening Szymon told his parents he was

planning to move. They didn't try to talk him out of moving to Lwow. His mother asked him to say goodbye to his grandparents and family. So, Szymon spent half the next day visiting relatives and packing a small suitcase with his clothing, books, and other personal items. Then he went to the train station to purchase two third-class coach tickets.

On Sunday morning, Szymon attended church with his parents. The service was long, and although Szymon tried to listen to the priest's words, it was no use; he was too agitated. After the service, he spoke with Father Thomas at the door of the rectory to tell him that he would be leaving for Lwow and taking Barbara Podoseck with him. Father Thomas gave Szymon his blessing.

Having received the priest's blessing, Szymon left hurriedly, darting in and out of the crowd as he made his way to the Roman Catholic Church. The mass was ending. He saw Barbara in a small group walking down the center aisle toward the church's open door. Barbara walked up and gave him a quick hug. Her aunt and uncle were behind her, seemingly trying to avoid him.

"Do you want me to speak to them?"

She smiled bravely. "I already have. Come with me to say goodbye to them."

He accompanied her to the church's rear, where Barbara's Uncle Paul and Aunt Agatha sat high on the teamster seat. Her suitcase was on the seat next to her aunt.

"Good afternoon, Uncle Paul."

"Hello, Szymon." His response was curt, his voice gruff, the conversation brief. Barbara's aunt wept quietly. Szymon promised them that he would take good care of their niece. The old man was silent.

"Please don't worry about me, Aunt Agatha."

Szymon reached up to take the suitcase. "Where are Barbara's papers?"

Barbara's uncle handed her a small bundle, then the old man flicked the reins, and the horse pulled the cart away.

The young couple walked back to the church where Szymon's mother and father waited. It was time for their goodbyes. Szymon's mother wept. His father climbed down from the wagon and wished them good luck with a trembling voice. They kissed and hugged. Then, Roman reached up to take the handle of Szymon's suitcase, and with a final handshake, their parting was complete—for now. Szymon and Barbara walked to the train station, in control of their destiny, at last.

Only a slight glow of daylight remained as they arrived in Lwow. They carried their well-worn suitcases to the open restaurant nearest the station. A young girl, perhaps the owner's daughter, approached them to ask what they wanted to eat. The small restaurant was about to close, so they ordered ox tail stew—a meal that was already prepared - along with bread, coffee and dessert. The food was good and hearty; it gave the tired couple a needed spurt of energy. As Szymon paid the bill, he asked the young girl if she knew where they could spend the night. Barbara added that they were moving to Old Town and wanted to rent a small apartment. The young girl called to her mother. An older woman came out, introduced herself as the owner, and chatted with them for a few minutes. She wrote something on a slip of paper and handed it to Szymon.

They left the restaurant and walked for four blocks, stopping in front of an older, small apartment house. "This is it." He opened the door, entering a tiny foyer where a row of boxes hung on the wall to their right. In front of them was a narrow, wooden staircase. Szymon stopped momentarily and inspected the row of boxes, then pushed a button at the bottom. They waited. A woman's voice called out, "Hello?" She stood at the top of the staircase. "Who is it?"

"Hello. Can we inspect the apartment?"

"Who sent you?"

Szymon explained that the owner of the restaurant near the train station had sent them. The woman told them to come upstairs, meeting them on the landing where Szymon gave her the note from the restaurant owner. The woman instructed them to follow her up another flight of creaky stairs. They stopped in front of a big wooden door while she removed some keys from her apron pocket and, turning to her right, unlocked the door.

They entered a dark room and waited while she

turned up a wall light. The room was small. A table and three chairs sat in the middle, with a cabinet that didn't match the table against the far wall. She motioned them to follow her down a short hallway which opened into a large kitchen. To the right was a bedroom with more mismatched furniture. There was a table with a pitcher and a large bowl for washing next to a window. Barbara was engrossed in examining each piece of furniture when she heard Szymon's voice. "How much?"

"Do you have references?"

Szymon told the woman that he had been in Lwow for almost a year at the Garrison, and Barbara had worked at the Roman Catholic hospital.

"I can get a letter from someone if you need it."

The woman said it wasn't necessary, but when she paused, Barbara blurted out that she was going to have a baby and they needed a place to stay. Not smiling, the woman eyed Barbara, who stared back at her.

"For how long do you want the apartment?"

Barbara told her she was three months pregnant, and they hoped to stay if they found work. The woman told them they could have the apartment for one-and-a-half dollars monthly once they found jobs. Until then, she would charge one-half dollar a week. Szymon and Barbara looked at each other and smiled. Szymon spoke decisively. "We will take it. Do you have a bed so we can sleep here tonight?"

Barbara spoke up, causing her face to redden, "I have sheets." Then she unpacked their cardboard suitcases, putting Szymon's clothes on one shelf in the cabinet, with her clothes next to his. She looked up at the sound of feet shuffling along the floor to see Szymon and another man enter the room carrying a bed frame and mattress. They turned them topside up, in one corner. While Szymon talked to the man— the landlady's husband, Luke—Barbara pulled sheets out of her suitcase. She had spotted a blanket in the closet, which she neatly smoothed over the sheets, but they would have to sleep with no pillow tonight. Looking through the drawers in the closet, Barbara found another blanket and noted the chamber pot was on the closet floor.

Hearing Szymon and the other man leave the apartment, Barbara wondered where they were going and hoped Szymon would be brief. Next, she looked through the kitchen cupboards and drawers. She found a few plates, a bowl, and a pot with a lid. The stove had a kerosene tank that hung on one end near a shelf. It stood on tall legs and had an oven on one side. She liked the stove and wondered aloud if Szymon had matches. Small containers of pepper and salt were on the shelf. Inside the oven was a frying pan. Both the stove and oven were clean; in fact, the entire apartment had been scrubbed. She glanced toward a window hung with pretty curtains. Under the window was an ice box, and to the right, a door that led to a porch. When Szymon returned, Barbara was leaving the kitchen to look around the other room.

"What do you think, Barbara?"

She told him that she liked the tiny apartment, described her discoveries, and was happy to be there. Then she asked what he and Luke had talked about.

"He told me that there was a shopping district nearby. Everything we need is within a few blocks. Also, I asked him about locating a job. Barbara, would you like to go out for breakfast in the morning?"

We should buy a few groceries instead of going out for breakfast. She remembered to ask him if he brought matches and he assured her they were in his suitcase. She showed him around the apartment and the discoveries she'd made, which made him smile appreciatively.

"I like it here. Oh, we will share a bathroom with the landlord."

It would have been too much to ask to have their private toilet, but the common bathroom was just out the apartment door, down the stairs, and a few steps down a hallway.

After exploring their apartment together, they returned to the bedroom and sat on the edge of the bed. Szymon kissed and fondled her for a long time. "Is this a good home for you?"

"Yes, I like it and am happy, Szymon."

He kissed her again as they lay back on the bed while he whispered reassuringly to her. "Barbara, I love you. I want you to be happy. I love you."

They awakened to a clear day just as dawn was breaking, having slept soundly through the night. Pulling her close to him, they nestled in the warmth of each other's arms. The room was bare of any comforts other than the bed, but to Barbara, it seemed like a palace. Neither of them had experienced the joy of spending such a luxury of time with the one they loved. Barbara wanted to remain in bed next to Szymon. She loved the feel of his body against hers. It aroused wonderful sensations in her. But, she thought they should go out to explore the neighborhood and shop for the essentials they would need to set up housekeeping. Love alone could not sustain them. "Why don't you go bathe first? I want to lie here for a little while longer." But after just a few minutes, she jumped out of bed to see what was provided in this little apartment and what items they needed to shop for. She discovered matches on the stove, and in the cabinets, she found two big cups, small bowls, another pot, a lid for the frying pan, and various baking pans.

Remembering that she had taken the rolls from the restaurant, she heated water, poured it into the two cups, and put out the rolls for their breakfast when Szymon walked through the door. As they ate their simple meal, they discussed how much they could afford to spend for the apartment and the job leads their new landlord had given Szymon.

"Well, Barbara, we should think about going out into the world.

"I'm so excited!" With that, Barbara got up to wash

and get dressed while Szymon searched for places to buy groceries and pillows. She had finished bathing and combing her hair when Szymon returned. He had talked to a man named Josh, who lived in a building down the street. Josh had given him some useful tips, and, best of all; he had a couple of job leads.

They headed into the town up Zamarstynowska Street, which was lined with small residential buildings and shops. They turned off the street but soon realized there were more shops on Zamarstynowska Street. So, Szymon turned at the next corner, and near the intersection, he spotted people coming and going from shops. There was a corner grocery store, and just two stores beyond, they saw some furniture and a baby carriage in front of an entrance. They walked into the shop and waited for the storekeeper to finish a sale. Barbara's eyebrows raised while looking at the items nearest the entrance. "This is too expensive."

The shopkeeper came over, and Barbara asked if the price of the sofa was firm.

"Yes."

Szymon shook his head. "That's too much for us." The young couple quickly left the store, embarrassed to inquire about other merchandise. Walking down the street, they spotted another furniture store, but the prices were no different. Concern spread across Barbara's face. "What will we do?"

Reality hit home for Szymon, so he suggested that they buy only what they needed right away, and the following day he would, hopefully, find a job.

It occurred to Barbara that they should go to Rynok Square. A large general store she remembered from when she shared an apartment with three other young ladies from the Roman Catholic Church was located there. As they walked along Rynok Street near the square, they noticed activity. Here and there, small tables were set up with various household items laying helter-skelter on them. Szymon's face brightened. "I'll bet there is a fair today."

Taking out his pocket watch, he noticed it was approaching ten-thirty. They watched people setting up their stalls and began looking for furniture items they might want. A small wagon came alongside where they stood. In the cart were several pieces of furniture. Szymon approached the driver, who was beginning to unload his wares. "Do you have a couch?"

The man had a couch and a comfortable chair. They didn't match, but both were in good condition. Szymon saw the look on Barbara's face. He could tell that the price was right. "I'll pay twenty-five cents more if you will take them to our apartment."

Without hesitation, the man agreed. Szymon helped the man push the furniture back into the wagon, assisted Barbara up to the teamster seat, and they left to take their newfound treasures home. After the furniture was deposited in the apartment, the seller took them back to Rynok Square so they could shop for other items they needed. As they rushed away from the wagon, eager to find more bargains, they heard the seller's voice and glanced back to see him wave his arm. "Good luck!"

Barbara and Szymon shopped around for another two hours, determining that the fair was the place to shop and find good things to eat and drink. They located a booth where a woman was selling pillows and another where forks, knives, spoons, and various baking utensils were displayed. They bought two forks, two knives and two spoons, two sharp knives, a large serving spoon, a rolling pin, a spatula, two big towels, two small towels, and clothes for washing dishes and bathing. Szymon suggested they find something to eat here instead of cooking at home. "It will cost less and save time."

As they ate sausage and cheese with bread and drank coffee, Szymon wanted to look at tools. So, when he finished eating, he went to talk to some men about what kind of work was available while Barbara continued looking at women's things. She was standing at a booth chatting with a woman who had hand-stitched designs in a Ruthenian motif in the brightest of colors on aprons, shirts, and vests, and thinking she wanted to make a vest like that for Szymon one day when he came up to her. "Are you finished shopping?"

As they walked toward the Rynok Market grocery store, Szymon told her about his conversations with the men. They had given him several leads on job openings. Four or five projects in the city were where he could look for work.

Returning to the apartment building, they walked up the narrow staircase with their newfound treasures. Although they had spent very little, they bought enough groceries for several days. After the groceries were put in the cabinet, Szymon went out to buy ice.

Upon returning to the apartment, he told her he had inquired about a few jobs, but no one was hiring. "Everyone tells me that winter is here and soon it will be snowing, so it is too cold for outdoor construction work." He saw her crestfallen face and apologized for not considering the disadvantages of moving there in winter.

"What can you do?"

He didn't have an answer, and she could tell by his face that he was also disappointed and a little worried. Szymon was quiet for the rest of the afternoon, but she overlooked his silence, thinking he might be tired.

That evening, it began to rain, followed by much colder temperatures. By early morning the rain had turned to snow. It snowed for the next three days, leaving the snowbound city of Lwow looking like a fairyland frozen in time.

Venturing outside the following morning, they encountered almost no one on the streets and discovered the side streets were nearly impassable. Regardless, they walked to Rynock Square. Tree limbs laden with snow had broken and fallen everywhere. Rooves on small sheds, older buildings, and garages did not match the heavy snow; some had caved in under the weight. They decided to walk up another street to their apartment on the return.

"This is a disaster, Barbara."

It was the same on this street. Dozens of huge tree limbs and branches were blocking drives and alleys along the sides of buildings. Ahead, there were two men on a street corner. They frantically waved for Szymon to hurry. Leaving Barbara's side, he ran up to the men. All three men turned right. Barbara decided to hurry after them to see what was happening. As she drew closer, she saw that they were pulling limbs and a roof section from atop a young child.

Concerned for her safety, Szymon ran toward Barbara, took her hand, pulled her toward their street, and told her to go home to wait for him. "It's dangerous out here. You could fall and get hurt. I'll tell you about the situation here later."

Then, he returned to help lift the little boy into the back of a wagon he had asked to borrow. The men headed for the nearest hospital, which happened to be the same one to which Szymon had been taken when he was found injured more than a year before. As they carried the boy inside, Szymon told the other men he needed to return the wagon. It was then one of the men handed Szymon one dollar.

Sitting high up on the teamster seat, looking out at the incredible damage, he spotted a man trying to free a horse from a shed leaning precariously to one side. Szymon halted the wagon and ran to help him. They removed thick limbs by tying a chain around one end of the limb and the other to the wagon until they could move the damaged door enough to free the horse. To thank him for his help, the man gave him fifty cents. Next, Szymon helped pull tree limbs and broken light poles to the road's edge so wagons could pass. He worked quickly, earning four dollars an hour.

Heading home to return the mule and wagon, Szymon watched as a huge, snow-laden limb fell about a hundred yards before him. His heart jumped as he realized how dangerous it was on the streets. He didn't stop but took the wagon back to Luke to explain what had happened and gave him part of his earnings. Luke's face lit up.

"I can make more and will give you part of what I earn."

Luke told him he could take the wagon for two dollars for the rest of the day. Szymon readily agreed.

As it continued to snow over the next two-and-a-half days, Szymon earned twenty dollars. Working from dawn to dusk, despite the snow, Szymon had earned in three days what he likely would have made in two months. Bone-weary from working ten hours daily, he sat beside Barbara and counted the money. That first day, almost no one else was trying to clear the streets except Szymon. On the second day, although the snow kept falling, men who worked for the city were on the streets. They were more concerned about damage to street lights and other city property than clearing tree limbs or snow. By the third day, neighbors were helping neighbors, frantically running errands. Word quickly spread around the neighborhood that Szymon could be called to help in an emergency. He was willing to transport critically ill persons to a hospital, help free trapped horses or mules, clear debris from drives and walkways, haul tree limbs away, and carry oil to fill heaters.

As Szymon told Barbara what he had accomplished each day, she considered him with a look of amazement and disbelief. She knew Szymon had worked very hard to make so much money. As a result, they didn't need to worry about immediately finding a real job so that Szymon could rest. It also meant they could purchase more than just basic necessities to make their apartment a home. In addition, they still had the money that Uncle Max held for them. Their life together settled into a quiet, comfortable routine.

Old Town was shrouded in a frozen, white blanket of snow. Because they had no money worries, they escaped the cause of so many young couples' unhappiness. Lwow was the perfect place to live, and life was treating them well. For the next few weeks, they spent hours walking, talking, and getting to know each other for the first time. He was quiet, but he became boisterous after a couple of drinks. Szymon could be sentimental and loving or funny and sarcastic. She was quiet, soft, and gentle. Her hardscrabble life had taught her to be frugal, patient, and ready for whatever life might throw at her.

It was early December; Barbara's birthday was on the fourth. Szymon surprised her with a pretty necklace of colored glass beads and a chocolate dessert. He suggested they do something extra special for her birthday. For months, he had been bringing newspapers home to read to Barbara. The papers were full of stories and pictures about the Royal Exhibition of Home Agriculture and Industries being held in Lwow. Stories abounded about the wonderful displays of innovations being introduced into everyday society. The exhibition had opened on June 5th while they were still living in Bukaczowce, but it would soon close. So, he decided to celebrate Barbara's birthday by visiting Striyskyi Park to see it. Displays included peasant costumes, pottery, domestic tools and utensils, blacksmith ironwork, and festive objects like Easter eggs. Photographs or artist drawings and descriptions of each object were also displayed.

The following Saturday, they woke early, ate a quick breakfast, and then hurried up the street to the central trolley station near Svobody Street. Throngs of people waited at the stop as people hurried in from all directions. The electric tram was built for the convenience of moving visitors to and from Striyskyi Park south of the center of Lwow. Fares were reduced for riders throughout the six months of the exhibition, and since Saturday was the last day, even further discounts were advertised in the newspaper; five cents for round trips. The ride took about twenty minutes, and when they arrived at the Striyskyi Park tram station, large crowds were heading up the walkways toward the entrance.

Barbara and Szymon had decided in advance that they wanted to see the replicas of houses from different parts of Galicia and the pavilion devoted to the exhibit about Galician life throughout the decades. They crowded into the special cable car that transported fairgoers along the walkways to the cultural section. Barbara was anxious to see the Brides Room, and the wait to enter the exhibit was well worth it. After they had visited the cultural center, including the Ruthenian displays, Szymon suggested they find the farming and dairy exhibits, where he spent time looking at farm products, tools, and dairy farming innovations, as well as picking up brochures about agricultural schools, organizations, and societies. There was also a model of a modern farm and farmhouse that Szymon wanted to visit. Barbara met a friend from her days working at the hospital who was also pregnant. The two rested while talking about the exhibition and exchanged addresses before parting ways.

After exploring the farming and dairy exhibits, Szymon found Barbara sitting on a bench outdoors, where the temperature was dropping, but inside, it was comfortably warm. Near the farming displays were gardening, dog, and horse shows, so he suggested they go to the horse show area. One of the most spectacular events was a performance of the famous Lipizzaner horses.

It was 3:30 P.M. before they stopped to eat. Szymon bought sandwiches and coffee, which they ate while sitting at long tables among crowds of people. Visitors to the exhibition talked over one another, excited about the exhibits they had seen.

After rushing from exhibit to exhibit, the time had come for the Royal Exhibition to close. The local newspapers had covered the exhibit regularly, and Szymon read in the Gazeta Lwowska that during the six months of the exhibition, over a million people had attended the fair. Adults and children came from all over Galicia and major cities throughout Eastern Europe.

Throngs of people made their way to the square, where a huge crowd assembled in the dark to await the start of the Water and Music Show. Colored lights illuminated water fountains as they splashed and danced up and down, synchronized in time to music played by an organist and live band. It was a beautiful, spectacular sight.

They rode the electric tram the short distance to Svobody Station and then hurried, shivering, up Zamarstynowska Street to their tiny apartment. Tired and hungry from their busy day, Barbara heated a pot of kidney stew. They sat at the kitchen table, discussing everything they had seen that day. Barbara had kicked off her shoes. "We could have gone daily for a week, yet still not have seen everything. Did you enjoy it, too, Szymon?"

"I wish we could go again."

Barbara's favorite display was the silk hangings from the weaving mills of Buczacz. Polish Countess Anna Potocki cleverly arranged several silks, with other artifacts and furniture, in the Bride's Room. Szymon read a note from the program to her, which stated the Countess displayed these items so people would know that a beautiful and useful dowry could be made at home.

"It makes me want to learn to weave." She knew she could learn but thought the beautiful designs exceeded her talents. "The scarves are made and sold in Buczacz but are very expensive."

She longed to make a handkerchief for Szymon but doubted she could finish it for his birthday, which was just a month away. Barbara had chatted with a new friend, Maria Marcin, whose handicraft she had admired at Rynok Square. Maria enjoyed showing the colorful vests she made and demonstrated how to stitch Ruthenian designs and symbols. The older woman took a liking to Barbara and gave her a pattern to trace on a plain handkerchief. She even provided yarn to make a bandana for Szymon's birthday present. Her gift was a complete surprise to him, and he lifted her off her feet, dancing around the room in a moment of sheer joy.

Winter slowly passed without more blizzards. Although most snow had melted, the weather abruptly turned very cold. For several days, Barbara felt it unsafe to venture outside. Szymon's reputation for helping others continued to spread. People occasionally came to the apartment building to hire him to unfreeze a water pipe, drag away a fallen tree limb, or help the owner of an apartment building haul garbage or trash, enabling him to earn a few dollars over the next few weeks of winter.

Approaching her sixth month, Barbara felt the effects of pregnancy—even clumsiness. Occasionally she encountered acquaintances from the years she had previously lived in Lwow. Once, she saw Sister Agnes from a distance at a busy intersection, but she turned the corner to avoid a face-to-face encounter with her.

As the days passed and temperatures moderated, they often walked to Rynock Square to explore—especially on fair days. It was pleasant on the first Monday in March, so, as was their custom, they walked to the fair. As they reached Rynock Square, a voice called out to them. They turned to see Joe Korlaszcz waving to them, and they hurried over to hug and kiss him. Szymon was curious about why Joe was in Lwow. "Did you move?" Joe explained that he was only there for a few days in order to make arrangements to enter the Seminary. Since it was nearing dinner time, they decided to get kielbasa sandwiches and hot coffee and sit on one of the benches scattered along the sidewalk to eat their meals while Joe filled them in on all the news from home. His brother Wally and Szymon's sister Anna were doing well, as were Szymon's parents. Even Steve was staying on the wagon.

"How about your Aunt and Uncle, Joe? Are they well?"

After the pleasantries, Joe told them about his plan to move to Lwow in June, which excited Szymon.

"That's great!" Szymon said he had spoken to a superintendent at a construction project near downtown. "I've got two more leads and plan to go tomorrow and Wednesday to see if I can find a full-time job. I have experience working with Max and a letter of reference from him to give to the construction boss. There's a tremendous amount of construction going on in the downtown center, and I've heard there are plans to expand the barracks at the Garrison."

As the three chattered easily, they didn't see a middle-aged man and woman approach from a side street. "What the hell are you three doing here?" called a gruff voice. Startled, they looked up to see Sergeant Schoeppler. Szymon and Joe were happy to see Sarge, who introduced his wife, Magdalena. Joe, in his usual friendly manner, chatted with her and soon discovered that she attended mass at the same church Joe did before he left Lwow to go home.

"So you are going to do it, Joe?"

"Yes, sir!"

"I'll be stationed here for a few years, so I suppose we'll see you in church occasionally. How is that ticker of yours, Joe? Do you remember to drink lots of water?"

"Yes, sir."

Schoeppler let out an exaggerated laugh. "Remember, Joe; I'm not your mother."

Szymon asked Sergeant Schoeppler what he knew

about possible construction at the Garrison, and Sarge suggested he talk to Commander Schwartzdorf. "He knows everything."

After Sarge and his wife had said their goodbyes, Joe mentioned a church dance that weekend. "Lent begins next week, so this will be the last fun weekend for a while," Szymon asked Barbara if she felt she could go; she told him she thought it would be fun.

After the three friends had gone their separate ways, Barbara broached the subject with Szymon about his job prospects. He was encouraged that his prospects for decent employment were good. The next day, he followed up with Commander Swartzdorf, who told him that projects were on the horizon; however, something had yet to be scheduled. So, he suggested Szymon find another job but encouraged him to check back occasionally. Szymon had a couple of opportunities for employment as a laborer on construction sites that were due to start the next day. He decided to take one of the jobs as a laborer and, in the meanwhile, kept trying to locate something better. The next morning, he left home shortly after daybreak, wearing his work boots. It had been a while since he had done hard labor, and when he finished his first day's work, he was damned tired. He reached their apartment just after dark, entering their little apartment hungry and tired. She was waiting for him with dinner ready. After a week or two of his new work routine, he looked forward to each evening when he returned to a homecooked meal and his pretty wife. Life settled into a pleasantly predictable routine.

Barbara missed their long, lazy days together, although she had known it couldn't last. They had been careful to live on the small income from Szymon's side jobs so they didn't have to dip into their modest savings. They attended services at a neighborhood Roman Catholic Church occasionally and made friends with their neighbors, often joining them at local dances. Szymon also visited reading rooms in Old Town, where he read newspapers to keep up with current political news.

They were happy together. She loved sleeping with him, their sweet sex, and snuggling close to him— especially on cold nights. They were content to enjoy the simple things in life. She knew there would be changes when their baby arrived, but life was peacefully uncomplicated for now.

However, worrisome signs surfaced occasionally. One occurred unexpectedly on a cold February evening, the Saturday after Lent. Szymon's fellow workers invited them to a dance at a local hall that featured lively Ruthenian dance tunes. Barbara didn't recognize anybody. Szymon's group of co-workers was much poorer than most of the people they had met during their few months living in Old Town. Their clothes were shabbier, their language coarser; they were a rough crowd. Several people sitting at a long table and drinking heavily invited Szymon to join the group. Barbara hesitated because some men were drunk, but she didn't protest. Szymon was eager for their companionship. Ultimately, she regretted going to the dance.

Szymon got very drunk that evening. His demeanor was ugly, he became belligerent, and it was all she could do to talk him into leaving the hall. On the way home, he slurred his words as he staggered up the street toward their apartment. His voice grew louder as they reached their apartment building. In a quiet, firm voice, Barbara told him to be quiet, not to awaken their neighbors. He stumbled and fell when they started up the stairs toward their apartment, missing the first step. And he cursed loudly when she reminded him that people were asleep. Somehow she managed to get him into their apartment, and with a great sense of relief, she pulled off his shoes, threw a blanket over him, and changed into her nightgown. The room was cold, so she turned up the kerosene cook stove for extra warmth. After several minutes sitting next to the stove, she was still cold, and although shaken by Szymon's behavior, she crawled into bed next to him. Disappointed that their fun had been ruined, she couldn't fall asleep and began chastising herself. Szymon had asked her if she wanted to go to the dance, but she knew she couldn't dance because her baby was due in two months, so she shouldn't have agreed to go.

Barbara finally fell into a fitful sleep but was awakened by a crackling noise coming from the kitchen. She bolted upright in bed, raced toward the sound, and stared at the stovetop, which glowed bright orange. Running to the bedroom, she frantically called his name. Szymon bounded into the kitchen to the kerosene cook stove. Looking around for something to protect his fingers, he grabbed a towel and, working quickly, was able to shut off the kerosene flow. Barbara shivered and trembled beside him, her heart pounding and her stomach rolling over.

Szymon turned to her. "Why didn't you ask me?"

Barbara felt threatened. "I only was trying to turn up the flame so we wouldn't be cold. You were drunk, so I tried to do it myself." Her response was abrupt, and she looked away as her eyes filled with tears.

This was their first misunderstanding, so the crisis passed quickly. He saw her upset and tried to find words to comfort her. He led her back to bed, holding her close to him, gently stroking her hair until they both fell into a peaceful sleep.

Chapter 18

Over the next two months, Szymon continued to look for a better-paying job, but something still needed to materialize. It was now late spring, and the baby was due anytime. Their landlady suggested a woman who lived on the next street could midwife the baby. But Barbara hesitated. She began to worry about how they could have their baby christened since they had not married. At first, being unmarried hadn't bothered her, but as her due date approached, she felt she was living in sin. No one knew of their prior lives. No one knew that she and Szymon had made love that warm, late summer day on the bank of the little lake in the woods. On the surface, it appeared they were living a beautiful, romantic life together, but under her happy façade, Barbara's conscience gnawed at her. She was certain that people knew her deepest secrets, especially the parishioners who occupied the surrounding pews on Sunday mornings. She felt everyone was watching her. Their once-happy lives were tainted. Thoughts of living in sin nagged her day and night. She couldn't tell Szymon how she felt, but he had already guessed the truth. He knew the reason for her thinly-veiled anguish. And, if the truth is told, Szymon was uncomfortable attending mass at Barbara's church. He always wanted a wife who would attend Greek Catholic services with him but had never broached the subject with her.

Barbara could feel her unborn baby moving into her womb in late May. She longed for a female friend she could confide in and answer her questions. This was her first baby, so she didn't know exactly what to expect. However, she suspected the kicks and bumps she felt were abnormal. She was becoming fearful and regretted that they hadn't made any arrangements for birthing their baby.

She asked Szymon if he would go to the Rynok Market Fair to find her friend, Maria Marcin, who had been helping her learn embroidery and stitching. Szymon's face took on a puzzled expression. "Why? What's wrong?"

"I'm so afraid. I think something is wrong."

"Why didn't you tell me?"

As she explained her suspicions about the baby, his eyes widened. Szymon gently placed his hand on her belly. "Tell me how it feels."

Barbara explained that she thought something was wrong because the baby was active almost all the time—even in her sleep, but she didn't tell Szymon about her guilty feelings related to not being married. Szymon felt the baby kicking and noted her pale face, so he agreed to find Barbara's friend. "I'll be home as quickly as I can." Feeling exhausted since she barely slept due to worry, guilt, and the hyperactivity of their unborn baby, she rested while he was away.

True to his promise, Szymon returned with Maria Marcin. Barbara cried when Maria came to her bedside. Maria's voice was soothing and gentle, and Barbara's fear lessened as she spoke in low tones. Szymon left the two women alone.

"Please call me Maria. Tell me, what makes you so fearful, dear?"

Barbara's voice was barely a whisper. "I'm so ashamed,"

Maria took her hand and told her not to be afraid. Barbara began weeping and pouring out her heart. In a voice full of anguish, she told Maria that she was not married to Szymon, to which Maria merely nodded as though she already knew. "You won't think that I'm a bad person, will you?"

"No, dear, I've known many good young ladies who have told me a similar story."

"How is my baby? Is everything alright?"

The older woman felt Barbara's belly and then looked at Barbara quizzically.

"Have you fallen?"

Barbara told Maria she hadn't fallen but had ridden with Szymon in a neighbor's wagon the previous weekend. "We went for a long ride in the countryside; the road was rough, so the wagon lurched from side to side. That made me feel dizzy, and I tripped getting down from the wagon. Do you think God is punishing me for living in sin?"

"No, dear, I do not. It feels to me that your baby has turned, but to be certain, you should see a doctor." Barbara knew what breech births were. She knew that sometimes a baby needed to be turned to position the head properly so it was ready to enter the birth canal before it was born.

"But do you think the baby is alright?"

"Yes, I do."

Barbara's fears were calmed, but her peace of mind did not last long. She continued to have irrational fears. In the early morning hours, about a week after Maria Marcin's visit, Barbara's water broke, but in the two hours following, she experienced no labor pains. After he awakened, she told Szymon about her water breaking but wanted him to go to work. Szymon's eyes didn't lie; he feared for her. It was too early to find Miss Marcin. He hurried to tell his boss that his wife was ready to have their baby and promised her he would return as quickly as possible.

When Szymon left the apartment, it was still dark, and there was hardly a soul on the streets. Arriving at the construction site, he hurried to find his boss to explain that Barbara was in labor. His boss gave him the name of a friend whose wife was a midwife. On his return, it occurred to him that it wasn't a fair day, so that he couldn't find Maria Marcin there, and Barbara did not have her home address. Reaching the tiny apartment, he found Barbara in bed, still not experiencing contractions. He helped her to a chair in the kitchen and made coffee. They sat and talked, finding that talking helped them remain calm. As daylight neared, Szymon knew he must find someone to help Barbara through labor. He looked at the address on the paper his boss had given him and was relieved to learn that it was only two blocks from their apartment.

An older woman opened the door. He recognized her from the dance they had gone to the night he got drunk. She remembered him, too. They spoke briefly while the woman hurriedly found her coat, and then they rushed to Barbara's side.

Introducing herself as Olena Ganarszcz, the older woman said she was from Oskrzesince and knew some Swaczys who lived there. Szymon beckoned to her, and Miss Ganarszcz followed him to the hallway, where they decided to help Barbara walk to Olena's home to deliver the baby. Once there, Olena suggested that Szymon return to work because the baby would likely be born late in the day.

Olena examined Barbara and felt her belly. She was certain it would be a breech birth because it was too late to turn the baby. She sang and whistled songs familiar to Barbara. "Do you want to come with me, dear?" She assisted Barbara to a small room with a small table, chair, and chests. The room was clean and quiet. On the top of one cabinet were stacks of folded towels, containers of cotton, and bandages. Bottles, large and small, were lined up along the wall.

Some tools and instruments lay on the top of the other cabinet, alongside pans and pails. Olena handed Barbara a flannel robe. "I'll help you put this on, dear."

Barbara felt cold in this room but didn't complain. As she lay back on the table, she experienced cramps similar to her period. Olena appeared pleased with that bit of news. "I hope that is what I think it is." Then, Olena resumed singing and whistling her songs.

Several hours passed, and the contractions came regularly, but they needed to be stronger. Olena examined Barbara, noting that her cervix had not dilated much. "Why don't we go for another short walk? It might help move things along." After helping Barbara to dress, they walked around the backyard of the apartment building, talking as they walked. Olena told Barbara that she had known two Ruthenian Swaczy families living in Oskrzesince about ten years ago. She promised Barbara that she would find the name of the head of the family.

"They are Greek Catholics, and we are Roman Catholics, so I didn't see the family often."

Barbara was interested in learning about this Swaczy family so she could pass along the information to Szymon, who was related to many Swaczys in and around Bukaczowce and Oskrzesince. The two women walked slowly around the yard's perimeter, out into the alley, and around the building. After thirty minutes, they reentered the vestibule and started up the stairs. Suddenly, Barbara stopped, clutching the banister.

"Don't worry, dear; I'm here."

It was dark when Szymon arrived at the Ganarszcz's apartment, so he didn't see the man standing near the door. The man startled him when he spoke. He introduced himself as Piotr, said that Barbara's pains were increasing, and suggested they find a restaurant for supper that night.

Upstairs, Barbara's pains were closer together and more intense, but her cervix still had not dilated very much. Oleana taught Barbara some breathing exercises to help her cope with the pain better. "Am I doing alright?"

"Just remember to take deep breaths and blow them out slowly."

She began to whimper, and Olena sought to comfort her.

"Now, now. Be brave; this isn't so bad."

Barbara gasped through clenched teeth. "But it's been such a long day."

Her labor continued for hours. "I have something I can give you for pain, but I don't want to give it to you too soon. Can you hold on for a little while longer?

"I promise I'll give you something to help manage the pain." Barbara was barely able to nod. For the next several hours, Olena helped Barbara to stand up and walk around the small apartment and to steady her when she stopped and hung onto the walls.

Settling her back on the table, Olena examined her again. "Your cervix is dilating." Three more hours passed. Barbara was terrified; the pain was excruciating, overtaking her. Olena ordered her to push harder during each contraction. Barbara cried out that her ordeal was unbearable, but Olena kept encouraging her. "Breathe in, blow it out slowly. She secured Barbara onto the table, left the room briefly, returned with a chair, and handed her a cup containing laudanum. "This is bitter, but it will help with the pain." Barbara stared at her. Olena could see the anguish in her eyes. "I promise that laudanum will help you, dear."

Barbara tried to position herself with Olena's help. She could hear her voice,

"Push! Push harder!"

It became a blur of pain, pushing, and more pain. The last thing Barbara remembered before descending into darkness was attempting to move from the table to the chair. She was exhausted, almost unable to stand. Barbara's delivery had taken more than twenty-four hours, but their son Joannes was born at noon on June 3rd, 1895.

Late in the day, Szymon stopped at the tiny apartment before going to work. Olena showed him his little son, then took him into the bedroom to stand by Barbara's bed.

"Barbara looks peaceful."

"It was a long, hard ordeal. I don't want to tell her how difficult it was. Thanks to God, your son is healthy. You are a lucky man, Szymon."

Her voice trailed off as they continued to stand there in silence, Szymon's lips moving in prayer, Olena crossing herself. Hours later, Barbara awakened to Szymon's voice. "It's a boy!"

Through tears, she smiled up at him bravely as their baby boy slept soundly in a makeshift bed on top of a cabinet in their bedroom. "Szymon, it wasn't so terrible.

Barbara's recovery was fast and without complications. For the next week, she rested and nursed their baby. Szymon shopped, cooked, and washed their laundry. He even found time to go to Rynok Square, where Maria Marcin told him she would come to lend Barbara a hand. Their landlady helped with the baby, and Olena Ganarszcz checked on Barbara and the baby several times. They managed very well, so Szymon needed more work.

Two weeks after the baby's birth, Barbara could do light housework. She loved being at home with her baby. Rosina, her landlady, came to help prepare a dinner for the first week and continued, from time to time, to bring a plate of food for their evening meal. Maria Marcin visited and brought Barbara another bandana and enough yarn so she could stitch and embroider during her free time. She showed her how to use appliques and ribbons for fancy vests and shirts. Her favorite time was when Olena visited.

Olena had become her surrogate mother. Barbara confided in Olena about her unhappy childhood and the abusive Uncles who raised her.

A few days later, Olena told Barbara she could begin taking short walks. Excited to leave her bed in the small apartment, she wanted to shop for a baby carriage and clothes.

Three weeks after Joannes was born, Barbara walked down the staircase, proudly holding her baby boy, to take him on his first venture out into the world. At the foot of the staircase was a baby carriage; next, Szymon stood proudly beaming as she placed the little bundle wrapped in soft blankets into the carriage. It was the end of June, and the weather was picture-perfect as they walked up Haidamatska *Street* toward the park dedicated to the Church of the Entry of the Most Holy Theotokos into the Temple Szymon pushed the carriage. The walk was short—only about 10 minutes. They sat on a bench in a secluded place under a shady tree where it was quiet. Szymon reached into the carriage and pulled out two bottles of honey-sweetened tea. The new parents talked about the pretty day, the beautiful park edged with seasonal flowers, the birds flying overhead against a deep blue sky, and a rabbit playing hide and seek with himself, completely oblivious to them.

"Szymon, do you remember the first time we went out together? We went to a park just like this." Szymon looked at her, only smiling and slowly nodding.

"I think of those days often, Szymon. They are my favorite memories."

They continued to talk just as they had those many months ago, even though their lives certainly had changed. Szymon worked six days a week as a construction laborer. He made enough money to provide for all the necessities of life and managed to buy some additional used furniture for baby Joannes.

Joe moved to Lwow in August when Joannes was two months old. He never talked about religion to Szymon and Barbara, but deep inside, it bothered him that their baby wasn't baptized. He wished they would find a church to have their baby christened. Joe knew Szymon was Greek Catholic but never had discussed Barbara's preference for Roman Catholicism. There was little time for the three friends to visit because of the disparities between Szymon's work schedule and Joe's studies and responsibilities after he entered the Seminary. One afternoon in late summer, Joe knocked on the apartment door. Barbara opened the door and threw her arms around him, so glad was she to see him. Joe suggested they take a walk. Barbara found her sweater and bundled the baby into the carriage. It felt so strange to have someone other than Szymon at her side. The friends talked as they walked up Zamarstynowska Street and then turned onto Haidamatska Street toward the entry of the park dedicated to the Church of the Entry of the Most Holy Theotokos into the Temple.

Sitting on a bench with Joe, Barbara suddenly

found she felt self-conscious and shy. Sensing her discomfort, Joe told her about funny things that had happened to him after he entered the Seminary. The stories were about how people reacted to him when he came upon them cussing and swearing or when he accidentally caught a man with a woman other than his wife. Joe related to common people had a great sense of humor, and could paint funny pictures with words about almost any situation. He was often irreverent, almost always witty, and cleverly found humor in awkward situations. The two friends laughed at the stories he painted. He told about elderly retired priests who often forgot parts of the mass when officiating. Barbara laughed at the mental picture of one old priest, possessed of a big, red, bulbous nose, who often got into the sacramental wine, becoming more than a little tipsy. Then, the altar boy tipped over a tray with the wine challis and pitcher, causing a very large red splotch on a pristine white cover, as the congregation stared at the wine dripping slowly from the table to the edge and onto the floor. The altar boy was so frightened he ran from the altar around to the back door, where the parishioners saw him run from the church in his altar-boy frock. Joe loved to tell these stories to friends and family. Time passed quickly, and soon it was time to part. Before saying goodbye at the entrance to her building, Joe picked up the little bundle from the carriage and gently rocked him while singing a sweet children's lullaby. Barbara was once again reminded of how sweet Joe's voice sounded. She told him that Szymon would want him to return for dinner soon.

"Tell Szymon to just stop by the parish office, leave a message for me, and I'll be there on any Sunday afternoon."

When Szymon arrived at home that evening, he had his own bit of good news. He would start a new job as a bricklayer on Monday; it would pay a bit more money each week. Szymon worked as an apprentice bricklayer for several months until about mid-winter. This time he was prepared for the long months when construction slowed down, and most outside workers were laid off. Little Jan—they decided to call him Jan at Joe's suggestion—was six months old and an active, curious baby boy. He was also quiet and happy, which fit into their peaceful, uncomplicated life. Szymon was given a little playpen and crib for Jan from a fellow at his workplace. Although there was not any snow yet, the weather had turned cold, and shortly after the holidays, Szymon was laid off.

Szymon had considered buying a mule and wagon in order to earn some money doing odd jobs during winter but only wanted to pay for feed if he was positive he could use the animal to make extra money. In the meantime, he looked for other ways to earn money so they wouldn't have to spend their savings. Although cold weather lingered, no snow materialized until after March 1st, when a snowstorm finally blew into the area. It was in and out in one day. Szymon calculated the possibility of more snowy winter days and decided not to invest in a mule and wagon. His landlord, Luke, told Szymon that he could pay him the same as last winter for the use of his mule and wagon when he needed it. So, he felt fortunate when ten inches of fresh snow blanketed Lwow one day toward the end of March. The storm was a fluke, and the town was brought to a halt for one day until streets could be cleared. Szymon managed to make ten dollars clearing driveways and sidewalks and transporting people who needed help with things like fetching a can of heating oil or seeking emergency medical treatment.

Szymon realized that he could not depend upon snowstorms during the winter months to find enough temporary work to tide them over the long winter. Szymon couldn't come up with other ideas over the next few weeks, but by then, he realized there was no need to conjure up a scheme to find temporary work. Rather, it was time to make the rounds of construction sites to learn what full-time positions were available because the building season would soon be in full force. To Szymon's surprise, he learned that construction work at his old job had been halted, but he was told to check back in a week or two. Instead, he decided to seek out another project to secure work. The next morning, Szymon arose before daylight, put on his work boots, and headed up the dark streets toward town. He was determined to find a job that day. It had been the right move. He was hired as an apprentice bricklayer on a small project that would raise a small church in an Old Town neighborhood. In its place, tenement housing for the expanding population of the city was scheduled for construction.

Szymon felt strange demolishing a church that he could see had been a beautiful building at one time. Nevertheless, he joined seven or eight men who waited for the crew chief to arrive. The boss, Jerzy, showed up drunk. Not only was he drunk, but he carried a small bottle of vodka in his coat pocket. The men—disgusted when they saw his condition—stood idly by, wondering if they would lose a day's pay. One man stepped up to try to get the job going. He sent someone to locate the project manager to determine what they needed to accomplish that day. No one knew what was to be salvaged, and no wagons were in the yard to haul the wreckage away. By the time the project manager arrived, Jerzy had passed out on a pew inside the church. A man spoke up and told the manager that Jerzy was his neighbor. "What the hell are you waiting for? Get him the hell out of here!" Finally, at 10 o'clock, the crew was busy salvaging anything that could be reused on another project. By the end of the day, the men gathered around the project manager while he told them to arrive early the next day to finish clearing the church and leveling the building.

Szymon laughed as he told Barbara about his day at the construction site. He was surprised that the crew wasn't sent home for the day. He hoped that Jerzy wouldn't get fired, if only because he was happy to be working again. Szymon was lucky to find work as a bricklayer and silently thanked Uncle Max for writing a reference letter. No doubt, he would not have been hired without it.

Szymon read the building plans and saw how the building would be constructed. He knew where the sewer lines came into the building and traced the pipes and electrical lines on the drawing with his finger. Once again, he thanked Uncle Max for allowing him to learn what promised to be a trade for him.

Day after day and week after week, time moved forward without consequence. Nevertheless, Barbara grew concerned that Jerzy was a bad influence on Szymon. At least once a week, Szymon told her stories about his unpredictable behavior. Jerzy was the kind of person who would push authority as far as he could get away with. Szymon had joined him and a few of their co-workers twice to stop at bars after the work week ended on Saturday. Barbara worried about his drinking. Jerzy had a good personality and was equally good as a crew chief when he wasn't drinking. He made good decisions that saved time and money, and the crew always followed his orders, even if they had to change course or begin a task anew. Unfortunately, Jerzy was unlikely to be fired because he was a master bricklayer who excelled at his job. Eventually, Szymon fell under his spell.

Szymon agreed when Barbara told him that Joe would come for dinner on Sunday after church. From time to time, over the past year, the three friends had gotten together, usually for Sunday dinner. They enjoyed each other's company and often exchanged letters they had received from home. On this particular Sunday, Barbara was apprehensive because Szymon had gotten home long after the taverns closed on Saturday night. She couldn't sleep for some reason, and when he wasn't home by midnight, she began to worry.

Szymon staggered up the stairs and nearly fell into the doorway when she opened the door to let him in. He was astonished to see Barbara waiting for him. She was on the verge of tears but controlled her anger and led him to their bedroom, where she undressed him and put him to bed. She realized it wasn't the time to start an argument. She was tired the next morning when she awoke to pick up baby Jan and sit in her comfortable chair to nurse him. Barbara was depressed about their situation. Szymon didn't realize that he was jeopardizing their happiness and marriage. She felt trapped, not knowing what to do next. She thought about taking Jan with her on the train to Bukaczowce to talk with Szymon's mother but stopped herself. It was a fool-hearty notion; besides, nothing was to be gained. Helena Swaczy wouldn't be able to change the situation, so why cause others to worry unnecessarily? She decided to put Szymon out of her mind for now and to bathe and dress. Barbara always enjoyed Joe's company because he was so much fun to be around. She hoped that after church, Joe would brighten her spirits.

Later that afternoon, as they sat talking, Joe was somewhat quieter than usual. Szymon looked as though he would fall asleep if there were a lull in the conversation. After Joe left, Szymon sat in his chair in the living room, watching Barbara. "What is wrong?" She sat quietly for a minute before deciding to tell him the truth.

"Szymon, I'm worried about you."

"Me? What are you worried about?"

"Don't you think you are drinking too much?" His face took on a sullen look, but he didn't speak. "Is something bothering you, Szymon?"

Szymon enjoyed going out with the other men and saw no harm in having drinks with them after work. But Barbara pointed out that he was coming home later and later each week, so she was worried that alcohol was beginning to overtake him. He scoffed. "That is stupid."

The next morning, Szymon arose a bit earlier than usual. Barbara awakened and carried little Jan to the kitchen, where she found Szymon preparing a cup of coffee for her. He was very pleasant, and the two chatted as usual. He asked how she would spend the day, and she told him about her plans, as well as what she would cook for supper. She avoided broaching the subject of Szymon's drinking. That Friday evening, Szymon didn't go out with his co-workers. He asked her if she wanted to go to church the following Sunday. The ruffled feelings had been smoothed out for now, but not for long.

On Sunday, they attended mass at the Catholic Church. She watched Szymon for signs of discomfort. It seemed that peace had been restored, but the following Wednesday, Szymon arrived home long after she had finished washing supper dishes and storing the leftovers—including Szymon's plate—in the ice box. As he entered the tiny apartment, he looked guilty and defensive. She thought he wanted to tell her something, but within an instant, he seemed to change his mind and asked her if she would heat the leftovers for his supper. She started to answer, but he brushed her away. "Let's talk about this another time."

A few weeks later, Joe came to visit late one morning. He was visiting some parishioners who lived nearby and decided to stop to see Barbara and Jan. He asked if she wanted to take the baby on a walk to the park. She was quiet on the walk up Haidamatska Street. While they sat on the bench, Joe asked if she was feeling well. She said she was alright but then took a deep breath. "Joe, I'm worried about Szymon." Not waiting for him to respond, she continued, "He is drinking heavily, Joe, and I don't know what to do about it."

"Barbara, I'm really worried about you. You have been increasingly distracted and withdrawn for the last few months. Do you want to tell me what is wrong?"

She looked at him and could see that his concern was genuine. "Oh, Joe, I'm worried about my baby." She had tears in her eyes but kept her composure.

"You don't know this, but Szymon and I never married." Joe just nodded. "We can't have Jan christened, and I'm worried that, if he died, he would go to hell."

She lowered her head and stared at the ground.

"Oh, Barbara, God will not punish your baby for what you and Szymon have done." She continued staring at the ground. "Have you ever spoken to Szymon about your fears?" She could only shake her head no.

"Do you think that God will forgive Jan for not being christened?"

"Barbara, why don't you talk to Szymon about this? Maybe he is worried, too. If you marry, you can have your baby christened in the church. It's not too late."

Barbara glanced at him. She had never thought about this. "Joe, the thing is that Szymon is Greek Catholic, and I love my religion."

"You must pray about this. I know it isn't easy for you, but God is merciful, and if you are sincere and ask God to help you, He will."

That evening as Barbara was prepared for bed, it occurred to her that she already felt relieved about the guilt she had been carrying with her every day. She didn't speak to Szymon that evening but vowed to do it soon. The next morning, she awakened well-rested and refreshed. She nursed little Jan while humming a favorite hymn. After preparing breakfast, she went to the bedroom to awaken Szymon. She returned to the kitchen, put the food on the table, and poured coffee as Szymon slipped into his chair.

"Did you sleep well, Barbara?"

Smiling, she told him that she felt well-rested. "How are you?"

He looked at her with a curious expression. "Why don't we go out tonight for supper?"

Joe stopped by that day to invite them to a choral music concert.

She sat silently, not answering for a long moment. "I'd like to go, but I don't know whether Szymon would want to. Joe said the concert was to be held in a German section of Lwow and that transportation had been arranged.

"Will you be singing, Joe?"

"No, but I guarantee we will really enjoy the music."

That evening Barbara asked Szymon if he would go with her to the concert; he surprised her by immediately agreeing to go. They decided not to dine in a restaurant that evening because they might have to pay someone to take care of Jan on the concert evening. Barbara smiled excitedly, and Szymon thought she looked more beautiful than she had in a long time. He took her hand. "Let's not argue, Barbara." She said nothing but continued to look at him sweetly.

The next morning, when Szymon awakened, he saw that Barbara was still sleeping peacefully next to him. He pulled her gently to him and, half awake, wrapped his arms around her, murmuring that he loved her."

On Sunday, they attended Barbara's church and afterward went home, where she prepared a quick dinner. Szymon took Jan upstairs to their landlady, and then they quickly ran down the stairs just as Joe came around the corner sitting high on the teamster's seat of a wagon pulled by a smart-looking team of horses. Two other people sat in the wagon. Joe stopped once more at his church, where several priests and nuns were waiting. Finally, they were off. Barbara was thrilled to attend the concert, billed as an Evening of Sacred German Music. The team of horses pulled to the front of a stately building built in German architecture. Carriage after carriage pulled into the front of the building, each one more beautiful than the next. The interior lobby was elegant. They waited there for Joe to secure the team of horses. When he rejoined the party, he whispered something to the usher, who led them to their seats. Once seated, Barbara looked around at the impressive auditorium. There were magnificent gilded, mirrored sconces on the walls and spectacular chandeliers hanging from the ceiling. Beautiful, gilded balconies ringed the room. The royal box was empty except for a huge portrait of Franz Joseph draped in ruby-red velvet. The reflection of light from crystals hung from the chandeliers, and sconces shimmered all around the hall. It was the most lavish structure that either Barbara or Szymon had ever seen. But the best was yet to come.

A hush fell over the hall as the mighty organ sounded the first chord of the Austrian national anthem, 'God save Emperor Francis Joseph.' From that point on, Barbara was overwhelmed by the beauty of the sacred music. The organist, conductor, and members of the small orchestra were all attired in elegant black formal wear; the female soloists and choir members wore elegantly simple black gowns made of velvet and satin. But it was the music that moved the audience. She briefly caught a glimpse of Joe, who had turned his head. Tears streamed down his face, but he made no effort to brush them away. No one applauded during the performance, as was the custom, and when the music stopped, people rose to file out of the auditorium solemnly. A hush fell over the large crowd gathered at the huge front doors, but as the musicians and singers filed out of the building, a roar of clapping and cheers arose from those gathered. The conductor received the loudest applause, and all the musicians stood respectfully while the throngs of people stamped their feet and cheered. The roar of the crowd subsided as each small group of twos, threes, fours, or more faded into the black night. Barbara and Szymon turned around for one last, long look to see the stately building standing regally with its windows lit in the dark as the team of horses turned onto the main road. Joe found programs which he gave to all of the people who rode together in the back of that humble wagon. Szymon and Barbara stayed up late into the night talking about the wonderful music they had heard.

The next day, immediately after supper, Barbara sat next to Szymon on the small couch in the living room. She hesitantly began speaking, "Szymon, we have never spoken of getting married."

"Barbara, dear, I didn't know whether or not you would say yes. I asked you once, but you didn't respond."

"I am sorry, Szymon, but I was so afraid when we met. You were the kindest friend, and I worried I would lose you. I've had no one for most of my life, so I was just scared."

"Yes, I remember." He took her hand and kissed it. "Let's talk to a priest. Where should we go?"

She hesitated for a long time before answering him in a soft, low voice. "Szymon, let's go to your church."

Life in Lwow was quiet and solemn. It was Lent, and with Easter nearly upon them, it didn't seem appropriate to discuss marriage with a priest, so they decided to wait. There wasn't any hurry. Although it may seem odd, they continued to attend Barbara's church, which Szymon didn't seem to mind.

Joe invited them to visit his church for a Vespers service where they could listen to more sacred music. This time he would be singing in a choir. The church was adorned with lovely vases of flowers for the occasion. The purple drapes had been removed, and the solemnity of Lent and Easter gave way to more joyous music. The friends decided to linger awhile after the Vespers service. They discussed many things that afternoon. Little Jan was almost a year old, and they realized it would be two years since they moved to Lwow in November. Joe suggested they take a trip by train to Bukaczowce later in the year.

"I've been thinking about that, too, Joe." Barbara was surprised because Szymon had not mentioned going home for a visit.

"Let's go together!" They began chattering excitedly. "It's only seven months, Joe!" The three friends spontaneously broke into laughter. The next day Szymon wrote to his father. He told them of their plan to visit Bukaczowce at the end of the year and asked if they could stay with them. He received a reply within 10 days. His parents were just as excited as he and Barbara. More than that, they looked forward to seeing their new grandson.

That spring and summer were memorable for the good times they had. It appeared that their worst problems were behind them. Szymon liked his job and was making a decent wage. Barbara loved her life taking care of Jan and Szymon. She made the little apartment into a pleasant, cozy home. Except for an occasional argument about Szymon's drinking, they seemed to have no worries. On weekends and holidays, they spent hours exploring Old Town, Central City, and the environs. Lwow was a beautiful city where the influence of the German culture had never quite faded away, and German was still spoken. They walked to many of the area parks. Occasionally, Szymon, Joe, and Barbara ate dinner together in a German restaurant. Szymon also liked a beer hall in a nearby neighborhood where some Germans resided.

In mid-August, Joe invited them to visit his church for another Vespers service where they could listen to sacred music again, and he would be singing. They brought baby Jan, who adjusted well to the sounds of the music. He fell asleep despite people talking around him. The music was lovely, as usual, but there were more familiar hymns and secular music this time. The concert was held earlier in the afternoon, so it was still daylight when they left the church to walk home. They turned a corner to Zamarstynowska Street when Barbara recognized Sister Agnes approaching them. Sister Agnes was trapped.

Szymon made the first move. "Good evening, Sister." Sister Agnes must have been deep in thought because she was visibly startled when she recognized them. She slowed down and stared at Barbara, who addressed her politely. "Hello, Sister Agnes."

"Hello, Miss Podoseck."

"Are you well, Sister?"

It was obvious that Sister Agnes was uncomfortable, even squirming, but the street was narrow, so she couldn't easily pass Szymon, Joe, Barbara, and the baby carriage. This time Barbara decided not to run away. "Would you like to see our baby? His name is Joannes, but we call him Jan."

Szymon picked up the baby and held him out for Sister Agnes to see his face. She trembled, and her lips quivered as she spoke. "He is beautiful, but I'm sorry, I cannot talk. I have to return to the church." Sister Agnes abruptly said goodbye as Szymon moved to the side to allow her to pass.

It was painful to see Sister Agnes' turmoil overseeing this happy baby boy.

"Well, she must be suffering from a guilty conscience, Barbara, but I'm surprised she became upset."

"Poor Sister Agnes," It seemed like it was terrible for her to see our happiness. I wonder why? I feel sorry for her."

Joe spoke up. "I'll pray for her."

A small German touring company brought the circus to town on a Sunday afternoon in late July. Tents and rides had been erected. Szymon read a newspaper article about the event to her. On Szymon's day off, they hurried to the tram stop on Svobody Street. They barely made it before the electric tram started pulling away. Szymon asked the driver if he was going to the area near Striyskyi Park, where the circus was located. Then he helped Barbara fold the baby carriage and carried it into the trolley.

The ticket price was very affordable, as was almost everything they did for fun. The circus was small, with only two high-wire acts, three clowns, some acrobats and jugglers, a trained dancing bear, a very old lion, and some chimpanzees dressed in girls' clothes. Still, the day was fun. They had hidden their dinner and drinks in Jan's baby carriage. Since the circus was just a short distance from the area where the Royal Exhibition had taken place, they walked up the sidewalk and found that most of the buildings were closed. Szymon had read in the Gazeta Lwowska that the city was negotiating to purchase all the buildings in Striskyi Park. As they rounded a corner, they came upon the pavilion that housed the Ruthenian exhibit; it was open. They found a small group of people inside the building being escorted by a tour guide. The people who crowded around the guide were speaking the Ruthenian language. The tour was beginning, so they decided to tag along. Their guide was knowledgeable about the history and the current political and economic prospects for Ruthenians living in Lwow. As the group walked through the museum, Szymon listened with rapt attention, especially to information about the local political activity being promoted by several recently formed Ruthenian organizations in the Old City. Barbara paid little attention to that presentation. She was deeply engrossed in eavesdropping on a conversation amongst a group of ladies who had broken away to examine authentic Ruthenian costumes and handwork,

Both groups seemed eager to end their conversations once the museum manager interrupted to announce that the building would be closing in a matter of minutes. The crowd hurried to the exit doors. Szymon asked the man nearest to him whether he knew of any groups that would be meeting soon. The man stopped to talk to Szymon and told him that the most informative of all the societies would be holding a meeting in Old Town at the end of August and provided Szymon with the name of the meeting place. He then pulled Szymon aside and whispered something to him before walking away.

Szymon rejoined Barbara, and they walked briskly back to the electric tram station at the park entrance. Arriving back home, Barbara prepared a pot of stew for dinner. "Szymon, what did that man have to say about the meeting?"

Szymon looked at her quizzically. "Were you listening?"

She laughed and said that she couldn't help but overhear the conversation. "You were so excited you spoke in your loud voice."

"Well, Barbara, just be careful what you say and who you talk to about that conversation. Most of the people we know here in Lwow are Polish, not Ruthenian. Not everyone around here wants the Ruthenians to organize to get ahead—the rich people and nobles certainly don't want us to."

Barbara was rattled by Szymon's remarks, never suspecting that any of her neighbors might bear ill will toward Szymon because he was Ruthenian. They had never thought about the differences in their ethnicities nor even broached the subject. She asked Szymon whether he ever was concerned because she was Polish. He laughed. "You're too sweet to dislike anyone who is a Ruthenian, and I can't imagine anyone disliking you!" He bent over to kiss her, and as he did, he drew her close.

"How much longer before we can make love?"

She just smiled at him and snuggled closer.

The next evening, Szymon came home from work a few minutes later. She saw that he carried a bag with his bathing items when he walked through the door. "Oh, you stopped at the bathhouse."

He answered by asking if she had fed Jan.

"He is sound asleep with a full stomach, "she said.

"Let's eat quickly. I'll help you finish dinner."

"You smell fresh, like your soap."

After they ate dinner, she arose and said she wanted to find her rose fragrance soap and bathe.

"I'll help you with the dishes." He put his arm around her waist and pulled her toward him as they stood in the middle of the kitchen, kissing, wrapped in each other's arms. Barbara and Szymon were still in love.

Days were growing shorter, overcast, and much cooler. Szymon and Barbara began staying home on Sundays. Szymon often visited reading rooms and attended meetings of groups disseminating information about new organizations devoted to developing a vision, strategies, and programs to secure economic and political power for Ruthenians. Sometimes he held back information from Barbara because he knew that some of the activities could provoke violence. After one particular meeting, he lingered to listen to a small group of men discuss an upcoming district election for a representative to the local town council. A Greek Catholic priest from Ternopil, a leader in the political movement, spoke that evening. Father Joe was encouraging the men to attend the upcoming town council meeting. The men appeared to be wary, but Father Joe was relentless. He told them they would only achieve their goals if they got into positions of power. To help put their minds at ease, he volunteered to accompany them. The following week, a group of fifteen or so agreed to meet at the Ruthenian church and then walk to the town hall. Szymon told Barbara the next morning of his decision to attend.

Szymon was nervous that evening but believed Father Joe was correct. Nothing would ever change unless people stood up. The meeting was long, and the election for representatives to the council took place late that night. Father Joe spoke and placed Theodorus Kulyk's name in the nomination for the position. The room was dead quiet. Four others, a total of five candidates, were nominated for the seat. The person with the most votes would win. The vote was evenly cast, but Mr. Kulyk won by one vote, having received eighteen votes, compared to seventeen votes for the candidate who received the next highest vote tally. When the results were announced, the hall was silent. No one anticipated the outcome. In a matter of minutes, the town council president gaveled the meeting to a close, and the attendees streamed out of the Town Hall. Men stood around in groups of five to ten people discussing the meeting, but as the Ruthenians walked out of the building, once again, there was silence.

Szymon told Barbara about the meeting the next morning before going to work. She looked worried. "Szymon, what can they do?"

"I don't know."

Szymon brought home a copy of the Gazeta

Lwowska later that week. News of the election of a Ruthenian from the Halitska District was prominently published on the front page. Szymon read the article to Barbara after supper that evening. The article mentioned that a meeting of the Ruthenian Supreme Council was scheduled for the following week. After he finished reading aloud, Szymon looked directly at his wife. "I'd like to go to that meeting." Barbara was silent.

"Barbara, there isn't any other way Ruthenians will ever get ahead. If the Poles see a united front, they will decide to loosen up and start paying us more.

"I doubt it."

Szymon devoured the news. He continued to buy the Gazeta Lwowska weekly. He also read a couple of dailies, particularly the Ukrainian newspaper Star Dilo and, occasionally, the Yiddish Lemberger Tagblat. He couldn't get enough news about Ruthenian causes. Lwow was a bee hive of activity. Many societies devoted to the causes of Ukrainians, Poles, and even Russians were covered in the newspapers.

Joe visited one late morning in mid-October. He suggested they walk through Halytsky Square to a park south of their apartment, where they sat on a bench. Barbara reached into Jan's baby carriage and pulled out two jars of sweetened tea. They arrived just as a group of men sat at a nearby table. Joe and Barbara ceased their conversation to listen to their complaints. The men talked about the rising political activity of the Ruthenians with tremendous hate in their loud voices. They cursed the Ruthenians, making vile, threatening remarks about them. Barbara looked at Joe in alarm; he put his hand on her arm and signaled her to say nothing. As they continued to drink their tea quietly, Barbara picked up Jan to nurse him. After a while, the men stood and walked away.

"Joe, I'm afraid. I never knew how Polish people felt about Ruthenians."

"I'm sorry, Barbara. Some people don't like them, but all of this unrest is happening because Ruthenians want an equal slice of the pie—a better life for themselves and their children. That makes the Polish people feel threatened. It doesn't make sense, but it is what it is." Joe lowered his voice. "If the truth is told, the clergy doesn't help. On both sides, they preach the most hateful sermons against each other. Barbara didn't respond. In fact, she didn't even mention the incident to Szymon that evening. She didn't want to rile him.

Barbara went to Rynok Square to talk to Maria Marcin the following day. Maria was her usual, friendly self and very happy to see her. The two women discussed stitching, and Maria showed her a vest she was working on. It took Barbara's breath away. "Do you think I can learn to do this?"

"I'll teach you, dear."

As they finished their conversation, some ladies stopped at Maria's table and began discussing the Ruthenian issue. They appeared to be upset about the current activities in Lwow. Barbara became nervous and decided to say goodbye to Maria and return home. Maria called after her to come back soon so she could teach her how to make a vest.

On her way home, she heard sounds coming from a small group of young men and boys who were cursing and beating with clubs two men wearing yarmulkes because they were Jews. Barbara felt sick to her stomach and began racing home, pushing Jan's carriage. The carriage's right front wheel dropped off the sidewalk into an alley. As it turned over, she began screaming. The fight broke up, and several men rushed to help her upright the carriage. Fortunately, Jan was not hurt - just frightened.

Over supper that evening, Barbara told Szymon of the day's events. Szymon silently put down his fork. "Barbara, I think we should move."

Her mouth dropped. "Why?"

"I doubt people around here know I am Ruthenian because we have been attending your Roman Catholic Church, but we agreed to have Jan christened in a Greek Church. Then, our neighbors would know that I am Ruthenian, and they might not treat you so nicely." She started to protest, but he stopped her. "I haven't told you anything about those evening meetings I attend. At some point, there will be violence, and people will be hurt. I don't want you to be mistreated because I am involved in the political movement."

"Oh, Szymon, do you have to get into this?" Her eyes reflected fear; her voice, anguish. "Our life has been going along nicely. Do you have to do this?"

He stared blankly, and she didn't ask him again because they both knew the answer.

Chapter 19

Three weeks later, at supper, Barbara turned toward him, beaming. "Szymon, dear, I believe I'm pregnant."

But Szymon was in a cheeky mood. He smiled and lowered his voice. "That's what happens when you tempt me like you do."

Szymon began looking for another apartment. It wasn't only that he was worried about his neighbors discovering that he was Ruthenian, but they truly needed a bigger apartment, for their growing family. Barbara had another thing on her mind. "Szymon, it might be better if we find a Greek Catholic church first."

He agreed. That's what they needed; that's what his future children needed.

That weekend, Szymon located a somewhat larger apartment over a pharmacy on Bohdan Khmel'nyts'koho Street. Saint Paraskevia Greek Catholic Church was located nearby. Barbara and Szymon talked to their landlady about leaving, Rosina said she was sorry to see them go. "You took good care of everything." But while they were moving, her attitude changed. She wanted them to leave some furniture that Szymon had bought for the apartment. Rosina was upset and demanded that they leave almost half of the furnishings. While Rosina was arguing with Barbara, Szymon walked into the apartment followed by Luke. Rosina averted her eyes. Luke interrupted his wife and told her to go upstairs.

After they left, Barbara began to cry softly. "Do you think she knows you are Ruthenian?"

"No, I don't believe she suspects anything. She is just greedy."

The rent for their new apartment was the same. The flat was only slightly larger but, had four rooms. One of the rooms could be used as a bedroom for the babies because it adjoined a larger room that was intended to be their bedroom. The landlord had stored furniture in that room, so Szymon did not have to buy more. They moved in on a Sunday afternoon around the first of November with the help of Szymon's co-workers. At the last minute, Luke stopped Szymon and told him that he could use his wagon to move. When Szymon told Barbara, she started to say something about Rosina, but Szymon stopped her. "Barbara, don't be angry about this, Rosina was just upset because we are leaving. She probably wanted us to stay so she could collect rent money. Besides, Luke is not the person causing us problems and Luke told me that we can use the wagon to move our furniture. Please ignore Rosina's pettiness."

Within a few days, they had put the new apartment in order, and the place began to feel like home. This apartment came with window shades, and Barbara already planned to sew decorative curtains for the windows, otherwise, there was nothing left to do. Their new neighborhood was across Zamarstynowska Street, to the northwest. The buildings were older and the people were poorer. They also spoke the Ruthenian language. The food stores sold authentic Ruthenian products and the restaurants and cafes featured Ruthenian cooking. On a Sunday, a few weeks after they had moved, Barbara suggested they walk to the Greek Catholic church for Sunday service. They walked up the stoop through the big doors, into Saint Paraskeva Church on a cold, dull gray morning. The interior was dark compared with Barbara's church. The Paraskevia Church had fewer windows and they were smaller, as well. The mass was in Ukrainian and the homily in Ruthenian. The priest was old and stern. Barbara's heart sank thinking she had made a mistake. Little Jan fidgeted in her arms, which was unlike him. Barbara went out to the vestibule and was placing Jan in his carriage when a young priest approached her. He spoke to her in Ruthenian and she responded likewise,

"Good morning."

The priest inquired if she was leaving. She hesitated before saying that she was waiting for her friend. Barbara was in an awkward position. Not wanting to lie to a priest, she smiled bravely as she explained that she had recently moved into the neighborhood and was looking for a new church. She told him she and Szymon would visit the parish sometime during the week. He appeared satisfied with her response. She picked up Jan. "I just need to sit somewhere to nurse my baby."

After church, they walked to a genuine Ruthenian restaurant and ate a delicious dinner. They sat in the rear where they parked Jan's carriage. She lowered her voice and told Szymon of her conversation with the young priest. She asked if he were upset that she told him they would visit sometime during the week. "No, dear, but remember, we are planning to go to Bukaczowce soon. Maybe we should wait until after we return." She wondered if this was the real reason he hesitated.

Joe visited later that afternoon and the three friends sat around the kitchen table planning their big trip. Barbara noticed Szymon was being quiet. "What's wrong?"

"C'mon, Szymon," urged Joe.

Szymon hesitated before speaking. "I was wondering whether we should get married while we are in Bukaczowce."

Joe and Barbara were both stunned, but it was Joe who spoke first. "Holy Mother of Jesus! We can never read your mind. You're like a sphinx. You never let on."

"I don't know how it would work out. Ma and Pa are there and Mr. and Mrs. Podoseck are, too, but we haven't seen Ma and Pa for over two years."

"Szymon, dear, it would be something your parents would remember the rest of their lives. It would make them very happy. Don't worry about my aunt and uncle, just invite them and let them decide for themselves."

Joe chimed in. "I side with Barbara." The matter seemed settled but, Szymon wasn't sure. Joe changed the subject as he pushed a small box across the table toward Barbara. "It's a little early, but "Happy birthday! It's a very small gift, but I hope you like it." Inside the little box rested a beautiful rosary. "The bishop blessed it."

Their plans seemed to be finalized, but on Wednesday, a letter arrived from Szymon's father.

Dear son, Szymon,

We read your letter. Ma has been sick. Many people are sick. There is a flu epidemic here. Is it in Lwow?

Szymon put down the letter.

"Are you disappointed, Szymon?"

"Hell, yes, I'm disappointed, Barbara!"

That night Barbara was awakened by Jan's cough. She picked him up and went into the kitchen. He was flushed and his skin felt hot. Szymon came out of their bedroom, and stood by her side as she checked his diaper. "What's wrong with him?"

"We have been lucky; he hasn't been sick." She tried to nurse him but, Jan wasn't interested in feeding. "I wonder what time it is?"

Szymon checked the clock in the living room. "It's almost time for me to get up anyway."

"What do we have around here to give him for his fever and cough? I wonder if I should heat some juice and wine. That might help him sleep and make him sweat. Then, his fever would break, I think."

Barbara reached for the little box Joe had given her at supper. She opened the box and began reciting the rosary. "That was for Jan."

Unfortunately, Jan's fever did not break. They didn't have a thermometer, but his skin was still hot to the touch. Over the next day and a half, she watched him closely, applying cold compresses to his forehead, sponge-bathing him with cool washcloths, and giving him juice. She prayed constantly that he would recover. Early Saturday morning, she asked Szymon what they should do. He was uncertain. Barbara interrupted his thoughts. "Maybe Olena could come. Would you have time before work to go to her apartment to ask if she would come to see Jan?"

"I'll tell her we will pay."

It was almost nine o'clock that morning when there was a knock at the door. Olena was cheerful, but went directly Jan who slept fitfully. He cried softly as she lifted him from his crib. "He's beautiful, Barbara, but I can feel the fever. He is a sick little boy." Olena immediately took Jan's temperature, then whistled softly. "It's 104 degrees."

"That doesn't sound good."

As Olena examined Jan and prepared a space on a table to bathe him. Barbara sat close by saying the rosary and praying. Olena crossed herself as Barbara finished and began to ask questions.

Half an hour later, Jan was clean and wearing a fresh flannel pajama. Olena suggested they take Jan outdoors for several minutes. When they returned from a short walk, Olena mixed a concoction which she fed to the sick little baby, then, she put the bottles and thermometer into her bag.

As the two women drank cups of tea that Barbara brewed, Olena told Barbara she had looked for the names of the Swaczys she knew in Dzurow. "When Szymon comes to pay this evening, I'll give him a note with the information."

As she prepared to leave, she told Barbara she would stop by in the morning to check on Jan, and gave her instructions for his care for the rest of the day. Olena gave her a quick hug, and then, she was gone. When Szymon came home that evening, they discussed what they should do, if Jan didn't improve soon. They both were worried, but Barbara was choking back sobs.

"Szymon, we have to have Jan baptized." They both had tears in their eyes as Szymon reached for her hand. "I'm so worried." They didn't want to eat, but Barbara insisted that Szymon have his supper to keep up his strength.

"You eat something, too."

Several days passed, but Jan only slightly improved. Olena was summoned twice during the week. She said that blisters covered his tonsils, so she swabbed iodine in back of his red throat. At least his temperature was not quite as high. Olena had bought a medicine made from willow bark for that purpose.

"You never finished reading the letter the night Jan fell ill." That night Szymon read his father's letter to her. Szymon's father had written how bad it was there, and that many friends and family were still sick with the flu.

"I hate to write to them to tell what little Jan has been going through." Nevertheless, after Barbara went to bed that night, Szymon wrote about his son. He wrote that he didn't want to upset them, but they have decided not to travel to Bukaczowce. He wrote that Jan was better now, but still not well, and that maybe they'd have better luck if they planned to come in the spring or summer. Ten days later, Szymon received a letter from his father.

Dear Son, Szymon,

We were so sad to hear that Jan is still very ill. We pray every day, that he will be better soon. We think you shouldn't come to Bukaczowce until the weather is warm. Many here are sick. Several old people have died. Some of my great uncles and aunts are gone. I am sorry to write that Uncle Mikolaj Tracz died two weeks ago. Grandma Tracz is not well and she may not make it through the winter. This flu has been very bad around here. I would like it if you want to come to

Bukaczowce in April or May. The weather is warm then. If you want me to talk to Father Thomas, I would like to have the baby baptized at the same church where you were. We would like another letter from you soon.

Your father,

Roman Swaczy

Although Jan had mostly recovered from tonsillitis, he was still weak and not his usual happy self. Olena stopped by to see him once a week, until he was well. By the time Jan had fully recovered, it was almost the middle of March, 1897. Szymon wrote his father that, so far, Barbara was well, and that he hoped she wouldn't fall ill. Szymon signed off saying he would write again when they were closer to being able to travel.

Spring, with its warmer weather, was just around the corner and Easter was only a few weeks away. Jan would soon turn two years old. He had outgrown the baby stage and entered that of a toddler. Szymon had begun working again after a two-month layoff during the worst of the winter. And, best of all, everyone was well. Szymon and his father had exchanged several letters, and they decided it would be safe to travel at the end of April.

Everyone was fasting for Lent. Barbara and Szymon visited St. Paraskeva Church after Resurrection Day, in late April. They spoke with the young priest and told him that they would be traveling to Bukaczowce to have their son christened. Barbara was now about eight months pregnant. Once the weather improved and the days warmed, Barbara began taking Jan outside in the afternoon. Szymon had bought a used stroller from a fellow worker and stored the baby carriage in the basement.

Szymon and Joe decided they all would leave for Bukaczowce the following Friday on the late train. They arrived in Bukaczowce at 8:30 in the evening and pushed the stroller up the road to the turn that lead to Szymon's parent's house. Helena was surprised when she opened the door. Amid the tears and kisses Szymon explained that they had decided to leave for Bukaczowce on short notice. Since everyone was well and the weather fair, it seemed to them like a good idea to visit before anything changed. Helena brewed a pot of coffee and brought out a coffee cake she had made that morning. They gathered around the table, enjoying a wonderfully happy, family moment. Noticing that Szymon became quiet, Roman and Helena looked at him quizzically. He hesitated briefly before speaking. "Barbara and I are getting married this weekend." There was stunned silence. "We never married, which is why Jan is not baptized. I'll see Father Thomas in the morning to make all the arrangements. Do you think Michael would agree to be best man?"

Helena broke the silence. "What a shock!"

Barbara tilted her head downward and stared at the floor. "I became anxious and began to realize that, if Jan died (Barbara and Helena quickly crossed themselves) he would go to hell." Helena gasped.

"Ma, do you think it is too late to ride over to see Steve?"

"No, go now!"

Barbara said she would stay behind while they went to see Steve. Szymon and Roman left to saddle old Black, and within minutes Szymon was at Stephen's door. When Steve opened the door, he was shocked to see his brother. "What is wrong?

"Nothing, Steve." Stephan was slack-jawed. Tekla came to see who had knocked so late in the evening. "Well, will you, do it?" asked Szymon after he repeated to Tekla what he had asked Stephan. Once they got over the shock, Steve and Tekla agreed to be godparents for Jan.

"I'm going to ask Michael to be best man, and Barbara will ask Anna to be witness."

The following morning, Szymon arose early and made a pot of coffee. Barbara had brought Szymon's jacket and good pants. She told Szymon that she would dress in a hurry after she ate and bathed. They reached Saint Mary's Church about nine o'clock that morning. Father Thomas was just leaving the building when Szymon finished tying the horse and cart to the railing outside the church. Szymon took Barbara into the church and returned to speak privately with Father Thomas. "What brings you to Bukaczowce? Are your parents ill?"

"Father, would you marry Barbara and me and baptize my son?"

"Why did you come all this way back to Bukaczowce to marry and baptize your son?"

Szymon spoke haltingly, explaining briefly what happened over the last two years, and that Barbara had become sick with worry about Jan when he was seriously ill and taking too long to get well. "We were afraid he would go to Hell, if he died because he wasn't baptized." He went on to say that he always wanted his wife to go to church with him, and that before Resurrection Day Barbara had agreed to join the Greek Catholic Church. "We were going to come months ago, but the baby fell ill during Lent. You're my favorite priest and I want my family to be around us for these ceremonies. While Szymon spoke, Father nodded slowly.

After Father agreed to marry them, Szymon joined Barbara, and took her hand. "That was one of the hardest things I've ever done, but I think everything will be alright."

She squeezed his hand in return. "Thank you."

It was a wonderful weekend. Stephen, Tekla and Szymon's mother and father rode together to the church. Uncle Max and Aunt Katarzyna came. During the ceremonies late that Saturday afternoon, Szymon and Barbara both had tears in their eyes. Barbara lost her self-consciousness over being eight months pregnant and by the end of the service she was smiling as she brushed away her tears. Even Father Thomas couldn't suppress a wisp of a smile. Joe Korlaszcz, his brother, Michael and Szymon's sister

Anna were all smiling, as well, and joined them at Szymon's parents' house for the refreshments Aunt Katarzyna had prepared for the occasion.

Alas, their joy was short-lived. After returning to Lwow early in May, their second child, Eustachius, was born on May 8, 1897. He survived only one day. The baby was badly deformed. His hands and feet were not fully developed, and he had severe respiratory problems. He died quietly in his sleep on May 9, 1897.

Barbara was devastated and exhausted from all the emotions she had spent over many months. She took solace in knowing that Eustachius had been baptized and believed with all her heart that he was in heaven. After his death, she and Szymon began attending church services regularly and decided to speak to Father Bohdan. The priest was young and charming. When Barbara began crying while telling about Eustachius' death, Father Bohdan seemed genuinely moved. He reached out, took her hand, and held it, until she finished and composed herself. He told Szymon that he knew he was trying to do what was best for his family. Then he blessed them. The weight of the world seemed to lift from their shoulders as they walked out the doors of the church, for they had found the needed strength to begin the next chapter of their lives anew.

Barbara became quieter following Eustachius' death. She knew she could face adversities so didn't feel as vulnerable as she once had. She didn't break down in tears about life around them, knowing that everyone suffered troubles at some point in their lifetime. All around them was the wreckage of once young, strong, happy-go-lucky, hopeful lives. Often tragedy struck long before one reached young adulthood. After living through her own recent tragedy, she could look empathetically upon those around her who carried the scars of illness, injury, or disability. She saw people with no legs or arms sitting in the market square or on the steps of the churches, hat in hand begging for money. Families more than likely cared for their sick or elderly parents, aunts, uncles, even grandparents, while raising their own children. Life was hard.

It had been foolish, considering all the evidence around them, not to realize that beyond the bliss of falling in love and selfishly grabbing every moment for themselves, the challenges of life were silently waiting for them.

In spite of so much personal tragedy, Lwow was thriving as more and more people crowded into the city looking for opportunities. Lwow was growing and experiencing a building boom the likes of which no one had ever seen. Every center city lot was built upon. Old buildings were razed to make way for the new. Gazeta Lwowska carried articles about plans for residential housing and an opera house soon to be built. Szymon visited the office of the project manager to view the model displayed in the lobby. He sought out someone who could tell him where to inquire about a job. Szymon was disappointed to learn that all the skilled craftsmen would be brought in to work on the opera house and ordinary laborer jobs would pay no more than what he already was making. He was disheartened that he had been unable to secure a better paying job, perhaps as an apprentice brick layer. Construction companies in the Lwow area tightly controlled labor costs by bringing in skilled craftsmen from as far away as Vienna or Prague to whom they paid even lower wages than other cities in the region. A master bricklayer received, on average, half the wages paid to his counterpart in Krakow. And the common laborer was paid approximately forty percent of the master bricklayer's pay. What is more, it would be very difficult for a Ruthenian in Lwow to find an apprenticeship for a brick layer, let alone a position as a master brick layer. Nowhere in Galicia were decent wages paid to either skilled or unskilled workers. In all of Europe, no city paid its workers less than Lwow.

These were the facts of life in Polish controlled Galicia. How could Szymon have known these facts? Decades of living under Polish rule, within the Austro-Hungarian Empire, had created bitter resentment among the Ruthenian people. They were oppressed, and the impossibility of finding a better job, even in the construction industry which paid better wages than other fields during bad times, perpetuated their anger and resentment. This was the Lwow that Szymon found himself in 1897 and he wanted desperately to do something to improve his economic situation, and to create hope for his children's future.

He attended Ruthenian council meetings and spent most of his free time pouring over the newspapers and reading materials in the reading rooms. Unrest was barely suppressed, so it didn't take much to provoke violent reactions to perceived slights. Ruthenian Council meetings promoted the notion of equality in government and more representation on planning boards which approved projects in the districts. Although highly unlikely, he held out hope that wage floors and hiring quotas could be written into contracts.

Whenever notice of new construction was posted, Szymon raced to the project manager's office to learn what jobs were available and what wages would be paid. He had done this for months, from spring until almost winter of 1897, but nothing promising had materialized. Szymon was terribly disappointed. Little or no progress was reported from the two or three evening meetings he attended each month. Szymon became angry, and worse, he stayed out after the meetings to drink with other men who were equally unhappy with their lot in life.

At times, Szymon moved around in a half drunken daze. Not completely sober from the night before, he often walked to work before daylight trying to sober up. Barbara understood, but that didn't improve matters for them at home.

During one particular Ruthenian Council meeting in late in 1897, several grievances were aired early in the meeting. Small gangs of Polish rowdies were harassing older youth in the Hatymaska District where several Ruthenian families lived. During a fight, a Ruthenian boy of about fifteen had been hit with a club on the back of his head. He was severely injured and in a coma. The authorities did not punish the Polish boys; instead, they went house to house warning Ruthenian parents to keep their teenage children under control. Gazeta Lwowska published an article which seemed to get the facts wrong (or maybe not), blaming the Ruthenian boys for provoking the incident. This article sparked more unrest even though Ruthenian and Polish teenagers often harassed each other. A turning point came when the Ruthenian boy who had been clubbed over the head died.

The Greek Catholic churches did nothing to calm frayed nerves. An emergency meeting of the Ruthenian Council was announced. Nothing went right from the start of the meeting. Rowdies showed up and stood near the church while inside the meeting hall next door, men called for retribution. Many had been drinking, making it nearly impossible to maintain order. Suddenly the door of the meeting hall burst open and dozens of club carrying men pushed in, overturning tables and chairs, beating, punching, biting and kicking meeting goers, and scattering or destroying papers, pamphlets, and records. The melee ended abruptly when the troublemakers ran from the hall. Later that night a fire destroyed the building.

Throughout the city Ruthenians were stunned. Grim faced men showed up to work on building sites all over Lwow the next day. Men could not look each other in the eye. An eerie quiet hung-over Old Town.

Ruthenians knew better than to start trouble because their jobs would be lost if they rose up to confront the Polish authorities over the incident. So, temporarily, they quietly plugged along trying to immerse themselves in their families, churches, and fraternal organizations. There was more than the usual drunkenness as grown men faced the reality that they were powerless. For the first time, Szymon lost hope, quietly accepting low wages,

On the Sunday morning following the boy's death the Greek Catholic churches were full as clergy attempted to find words to comfort the disconsolate. Throngs lined the streets of Old Town on the day of the funeral as many hundreds more walked behind the casket to the cemetery and all the clergy gathered at the gravesite. Prominent among the mourners was Ruthenian Hatymaska District Council Member, Theodorus Kulyk, who sat with bereaved family members. When he rose to eulogize the boy, his voice soared above the crowd. His words lifted spirits and when he took Mrs. Mroz's arm to lead her to the open grave, tears flowed from the eyes of even the most hardened men.

A leader was born. Word spread and dozens of new faces showed up at the Ruthenian Council meeting. The next election to replace a Haidamatska district member was announced, and for the very first time several Ruthenian men threw their hats in the ring without being coaxed. The election date had been scheduled in advance and the leadership in the district didn't have enough time to rally the Polish community to turn out for the election. After counting the votes, it was announced that a second Ruthenian, Paulus Svajko had won by fifteen votes.

Lwow was mired in a cold January. No snow, just cold. Szymon was out of work, so money was scarce, and there wasn't enough snow to make extra money clearing sidewalks or running errands for people. They didn't have much to spend on St. Nicholas Day gifts, but Barbara knitted a hat, gloves, and matching scarf for Jan, who would turn three years old in June. Szymon built a little sled for him and painted it bright red. But Barbara and Szymon could not afford gifts for each other. In February, it turned even colder. The small kerosene heater in the apartment didn't keep the bedrooms warm. So they moved the beds into the living room and kitchen, kept the bedroom doors shut, and heated only two rooms,

Szymon began looking for any small jobs he could find. They spoke to Father Bogdan about getting charity milk for Jan. And, as if it couldn't get any worse, their landlord told them they would have to move by the end of March. He had sold his building to a developer who planned to build several new residential buildings in the neighborhood. Szymon cringed because he couldn't afford to rent an apartment in a building with modern conveniences. He had to do something immediately. The next morning, Szymon left early and went to the building site where he had worked until three months ago. No one was around, so he walked to the building site where he worked until late the prior year. Again, no one was around, and it was obvious that no jobs would be available until the weather warmed. He looked up Zamarstynowska Street, saw the gates of the Kaserne, and walked into the garrison to Commander Schwartzdorf's office. He greeted Szymon warmly and Szymon got down to what he wanted, asking him if he knew about any progress on the construction schedule for the new Kaserne. "Are you working now, Szymon?"

"No, sir, work has been very slow, and I have to get a job right away, as we are running out of money."

"Szymon, if you don't find something today, come back and I'll speak to the construction boss." Szymon left feeling more hopeful than when he arrived.

The next morning, Szymon was at Commander Schwartzdorf's door. "Not much construction is going on, sir." Schwartzdorf wrote something on note paper, handed him the folded note, and gave him directions to a construction manager's office in town. Szymon also carried the reference letter his Uncle Max had given him. The project manager read the note and the reference letter. Then, he raised his head and peered at Szymon over his glasses. "Have you done demolition and salvage work here in Lwow."

"Yes, sir." Szymon wrote the name of Petrus Damyan and handed the paper to the project boss.

"Can you begin work in the morning? We are tearing down three buildings in Old Town."

Szymon stood upright, composing himself. "I can do any job that requires demolition and salvaging materials, and a whole lot more."

Arriving home after reporting to the crew chief on the demolition site, Szymon skipped up the steps, picked up Barbara, and danced around the apartment with her in his arms. "I'll have to behave myself on this job. I think I answered the last remaining job opening left in Lwow."

Szymon reported to the demolition site the following day joining a crew of three men. The building was a dilapidated factory warehouse that was falling down. In addition to the warehouse, there were two other demolition projects. One was a church with adjoining buildings which had once served as a small charity hospital and school for children. The last site, located in the Haidamatska District, was smaller. On it stood a stone building from the early 1800s. It had once served as an orphanage, and more recently as a jail.

Neither Szymon nor Barbara wanted to move out of their neighborhood. Ruthenians lived there and they hoped to remain in the Paraskevia Church. So, each night after work, Szymon also visited an apartment owner or manager he had learned of during the day by word of mouth. Szymon had begun to worry a week earlier and had gone to visit Father Bogdan. That night at supper, he and Barbara discussed what they would do if nothing materialized. Barbara suggested that Szymon talk to Father, but he doubted that any good would come of approaching him again. Since there was nothing else on the horizon, Szymon walked through the big doors of St. Paraskevia

Church. Scattered throughout the sanctuary were a few people reciting the rosary and praying, so Szymon sat down near the back of the church. He briefly nodded off, awakening with a start when he heard a man's voice beside him. "Are you alright, Szymon?"

He was momentarily uncertain of his whereabouts, until he realized it was Father Bogdan who had spoken. "Father, we need to locate an apartment because we have to move next week.

"I'm sure you must be worried, Szymon."

He explained to the priest that he and Barbara wanted to stay in the neighborhood because it was close to the church and his work. Father reassured him, saying that he might be able to help.

Returning home that evening, Szymon was surprised to find Joe Korlaszcz chatting with Barbara. Barbara had told Joe about the difficulty Szymon was having locating a nearby apartment. She was embarrassed because she didn't have anything to offer Joe for supper. Aware of their circumstances, Joe said he wasn't hungry. While Szymon ate, Joe talked about what he was experiencing. "The Polish people are having difficulty paying for rent, too."

Joe gave Szymon leads on two vacant apartments. Fortunately, the rent was almost the same as he presently paid. One of the apartments was a small, second story, four-room flat, over a corner grocery store, almost the same distance to Szymon's current job, so on April first, 1899, Szymon rounded up three men and within two hours they had moved—for the fourth time in three years.

Barbara and Szymon soon learned to love the little neighborhood where they now lived. Martyniak Street was only one block long and dead ended into a wooded field belonging to the military garrison. No one knew why the property was vacant, but Barbara didn't ask questions. She liked to play with Jan who was an active, healthy toddler. She often walked, holding Jan's hand, to the edge of the property which was like a small wooded park. Sometimes, Jan would sit high upon Szymon's shoulders as the family strolled along the city streets before ducking into this secluded refuge to enjoy the sandwiches and drinks they had brought. Jan was a talkative, curious, little boy who asked question after question. This peaceful interlude, in their oftentimes frenetic life, allowed Barbara to regain her strength and good nature. They didn't have much money now, but neither she nor Szymon seemed to worry about their financial straits. The winter passed and the days lengthened, as spring melded into a perfectly lovely summer. The young couple asked for nothing except to live a healthy, normal life free from sickness and death—at least for a little while.

During the week, while Szymon worked, Barbara and her friend, Maria Marcin, fabricated colorfully patterned vests. Maria showed her how to sketch designs and demonstrated the various methods for applying appliques or beads. Maria showed her pictures of shirts with beautiful designs comprising

Ruthenian symbols of birds and foliage, embroidered on the sleeves, cuffs, collars, and fronts. Within three months, she had learned enough to design patterns herself. Maria was encouraging and told Barbara that her handiwork was excellent and suggested that she sell her scarves, vests and shirts at the Thursday markets. Barbara smiled shyly and told Maria that her work did not measure up to the fine quality of Maria's designs. "Dear, you will make beautiful pieces, better than mine, in no time. All you need is practice, and practice will make you self-confident."

One day, as they sat on a blanket in the park watching Jan drop small pebbles onto a growing pile, she inquired, "Szymon, do we have enough money to go to a Ruthenian dance? He glanced at her curiously, but before he could respond she continued, "I want to see the authentic Ruthenian costumes the dancers wear.

Szymon always seemed to know what was going on socially in the Ruthenian community. That weekend, on a warm, late summer, Saturday afternoon, they visited the Ruthenian Community Hall. A five-piece band played authentic Ruthenian music on genuine Ruthenian instruments. There was cheap beer and a covered-dish dinner. Barbara brought a pot of her home-made noodles and gravy. As she ate, Babara compared her shirt with the other ladies' costumes. As usual, families sat at long tables intermingling with other families. The lady sitting next to Barbara, Olena, wore an elaborate, but worn, traditional costume. Her husband, Hryc, introduced himself.

Barbara expressed her interest in their costumes. It turned out that Olena and Hryc were celebrating their wedding anniversary of twenty-five years, and their costumes had been wedding gifts from a wealthy relative. Barbara closely examined the shirt and matching dress. Both were blue linen with exquisite, mostly grey, silk embroidery accented by touches of red, yellow and ochre. The couple wore matching red bandanas, and finished off their outfits with old, but impeccably polished, black boots.

"Thank you for letting me examine your clothing."

The couple was used to people admiring the colorful, intricate designs on their shirts and went on to explain that they hadn't worn the costumes for a few years, but had dressed up to celebrate their anniversary.

The musicians began to tune their instruments when Hryc excused himself and briskly walked to the small platform at the front of the hall. Barbara and Szymon glanced at each other. They hadn't suspected that he was a musician with the band. Olena smiled at the younger couple. "Oh, my husband plays the bandura."

The afternoon turned out to be a lot of fun. When the band took breaks from playing, Barbara and Szymon chatted with the other couple. They learned that Szymon and Hryc both loved music. In addition to playing the harmonica and Jewish harp, Szymon played string instruments – the mandolin and tambura too. And both men drank a few more beers than they should have. By the end of the dance, the two couples felt as if they had known each other for years rather than hours. So, when Hryc suggested they visit their apartment in a week or so, Szymon and Barbara readily agreed to a Saturday evening after the first of the month.

On Thursday, the following week, Barbara went to the fair, excited to tell her friend, Maria Marcin, about meeting Olena and her beautiful Vyshevenka. Maria invited her to come to her apartment the next morning to examine two garments. "Did you embroider them yourself?"

"They belonged to my mother-in-law and are of exquisite quality."

Barbara was excited the next morning as she pushed the stroller along Martyniak Street to Maria's apartment. She was anxious to see the garments Maria mentioned, and the thought of making such beautiful shirts to sell at the fair lifted her spirits even higher.

Maria had everything ready for her. She carefully uncovered each box, unfolding the white paper wrapped around the shirts and skirts. She carefully laid out the first shirt which was a slightly yellowed white. Maria described how she would use a cloth with lemon water to dampen the fabric around each embroidery pattern and lay the garment out in full afternoon sun to bleach the yellow out of the linen. The blouses were exquisitely embroidered with a black and white motif. A dress of royal blue was embroidered with mostly gray on a red and gray woven motif. Additionally, Maria had several skirts and vests embroidered with traditional red and black Ruthenian symbols. All the pieces had been immaculately kept. Barbara inquired about caring for the garments.

"Always wear undergarments so body oils don't stain them. And when I wash them, I hang them in full sun to dry."

"Do you sew your own?"

"If I find a wonderful bargain, I'll buy one or two ready-made; otherwise, I make my own."

"Do you own a sewing machine?"

Maria let out an exaggerated laugh. "No, but I wish I did," Maria told Barbara that she would explain some of the traditional meanings in the embroidery as they went along, and before she left Maria's apartment, they agreed to meet the following Tuesday, and going forward, whenever they could arrange time to work together.

Barbara was anxious to begin her project in earnest, with a goal to earn some money to help provide a few extras for her family. On fair day, she put Jan in his stroller and hurried to see what bargains she could find. But at Rynoc Square she found nothing affordable, so she walked to Haidamatska Square and dug through a pile of old, used clothing. She was ready to give up when she came across a gray, traditional, linen shirt with some worn embroidery on the cuffs and collar. The shirt was no more than a few cents, so she thought she would buy it if only to practice embroidering. She could see the potential of making a finished product by turning the cuffs and collar. The shirt was a larger size than most ladies wore, so she would have extra material to use for linings, if needed. At the bottom of the pile of worn clothing she found a badly stained shirt with some lovely buttons that she could cut from the garment to reuse on another. Altogether her purchases cost a fraction of what she would have had to spend for one used, plain, linen shirt in good condition. She had to start somewhere.

Before leaving the Square, she shopped at a large food market for some fresh onions and turnips, and ended her shopping spree by stopping at the street-level grocery shop under their apartment, where she bought a bag of neck bones.

One-day Joe visited, and when he came up the stairs to the apartment over the grocery store, he found the door cracked open. He poked his head in and found the two friends, their heads bent together over the kitchen table. They were deeply engrossed in something and he heard them speaking in low voices. The older woman seemed to be instructing Barbara. Joe tip-toed into the apartment behind them, and then in a quiet voice he whispered, "Boo!" Once he saw the women had recovered from being startled, he curled up his face and began to laugh. Soon, all three of them were laughing uncontrollably.

"Joe, you have a wicked streak in you!"

"Do you think it will keep me out of heaven?" he

asked crossing his eyes and causing them to break into laughter again.

Barbara and Maria stopped working on their project for the day and Barbara made a pot of tea. Jan came into the kitchen rubbing his eyes. "Mama, what's wrong?" Once again they began laughing. It was close to 5 o'clock when they heard the sound of Szymon's heavy boots on the stairs. Jan played horsey, riding on his father's leg, while Joe and Barbara talked over each other. Maria quietly gathered her embroidery as Barbara served tea. It was a simple homey scene.

Chapter 20

In the late in fall of 1898, the air had taken on the smells of autumn when Barbara suspected that she was pregnant again. She vowed this time she would try to remain calm by not letting life get the best of her or cause her stress. Szymon's work was steady, and he had done some snooping for opportunities to make extra money to help tie them over the long winter months. There was not much more he could do other than to watch their spending.

During the summer months, he had slacked off from attending Ruthenian Council meetings, but after reading an announcement for the next scheduled meeting in Gazeta Lwowska he decided to attend. Before he left to attend the meeting, which was being held in a small building behind the Paraskevia Church, Barbara spoke up and asked him to please try to stay away from trouble. That was easier said than done. An issue could be brought up at almost any meeting which might cause uncontrollable outrage among Ruthenian men – and there were always bona fide issues in Lwow in 1898. It was announced that during this particular meeting, the men would be preparing a list of demands, stemming mostly from unresolved requests and grievances, to be presented at the November 22nd meeting of the Supreme Ruthenian Council. However, when Szymon arrived early on the evening of the meeting, no one was at the church and no men were gathered outside next to the hall. Szymon heard horses approaching, so he quickly slipped around to the rear of the building. Not knowing who was approaching, he didn't want to be seen alone. A few men rode up on horseback, dismounted, and ran into the building. He heard pistol shots ring out, saw the men run from the building, mount their horses, and ride away. He was stunned and bewildered by the sudden violence. Cautiously, he went around to the side of the building and located a window. It was dark and there appeared to be no movement inside the room. Szymon listened for sounds, but it was eerily quiet. He decided to leave immediately. He lived close by the church and had walked to the meeting, so he was confident that no one had witnessed his arrival. Turning toward his apartment building, he tried to reason why no one was at the hall. He feared that tonight it wasn't safe to walk the streets of the neighborhood. Glancing behind him several times as he walked the empty streets, he imagined there were people hiding in doorways or alleys who would pop out unexpectedly to attack or rob him. He feared not knowing what was going on, but had no choice except to keep walking, telling himself to hurry because it was unsafe on the streets. By the time he arrived at the apartment, his heart was pounding.

One thing was certain, he would not tell Barbara, but what excuse would he give for being home early? Naturally, Barbara was curious about his early return home. He decided to tell her that he hadn't felt well, so he sat on the grass in from of the church for a while and then came home before reaching the meeting hall.

Exhausted, realizing he was beginning to despair, he sat at the table and poured himself a drink. He had been slow to understand that it wouldn't matter if Ruthenian wages rose. The major problem was that Ruthenians were repressed and nothing would ever be right as long as they were powerless, but he wasn't certain about what it would take to bring about real change. Without a catalyst, nothing would ever change. Unfortunately, people would have to suffer a lot more pain.

It took days for unrest to settle down. Fortunately, no one had been killed in the bizarre incident, but the meeting hall had been vandalized and bullet holes were found in walls and posters hanging on the wall. Szymon felt foolish because people regarded the vandalism more like a prank than a serious crime. However, things had gotten out of hand between the factions, so he thought it just as well that he had missed the meeting. He learned the meeting had been cancelled to enable members to attend the Haidamastka District meeting instead. A seat had opened due to the retirement of one elderly, long-time member. The meeting had become contentious until, in an effort to calm tensions, the president called for a vote to adjourn early and reschedule the meeting.

Szymon remained convinced that nothing would ever change until the Ruthenian situation got much worse. He didn't tell anyone about seeing the men enter the meeting hall and hearing the shots ring out. Since he hadn't recognized the men, he tried to put the bizarre incident behind him, which was easier said than done. He had nightmares for weeks reliving the incident and knowing he had managed to escape being drawn into reciprocal gang warfare.

Barbara was so involved with her project that she didn't notice how despondent Szymon had become. He drank openly. It was common when visiting the home of a Ruthenian or Polish family to see a bottle of vodka sitting on the table. Liquor was cheap and men turned to booze to numb themselves against their miserable, hopeless circumstances. Once the reality of economic and political circumstances sunk in, Szymon decided it was enough that he was able to work six and a half days a week. He didn't see how Barbara could make enough selling shirts to make a difference in their household income; he was also ashamed that he couldn't provide for more than just the barest necessities of life. Furthermore, he didn't want her to work, but knew he couldn't change her mind.

Vlad stopped by one evening and Szymon repeated the invitation for Hryc and his wife to visit their apartment the following Sunday afternoon. Olena brought her Vyshevenka. While Hryc and Szymon sat at the kitchen table talking and drinking, the two ladies took Olena's outfit into the living room. Sunlight shined through the small window directly onto Olena as she removed the white paper from the shirt and showed Barbara damage on the cuffs of the sleeves. Examining the dress, however, Barbara found it to be in perfect condition. Olena asked Barbara what could be done to repair the cuffs. "Let's take the dress and blouse into the bedroom where you can put them on." While Olena was changing, Barbara showed her the unfinished Vyshevenka she was making. Olena was enchanted by the beautiful embroidery on the cuffs and collar." "Please try it on."

"It's lovely." Barbara could not believe her ears. Olena wanted to buy the Vyshevenka, in addition to wanting Barbara to mend the frayed cuffs and collar on her shirt. Barbara's spirits soared. She couldn't believe that she would make two and a half dollars for the shirt and fifty cents for the mending.

When Vlad and Olena left that evening, Barbara excitedly told Szymon what had happened. Szymon smiled at her and quietly pulled her onto his lap. "I love you," he murmured as he fondled her breast and smoothed her hair.

"Come, Szymon, look at my blouse." She led him to the bedroom where the two shirts hung.

After she showed him her handiwork, he pulled her toward him, picked her up, and laid her on their bed. "Do you still love me?"

"What do you think?"

The next morning, Szymon sat drinking a glass of vodka while Barbara prepared their breakfast. She was beginning to show that she was several months pregnant. She's a good wife he thought. He liked her grit and determination and her willingness to find ways to get along in a marriage which was at the mercy of sudden, unforeseen hardship. Be it sickness, death, financial woes, or whatever misfortune came their way, she proved over and over again that she was in it for the long haul. He liked her quiet demeanor and her patience but, she also was a pretty woman who liked to put on a nice dress and a little rouge on her cheeks to go to church or to a dance. He was proud of her. She interrupted his thoughts. "Szymon, I think I am four and a half months pregnant." Despite all their challenges, they were both happy to be having another child. She loved Szymon and he loved her. They knew that their devotion to each other was the glue that held them together.

They had managed to find an inexpensive toy tow truck for Jan and Szymon made a little garage for him to park it in. He painted the truck red and black and the garage brown. Szymon's job appeared to be as secure as anyone could expect. After he finished with the demolition and salvage project, the owner, Damian Sawchuk, hired him on full time as a laborer at a slightly higher rate of pay. And, surprisingly, Barbara had managed to sell her shirt to Olena and began taking a few items to the Rynoc Fair two or three times each month, setting up a table near Maria

Marcin's. Maria said it was good business. Barbara made a few cents, and although it wasn't much, whenever she sold an item, she was thrilled to add the proceeds to the other coins had placed in a covered jar tucked away in back of her vanity drawer.

While eating supper one evening, Barbara reminded Szymon that they had been living in Lwow for more than four years. He looked up from his plate. "Yes, I was thinking about that a week ago." Their lives had settled once again into a predictable routine. They reminisced about the past four years, both the good and bad fortunes that had befallen them.

"Are you happy, Szymon?"

"Why would you ask?"

A wry smile crossed her face. "Well, you know how I worry."

"Barbara, what can we do about this now? Do you think I would go anywhere else?"

"That's not what I asked, Szymon." He was silent. He admitted that he wished that life could be better, but he didn't blame her for their misfortune.

"Lately, it's been more good than bad."

"We shouldn't speak about things like that. It's bad luck. You don't want to jinx things when they are going along in the right direction."

Szymon slapped the table and shrugged. "Just like a woman. Why did you bring it up?"

They hadn't had any extra money to spend for

many months. Barbara worried about how they would pay for their new baby. They were sitting quietly when there was a knock at the door. Szymon answered and returned with an older woman. "Are you the young woman who embroiders shirts?" Szymon and Barbara looked at one another.

"Yes, can I help you?" The woman told Barbara that she had been recommended by her sister who had examined her shirts, skirts, and vests at the fair the previous day. Barbara's expression changed. "Oh, yes," Barbara showed the old woman two garments that she was working on currently. The woman was impressed and asked if she could make a pure white Vyshevenka skirt and vest. "When do you need them?"

"By Easter."

It was Lent and people were living quiet, reflective lives. The older woman told Barbara that her sister would marry after Easter, so there was plenty of time to get the materials together. They agreed to meet at the fair the following week to make a firm decision about the garments.

Barbara was standing at the door the next day, as Szymon climbed the stairs followed by Joe Korlaszcz. They hadn't seen Joe for several months and were surprised when he told Szymon that his time at the seminary was almost finished. "What's the next step, Joe?"

"Maybe another year or two."

Barbara was the next to speak, "Will you stay here?"

"I hope so."

Szymon could tell by Joe's demeanor that he wasn't telling the whole story. "It sounds like we might have to go to Lake Minorek and throw pebbles into the water."

Barbara looked puzzled, but had the good sense not to ask any questions, and the subject was dropped. "Well, since we can't go to Lake Minorek, let's take a walk to our own private park."

The friends gathered up Jan, some drinks and a blanket and walked to the edge of the wooded property belonging to the garrison. Szymon and Joe left Barbara for a while to walk through the woods. As they walked and talked, Szymon suddenly remembered Joe's health problem. 'Joe, you haven't mentioned your heart recently."

Joe lowered his head. "I'm having palpitations, but try to overlook them."

"Do you have a doctor you can ask about what you are doing that might cause the palpitations?"

"I go to a doctor who is a member of my parish, but he only says to avoid stress."

"Are the palpitations getting worse?"

"No, they're about the same. The two friends were silent for a minute or two. "I'm not worried, Szymon. It's in God's hands."

The next day at the fair, Barbara was on the search for used clothing. She had found two shirts in excellent condition, but neither was white. She gave up and walked back to the Haidamastka Square where she found several tables and stalls selling used clothing, but nothing suitable for her needs. Then, a thought occurred to her: all men wore white linen shirts. So, she decided to check for new clothing.

She didn't know why she hadn't thought about that earlier, as she could have saved herself time. White linen shirts were readily available, and many were of good quality for a fair price. She thought again about how much fabric she would require. She became confused and a bit concerned that if she misjudged how much fabric she needed for the complete outfit, she might squander all the money she had tucked away. She decided to wait and return to the fair again next week. That turned out to be a wise move because the old woman came to the Haidamatska Fair the following week and sheepishly told Barbara that she couldn't afford to have the clothes made. The entire situation upset her. Barbara felt sorry for the older woman, who she thought must have been very poor. It was a sobering experience, but the next day her spirits brightened again when she realized that she would have been able to sell the garments and undoubtedly recoup all her investment.

When she next visited Maria Marcin to work on her project, she told her about the older woman's dilemma. Maria said she had faced the same situations when she began embroidering and sewing items for sale. "Today, if I am asked to make a garment that is expensive, I ask the person to give me a down payment. I have lost customers, but once your reputation is established, you will almost always find people willing to put a deposit down on your sewing." Barbara was grateful to have a friend such as Maria. She appreciated her advice and found herself depending on Maria to help her make decisions on materials, embroidery thread, and designs. She even brought one vyshevenka to seek Maria's advice about cutting down a used, oversized shirt to make one for a much smaller woman.

It could be unpleasant to rummage through old, dirty clothing, rip the threads to separate the pieces of the garment, remove collars and cuffs to turn them, pull out the old embroidery threads and sew the whole thing back together in the appropriate size. Then she had to wash, starch, and iron the partially finished shirt before beginning the embroidery. Nevertheless, Barbara tried to overlook the unpleasantness and to find gratification when a completed garment was as perfect a vyshevenka as she could design.

Szymon began to socialize with friends from work, going to the bars on Friday nights and Saturday afternoons. Barbara had decided that it was not healthy for her to go to dances or to drink alcohol. She somehow linked attending the dance and alcohol with the death of Eustachius, and overlooked her fall just prior to his birth. She wanted to remove herself from stressful situations as much as possible and to rest. Szymon accepted her wishes without argument. He controlled his alcohol consumption, at first, but as in the past, his ability to maintain self-control melted away, if an afternoon of drunken revelry with his friends presented itself. Barbara understood what was happening, but she ignored it, feeling she'd be better able to confront Szymon after the baby was born. And, at this point in time, Szymon didn't care about what Barbara thought. He was having too much fun.

Once again, Szymon began attending political meetings with his friends.

Late one Saturday night Barbara was awakened by a loud commotion. She heard the sounds of breaking glass followed by excited voices coming from the street outside the grocery store. Since the apartment was located on a well-lit intersection, she peeked through the curtains to see what was happening. There were more than a dozen men on the street and sidewalk. Shots rang out and the men raced away from the scene. About twenty minutes later, Barbara heard a noise coming from the back porch. Szymon hurried up the stairs and unlocked the apartment door. Everything was a blur. It all happened so fast.

"Don't tell them I'm here," he whispered. Barbara's heart jumped into her mouth. "There were fights between Rusyns and Poles tonight, and a man was killed." Szymon squatted near the window, watching the streets below. "Barbara, go in the bedroom, close the door, and stay there. Don't turn on lights. Try to keep Jan quiet. Do as I say." She knew by the look on his face, that there was serious trouble. Szymon was deadly earnest. "Don't worry, I'll tell you all about it in the morning."

Barbara didn't get much rest that night, falling asleep sometime before dawn. Szymon remained in the living room all night. Fortunately, no one came to the apartment in the middle of the night. It must have been nine in the morning before she heard Jan whimpering. Barbara was upset with herself for neglecting him. He came to her bedroom and stood at the side of her bed crying. "Mama, get up." She awakened confused and felt the bed beside her. Realizing he wasn't in bed, she remembered the incident of the previous night. She picked up Jan, tucked him under the covers with her, and snuggled with him. He loved to sleep with his mother and Barbara wondered what he would do when he had a little brother or sister. As usual, Jan asked dozens of questions, never waiting for an answer to any of them. Unable to resist the charms of her beautiful, blonde, curly-headed, blue eyed little boy, she chattered away with him, never getting enough of her loveable son.

On Sunday, Barbara awakened Szymon early in the morning. "Church will do Szymon a lot of good," she thought. Jan discovering his father asleep on the couch in the living room ran to the kitchen and tugged on her apron. "Mama what's wrong with Papa?" Just then, Szymon walked into the kitchen. He picked up Jan, put him in his chair, placed a cup of milk in front of him, and was just about to pour himself a cup coffee when a knock was heard at the door. A man stood in the hallway. He and Szymon walked down the stairs together and after a brief conversation, Szymon returned to take his seat at the table. "What is going on, Szymon? That was someone from the police."

I don't want to tell you anything because you are going to worry."

"I'll worry anyway. What is going on?"

He explained that the Ruthenian men had gathered at the meeting hall in back of the Paraskevia Church, to plan ways they could defend themselves against beatings. "Our young boys have to fight every week. It doesn't matter if we tell the police; they do nothing to stop the Poles."

That Sunday, as they left church, he saw men running toward the small building behind the church. Barbara tugged on his sleeve to discourage him from joining them. Just like in the past, the incidents between Ruthenian and Polish factions continued. Not only were there beatings, but it now was common to find property vandalized. When the window was broken at the grocery store, several months ago, Szymon helped the owner repair it. Only two weeks later, the window was broken again. The store was vandalized a third time. Rotten garbage was strewn throughout. Food items were removed from the ice boxes and thrown around. The severity of injuries, as well as, the dollar value of property damage escalated.

A week later, the Ruthenian men attended a Haidamatska District meeting. The President of the Council announced at the beginning of the meeting that order would be maintained and anyone becoming loud or unruly would be escorted outside. Several members of the public spoke early in the meeting describing the plight they faced and the effects on their children. District Council Member Theodorus Kulyk rose to speak. Not only did Kulyk speak, but he showed the Council members a hand printed sign which read, 'Filthy Ruskey's Get Out.' Although there was snickering among those who attended the meeting that night, the council appeared to take it seriously.

Mr. Kulyk told the district members that the Ruthenians were not starting trouble, but they weren't getting any relief from the police who ignored their reports of vandalism and property damage caused by gangs of mostly young, Polish men. "It seems there isn't much we can do except fight fire with fire, and we don't want to do that. Quiet prevailed. Szymon thought that he could hear a pin drop. The President of the District Council seemed concerned and promised that something would be done to stop the harassment and vandalism. However, not even a week later, more fights broke out and many properties were damaged.

When the news got around that garbage was dumped in front of two Greek Churches and inside on several pews, the Ruthenians poured into the streets. Crowds of people walked down Zamarstynowska Street singing Ruthenian songs about overcoming adversity and triumphing over enemies with the help of God.

Everyone knew the Ruthenians had had enough. As

strange as it felt, an uneasy truce hung over Old Town. For the moment, the harassment and vandalism stopped. It was as if an all-powerful force hovered over the neighborhoods. Szymon reasoned that, if things carried on unabated, a line would be crossed from which there would be no return. And so, for now, cooler heads prevailed.

A series of articles appeared in Gazeta Lwowska and other newspapers. The reading rooms prominently displayed pamphlets in both the Ruthenian and Polish languages with stories about the authorities' attempts to maintain peace. Individual letters pleading for peace on the streets of Lwow, written by ordinary citizens, were published. Both sides wanted a peaceful solution to the unrest.

Open meetings were held in several parks throughout the city. One afternoon, there was a knock at the apartment door. The Haidamatska District President was visiting Ruthenians in the neighborhood. Theo Kulyk stood at the President's side. The visit was friendly. After introducing themselves, Mr. Kulyk said, I've seen you at District meetings, Szymon. The Haidamatska President and Mr. Kulyk told Szymon and Barbara that the Council was doing everything in its power to maintain peace in neighborhoods. They inquired if they knew of any recent incidents or troublemakers who were causing problems. Szymon and Barbara stated they didn't know of anything. Mr. Kulyk ended the conversation politely by saying, "Szymon, we would appreciate your help, if you see or hear of anyone starting trouble."

"Why didn't you tell them what you know, Szymon?"

"They are just snooping for information in the Ruthenian neighborhoods and we don't know what the hell Poles are telling them, so I'm not telling them a damn thing," Szymon said, frustrated.

Barbara changed the subject as soon as she sensed the frustration in his voice. "Szymon, the baby will be here soon. It's already the first of May and I feel like it's almost time. We should locate a midwife in this neighborhood. I can help pay for someone."

He stood and took her hand. "Barbara, please, don't do this. I will take care of you and our family." There was a sudden sadness in his voice and eyes, which made Barbara feel a tinge of guilt.

"Szymon, I know life is hard and I just want to help."

"No." He was firm and wouldn't back down. He felt as a man, it was his responsibility to take care of his family.

That evening, he left the apartment early. He was gone for only forty-five minutes and when he returned, he told her that he had located another job for a few days.

"Where?"

"I'm not telling you, so don't ask. Now, Barbara, I want you to locate a midwife tomorrow."

The next day, Barbara asked her landlord where the midwife lived.

Barbara and Szymon walked to the Paraskevia Church the following Sunday morning. Warm, spring weather had arrived a few weeks earlier than in previous years. Leaves covered the long, gray branches of trees in the parks, and early blooming flowers were displayed in pots in the squares. The winter had been mild, but with plenty of rain. Grass was just beginning to grow so they couldn't go to their favorite park. They had no money to spend on restaurant meals, so they decided to take a long walk after leaving the church.

The day was pleasant and they were not in a hurry. Szymon brought up Joe Korlaszcz. "We haven't heard from Joe in a while. I wonder how he is doing and if he resolved his issue?" Barbara asked what Szymon thought was on Joe's mind.

"He seemed to be a million miles away and that is unlike Joe. He mentioned to me that a doctor visited him and told him to reduce stress."

"That's the same as another doctor told him years back. Well, he doesn't bring it up, so maybe he doesn't want to tell anybody about his problem."

"He never talks about his heart palpitations anymore. I hope he is well."

"Do you think there is something wrong concerning his health?" Szymon shrugged, and they walked along quietly, each absorbed in their own thoughts about their friend. But they didn't get very far because after walking for a few more minutes, Barbara's water broke. By the time they arrived at the apartment of the midwife, Olga Stasiuk, Barbara was already having contractions. Szymon took Jan home with him and prepared their dinner. Just as they finished eating there was a knock at the door. It was Barbara and Olga Stasiuk. Mrs. Stasiuk explained to Szymon that she believed the birth would be quick so Barbara could deliver at home. "You can take Jan out for a while and we will prepare for the baby." Jan was happy to go with his Papa.

Barbara's contractions were already close, so after Szymon and Jan had gone, she showed Olga where she had put items from her two previous births, and the two ladies set about preparing for the newborn. They lined up jars with cotton, gauze, and swabs on the tops of a table and dresser. They made neat piles of clean rags, wash cloths, and towels alongside basins and pails. Olga poured buckets of water into a large pan on the stove top and lit the burner. Barbara asked Olga if she had laudanum, alcohol and other items she remembered Olena used when Eustachius was born. A sharp contraction surprised her, reminding her to tell Olga about the death of Eustachius. "Every birth is different, Barbara, don't worry."

She was right. Josephus was born at seven thirty on the night of May 8, 1899. It was the easiest birth of all her children. Just as the baby was born, Szymon walked upstairs carrying a sleeping Jan. A very happy Barbara smiled at her husband, "He's healthy."

"Another son!" Szymon was clearly delighted. When Jan awakened, he carried him into the bedroom. "Jan, say hello to your brother, Joe." Jan did not stir. Soon, the newest family member joined his brother in their small bedroom as everyone peacefully slept.

Barbara wasn't interested in what was going on in the neighborhood. It always seemed the news was bad. Evidently, people could not get along. Most folks felt like Barbara did, so stayed in their familiar groupings of family, friends, and neighbors. Jan was a sociable little boy who made friends easily and was much too young to be involved in fights. Barbara hoped that conditions would improve before he entered school and certainly before he reached his teenage years. Szymon and Barbara's friends were Ruthenians who were extended family, close neighbors, fellow church members, or others like Hryc.

So, it was like a thunderbolt out of the blue, when Szymon learned a stunning secret. Szymon was invited to join several co-workers the following Friday evening. They went to the Halychina District which had a large Ruthenian population. The men were drinking beer, throwing darts and playing cards when Hryc tapped him on the shoulder. The two men exchanged pleasantries and then, Hryc invited Szymon to join him and his friends. The crowd was talking openly about fights which had broken out the previous weekend and the brutal retribution they were planning for unsuspecting Poles. Some of it sounded so extreme that, undoubtedly, it could cause someone to be seriously injured, or even killed. He didn't like the things he heard, but didn't feel he could tell Hryc, who was a leader of this tight group of rough men, so he decided just to listen. Not only did he think that the Poles deserved to be punished, he believed they deserved the harsh punishment that the Ruthenians were about to perpetrate on them.

The scenes of the fights and beatings he had witnessed over the past year and the ghastly injuries Ruthenian men and boys had sustained - injuries so serious that many were blinded or crippled for life - haunted him. But Szymon hesitated to commit to this kind of brutality and wondered where the violence would end.

He walked home through the quiet, dark streets, stunned that Hryc was completely consumed with - even enjoying - the violence between Ruthenians and Poles. He never suspected that Hryc had such a dark side to his character. It was almost frightening, and he wondered what had happened to him to mold him into such a brute. Hryc was an ugly man with a long scar running from below his eye to his mouth. When he was drunk and fighting with the Poles, he presented a frightening figure. Hryc was aware of his disfigured face and, when he shaved in front of a mirror, he hated himself. He often wore an eye patch, but when he saw his reflection in the mirror, he knew there was nothing he could do to improve his appearance. Szymon was glad Barbara wasn't awake when he arrived home, and that she didn't stir when he slipped under the covers next to her.

News of the fighting trickled out slowly. Articles in Gazeta Lwowska described an incident which occurred over the weekend. The fighting didn't sound serious, but Szymon suspected that newspaper played down the true nature of the clash. People had become accustomed to fights almost every Saturday night, but Szymon did not talk about it. Barbara was kept in the dark until she overheard a conversation on a fair day. Two women who always came to look at Barbara's garments spoke about an incident that evidently was far more serious than any prior one. Two men were attacked outside a tavern frequented by Polish men. They were the last to leave and had begun walking home when they were jumped by several men. One of the injured men lay in a coma in the hospital; the other was blinded so couldn't provide details about the attack. Both men had been beaten with iron pipes and the blinded man's clothing had been set on fire causing severe burns to his face and hands.

At supper time that evening, Barbara mentioned what she had heard. "Do you know about this?" Szymon said that he heard about the latest attack, but didn't know the details. "Szymon, this is getting out of hand." He said nothing. "What is going to happen now?"

It didn't take long for her question to be answered. The following Friday night, there was a horrific incident.

Men came armed with clubs, iron chains, and homemade brass knuckles. People were genuinely shocked. Barbara told Szymon that she didn't want him to go out to the bars because she feared that he was going to be permanently injured if things continued spiraling out of control.

An indefinite curfew was put into effect in Old Town on Friday and Saturday nights. Although violent incidents halted, and no alcohol was served, men still crowded into the taverns. They knew that someone would have to pay.

In spite of the unrest in Old Town, Barbara continued searching for bargains on old linen clothing to remake them into handsome Vyshevenka and skirts. She and Maria met at each other's apartments, where they chatted while they worked. Although the work was slow, they could always see some small amount of progress being made.

It was October, nearing their fifth-year anniversary in Lwow. Szymon talked about moving to another city. His young family was growing, as was the cost of supporting them. He knew he was fortunate to have the job he held, and likely couldn't make better wages elsewhere – he might even be paid less. As had been true for years, they had a difficult time making ends meet. Nevertheless, their family life had settled into a comfortable routine. They had enough to eat and there was always something to do and somewhere to go. But there was also uneasiness in the air. Szymon asked Barbara if she wanted to visit his mother and father. "Yes, but we can't afford it?"

He wanted to visit his family, too. "Let me worry about that." He knew where he could get a few days' work, but the thought almost sickened him. When Barbara required a midwife for to help birth Eustachius, he had worked several nights cleaning out houses on construction sites. He could do it again, but didn't want Barbara to know. The next day he checked on the round-trip train fare to Bukaczowce and realized that children traveled free. He was certain he could make enough working three nights to pay their travel expenses.

Szymon then stopped in the Rectory at the Catholic Church to leave a message for Joe Korlaszcz. Joe hadn't visited for many months and Szymon wondered whether he had been able to resolve whatever was bothering him. Joe happened to be in the office when he arrived. The two friends embraced and Joe promised to visit on Sunday. He seemed his usual cheerful self so Szymon forgot about his friend's issue for now. Not surprisingly, Joe brought up the violence between the ethnic groups.

"It's worse than you can imagine, Joe."

"You aren't involved, are you?"

Szymon hesitated because he didn't want to lie to his friend and avoided Joe's gaze. "Not in the worst of it—so far. I'm trying hard to stay away from it."

Joe quietly, skeptically observed Szymon. Neither spoke. Szymon lowered his head. "It's hard, Joe."

That Sunday, Joe caught up with Barbara and Szymon as they were walking home from church. Joe had only seen baby Joe once, and was amazed to see how much both children had grown. During dinner, the friends talked about a trip to Bukaczowce. They agreed to go while the weather was still warm because it would be easier to travel with lighter weight clothing. Joe said that they could count on him to help carry the baby's bed. All they had to do was notify Szymon's father and Joe's Aunt and Uncle. By the time they had finalized their travel plans, all three were excited and looking forward to the visit.

However, Szymon came home from work three days later and told Barbara that he had lost his job. She lowered her head and cried. "I'm sorry, Barbara, I don't know what happened."

She felt sick in the stomach. "Just as everything was going so well..." She wondered what could have happened, and felt anguish like she hadn't experienced in years. A letter arrived from Roman Swaczy about ten days later, in which he wrote that they looked forward to seeing Szymon, Barbara and the boys, but it would be better to wait until St. Nicholas Day." Roman was still working and couldn't afford to take time off from his job.

A few days later, Szymon read a notice in Gazeta Lwowska about the impending construction of an expansion to the kassern and other major projects at the Lemberg Garrison. That evening at supper he told Barbara that he was going on active duty. "They need men to come in for one or two years to build several structures and facilities on the base." Then, he read the article to her.

"It says that I would be able to come home on

Saturday nights, and the work would be steady through the winter months until the end of my enlistment."

The very next day, October 30th, 1899, he went on active duty. Szymon brought mail home with him that evening. He had stopped at the post office to mail a letter to his father, and read a letter from the War Department. It was a notice to report to the office of military affairs near the garrison. The next afternoon, he spoke with the clerk and showed him his re-enlistment papers. Everything was in order.

Barbara's spirits soared as she breathed a sigh of relief. She had continued meeting with Maria Marcin to work on her projects, and had finished two more Vyshevenka along with several vests and bandanas. She was always able to sell items at the fair and each evening upon returning, she tucked her coins in the vanity drawer.

Shortly thereafter, Szymon was surprised to answer the door and find a smiling Hryc standing in the hallway. Hryc was wondering what had become of him, and said the group was growing as unresolved complaints continued to fester. Hryc described the present situation: there were more brawls and vandalism.

"Sounds serious. What are the police doing about it?"

"We are careful not to get caught after the last incident. Lucky for me, I have connections."

Szymon was relieved to not have to go the

following Saturday evening. That was fortunate for him because Hryc's friends were caught by the police brawling in a Polish beer hall. Szymon knew that he would have to be extremely cautious. That evening he overheard loud shouting coming from the direction of the grocery store. He told Barbara to be quiet and went to the dark living room to peer out the window. Three men were fighting and yelling in loud voices under the street light below. Evidently, they were drunk. He watched the fight, which was lop-sided, and then saw the police arrive and arrest all three men.

"I will be happy to get away from this," he thought.

About an hour later, Szymon answered the door to find a policeman standing there. Szymon told the officer that he hadn't gone anywhere that evening. After identifying himself, the officer said he knew Szymon was part of a group of men who had harassed people in the Polish neighborhoods.

"There isn't any truth to that." Szymon's mind raced. "How would anyone know what I'm doing?" The officer didn't give Szymon a straight answer, so he suspected that someone had pointed a finger at him, but couldn't imagine who would do such a thing. "Who told you this lie about me?"

"You are on a list of known trouble makers." The officer went on to say that the police were watching him, so he needed to stay on the straight and narrow.

Szymon wanted to punch him in the face, but knew better. That would ruin his military record. The more he thought about someone doing this to him, the angrier he became. The police sought him out several more times, but eventually things settled down and the unrest stopped.

Going on active duty had made a difference, but adjusting to their new schedule was more difficult for Barbara than either of them had thought it would be. Neither was he able to get home during the week, nor could he spend much time with the family on weekends. Although Barbara was happy with her growing family, she had to admit it was difficult to get everything done, and find time for her sewing and embroidery. Her friend, Maria Marcin, stopped to visit her once a week just to bring groceries. Szymon brought food on weekends, but that still wasn't enough. So, he visited Joe Korlaszcz to ask if he could find time to help the family for a while. Joe visited once or twice a week, and, as usual, Barbara and Jan enjoyed seeing him. After the first month, Joe told her that he would be able to come only once a month because his duties were increasing. She felt sad because Joe was a real friend and she would miss seeing him more often. It was Joe who suggested that she visit Father Bogdan at the Paraskevia Church.

Her face brightened, and after Joe left she got the stroller from storage and walked with her sons to the Paraskevia Church. She was disappointed not to see Father Bogdan, but Anton, one of the Brothers, said that he would give Father Bogdan her message. Father left a message for her when she wasn't home, so Szymon read it to her on Saturday.

Szymon liked living at the base and seeing

Commander Schwartzdorf and Sergeant Major Schoeppler. One day, Schoeppler stopped Szymon as he was hurrying to the construction site. He seemed genuinely pleased that Szymon was doing well.

That Sunday after church, Father Bogdan called after Szymon as they were walking down the stairs to return home. When he heard of their dilemma, he said he would be pleased to locate someone to help with shopping. It appeared that most of their problems were solved for now. When they arrived back at their apartment, Barbara confessed that she could probably solve the problem if she did all of the grocery shopping at the corner grocery store.

"Why haven't you been shopping there?"

"It is more expensive than shopping at the Square," she answered.

Szymon stopped in a reading room and read an article in Gazeta Lwowska stating the Ruthenian Council was calling for a general strike of construction workers. Not only did the council back the strikers, but so did the Greek Catholic parish priests, as well as, university students and professors. Szymon was itching to get involved. He talked Barbara into going with him to an emergency meeting of the Prosvida Society. The Prosvida Society was created in the nineteenth century in Ukrainian Galicia for the purpose of preserving and developing Ukrainian culture. So, she joined Szymon on a Saturday evening after supper. They took Jan with them, while Maria Marcin watched Joey.

Barbara was surprised to find that the meeting was orderly and peaceful. The hall was crowded, with people extending outside the doors and into the street. Several speakers described how demonstrations were planned for November 25th, 1899, and how they would proceed. It would be impossible for Szymon to participate because he would be working that day.

The demonstration went off smoothly, as though it had been rehearsed, and was considered a success as it halted construction on virtually every project in Lwow and in several surrounding communities. The crowds in Rynoc Square, and other parks and other squares all over Lwow, were huge. Speakers sounded warnings that the pressure would not let up until wages were increased. People appeared to be firm in their resolve to stay off the job. There was a noticeable difference at the construction sites. Both sides were pleased with the way the strike went. It was difficult for most men to miss any days of work because most families lived from payday to payday. Still, they planned to stay off the job for three days, but the organizers called off the strike the next day because their point had been made.

Newspapers and church pulpits all over the region reported the remarkable event and the construction companies' reaction.

Hryc popped up again. Seeing him at their front door often seemed a bit sinister, and Szymon wondered why he kept coming around. This time, he insisted that Szymon join him and his friends at the tavern on Sunday afternoon. Szymon explained to him that he'd gone back on active duty. Hryc snarled, "Why would you do a thing like that?" He was insistent that Szymon give him an answer.

"I lost my job and was tired of the uncertainty."

"What's that going to get you?"

Without hesitation, Szymon responded, "Steady work and food on the table for my family."

In the end, Szymon joined Hryc at the tavern. They sat at a long table with ten other men, all strangers to Szymon. But the tavern was closed, so the men announced they were going to a private hall where they could have a couple of alcoholic drinks. Szymon knew he shouldn't go, but Hryc insisted so Szymon gave in. The next thing Szymon remembered, he was home in his own bed and Barbara was upset. "Hryc is not a good friend. He is a bad influence, and a selfish person who instigates trouble.

The calendar turned to January 1900. Saint Nicholas Day came and went. Szymon had no money for gifts because he spent it all on his drinking. The family struggled to pay rent and buy food. Nonetheless, Szymon made it to work every Monday morning. His job was that of a laborer—hard labor at that. He didn't have to think, just use his back to lift, push, or pull anything that needed to be moved. He mixed mud for the master brick layer - the job that he really wanted. He was warned against fighting in public and told that it wouldn't be tolerated. When his superior told him that his appearance was shabby, he shot back, "Why do I have to clean up for this shitty job?"

That afternoon, there was an accident. Several men were working on the second floor of a new building when a tier of scaffolding fell. Szymon, who was working underneath, sustained bruises on his arms, back, and face. Fortunately, his head wasn't injured. Only a few men suffered serious injuries, and all but one survived. Szymon sat on a bench at the hospital awaiting treatment; it was a long wait. When the nurses reached him, he was laying on the bench trying to get comfortable and relieve some of the pain in his shoulder. One of the nurses teased him about his black eye. "I guess I had to add a few more bruises to show my wife." A doctor examined his arm and shoulder, put the injured arm in a sling, and sent him to his unit with a note. Szymon was discharged and allowed to go home later that night.

When Barbara opened the door and saw him, she was shocked. "The doc told me to stay home for two nights and not to use the arm. They gave me something for the pain, too."

She remarked that she thought he had been drinking.

He laughed. "Why would you think that?"

Was she onto him?

Barbara wasn't amused. Jan got up from his nap and hopped onto his father's lap. He wanted his father to play horsey, but Szymon's upper body ached when he tried to give him a ride. "Pa's got to rest, son."

The next day, Szymon wanted to go out, but Barbara told him not to.

He was mad, but she ignored him. "You can't go out and get drunk. You will get kicked out of the army, lose your job, and then what will we do?"

Szymon didn't respond. He knew that she had a point and arguing with her wouldn't make her back off. The following day, he arose, cleaned up, ate breakfast, and left early in the morning. He didn't have trouble walking but was uncertain he could lift on his job. The doctor examined him and said he should rest another day.

"You will be fine after that."

He left the infirmary and went to the construction site, where he gave the construction boss the doctor's note. "See you in the morning."

Szymon couldn't resist, so, on the way back, he took a detour and stopped in a nearby tavern. Fortunately, his landlord was there drinking an "eye opener." Szymon sat down and sheepishly told him about the accident saying that he stopped to get a drink to deaden the pain. After two beers, the two men walked home together. Barbara had dinner on the table. They ate in silence.

The following Saturday evening, Barbara was watching him when he growled at her, "What the hell are you staring at?" She didn't argue nor have anything to say to him. On Sunday afternoon, Hryc showed up wanting Szymon to go with him. Szymon looked at Barbara, but did not speak.

As usual, they wound up at the private beer hall, where plenty of liquor was available. Szymon was already drunk when a fight broke out. Men ran out into the street, but Szymon hung back. Even though he was drunk, he could sense that the situation could get out of hand. But Hryc was aching for a fight and pulled Szymon outside with him. Immediately he was thrust into the melee. He didn't remember how it happened, but when it was all over, Szymon sported another black eye.

Barbara was furious and the superintendent at the construction site warned Szymon that this was the last time he would allow him on the job with a swollen, black and blue eye. Barbara was beginning to have sleepless nights. She wouldn't listen to anything Szymon told her and made it clear that she didn't want anything to do with him. He had never seen her so angry. She ignored him and on Sunday morning, she dressed and walked to church alone. As was his usual routine, the next Saturday afternoon Hryc showed up at their apartment again. Szymon told him that he decided not to go anymore. Hryc didn't like it, but left him alone. The following weekend, Szymon could not believe his eyes when Hryc appeared at the garrison.

When Szymon told him he had decided to quit going to the taverns, Hryc became argumentative. He called Szymon a weakling and a fucking pretty boy. He also called Barbara a fucking whore. Szymon stood for a minute then told Hryc to take back his words. "This time, you've gone too far!" The fight between the two former friends became loud. Szymon was strong, and since he had not been drinking, he was able to get the best of Hryc. Hryc struggled to stand, backed away, and then began to lose self-control. Szymon had never witnessed this kind of behavior. "Hryc, I'm warning you, don't come after me again."

Before Szymon could think Hryc had pulled a gun. He threatened Szymon, cursing and swearing, and called Barbara more filthy names. He fired one shot and lunged at Szymon. Several men stood on the sidelines watching. "Hryc, I'm warning you to go home." Hryc lunged once again.

Szymon easily side-stepped him, which only infuriated Hryc, and as he lunged Szymon tripped him, wrestling the gun from his hand. Hryc kicked the gun from Szymon's hand but lost his balance when Szymon grabbed the weapon. The gun misfired. Hryc spun around. By this time, the military police were running toward the two. Szymon was placed in restraints, forced to walk to the base police station, and placed in detention.

Szymon was uncertain what version of events Hryc would tell the police, but he was certain it wouldn't be the truth. Sergeant Schoeppler got wind of the brawl and came to see Szymon the following Monday. "I don't know what happened, Sarge. Everything was going great and this guy started coming around harassing me. Then, everything fell apart. I can't tell you much more than that, except that I began running around with a bum, and drinking influenced my behavior."

Szymon was drifting off to sleep when a guard came to his cell, unlocked it, and allowed Joe Korlaszcz to step into the small space. Szymon's eyes filled with tears. As Joe tried to comfort him, Szymon choked on his words. "I don't know what to do, Joe. I'm so sorry and ashamed."

"Have you seen Barbara?"

"Joe, I don't want her to see me like this."

"She's distraught and worried about you. You should speak with her, Szymon."

"Joe, I'm ashamed of myself."

"Szymon, Szymon! Pull yourself together." Joe interrupted Szymon several times and finally spoke firmly to him. "You have to make it right with Barbara. You can't let her stay alone and not tell her what is going on. For God's sake, Szymon, tell her the truth."

Joe took matters into his own hands. He went to see the priest at the Garrison Chapel, and then to the rectory to request a Greek Catholic priest speak to his friend. That evening a stern, no-nonsense priest was sent to Szymon's cell. When he left, he promised Szymon that he would speak to Barbara and try to make arrangements for them to have a few hours of privacy. A few days later, a pale and haggard Barbara stood outside the cell waiting for the guard to unlock it. She entered, sat down, and looked expectantly at her husband.

"I'm so sorry, Barbara." Their conversation began stiffly. Szymon inquired about the children and Barbara asked what she could bring to him. Then, he lowered his head and sobbed. No one was certain about Szymon's fate, even though several men vouched for him, swearing that it was Hryc who harassed Szymon. But all of that didn't matter now.

He was told that his chances of remaining in the common army were slim.

Two weeks later on a Sunday afternoon, Barbara brought Jan to see his Papa. By now their financial situation was desperate. The priest at St. Paraskevia Church found a charity to help the family, but it was uncertain where they would be living in another month. Someone had paid the rent for the previous two months. It was now July and she worried every day about how much longer they could survive with Szymon imprisoned. Barbara would wake up in the middle of the night and cry. She was desperate; she prayed to God for help.

Letters arrived for them. Because she didn't read, she was unsure who had written, but thought she recognized the handwriting as Szymon's father's. She walked holding Jan's hand and let him carry one letter Sunday after church. They were going to visit Szymon. Just as they reached the garrison, Joe Korlaszcz crossed the street and called out for them to stop. The two friends walked together. Joe held Jan's hand as Barbara pushed the stroller. "Have you heard anything yet about where you might go?"

"No, Joe, and I'm very worried. I just want this to be over no matter what Szymon faces."

They reached the prison and the guard took Barbara to Szymon's cell while Joe waited in a small visitor's room with the children. For the first time in a long time Szymon seemed upbeat, even a little cocky. "An officer came to see me, and I think a decision will be made next week. He interviewed me, asking all kinds of questions about the fight, my background, and my family. I promised him that I would not get into trouble again."

Barbara handed the letter to Szymon. His face reddened. The letter was from Hryc. When Joe entered the cell, Szymon passed the letter to him to read. "Hryc is a very bad person. Stay away from him, Szymon. He is an evil, troubled man. Szymon, you have to give this letter to the advocate."

Joe Korlaszcz and the family spent an hour together. The time was too short and after tearful goodbyes, Barbara and Joe walked back to Barbara's apartment. Joe helped her store the stroller and get the children situated. He stayed to have some cheese, freshly baked bread, and a cup of coffee, then he said goodbye.

As he left, Barbara had a feeling that something was not right with Joe, but she couldn't put her finger on it.

The following Tuesday evening, Szymon came home. "Barbara, I'm on probation, but I think I'll be all right. Szymon went back to his job under a strict curfew. He could only spend daylight hours off the base, and he could not be outside after six o'clock in the evening. Szymon felt fortunate to be back in the army. He discovered that Sergeant Schoeppler had sent his record from his prior military service to the military court. Szymon also learned that when the gun discharged, the bullet hit Hryc below his abdomen in the right pelvic area, but did not cause a serious wound. He tried to put Hryc out of his mind, but couldn't help replaying the threats outlined in the letter he had written:

"You cannot get away from me. I will hunt you down. Next time, I'll slash your pretty face, you fucking son of a bitch!"

Szymon's mind was wandering when he remembered what Hryc had said to him after their fight a year ago. He had told Szymon that he had connections. Szymon shuddered, transfixed for a moment. Maybe Hryc's connections are why the police came around and told me that they knew I was involved in fights in the Polish neighborhoods. The picture started to become clearer. It had to be. It had to be Hryc who told the police that Szymon was involved in the Saturday night brawls. "Jesus Christ! But why? Why does he have it in for me?" Szymon was stymied.

It was the fall of 1900, and the weather was pleasant as Szymon and Barbara returned to the park near the garrison. Jan was now more than five years old; little Joey was more than a year old, and walking. The family had brought the baby carriage where, alongside Joey, they had tucked a hamper full of food. The grass was still lush because there had been good rainfall all summer long. They spread a blanket and, as Barbara set up the picnic dinner, Szymon played with the boys. It was fun to hear their squeals and laughter. Joey hovered near Barbara, while Jan played catch with Szymon. Barbara had splurged, buying sausage and cheese, and had made delicious, freshly baked bread to go with it. She made a pot of beans sweetened with honey, mustard, and some lightly fried onions. The day was glorious. With no wind, just the warmth of autumn's sunlight, the scene was perfect. "If only life could stay this way it would be wonderful," she thought apprehensively. She didn't know why she was nagged by all this doubt, but suspected that their lives might not ever find a path to the good life.

In the middle of October, Szymon was notified that he was eligible to extend his reserve duty, so he went to the office of military affairs and signed up for an extension. He and Barbara celebrated by having Sunday dinner in a Ruthenian restaurant while Maria Marcin watched the children. They drank toast to Szymon, raising a couple of beers. The beers may have been a mistake because Szymon began stopping in taverns each Saturday after he left his job. Although life had been more peaceful in Lwow during the past two months, he still read about sporadic fights between Poles and Ruthenians, but they were not as serious as they had once been. The night that Szymon next went to a tavern was an exception. He was barely able to get out before the fighting turned ugly. Newspaper articles described the fighting as serious – as serious as it had ever been.

On a Sunday afternoon a few weeks later, Szymon told Barbara that he was going to the garrison early, but instead, he stopped at a beer hall. As he opened the door, he bumped into Hryc, who surprised him by being cordial. Szymon mentioned that he had recently reenlisted for another year. After just one beer, Szymon said that he needed to be on his way to the garrison, and Hryc didn't object when Szymon got up to leave.

"Oh, shit, what do I do now?" wondered Szymon.

For the next few weeks he avoided taverns, staying home to play with his children and read newspapers or other publications. He read a few articles to Barbara. Looking over his shoulder, she asked him about one of the drawings. She had spotted an illustration of a vyshevenka in an advertisement. Szymon read the short article which described a store in Rynoc Square where these vyshevenka were sold.

Szymon returned to the base on Sunday evening, and early on Monday morning Barbara placed little Joey in the stroller and told Jan to hold on as they walked to Maria's apartment. She had brought the illustrated article with her and showed it to Maria. The two friends decided to go to the Square about 10 o'clock, just as the stores were opening. Jan was tired of walking and began fussing. She told him firmly to stop, that it wasn't much farther. She also bribed him by saying she would buy a candy for him. Jan's eyes widened because his mother had never said anything like that before. Barbara knew she should not have promised him a candy, but she wanted to see the vyshevenka. In the end, she was happy that she had made the bargain with Jan because he raced up the sidewalk.

When they arrived, the store was just opening and there were only two others waiting outside the door. All of them wanted to see the Vyshevenka. Barbara thought they were worth the walk and the bribe; they were beautiful. Maria and Barbara examined each of the garments. The colors used were not traditional, but the embroidery was exquisite. When the store manager approached them Maria explained that they were sewing garments to sell at the fair. Barbara interrupted. "Maria's Vyshevenka are just as nice as these." The manager called to the owner who came over, spoke with them about their work, and asked if they would return with some samples. Barbara excitement created a knot in her stomach, but Maria, who was familiar with such conversations, was calm. As they prepared to leave, Maria promised that she would return with two garments.

The next day, the two friends again walked to the dress shop. The owner was pleased as he examined Maria's sewing and embroidery. "How much will you give me for the two?" After some haggling, the owner agreed to pay her $7.50 each.

Within minutes, Barbara found herself walking alongside Maria back toward her apartment. "I learned a lot today."

"When you are ready, you will do just fine, Barbara. Just don't give your beautiful garments away."

As the weather turned cooler and the days shorter, people began to look forward to the holiday season. This year neither Szymon nor Barbara was worried about their finances. Barbara continued to work on Vyshevenka to sell at the fair, but Maria now went to Barbara's apartment to work on their projects because of the two young children, and for convenience, Barbara continued shopping at the corner grocery store. Szymon came home on Sunday mornings. Occasionally, the children had colds or earaches but, nothing serious. Jan was now in first grade at the grammar school. And Barbara was pregnant again. She wondered how that could happen since they had very little privacy or time to be alone.

When she discovered that she was pregnant, she went to the Roman Catholic Church, lit a candle, and said special prayers that she would have a healthy pregnancy and delivery. "Just a little girl, please."

On Sunday evening, as Barbara was saying goodbye to Szymon, the owner of the corner grocery store approached her. He asked if she had seen anyone lurking around the streets after dark. They chatted for a few minutes, and when she turned to walk upstairs to their apartment she thought she caught a glimpse of Hryc. She hurried inside and rushed to the living room to see if she could see him through the window with the aid of the street light. A man was slowly walking away. She watched until he got to the corner and turned right toward Zamarstinowska Street. Even though she was sure Hryc hadn't seen her glance at him, a chill came over her. The next morning she awakened thinking about Hryc. That night she saw his face peering in the window, but when she awakened she realized it had been only a bad dream.

Barbara continued her normal routine all week. Maria came over every Tuesday, and sometimes on Thursdays when Joe called on the sick and infirmed, he also visited her. On this particular Thursday he was in the neighborhood, so he stopped to see her. Joe suggested that they walk to the nearby park. She put little Joey in his stroller along with two bottles of sweetened tea, but the day turned chilly so they decided not to stay. When they returned to the apartment, they saw Hryc hurrying away from the building. Barbara put her hand on Joe's arm and told him she saw Hryc.

"There he is again! What's he doing here on a Thursday morning, Barbara?"

"I don't know. Joe, do you think Szymon should be told right away?"

Barbara was upset and unnerved. She and Joe sat at the kitchen table drinking tea and discussing Hryc. "On my way back to the church, I'll stop to leave a note for Szymon at the construction site."

She continued to worry all that day and the next. Whenever she stepped outdoors, she searched the streets to see if Hryc was anywhere around. On Saturday evening, realizing Szymon would be home in the morning, she began to relax. She ran down the steps to the grocery store and bought a few items to prepare a pot of soup for their Sunday dinner. She hesitated as she reached for the door handle, and was relieved that he wasn't behind the downstairs door. But when she reached the landing on the second floor, there was Hryc, lurking in the dim light. He spoke quietly but menacingly to her. "I want to leave a message for your pretty boy husband."

Her heart pounded. She screamed. "Leave us alone!" He put his hand over her mouth, forced her head back, and looked straight into her eyes. His alcoholic breath nauseated her.

"You tell pretty boy that I'm going to get him." He let her go.

"You hurt me! Why won't you leave us alone? What have we ever done to you?" He stared back; his scarred face frightened her.

"Just give him the message," With that he turned, bounded down the stairs, opened the outside door, and ran down the street.

Barbara immediately felt sick. She wondered if she should tell the owner of the grocery store, but decided to just go upstairs and not say anything. That night she had nightmares. On Sunday, Szymon came home as usual. Barbara couldn't help herself. No sooner had he arrived than she began crying. "What is wrong?"

"Hryc was here, and he hurt my neck."

As Szymon examined her bruises, he became

enraged. Hitting the wall in his fury, he knocked over a chair.

"Szymon, don't make so much noise. People can hear you a block away."

That night she barely slept, but just as quietly as he appeared, Hryc disappeared. Three weeks passed, and Szymon had not seen nor heard from Hryc. It appeared he was playing a cat and mouse game. Barbara began going to church during the week. It helped calm her. She decided to tell the priest about Hryc stalking her and Szymon. The priest asked where he lived, but she wasn't sure if he still lived in his old apartment. Hryc's wife, Olena, had left him long ago. He never told her the reason, but Hryc had told Szymon that she visited her family about a year and a half ago and never returned to Lwow.

As she walked down the stairs to return home, Father Bogdan stopped to ask about Hryc and whether the incidents of harassment had been reported to the authorities. She explained to the priest that Szymon was afraid of starting something he couldn't finish. The priest looked at her quizzically. "What do you mean?"

Father Bogdan had been told by Joe Korlaszcz about Szymon's problems with Hryc but, she wasn't sure Father knew about Szymon's drinking and fighting in the taverns. "Father, Szymon has been fighting. He even went to work with black eyes. His boss didn't like it and told him that he had to stay away from trouble or risk being thrown out of the army." Father told her that he understood why she hesitated to tell the military authorities about Hryc. "I'll speak with Szymon for you."

The mood was somber as Lent arrived. Joe Korlaszcz invited them to go to the sacred music concert again. But, this time she told him that she hadn't been feeling well for several weeks and thought she needed rest. Joe wondered if that was the real reason she declined. Szymon had little money and both wore shabby clothing. Maybe Barbara was embarrassed. Joe's heart ached for his friends.

After Lent, Joe again invited them to his church and this time Barbara agreed. They had no money to buy extra food for a nice dinner, so they met at the Catholic Church. When they arrived, Joe was startled to see that both Barbara and Szymon looked thin, worn and tired. He was especially worried about Barbara losing another baby, so he borrowed a small cart to transport them back to their apartment. He was happy and felt rewarded when both Szymon and Barbara expressed many thanks for taking them to a concert and transporting them back home.

This concert was the first that either had been able to attend in almost two years. He could feel the weight they carried every day. Although she obviously enjoyed the music, when the concert was over, Barbara asked if they could return to the apartment, saying she needed to rest. She was now seven months pregnant.

Joe felt sad for them and, with a heavy heart, he

prayed for them every day.

That weekend Szymon came home on Saturday evening. The family spent a quiet evening together. The next morning as they were dressing for church, Szymon caught a glimpse of Hryc from the living room window.

"That son of a bitch is out there again! He must have waited for me at the garrison and when I didn't come out the gate he snuck over here."

"Do you think we should go to church?"

"Maybe not. Damn it! I don't know what to do."

"Szymon, we can't take the children. I wouldn't want to risk them being injured if a fight broke out. Please, let's not go. The boys will be scared to death."

Barbara was becoming hysterical, screaming about Hryc. Szymon tried to soothe her. He took her into the kitchen and made a cup of tea for her, into which he put a drop or two of laudanum. They sat together until Barbara stopped shaking. "Barbara, I want you to lie down. You are terribly upset. Please think of the baby."

She didn't argue with him, and within minutes she was sound asleep. He tucked a quilt around her and let her sleep until about two o'clock in the afternoon. While Barbara rested, Szymon happened to catch the owner of the grocery store who unlocked the door and allowed him to buy a few grocery items even though it was Sunday. Szymon explained that Barbara was upset because Hryc was loitering around their apartment again. "Don't worry, Szymon, I'll keep an eye on her for you." When he returned home Szymon made a pot of soup for dinner and served the small dessert he bought as a treat for her.

After dinner, they sat together and talked for a while, trying to imagine a normal life. During the past weeks, Barbara and Szymon had repaired their relationship, and any hard feelings had softened. She kissed him goodbye as he left for the garrison that evening. He wrapped his arms around her and pleaded with her not to worry so much. "Everything will work out."

But Szymon didn't make it inside the gate. Hryc was standing outside and stopped him. He was falling down drunk and holding a knife. Szymon pushed him aside, but Hryc was on his feet again, kicking and slashing at his face. Szymon tripped him and pulled the knife from his hand. "Stop, Hryc! I'll have to kill you, so just stop." An officer arrived and pointed his weapon at Szymon and Hryc. Szymon handed the knife to the officer. "This is Hryc's knife. He jumped me as I was walking onto the base." Hryc could barely speak or stand upright. He stumbled and staggered behind the officer, screaming that he was going to kill Szymon's fucking wife. Arriving at the detention center they were both processed. Once again, Szymon was behind an iron gate.

On Monday, he contacted the advocate who had overseen his previous court martial. Szymon explained his family's dire financial situation. "I don't know what the hell to do. We can't keep going on this way."

Again the wheels of justice ground slowly. Although Szymon had explained that his family had very little money and his wife was about to give birth, there was no progress on his case. Sometimes, he felt abandoned.

Father Bogdan and Joe Korlaszcz came together. They asked to speak to someone in the advocate's office. Joe vouched for Szymon and told of witnessing Hryc loitering around their apartment on several occasions. Others vouched for Szymon as well, but his previous record of drinking and fighting didn't help his case. Things finally came to a head when Barbara went into labor.

She was visiting Szymon in the military prison when her labor began. As a result, she was taken to the garrison hospital. Barbara was also suffering from nervous exhaustion due to weight loss and malnutrition. On August sixteenth, 1901, with the assistance of a midwife named Petronella Mraz, Petraeus was born. He was baptized two days later in the Peter and Paul Garrison Church, also known as the Mission Church. Sadly, Szymon's incarceration dictated that the family couldn't be together at the christening. Afterwards, the advocate assigned to Szymon came to the military prison. A guard led them to a small room where they could discuss Szymon's case. Unfortunately, Szymon's chances of receiving leniency were significantly diminished because of his prior offenses. Szymon was brought before the judge a month after his arrest. The judge told Szymon that he would be discharged from the army. Szymon tried to interject his grim personal circumstances before the final decision was rendered. At the trial, the advocate presented the plight of the family: their newborn son, two other children under six, a terribly ill wife, no financial resources. Despite the advocate's plea for mercy, the judge rendered a dishonorable discharge, not only because this was Szymon's second court martial within a year, but it was also discovered that Szymon had been associated with groups suspected of engaging in subversive activities. Although these accusations were mostly true, his participation long preceded his going on active duty. After the court martial , he was allowed to see Barbara. Her appearance shocked him; she was terribly thin and weak. She was asleep, and Szymon didn't want to wake her to tell her the truth right then, so he slipped out without saying a word. He had no idea what he would do next, only that he had no choice but to immediately begin making plans for his and his family's future.

Szymon had few options. He arranged for Barbara and Petraeus to remain in the hospital. However, Jan and Joey would go to an orphanage. He got a job cleaning outhouses on construction sites in and around Lwow, and did what he could to save money. He sought out Father Bogdan and bartered some work for a place to sleep. As bad a situation as this was, Szymon faced worse. Since his recent work was for the military, each time he applied for a job, he had to produce his military papers. Due to his dishonorable discharge, he knew he needed to have a fresh start somewhere other than Lwow. The only certain employment in rural areas was as a farm laborer, which meant moving to a village. He would need to buy a wagon and a team of mules to transport his family into the countryside.

Eventually, Barbara regained enough strength to be discharged from the hospital, but she still required considerable rest. Little Petraeus remained because he needed a wet-nurse since Barbara was unable to nurse him. Szymon visited her. He hated seeing her so weak, and sobbing uncontrollably. The two held hands and wept together. Life seemed hopeless.

On a Sunday morning about a month later, Barbara, Szymon and their children ascended the steps and proceeded through the big doors of the Paraskevia Church. Barbara pushed the baby carriage with Joey holding on, and Jan walked alongside his father. After Church, the family returned to their apartment over the corner grocery store. Arrangements had been made with their landlord to allow them to stay for another month or two. It had been a long time since the family had been together at home, and it felt good. Szymon had cleaned the apartment, Father Bogdan and Joe Korlaszcz arrived with some groceries they had bought for them. After dinner, Papa gave Joey horsey rides and Jan played with his toy truck and garage while their infant brother Petraeus slept. Someone had left a newspaper on the dining room table. It was quiet and warm, sunlight filtered through the curtains while Szymon read to Barbara. That evening, they knelt in prayer next to their sleeping children's beds. They thanked God that they were together again, and asked for God's blessing on the next phase of their lives. The next morning as they drank their coffee they planned – for exactly what, they did not know. They couldn't take furniture with them as Szymon would be lucky if he found a job on a farm owned by a nobleman where decent farm worker's housing was provided. They decided to sell all of their furniture at the Thursday fair. Everything would have to be sold, and the money used to pay for the costs of moving so they could begin life anew.

The costliest items Szymon needed to buy were a wagon and mules. He had already begun his search when one afternoon as he headed to an auction in a nearby village, it occurred to him that he had no place to keep a mule. But he decided to go to the auction anyway. Shortly after arriving he located a mule and wagon, but the wagon seemed too large for his needs and he wanted mules, not a horse. Only one small herd of milk cows remained to be sold at auction so, he hung around until the end. Szymon told the auctioneer what he wanted. The auctioneer advised him to shop around Lwow, and gave him the name of a farmer in a community in the northwest corner of Lwow. "If that doesn't look like it has what you want, go to Junkyard Street."

The following day, Szymon walked up Zamarstynowska Street, crossed over into the oldest section of Lwow, Pidzam. Several blacksmiths and wagon makers were located here, so he thought he would have no problem finding a wagon to fit their needs. He went to blacksmiths' shops where he learned horses and mules were plentiful; even though Lwow was becoming more modernized, people still used them to draw wagons, carts, and carriages.

The next morning over breakfast Szymon and Barbara discussed what he had learned, and when would be best to sell their furniture. Barbara was feeling anxious about moving.

"Why do we have to leave so soon? We still have a month."

"I have to find work and begin making some money, Barbara. There is a lot to think about.'

He had no reason to go to the Zhivkov suburb before now, however, its reputation as a place where the poorest, most undesirable of society lived and worked was known to him. He also thought it likely there would be a large junkyard with used tools, equipment and, machinery, where he might also find a broken-down wagon and whatever parts were needed to restore. He had no problem finding the junkyard; it was located on Junkyard Street. He inquired inside a rusty shed and was told to feel free to look around. Signs everywhere warned, "Don't steal. If you do, you will be shot!" He found some wagons, but only one he thought might be salvageable. He attempted to speak with the old man in the rusty shed, but the man cut him off. "Don't ask any stupid questions!"

Szymon interrupted him to say he wanted the wagon located around the corner. "There is another damaged wagon with iron rimmed wheels on it. Would you sell the wheels, if I removed them?"

"Yes, just make sure that the size is right before you remove them."

"How much?"

Altogether, the price of the wooden wagon bed, four steel rimmed wheels, and all hardware needed for repairs was significantly less than a good used wagon. Then he bought a team of mules, a used harness, reins, and a long whip. He harnessed the mules to the wagon. Ready to get on the road, he reentered the shack to thank the man for his help. They shook hands and the junkman wished him good luck.

Szymon spent the next week measuring—again and again—the length and width of the wagon bed and axels, stripping parts and transferring the frame, axels and wheels from the broken-down wagon to the wagon bed which he blocked upside down on wooden horses. When his work on the wagon was completed, Szymon sat atop the teamster's seat and drove the wagon down Zamarstynowska Street. As he passed the road to the old castle, he remembered that the Mission Church was on nearby Teltralna Street. He halted the mule and tied him to a post near a back entrance to the church offices. He found the door where Joe's office had once been located. A young priest greeted him.

"I'm looking for Father Joe Korlaszcz." Shortly thereafter, Szymon saw a tall priest strolling toward him. It was Joe! The two friends embraced, and then Joe led Szymon to a small secluded sitting room. The two friends briefly took stock of each other. "Joe, you are thin. Have you been well?" Szymon sensed that Joe was in frail health. Joe acknowledged that he often he had shortness of breath, irregular heartbeats and, at times, chest pains. His heart condition would not improve. Szymon told Joe that he and Barbara often suspected something was troubling their friend and wondered what it was. Szymon said that they prayed for him often. Joe reached out and took Szymon's hand. "Please don't worry about me. My God looks after me; my fate is in his hands."

As Szymon told Joe about his court martial, both men had tears in their eyes. Father Joe saw the pain etched on his friend's face. "I've prayed for you and for Barbara, too." Szymon could not stop his tears. "Oh, Joe, this isn't the life I imagined for us. And, I'm certain that I have disappointed Barbara and you.

As their brief visit came to a close, Szymon rose and the two unlikely, nevertheless, closest of friends, walked to the door where Szymon turned to say goodbye. "This is not the last time we will meet. In my bones, I know we will see each other again." Joe smiled, they embraced, and then Szymon headed toward the apartment building. It was difficult to part with his best friend, but he found comfort in the belief that somewhere, sometime, they would meet again.

Szymon stopped the mule-drawn cart in front of their apartment building, ran upstairs, and asked

Barbara to bring the children down to see the wagon. She smiled and hugged him. Reaching the street, Jan and Joey looked up wide-eyed at their father sitting high upon the teamster's seat. "Papa, can Joey and I go for a ride?"

Szymon laughed. "You soon will get all the rides you want for a lifetime."

Chapter 21

They had never before been thrust from their home, not knowing where they would land the next week—or even that evening. Szymon planned to travel west before eventually turning south...but where? Barbara shivered with trepidation as Szymon flicked the reins. The mule pulled the wagon down Zamarstynowska Street until they got to the main road heading west out of town. It was the end of November 1901. Szymon thought to himself, "I'm thirty-four years old with a wife and three children, no money, and I don't know where the hell I'm going." He turned his head to see Barbara holding their newest baby and smiling up at him. He bent down to kiss her, as she nuzzled closer to him. For now, at least, everything seemed alright.

The first day of their journey went smoothly. They had progressed about fifteen miles. Around four in the afternoon, Szymon began looking for a place to stop for the night. He pulled off the road next to a locked gate, where there was enough distance between the road and the fence to park the wagon.

The mules would be able to forage on the grass alongside the fence. Just as he was pulling to a stop, a carriage drawn by a smart-looking stallion reined in.

"Where are you going?" asked the stranger. Szymon hadn't given any thought to how he would answer such a question.

"I'm looking for a place to spend the night with my family. Is there a pond and field of hay nearby for the mules?" Jan and Joey regarded the well-groomed stranger with wide eyes. The man walked over to the wagon and noticed that the family appeared to be moving. "Not sure yet where we are headed. I'm looking for work."

"What kind of work?"

Szymon slid down from the seat and walked a short distance with the man. When he returned, he climbed back up to the seat, picked up the reins, and cracked the whip. "That was the property owner. He gave permission for us to stay overnight. We will stop up the road, where there is a small lake and a field of hay."

Barbara took out the dinner she had prepared at home. The boys remained in the wagon while she poured some juice into cups and handed each their portion. After they ate, Szymon unhitched the mules, led them to the pond to drink, and tied them to a tree so they could forage. Then, he prepared the wagon so they could sleep. He tucked the boys under the teamster seat, and pulled a canvas cover he had found in the bottom of a wrecked cart over the back of the wagon. Then, he put a bullet in his gun and tucked it under the mattress on his side. They slept with Petraeus between them on a mattress made of canvas filled with straw. In the morning, they were both surprised they had slept so soundly.

Later that morning, Szymon stopped at a dairy farm to inquire about a job.

"Nothing here, but the boss said I might try a very big farm owned by the Potocki family. I worked for the Potockis in Bukaczowce. They traveled another hour before stopping in front of the entrance to a farm. As Szymon climbed down, a guard approached. After a short conversation with the guard, Szymon called up to Barbara, "We'll turn in here."

Szymon was well acquainted with dairy operations. His entire family --father, uncles, grandfather, and now the younger generation of brothers, cousins, and nephews—all worked on dairy farms for noble families in and around Bukaczowce. And Szymon had worked on farms before he entered the Austrian Army.

They moved into a dilapidated house with sparse furnishings. The house contained a fireplace, one big bed and a smaller one where the boys would sleep, a worn couch, a small table which could be used for eating their meals, and a white porcelain pan which could be used for bathing. Outside, there were several small buildings around a well; an iron kettle hung over a fire for washing laundry. Farther up the road was an outhouse. Standing in the little building,

Szymon turned to Barbara and shook his head. "Well, this is all we have." Barbara just smiled ruefully.

The little house was cramped but warm whenever he could afford to burn wood the entire night. Jan attended class five days a week in a 4 room schoolhouse, and the children were healthy, other than occasional sniffles. It was just the beginning of spring, a time when there always was a great deal of work to be done on a dairy farm, so Szymon decided to look around for another job. It wasn't that the work was hard; rather, he hoped to find larger accommodations than the one-room house he currently rented. They stayed on the Potocki farm through the winter, until the end of April, 1902, when he learned about another dairy farm which was owned by the Catholic Church and located about twenty-five miles farther down the road. So, on a cold April day, Szymon packed up the wagon and started out.

He located the other farm and discovered that there was a natural, warm spring just outside of town. He decided to visit the spring first, so he told the boss that he would return in a few minutes. A mile down the road was a sign at a crossroads that simply read 'warm water.' Szymon turned the mules to the right and a mile down the road pulled the wagon into a yard just beyond a second, similar sign. He went to speak to the property owner to ask if he could pay to bathe the children. The owner was gruff, but his wife overheard their conversation, yelled at him to shut up, and came out of the back room to speak to Barbara. The women chattered away in Polish. She said her name was Celia, originally was from Poland, and her husband was Jacob Janereska from Prussia. Celia was a big woman, tall like her husband. She was immediately drawn to the children. She took Barbara into the back room which led outside onto a crudely built covered patio. It was obvious the owner had built the structure. Beyond the patio was the entrance to a shed where water flowed into a pool. Szymon followed along a narrow path behind Barbara and the older woman. Barbara was almost overcome when she felt the warmth of the water. "

"How much?"

The older woman hesitated. Her eyes shifted from one child to another, finally resting on the baby Barbara held in her arms. "Would five cents for everyone be too much?" Barbara beamed. The older woman and Barbara chattered away as they inspected the area where they would soak in the warm water. It was heavenly. Before Szymon turned to go with Mr. Janereska, Barbara whispered to him to go back and tell the boss at the Roman Catholic farm that they would come back another time.

Szymon paid Celia, and left Barbara and the children in the building while he went to the Catholic farm to let the guard know they would not be returning that night. Mr. Janereska came over to the wagon just as Szymon pulled the mule to a halt. "Could we pay to stay here tonight?" Szymon explained to him how he had put together two wrecked wagons to make one sturdy one. He could see that the old man, who at one time may have been capable of taking on such a strenuous project, was impressed.

"Where are you heading?"

Szymon told him he might travel down toward Ivano Frankivs'k.

"I'm going to go home, eventually, but I want to look at places around here before I make up my mind."

"Where's home?

"Bukaczowce."

"Where did you come from?" Szymon told him the truth.

They walked to the spring, and Szymon listened as the old man told him where he wanted to build terraces and walkways. The two men continued to walk and talk for another hour. They passed a barn, a small herd of cows grazing in field. Everything on Jacob's property was neat and well-maintained. Then, out of the corner of his eye, Szymon saw Barbara approaching.

"Mrs. Swaczy, I'd like Szymon to do some work for me." She looked from Szymon to Jacob and back again. "Your husband will tell you what I'm willing to pay, so you can discuss the details with him." With that, Jacob left them alone.

"Do you think you would like to stay here for three or four weeks?"

"We're not in any hurry. Do you think you can trust

him?"

Szymon nodded yes. "He wants me to build the paths and a terrace. He will pay me fifteen dollars. We can use the warm springs. It might be good for you to rest and sit in the warm water." They knew that rich people went to spas to help cure their aches and pains and restore their health.

"The boys would like it, too."

"How would you cook and bake?"

"We will have to ask Jacob about these things, and then we can decide."

According to Celia, Jacob had moved to Lwow two years earlier from Brandenburg, Prussia. He bought more than one hundred and fifty acres near Stare Strzeliska with the idea that he would turn the place into a dairy farm. A house and several other buildings were on the property, but it was soon apparent that he was not able to take on the responsibility of operating a large dairy farm alone. He was thinking of selling the place when he discovered the warm springs. He spent many months sitting in the warm water nursing his legs and back. There were two additional small, unoccupied houses, with fireplaces, which were clean and in good repair. One of the houses they used for storage, filling it with furniture and personal belongings they had brought from Prussia.

By evening, Szymon and Jacob had moved some furniture into the second house—more than enough to keep Szymon's family comfortable. Then Szymon brought the Swaczy family's few personal possessions in from the wagon, and placed them in one corner. They built a fire in the fireplace to use for both cooking and heating.

Jacob was eager for work to begin on the terraces and pathways. Only a few weeks earlier, he had begun to fear that his project would never be completed. His legs and back pained him, so he knew he needed at least, one other person to help him. When Szymon arrived and told Jacob of his personal circumstances, his hopes were raised. At last, there was someone who appeared capable of taking on his pet project. When Szymon found the reference letter from his Uncle Max packed away in a small suitcase, he presented it to Jacob who couldn't hide his favorable impression; he beamed as he read the letter, now convinced that Szymon was the right man for the job.

The previous summer, Jacob had bought wagonloads of bricks, stones, gravel, concrete, and sand, all piled neatly under a tin-roofed pole building; cut lumber was covered by waterproof tarpaulins. Jacob had bought all the supplies and equipment needed to do the work. They spent the first day measuring for frames and footers. In subsequent days they began clearing the land and moving bricks and stone alongside where the paths and terrace would be built. Szymon offered the team of mules to pull out trees and drag them onto a burn pile in a clearing. They dug trenches, poured concrete, and lined up stones of various sizes for the terraces, working quickly to mix mortar and fit the first row of stones.

They drew several sketches as they went along. The heavy work was hard on the body so each night both men soaked in the warm spring to ease their aches and pains. The terrace of stone rose with the contour of the land, so it appeared to be a natural feature of the surrounding landscape. They didn't talk much while they worked, as each knew what the job required. At dinnertime each day, they stopped and went to Jacob's house where Barbara and Celia had prepared a hearty dinner.

Each morning Barbara helped with farm chores, milking cows and feeding the farm animals. When that was done, she mixed dough to make bread and sweet rolls. In the early afternoon, Barbara and Celia cleaned house, played with the children, patched worn clothing, and soaked in the warm spring. If a few free moments remained in the day, Barbara would use them to teach Celia how to embroider, but there was precious little time to work on vyshevenka. Celia took Barbara to a market fair in a nearby town on Thursdays where they bought food and supplies. The women chatted as they worked together or played with the children. Everyone had a job. Jan, and even Joey, fed the chickens, collected eggs from the chicken coops, and ran errands between Jacob and Celia.

When the project was finished, the men poured kerosene on the burn pile and set it afire. The Swaczy family had remained at the warm springs for four and a half weeks. As they were preparing to leave, Jacob gave Szymon a tip on another dairy farm near

Strzeliska another 25 miles to the southwest. The farmer looked Szymon up and down. "Are you in trouble, young man?"

Szymon looked directly into the man's eyes and said, "No, Sir."

"Ever been in any trouble?"

"No Sir." Szymon could not help but wonder why in hell he had asked that question. A sense of unease prompted him to check his gun and make certain there was a bullet was in the chamber.

Szymon decided to return to the farm owned by the Catholic Church. They spent four months there. Jan attended second grade, and from time to time, the Swacsys visited Celia and Jacob. Jacob furnished both of the small houses and had a large, professionally painted sign made to replace the little one that had simply read 'warm spring.' In addition to the two existing houses, Jacob and Celia planned to build two more small rental houses, to enable visitors to stay for longer than a day or two.

As the time approached for Szymon's family to move on again, Barbara and Celia talked about how sad their parting felt. Theirs had been an unlikely friendship, yet they had shared their most intimate secrets with each other. Celia told about the emptiness she felt because of never having a child, and Barbara confided her feelings about the mother she never knew. They both appreciated how Barbara's baby, Petraeus, loved to be held by Celia, nestling in her arms close to her large bosom. They both acknowledged that Szymon needed to make more money, and deep down, they knew they wouldn't see each other again.

In this place, days shortened noticeably as summer waned. The days passed quickly as the time of their departure approached. It was Petraeus' first birthday. Celia had a difficult time relinquishing the beautiful child. Facing the day when he would be gone was made far more difficult given that she and Jacob never had children of their own.

That day arrived in late August. The landscape was breathtakingly beautiful – sun glinted off miles of trees bearing leaves of purple and copper; colorful wildflowers bordered the roadways. Celia and Jacob stood on the road leading away from their property, watching as Szymon flicked the reins and the mules pulled the wagon farther and farther toward the crossroads where they turned south. Barbara sat next to Szymon, tears running down her cheeks. The boys silently watched Celia and Jacob, then turned to watch their mother with mournful eyes. The family was once again on the road to an unknown destination. They turned southwest into the sun splashed landscape. The warmth of the sun provided comfort for her, but would stand in stark contrast to the unspeakable squalor they would find just a few miles ahead.

They encountered horrid living conditions and cruel, sadistic bosses. They would leave these places as they had left others in the past, and would do so again in the future. Conditions throughout Emperor

Franz Josef's Galicia could not be imagined. How could this revered man, who peered out kindly upon his subjects from portraits, neglect his people?

In early autumn, as Barbara's fifth pregnancy reached full term, they found themselves in unhealthy conditions. Filth, which caused dysentery, presented a real danger to Barbara and her children. She was remarkably well, considering all the bouncing around she had endured while traveling from town to town. Two weeks after moving into a small, dirty house, Barbara gave birth on September seventeenth 1903 to a six-pound boy they named Michael. Their baby was born healthy, for which they thanked God. Strzeliska was like every other town they had lived in with one distinction: considerably more Jews lived there. Greek Catholic Churches were increasingly accused of being anti-Semitic. The clergy railed against Jews, not only labeling them as Christ-killers, but blaming them for poverty and all other ills. As a result, people came to believe that Jews were dirty, putrid people. Each year their hatred intensified and incidents of beatings and vandalism increased. In addition to numerous incidents of personal violence against Jews, gangs of drunken men defaced synagogues, and burned homes, businesses, and schools. It was a rare person who did not hate Jews. Szymon never questioned what the Jews had done to him, personally, to make him so full of hatred. He conveniently forgot about the times in his childhood, when he had worked for Jews on their Sabbath and Passover.

It was at this time that he began to drink heavily again. The family had suffered through some unusually cold weather and hard times, so Szymon promised that they would remain in Strzeliska for a few months. As temperatures fell, he fitted the canvas cover over the back of the wagon tightly to shield Barbara and the younger children from the wind and cold whenever they went to a market square or church. The straw-filled mattress did little to cushion Barbara against the rough ride, but Joey and Petrus enjoyed playing with their mother and snuggling together to stay warm. Jan sat with his father on top of the teamster seat. Although Barbara dressed him as warmly as she could, he still had been cold. Jan was a strong boy who wanted to be with his Pa and Szymon enjoyed his son's company. Soon, he was teaching the eight-year-old how to check the wheels for loose bolts and adjust them. One day, Szymon climbed down from the seat to find that a bolt was close to slipping out of the axle. He called up to his son to move the wagon just a foot forward, explaining to him how to judge distance, and then returned to watch the back wheel inching forward. Szymon yelled "Stop!" in a booming voice. The wagon stood right on the mark. He removed his tools from a box on the side and made a quick adjustment. "Do you think you will be able to do this, son?" After that incident, he taught Jan how to listen for abnormal noises. "You can tell by listening to the sound of the wheels. If you hear unfamiliar noises, it always means there is trouble. Jan was a fast learner.

It had been a tough few months, traveling around

from village to village, farm to farm, looking for work. Szymon had done his best to ward off the worst of the cold and to make his family comfortable inside the wagon, but to his despair, he found that the farther south they travelled the worse housing conditions were for workers. Moving around in a wagon during the coldest months of the year over cobblestone or crumbling brick or broken pavement, often brought Barbara to tears. They traveled hours – even days— before finding a suitable job and house for their family. The small houses were often extremely dirty and drafty. Some had broken windows and no means of heat. One even had a front door that hung by one hinge, so it didn't close properly. And peasants were charged unfair rents for these deplorable living conditions.

They talked about getting off the road and settling down in Starliska—a bigger town that Szymon knew of which was located a bit farther to the southeast. Pregnant again, Barbara she was worn out. One baby after another over the past ten years had gradually taken its toll, draining her optimism, as well as, her strength. She found it increasingly more difficult to believe that eventually life would improve. Szymon was currently working on a farm in Brodozwce, where people were no different than any other place they had lived. The complaints were always the same: dirt, disease, poverty, and drunkenness.

One day, in a moment of deep despair, Barbara told Szymon that she believed there would never be any improvement in their lives, and dreaded to think about what that could mean for their children. Szymon believed her and could see that Barbara had taken as much hardship as was possible for any woman to endure. They went to see the priest at the Greek Catholic Church, but he appeared unsympathetic to Szymon's concerns about his family. All the priest could do was offer a few words of comfort. Szymon admitted to himself that his drunken behavior did nothing to buoy her spirit and he wondered if the priest knew he had been drinking.

That afternoon, he went for a long walk and tried to think. His mind was a drunken blur and he was exhausted. As he was walking away from town, he was accosted by a robber, but Szymon successfully fought off his assailant. This was the first time anyone had attempted to rob him in broad daylight. He returned to the wagon and his family, never mentioning the incident to them.

Barbara's pregnancy was difficult. She was sick the entire time and both feared the worst, so they were not surprised when the baby was stillborn. This in itself was a tragedy, but what made it worse was that the baby was a girl. Barbara's face was haggard and tired. They went to church almost every day for three weeks after the baby was stillborn, but the church offered her no solace. Barbara had named the baby after her birth mother, Katarzyna. It seemed fitting to name the child she would never know after the mother she had never known. Szymon believed that if the infant girl had lived, it would have revived Babara's spirit to live. She struggled along because she had a family to look after. Szymon decided to move again once early spring arrived. When they were living in a house, there wasn't time for anything except cooking—as best as she could—be mending and washing clothes, shopping for groceries, and taking care of her children. After she stopped nursing Michael, her health improved slightly. They continued to move from town to town. Occasionally, during the winter months, Szymon would give in and stop at a church to ask for a place to stay for the night to get his family out of the cold. Some churches offered a warm meal and milk for the children. They had been on the road for several years, moving from farm to farm. He kept telling himself that this was no way to live, when Barbara became terribly ill. She needed rest and a warm house; without them, he feared she would not live.

Returning to his home would be difficult for Szymon, but he realized that he had no choice. He would have to swallow his pride. Their last child, Marya, was born prematurely on December 18th, 1906—a little more than a year after Katarzyna had been stillborn. They stopped in a small village named Oskrzesince where she gave birth to the baby on a cold winter day in the back of the wagon. Szymon had taken the boys inside a church, so she was alone when faint labor pains began. "Please, God, No! No!" But her plea was too late. Szymon heard her screams and came out to carry her into the church just after the little girl was born. The church gave them a place to live and food to eat. Two days later, Barbara awakened to see worried faces surrounding her. She was lying on a bed in a small room. Szymon bent over her, and tried to smile.

The baby was named after Barbara's stepmother, whom she didn't remember. She had been told by relatives that after her mother died her father married a woman named Marya. Little Marya had been born so prematurely she was barely recognizable as a human. On December 20, 1906, the family huddled together while a priest christened the baby. They stayed in a room behind the altar that night and left the following morning for Bukaczowce.

They didn't talk much on the twenty-mile journey home. If it had been cold before Oskrzesince, the temperature dropped into the frigid range the further south they traveled. On a bitterly cold day in late December, 1906, Szymon, Barbara and their four surviving children arrived in Bukaczowce. Barbara wept tears of relief. After more than five years, their ordeal was finally over.

Szymon stopped to see his Uncle Max first. He had not been in contact with any of his relatives for six or seven years—he couldn't remember exactly—and he was embarrassed by the current condition of his own family. But it was Max who had helped Szymon find Barbara after he left military service, and he knew his uncle would help break the ice with Pa.

When his uncle opened the door, Szymon could read his face. It bore a look of contempt. All Max said was, "What the hell happened now?" Then, he called for Katarzyna, and the three of them helped Barbara down from the wagon. Seeing how weak she was, Max carried her into the house and gently laid her on a bed, before returning to the wagon to bring the boys in. Katarzyna set about preparing a meal. She put out some bread and cheese, and then heated some milk and a pot of soup she had made for the evening's supper. Katarzyna served the boys and Szymon, before going to see what she could do for Barbara. She was frail and so thin her eyes were sunken in their sockets; her breathing was shallow. Katarzyna recognized that Barbara was in such a weakened condition she was unable to speak. She gathered a clean flannel nightgown and some underclothes, fetched a warm wet towel, and did her best to clean Barbara's body which had not been properly tended to after the baby was born. Barbara had developed a hoarse cough, for which Katarzyna prepared hot juice with wine and rubbed her chest with a compound she kept in her medicine cabinet to relieve congestion. She wrapped a brick in heavy canvas, placed it in the foot warmer, and then slid it under the covers near Barbara's feet. Finally, she threw a couple of blankets and quilts over her before lowering the shade and closing the bedroom door. Szymon was standing outside the door. "Will she be alright?" Katarzyna stared past him, saying nothing.

That evening, Szymon gave his sons baths while Katarzyna prepared a supper for them. After he put his children to bed, he walked outside into the cold night air. He wanted a drink but couldn't bring himself to ask his uncle for one. Szymon took the mules and wagon around to the back of Max's house.

There was a field of hay adjacent to a barn and a trough of fresh water. Szymon filled two bags with oats he scooped from the feed box mounted in front of the wagon, and hung a bag around the neck of each mule. Szymon reached in his pocket for a cigarette, but he was out. He looked up at the star-filled sky, trying to remember how to navigate by the stars, a skill he had learned while in the army. When he felt the cold penetrate his warm coat he went indoors; the house was quiet. He checked the boys and noticed a few extra quilts at the foot of the bed. He was tired, so he wrapped a couple of quilts around himself, lay on the floor, and tried to sleep. He heard the sound of a clock on the mantle in the living room; it was 7:30. And then he fell asleep.

He awakened and looked out the window as dawn was breaking. The house was quiet and it was still too early to risk waking the others, so he decided to lay on the floor again and fell into a fitful sleep. When he awakened again, he heard the sound of the clock; it was nine o'clock. He got up and entered the kitchen, where he found a note in addition to some rolls, plates, glasses and a cup for coffee on the kitchen table. The note said that Max and Katarzyna had gone into town and would be back about eleven. Jan, having heard his father open his door, came to the kitchen. "Papa, I have to pee."

They found a chamber pot, and after Jan finished, they tip toed into the bedroom where Barbara had spent the night. Seeing that she was still sleeping peacefully, they left the room, closing the door behind them. Joey awakened next. Szymon thought he had better prepare a breakfast for his sons. He poured milk into four glasses and placed rolls on each plate. Soon Michael and Piotr were standing next to Szymon and Jan. He cautioned the boys to be quiet so Mama could rest.

Leaving the boys at the table to eat, he went out to the wagon to find clean underclothes and his shaving gear. He returned to the bedroom where he had slept, washed his face, and glanced at his image in the mirror before shaving. He didn't like what he saw. He was unkempt and haggard-looking; his eyes were red and bleary, and his skin was wind-burned from sitting in the cold air on top of the wagon for days on end. His clothing was filthy; he needed a haircut and a bath. He would have to bathe the best that he could, so he heated water on the stove and poured it into a basin. He looked up to see his sons peeking into the room. The boys giggled, but he didn't feel like playing with them. "I told you to stay at the table, and not to make any noise."

Clean and shaven, next he took the boys into the room and washed their faces, while wondering how he would get the money to buy some clothing for them. His stomach turned as he realized that he would have to go to the fair to barter his harmonica for some pants and shirts for them. And he would have to drive a hard bargain.

They were leaving just as Max and Katarzyna rounded the corner. Katarzyna chirped, "Good morning!" She wouldn't hear of Szymon leaving the house before he and the children had a decent meal. Szymon began to protest, but Max interrupted, clearly irritated. "Szymon, for Christ's sake, shut up! You are in no position to turn down a meal."

They went to the fair the next day. Szymon looked for clothing for his four sons before the auction started, and found some decent pants and shirts, holding them up to see if they would fit. "How much?" The price was reasonable, but the seller wouldn't trade for a harmonica, so he gave up for the time being.

Walking toward the auction grounds, he encountered a man speaking to a large group of men who appeared to be farmers from surrounding villages. Szymon stopped to listen. The man was promoting sailing to America to work in coal mines. In the towns where Szymon had recently worked, he had heard they were recruiting people to go to America and the company would pay for their passage. The man said the company would guarantee a job which paid close to four dollars a day, so Szymon asked the recruiter where he could get more information. It sounded too good to be true, but the recruiter said that a man could send money home to help his family and manage to save some, too. His head cleared as if he had been struck by a board!

The auction gave him other ideas he would not have thought about which would enable him to recoup his cost for one of the mules, and provide enough additional to pay for groceries for a couple of weeks. "Not so fast!" he thought.

He decided to wait until he went home and spoke with his father before he did anything.

After supper that evening, when the boys were in bed, Katarzyna, Max and Szymon were sitting at the kitchen table when they heard Barbara open the bedroom door. She was weak and had to lean on his arm as Szymon helped her to the table. Katarzyna thought she felt feverish, too, so wrapped her in a blanket and settled her in a comfortable chair in the living room. Barbara had awakened earlier in the afternoon and eaten some soup. Katarzyna now encouraged her to have some dessert with a cup of coffee. She had barely finished when she told Szymon she wanted to return to bed.

With Barbara settled back in bed, the other three moved into the living room, in front of the fireplace. Szymon started to tell them how grateful he was for their help, but Max waved away Szymon's remarks curtly. "Well, have you thought about what the hell you are going to do?"

Szymon swallowed hard. "Today I went to the fair to get some ideas." He went on for several minutes before he looked up to see Max's face.

"How do you intend to go about all of this? Remember you have a very sick wife. You'd better talk to your pa before coming up with lame-brained ideas."

"Alright, I'll go there tomorrow."

The next morning, after he bathed the boys he found some clean clothing on the chair in his room.

He knew it was Katarzyna who had bought the clothes. Later that morning he put the boys in the wagon and drove off to visit his father.

Szymon sat on the teamster seat surveying the familiar scene before him. He saw how little had changed in the six years since he had last visited his parents. There was something comforting about being home. And to think that at one time he had been scornful of his home, so was happy to leave all those years ago. Had it only been twelve years ago? It seemed longer ago and farther away, which made him feel like an old man.

He was snapped back to reality as the mules pulled the wagon around to the rear of his parent's house. He climbed down from the wagon. Jan already had jumped down and lifted Piotr out, while Szymon picked up Joey and Michael. Szymon's father came around from the front of the house. Joey and Piotr were shy around their grandpa; they stood awkwardly frozen in place next to their father. Their awkwardness was broken when Piotr and Joey said they had to pee, and scurried into the house. Szymon felt like a stranger on this land where he had grown up, and found it difficult to open up to his father. It took a long time for their conversation to flow freely. Everyone was tense. Helena, with Roman's help, prepared a simple dinner of Kielbasa, sauerkraut, and boiled potatoes with warm baked bread. After dessert, the boys lay down for a nap.

Szymon was holding Piotr as he told his parents how he had built the wagon from old wrecks and used parts, and bought the mules. His father wasn't interested in his stories. "How did Barbara wind up in such a mess?"

"Who told you? How did you know? Who told you about that?" Pa told him that he had met Max and Katarzyna in town on Monday.

"Tell me the truth, Szymon. No bullshitting."

Initially anger welled up in Szymon, followed quickly by tears of remorse. The horror of the past few months caught up with him and he was suddenly overcome. Glancing at his mother, he saw her skeptically eyeing him, and realized he would get no sympathy from her.

"I'm sorry, Mama. It was all my fault."

Szymon told his parents how he screwed up in the army and was booted out. He observed his father's body tense as he spoke. After confessing his poor behavior, he stopped, exhausted.

"Do you have any money, Szymon?"

"All I have are the mules and wagon."

His mother spoke next. "Is Barbara going to be alright?"

"She has improved and I believe she will get her strength back."

"Szymon, what is it you want?"

Szymon was uncertain how to answer his father, worried that Pa would not approve of anything he had to say.

He slumped in his chair, wanting to get up and flee as the feeling of sheer panic overwhelmed him. He looked up to see his mother's face.

She was pale, very thin, and looked quite old to him. "Ma...Ma...

what is wrong? You don't look well!" He stood up and fell to his knees at her feet. "Mama, are you sick?"

His father answered. "Yes, Szymon, your mother is very sick." Szymon was stunned as he realized she looked as though she were dying. "Your mother has been ill for quite a while."

"What is it?

"Szymon, she has cancer." They had learned about her cancer almost a year prior. Nothing could be done to help her and she was already living on borrowed time, as the doctor initially gave her six months to live.

"No, Mama!" His eyes filled with hot tears. "Oh, Mama, please don't die."

"Szymon, we couldn't write you because we didn't have your address."

Szymon's mind could not process all this information, but he realized that he couldn't ask his father for anything. He felt numb; there was a dull pain in the left side of his temple. He and his father talked for a short while before he said that he had to go.

"What are you going to do?"

"I don't know, Pa. When I figure that out, I'll stop to tell you."

Ma felt sick so Roman returned her to the bedroom to rest. Szymon sat paralyzed by panic and fear. His beloved mother was dying. Awakened by their grandfather putting Helena to bed, his sons came to the table, followed shortly by Roman.

"Pa, I am sorry about Ma. Is there anything I can do?"

"Just pray."

Szymon lifted his sons into the wagon. "I'll go to the estate to see what kind of job I can get." With that, they rode out of the yard.

Szymon was hired immediately. It was the same as it had been forever—poor wages and high rent for a wreck of a house. He returned to Max's house in the late afternoon, and told them about Ma, with Barbara at his side. She had improved and was dressed in one of Katarzyna's pretty robes. Szymon told his uncle that he would be working at the estate, at least temporarily. He looked up to see Max staring at him. "Szymon, why did you come here?"

"I wanted to talk to you first, before I made any decisions, because you have always given me good advice. I planned to ask Pa if Barbara and the boys could stay with them while I went to work in America. I planned to send money for them to live on. It seemed like the only way I could ever make enough money to better myself and my family."

"That's just like you, Szymon. I have to say, you never stop trying, but you always manage to derail your plans because of your drinking."

Szymon lowered his head. "But Max, what do you think of the idea? Do you think it is stupid?

Max was thoughtful in his answer. First, he asked Szymon what he knew about what it would take to go to America. Szymon answered that it would not take much, just a passport and possibly passenger fare. He had a promise of a job working in the coal mines after he arrived in America, but this information had to be kept quiet. If the officials at Ellis Island discovered that he had a job waiting as a coal miner, he wouldn't be allowed to enter the country. Szymon told his uncle about the wages and cost of room and board, and claimed he knew he could live inexpensively in order to send half his wages back to Bukaczowce.

When they finished their conversation, Szymon asked Barbara if she wanted to visit his mother. He hadn't spoken privately with her about Helena, but saw that Barbara seemed anxious to go out for a while. "Let's wait until tomorrow morning. You can get another night's sleep, Barbara, and the rest will do you good."

So, the next morning they arose, ate a breakfast, dressed the boys, and left before dinner time. On the way, he whispered to her that his mother was ill, just to prepare her. It wasn't enough of a warning; Barbara was shocked when she saw Helena. "Szymon, we can't stay, Ma needs to rest." Helena wouldn't hear of them leaving before dinner, but the only way Szymon would stay was if Barbara agreed to prepare the dinner with his help. They decided on a simple meal of corn meal mush and gravy. While they prepared the meal, Roman told Barbara about Ma's condition. With that, Barbara insisted that Mama sit down to rest, but as she tried to sit, Mama cried out in pain. Her entire body hurt, and there wasn't much anyone could do to relieve her of her pain.

Dinner was a somber affair. The boys sensed that their grandmother was sick, just as they had when Barbara was ill. During the meal, Helena became nauseated, so Szymon helped her to her room and brought her a bucket to vomit in. He had witnessed a lot of illness and death in his life, but this time it was worse—much worse—because it was his mother who was suffering.

Later that day, Szymon moved into a small farmhouse located on a nobleman's estate, just as he had frequently done over the past nine years. With only a few coins in his pocket, he wondered what they would eat until he was paid. He stopped to buy two loaves of bread and milk for his children. Szymon knew where he could go to possibly kill a couple of rabbits, so he took his gun and went into the nearby woods. When he returned to the little farm house, Barbara was boiling a pot of rice. They ate a skimpy evening meal of rabbit stew, rice, and bread. Afterward, Barbara prepared the bed for their sons, but before retiring Szymon gathered his family around him to say prayers for his mother and thank God for what little they had.

It was not quite daylight when Szymon arose the next morning. He heard a noise outside and went to the door in time to see his uncle dismount. He knew by Max's face that he bore bad news. "Szymon, your mother is in bad shape. She took a turn for the worse last night, and is calling for you to come."

Szymon took Max's horse and immediately rode off on it. Upon his return, he informed Barbara and Max that Helena had only a few days to live, and that Pa had asked for Barbara to come take care of her. Barbara took the three youngest boys with her, while Jan stayed with Szymon on the estate, where he cleaned the barns while his father milked the cows. Max and Katarzyna also provided help whenever 'theirs was needed. Mercifully, Helena's ordeal ended when she died quietly in her sleep one night after lingering for nearly two weeks.

Friends and family gathered in Saint Mary's church, and then walked behind the casket to the cemetery. Jan joined his uncles Stefan and Michael, along with nine other men and boys to carry the coffin from the church. Father Bogdan performed the short service. There were prayers, but no eulogy for this humble farm wife and mother.

Szymon was quiet for several days after the burial, reflecting on the goodness of his mother's life. He would always remember her for the kind woman she was, and not for the suffering she endured in her last days.

Szymon sold one of the mules and gave the money to his father. He asked if he also wanted the wagon, but Roman told him to sell it because it was too big for his needs. He made a decent profit on the wagon compared to what he paid for the two wrecks and the parts to put it in working condition. He gave Pa half and kept half to pay for his passport, travel expenses and, a room when he arrived for work in the mining town in Pennsylvania. He also put aside money to pay for passports for his family to come to America.

First, he sought out the recruiter from the Hudson coal mine, to inquire about a job. Then he wrote to his cousin Kate who lived in America. He told her he would be arriving shortly, asked her to meet him at New York Harbor, and wrote his arrival date and the ship's name on the letter. Then, he dropped off the letter at the post office on his way to the church. He knew his baptism record was in old St. Mary's Greek Orthodox Church.

Szymon brought his baptism record and military papers, as required, to the passport office. He feared he'd have to convince the passport agent to overlook his less-than-honorable discharge from the Austro-Hungarian Army, and give him a passport anyway. However, after reading his military papers, his application was easily stamped 'approved'. Many men in Bukaczowce had checkered pasts because of drinking and fighting, but that didn't seem to matter. More to the point, it may have helped the agent to make a favorable decision when Szymon handed him an envelope containing cash.

Barbara took his decision to go to America in stride. She wasn't nervous or distraught as she once had been. She was happy to be in a safe, secure environment with her children and Szymon's father. She knew it was best for the children to be living with their grandfather, rather than traveling around in the back of a wagon. For his part, Roman needed someone to take care of the house, cook, and look after him, as his health had been declining for several years. So it was a relief to her when Roman asked her and the children to live with him – a situation which benefitted them all.

Szymon took Jan with him to obtain his baptism record and passport, as he felt his oldest son should learn how to deal with bureaucracy. Afterward, they stopped in the German American Line office to get information about buying tickets for Barbara and the children to join him in America in future—perhaps in eighteen months. Jan would be eight-years-old in a few months. Szymon talked to him about accepting responsibility for his family and taking care of his mother, in his absence.

A week later, Szymon and Jan were shaking hands on the train platform, when Szymon suddenly put his arm around Jan and drew him close. "Son, you will be taking on a grown up's job. It won't always be easy. He explained that he could speak to Uncle Max whenever he needed help or advice. A feeling of awkwardness swept over Jan because his father had never shown him such emotion and intimacy. Jan interrupted saying, "Pa, I know that Uncle Max will never turn me away or let me down.

Szymon already had said goodbye to his younger sons and Barbara in the little house where he was raised. This time, Barbara didn't cry; she believed Szymon finally was on a path where something good might materialize.

Chapter 22

Two weeks after Szymon's thirty-sixth birthday, on February 2nd, he boarded a train to Lwow; one-and-a-half hours later, the train arrived in the station. He checked his timepiece and the schedule. The train to Bremen wouldn't leave for another three hours. He decided to walk into the old neighborhood. First, he bought the next day's dinner and put it into his cardboard suitcase, then walked up the street, turning onto Zamarstynowska Street. It was barely daylight, so he didn't want to linger because he could be an easy target for a robbery. Reaching the building where he and Barbara lived when they first moved to Lwow, memories flooded back to him. They did have some good times.

He remembered his visit to Joe Korlaszcz a few months previously, wanted to visit him again, and wondered if it was too late. A young priest outside the church greeted him. Szymon asked about Joe. The priest told him he would be awake and where to locate him. As he stepped into the rectory, Szymon saw Father Joe sitting in the living room near the fireplace. He was relieved to see that his friend's appearance had improved. The old friends embraced.

Szymon told Joe he was heading for America. Joe's face lit up, and he said that he envied his friend. They had an opportunity to chat for more than an hour before Szymon had to return to the train station to catch the train to Bremen. He promised Joe that he would stop to see him again when and if he returned to Galicia. There was a hint of a smile on Joe's face, even though the two friends obviously were saddened by the brevity of their visit, each recognizing that the other was having a hard time parting company.

Szymon asked Joe to recite the rosary for the two of them. After reciting the rosary, followed by the Lord's Prayer, the friends embraced, and walked together to the door. On the way to the train station, Szymon wondered whether he would ever see his friend again. An unbearable sadness overwhelmed him, but he forced himself to focus, grateful that he had to concentrate on returning to the station. It was quiet when he entered the building. He bought a copy of the Gazeta Lwowska to read, found a comfortable seat near the exit, and waited for the next part of his journey to begin.

The train arrived in Bremen in the early morning hours two days later. Szymon hurried toward the docks, his heart quickening as the ships came into view. At the ticket office, he showed his prepaid ticket. The ship wouldn't leave port for several hours, and passengers were not allowed to board until an announcement was made. He amused himself by watching other passengers, many carrying cardboard suitcases like his own. Some were traveling alone while others led a rag tag family with several children in tow. Most passengers were talking to people who would not be boarding the ships. There were tears and nervous glances all around. Everyone waiting in the boarding area was dressed shabbily. Most of the men and boys wore their hair parted in the middle, long, shaggy, and combed straight back.

Sobs and wails were heard throughout the crowd, as emotion overtook many. The scene was difficult to watch. A shipping company employee bellowed through a bullhorn for quiet. Visitors were told to leave the area where only passengers were allowed to remain. The man on the bullhorn kept demanding that people leave. Finally, the crowd dwindled and passengers were gathered in one large group. Passengers were interviewed individually by ship's employees seated at long tables. They were asked questions about their age, occupation, whether they had ever been imprisoned, where they would be going, and with whom they would stay with after arriving in America. Szymon was asked dozens of questions and the answers were recorded on the ship's manifest. Before boarding the ship, each passenger was examined for any obvious physical defects, such as limping, difficulty climbing steps, shortness of breath, signs of mental illness or even confusion. All this took no more than a few minutes for each passenger. The doctor gestured for him to proceed.

He walked up the ramp onto the ship, past the ship's engines, down three short flights of narrow steps, and into a poorly ventilated area. Bunks were fitted alongside the hull, with more rows of bunks hung in between. He selected the farthest, top bunk.

Szymon lay on the bunk with his cardboard suitcase propped up against the hull. The entire area was dismal and reeked of foul odors. He knew he could endure the voyage, if only because he was anxious to leave the hellhole that was Galicia.

Szymon stayed to himself for most of the voyage, which took six days. The Barbarossa was an ocean liner belonging to the German-American Line that carried both cargo and passengers. It was not at all like the small paddle-wheeler he remembered from his early military days when he was part of an occupation force. Riverboats plied the inland rivers in Europe. His travels to the military base, led him from the train onto a riverboat on the Saba River. He had never been on an ocean-going vessel and he hoped to see some of the interior and the engines. He was daydreaming when an employee of the shipping company approached him. He asked Szymon to move into a different part of steerage. Szymon responded that he'd prefer the quietest section. He wanted to keep to himself. He preferred to keep things that way.

Szymon moved, but as the ship began to fill up, he realized that he had been moved to the busiest, not the quietest, part of the ship. "Son of a bitch!" It might have been noisier, but it was nearest to the stairs leading up onto the decks. He considered that perhaps the man had done him a favor because it seemed to have better ventilation. As the ship got underway, passengers stood on the decks waving to those assembled on the docks, and afterward many remained until the ship's employees ordered them to return to their berths.

Szymon remained outdoors as long as possible. When he was approached by a ship's officer, he inquired about smoking privileges. "Announcements will be made, and smokers will be allowed outside to designated smoking areas; You can always remain outside until someone tells you otherwise." Satisfied with the officer's response, and feeling chilled from the ocean air, Szymon went below.

Most days he ventured outdoors, but concluded early in the voyage that the sea was monotonous. Only once did he see another ship on the horizon. As the days slipped by, the stench in the steerage compartments grew more and more intense. People vomited near the berths, toilets overflowed when they became seasick. There were broken faucets in the bathrooms, and those faucets which were not broken dribbled small trickles of salt water. At one point, during a light rain, Szymon stood outdoors on the deck to wash his face and upper body. Halfway through his bath, an officer ordered him down below, stating that the decks were slippery when wet, which could cause passengers to fall overboard. On this particular voyage two passengers were lost at sea, although no one knew what had caused the incidents. Since the only rain had been a brief, overnight shower on the same day Szymon tried to bathe, he wondered whether someone might have committed suicide.

On the sixth day, Szymon awoke knowing they were approaching New York; he hoped to see land. Although dawn was breaking, fog shrouded the harbor. He walked up the three flights of narrow stairs and peered outside the glass at the top of the exit door. To his surprise, he could see. He stopped to listen; the engines were running, but the ship wasn't moving. Wondering where they were, he opened the door to try to orient himself—to see something, anything, to help him determine where the ship was. He was startled to see several other anchored ships. The morning was still and peaceful. A ship's officer came toward him. "Where are we?"

"We're here."

"Where is here?"

"The ships are anchored in New York harbor."

"When can we leave the ship?"

"Don't know." The officer moved past Szymon.

He was leaning against the side of the super structure, when another officer approached. This time, Szymon said nothing. The officer reached into his pocket, taking out a cigarette. Szymon hated not knowing what was going on—he couldn't even tell what time it was. The sky was brighter, but he predicted the day would remain dull, overcast. He watched birds flying across the bows of ships in one direction - seaward - and thought to himself that they were looking for food.

Szymon took out a cigarette and offered one to the ship's officer, who refused. An hour later, Szymon offered the cigarette a second time, and this time he accepted. "Are we in New York Harbor?" Szymon inquired in German. The officer nodded. Szymon noticed some smaller vessels up ahead. The officer's actions indicated to him that something was about to happen. It appeared that the ships were lined up in some kind of order.

"Thanks, Buddy," said the officer with a nod as he briskly walked away.

Szymon remained topside with his suitcase beside him, so he wouldn't need to retrieve it later from down below. He watched while one at a time the ships were prepared to move toward Ellis Island. Szymon could see that the Barbarossa was now fifth in line, but the ships were halted and it was after one in the afternoon before they moved again. Szymon gave up and returned below deck to await the afternoon dinner announcement. People were excited. He asked the man who shared his bunk what had happened. "They say it will be late this afternoon before we get into Ellis Island, and probably will be allowed to leave there sometime late tonight."

After he ate, Szymon took out a pencil and paper. He wrote the date and approximate time he awakened, as well as, the time they headed for the docks of New York. Steerage passengers were tagged and queued into groups according to the ship's manifest, then herded onto barges and taken to Ellis Island.

At Ellis Island they walked up the staircase into a large room. As he walked up the stairs, he noticed a man at the top of the landing marking the clothing of an occasional passenger with chalk. Szymon thought it must be for trachoma, a dreaded eye disease which, if detected, would prevent a person from entering America. Passengers spoke with each other nervously, in low whispers. The large crowd continued inching forward, as each examination progressed. Szymon passed through all the examinations quickly, with no chalk marks on his clothing, but he noticed a small number of fellow passengers being led away to examination rooms. He really wasn't curious about where they were going, or why; he just wanted the process to be over and to meet his cousin Kate. He was directed to an area where hundreds of passengers had assembled. Passengers were queued and again put on the barges which took them to the docks where they finally stepped off in America. Szymon was sent to a large room where, out of the corner of his eye, he saw a young woman who was familiar to him. He was directed to a counter to show his ticket and passport, as the young woman walked toward him, "Hello, Szymon." It was his cousin Kate. Within minutes she signed an affidavit swearing that Szymon was who he had said he was. Then, he and Kate joined others at the rear of a large crowd. The barricades were lifted, and the crowd fell silent as they poured out into the streets, away from the harbor. Just as quickly another crowd ran toward them cheering and shrieking with excitement. Some cried, some laughed as they joined the oncoming sea of outstretched arms frantically grabbing for each other until they could finally embrace. Although weeping was mixed with laughter, this was the most joyous union that Szymon had ever witnessed. Unable to control his own emotions, his eyes filled with tears.

Many things could have gone wrong. He had taken a risk writing to his cousin Katarzyna Swaczy on such short notice, but his letter had arrived on time, and he was relieved that Kate had been at the port to meet him. Had his letter been delayed, no one would have known that he was coming, nor when and how to locate him. He would have been broke and stranded. As they walked along to the tenement buildings of lower Manhattan, Kate asked about her family in Bukaczowce.

Kate, who had been known to him as Kasha, had sailed to New York three years earlier with her cousin Paraska Swaczy. Not only her name, but everything about her had changed. She fit so well into New York with her sophistication, stylish clothing and hairstyle, that he might not have recognized her. He was captivated. "How long have you lived here?"

"Since I arrived in Manhattan, three years ago." He was too shy to tell her how much she had changed, so he just kept staring at her.

"Do you like living here?"

She told him how exciting living in New York City was. It was everything she had dreamed of.

He told her that he wouldn't be living in New York

because he had a job in the coal mines south of the city. She asked how long he planned to stay. "I have to leave tomorrow morning. The coal company is waiting for me to arrive."

They arrived at a tenement building on Exeter Street. She said that she and her husband were planning to move to a better neighborhood soon. He could understand why. The building was old and dingy; the rooms were small, narrow, dark, and smelled rank. Kate explained that they had lived in this location for several years because they wanted to save money. Rent was cheap, but they were planning to move to New Jersey for better housing and better paying jobs.

She told him that several neighbors and family members from Bukaczowce had come to New York in the past few years. Kate's husband arrived home from work later that evening. He, too, was from Bukaczowce. Kate said that they hadn't known each other while they lived in the old country, and Szymon, who had been away for many years, didn't recall ever having met him. Both Kate and her husband, who was several years older, were happy living in the United States. The couple assured him that opportunities to make money abounded. They talked for several hours that evening until Kate brought out two blankets and a pillow and laid them on the couch. Szymon would sleep on the couch that night. He was happy to be there and to have something, anything, to sleep on. She showed him the bathroom and brought a towel and soap. He bathed in a tub for the first time since he lived in Lwow many years ago. The next morning at 4 a.m. Szymon arose, dressed, drank a cup of coffee, and then left quietly.

He rode the subway to Midtown, to the Pennsylvania railroad station to board the train. He had directions instructing him where to transfer in Newark to continue on to Wilkes-Barre. He showed the conductor his ticket for the train to the coal fields of Lehigh Valley, Pennsylvania. As Szymon sat down his eyes were glued to the train window, awestruck by the magnitude of New York City. It was the largest city he had ever seen. As the train continued into the countryside, the scenery was breathtaking, with its rivers, rolling hills, and picturesque bridges. America, indeed, was a beautiful land, reminiscent of landscape paintings.

Wilkes-Barre was one hundred and fifty miles south of New York City. It took the train five and a half hours to reach his destination. Although he didn't speak much English, Szymon understood the simple terminology railroad personnel used to communicate with him, such as gate numbers or track letters. He had a train schedule which provided town names, as well as, departure and arrival times. With each exposure to the new language it became easier for him to follow verbal instructions. The conductor approached and told him his was the next stop. In Galicia, Szymon spoke Ruthenian, Polish, and a bit of German; he could communicate with Slovakians, as well as, speak a few words in other languages. So, he was not intimidated by the prospect of learning

English. It was three-thirty; he read the schedule and saw that the next stop was Wilkes-Barre. The conductor motioned for him to come to the front of the coach. "Wilkes-Barre!"

Once off the train, Szymon found a policeman who directed him to the address of the Hudson Coal Company's office. Then he left the station and walked up the street. Szymon joined several other single men, immigrants all, who had been recruited in Eastern Europe and brought to Pennsylvania to work in the mines. That night they were told about their jobs. Everyone agreed that the hours were long and the job was hard. In the morning he joined them in the back of a cart pulled by a team of mules for the ride to the mine. Inside the entrance was the small office of Mr. David Llewellyn, the mine's manager. He had arrived from Wales almost thirty years earlier. Grimy characters with blackened faces stood awaiting the new arrivals. One of them, Thomas Bowles, took over the new recruits. "No time will be wasted filling out paper work. You do that on your own time."

They followed Bowles to a bank of lockers where he distributed a pick ax, work clothes, a cap, an oil lamp, and gum boots for each man. "You are responsible for charges for the equipment. Change your clothes and get to work.

They rode in an elevator that seemed more like a cage, down 349 feet into the bowels of the earth. Szymon stepped off the elevator onto a dirty gangway which led to a dusty, noisy world of hell. The sounds were deafening. He followed along through a maze of narrow passages where a different grimy character greeted him with a grunt, then turned to yet another grimy character. They spoke in raspy, loud voices, in a language Szymon didn't understand. "What's this?" Szymon wondered.

The men were led farther through the dark, the only light provided by lamps on the miner's hats, toward the noisy center of hell. No one looked up or said anything to him. Szymon was fixated by the eerie shadows in the dim light, until someone yelled, "Get to work, you son of a bitch!"

He joined dozens of men banging away at the walls. Thank God it was cold this deep in the mine. The ceiling was low, water dripped from the walls into a gutter, rendering the floor a dirty slush. The work was monotonous. Hours later, the men took a break. Sitting on the floor of the mine, each man reached for his pail, then greedily devoured his dinner, holding a sandwich in his dirty hands. Looking down the passage, he saw the flickering light of an oil lamp mounted on a miner's cap. It was one of the grimy characters watching them. The man on his right introduced himself as Jacz from Poland.

Just then, Szymon heard an explosion that caused him to jump. "Don't worry," reassured Jacz; they're just blasting out a new breast. We'll probably be working there tomorrow." Minutes later, the men were on their feet, pickaxes in hand, pulling out coal which dropped around their feet. Szymon heard the muffled sound of hooves going past him. He glanced back to see a wagon pulled by a team of mules. The boss man blew a whistle; everyone stopped, and then began loading the coal into the cart. Before the mules pulled away, Jasz told him to only load small to medium sized chunks of coal, showing him the correct size. When the first wagon pulled away, another came along side to take its place.

The hours ticked by, but the day was long and Szymon was hungry, since he hadn't had anything to eat. When the whistle finally blew, signifying the end of the workday, the men began walking away and Szymon followed.

They reached the lockers, but he couldn't remember if he had stored anything in one of them. He started walking away when Jasz pulled on his arm. "Get your stuff." Szymon shook his head, too tired to think straight. He had worn his own clothes in the mine, only changing his shoes for boots. Jasz pointed out to him the locker in which he had placed his shoes.

On their way to the elevator, Jasz told him not to forget to pick up his lunch for the next day. They rode in a cart to a big rooming house, where Szymon was assigned a bed. Then he proceeded to a room where twenty or so men sat eating. Szymon sat next to a man named Joe who told him that he also was from Galicia. Szymon spoke to him in Ruthenian. "Where do I buy a pail and sandwich for tomorrow?" Joe told him that the kitchen would have a lunch for him in the morning. He followed along with whatever the others did that evening, which meant that he washed his face, arms, and upper body in a basin, found his bed and laid down. The next morning, he did not remember having fallen asleep.

Szymon arose and joined the other men in the kitchen eating a breakfast of hot cereal, scrambled eggs, bacon, and bread. Jasz joined him after breakfast, queueing up to pick up their dinner pails. On the walk to the mine, Szymon remembered that he hadn't begun filling out the forms Bowles gave him. Sure enough, as soon as he arrived at the mine office, he saw that the completed forms were being collected. "I'll have mine for you tomorrow."

The work day began the same as the previous one. Jasz was right; Bowles led the men to a new passage. Aside from being moved to a new part of the mine, they would start preparing the breast by drilling holes, inserting dynamite, and setting off the charges. There were two teams of miners and helpers. Alongside him and Jasz were Mraz and Tymko, both certified miners. The two certified miners consulted with each other on where to drill the holes so as not to endanger the supports and beams when the dynamite was detonated. A two-year apprenticeship trained new miners how to work safely, as well as, where and how many holes to drill in the breast to accommodate dynamite charges. They learned how to build supports and did other carpentry. Lastly, they learned first aid to save lives.

It went on this way for four months, until one day a grimy man came over to him and tapped him on the shoulder. "Swaczy, c'mon with me."

Bowles took him up the elevator to the breaker. Szymon's new job was washing coal, breaking the bigger pieces into smaller chunks. This job was not as hard on the back because he could stand up straight. Szymon didn't have to wear his canvas hat with the oil lamp. He hated the damned thing and thought it was dangerous because the open flame could cause an explosion. Szymon's job changed again before the day was over. Szymon heard the whistle and wanted to leave, but the boss told him to come in on Sunday. He started to say that he was supposed to work only six days a week, but decided to remain silent as the extra earnings would pay for his food, and maybe more. However, the company cheated him out of part of the pay he was supposed to receive. He was mad as hell, but again kept his mouth shut.

Szymon was moved back into the mine a few days later. The men greeted him like a hero. When he didn't understand why, everyone laughed. It was Jacz who explained. "You thought you were getting one up on us, but everybody gets yanked around like that. They cheat us all the time on our pay, our oil work clothes, our gum boots, everything!"

When Szymon returned to working six days a week, he was on track to become a certified miner which would mean a substantial increase in pay after two years. He also started going to church on Sundays. He was accustomed to a six-day work schedule, because he had worked six days a week in Lwow. Working in the mines was, by far, the hardest work he had ever done. He gradually adjusted to it, yet it still didn't feel normal to him. At thirty-seven he was still young enough to perform such tasking work. Older miners couldn't keep up the same pace for long before they either switched to easier, but lower wage jobs, or retired from mining altogether. Many older men worked as breaker boys making the same pay as the young boys who barely scraped by.

He sat in St. Mary's Church, which was the same name as his church in Bukaczowce. Sitting in the familiar setting, observing the rites and rituals comforted him. He had to admit, that attending church made a difference. After church he returned to the boarding house and was about to eat supper when he heard a commotion outside. One of his fellow employees ran into the building yelling, "Cave in! Cave in!"

Everyone cleared out, running in the direction of the mine. The men congregated around the mine shaft near where Szymon worked. Information was scarce; all anyone knew was the entrance to the shaft was blocked and the airway was in danger. No one knew how many men were trapped. The men standing by the entrance were grim and white faced. "It could have been me." was a frequently repeated statement. The night grew late, and although there was no news about the trapped miners, the other men stood vigil in the dark. Someone built a bonfire away from the mine entrance, so they could slip away to warm their faces and hands. A trickle of news emerged from the office; it wasn't particularly good news. A crew was tunneling through the airway where the cave-in happened, but it was slow work with picks, shovels, and axes, so it would take precious time to reach the miners. Llewellyn came outside to address the men. There had been four men working in a breast a few hundred yards from the airway entrance. Llewellyn told them that they would be working throughout the night. "Go home, men, it will be tomorrow before we know more."

"Can you hear voices?" No one answered. "Son of a bitch! You treat us like dogs."

When the crew made it to the mine in the morning, the scene was eerily quiet. No one was around. Szymon climbed down from the cart and walked to the mine office along with the other men. Llewllyn walked out and simply told them that the situation was hopeless. "We'll continue to dig, but no one will be alive." Several men crossed themselves. No one said a word.

The entrance to the breast had caved in trapping the miners. Szymon's stomach churned. "Those men could still be alive." No one answered him. Szymon thought the other miners must know something he didn't. No one brought up the subject again that day. Szymon couldn't eat lunch. At the end of the day, Jasz walked alongside him. "You have to get used to it, Szymon."

December was a bad month for accidents in the mines in Eastern Pennsylvania. Two breaker boys were injured. One lost his arm when his hand got caught in the mechanism that smashed the coal into smaller pieces; the other boy slipped and fell from the breaker smashing his skull. A runaway mule ran over two miners breaking their legs. And a support beam gave way falling on a miner working in the same area as Szymon. Even one of the grimy men injured himself slipping on the wet floors off the passage near Szymon's crew.

"Oh, my God," Szymon exclaimed. "It really could have been me. That's the way it is."

Szymon wrote letters to Barbara, but he knew his father would have to read them to her. His father wrote back lengthy letters about what the family was doing so that Szymon might sometimes feel as though he were at home. In the letters between Szymon and his father, he never mentioned accidents or serious mishaps. If his family knew how dangerous his work was, he could not imagine how it would affect them— particularly his sensitive boy, Piotr. The only reason anyone would want to work in these mines was to support a family, if no other decent paying jobs were available. After the accidents, Szymon found it difficult to think about anything but home.

The calendar was about to change over to the year 1907. He had been working in the mine for almost one year. Occasionally, Szymon socialized with a couple of Polish men who were married and whose families lived in Galicia. During the holidays they reminisced about Christmas celebrations in Galicia, contrasting them to the way Americans celebrated. It reminded him of the year he spent in Pljevlja, when he was in the Austrian army, many years ago. Maybe Americans celebrate Christmas like Poles and Germans, he theorized. Szymon missed his family more during the holidays. He hoped that Barbara and his father could spare some money to buy each boy a gift for St. Nicholas Day.

The next time the miners had an opportunity to go to the tavern, Szymon joined them, but he drank too much. When he got back to the boarding house he was very drunk. He hadn't gone to church that day and was already feeling guilty about his choice to spend money in the tavern. "Drinking has gotten me in trouble before, so maybe I should stay sober. It's too easy to get hurt in this kind of work."

As if to hammer the point home, one of his drinking friends was seriously injured in a freak accident. The man had stumbled and fallen in the path of a team of runaway mules hauling coal from one of the breasts near the shaft opening. The injury crushed his right foot, ending his ability to work. Szymon wondered if perhaps the man had been hungover from the night before. He resolved not to spend money on booze, and didn't go to the taverns for the next four months.

There was talk of a work stoppage. Szymon hoped that a strike could be averted, for as much as he disliked the nature of the work, he very much wanted to earn money to send to his family. Workers in the mines in the United States were unionized. At first, the thought of working under union rules mystified him. He could not believe that miners would unite and stand firm against the mine operators and owners. The only time he could remember anything similar to this, was in Lwow when the Ruthenian Council called a general strike in the construction industry in an attempt to pressure company owners to increase wages. In the end, the workers gained very little for their efforts. Construction workers did not receive a wage increase; he reasoned that the companies thought that minimally improving social unrest should be enough to dampen legitimate worker demands for higher pay. Here in the U. S. in 1907, companies could never get away with that.

What made the mines unsafe was the potential for natural gases to build up hundreds of feet below the surface and explode. However, miners understood that the owners could do very little to protect them from such explosions. Nonetheless, miners organized, mine safety became cause for striking, and safety precautions generally improved.

Szymon bought a calendar which he put up on the wall next to his bed. He marked it with the dates of his sons' and Barbara's birthdays, as well as, special days such as St. Nicholas Day and Resurrection Day. One Sunday after church, he lay down on his bed to rest because he felt ill due to an outbreak of influenza. He glanced up to see the calendar and remembered that it was already nearing the birthday of his premature, stillborn daughter, Katarzyna. Although she was stillborn, Barbara wanted to have her baptized. She would have been one-year-old. His mind wandered and he thought he would buy each son a small gift and mail it to Bukaczowce in time for

Christmas. He was homesick and feeling sentimental, so wanted to do something for his family. Some of the men who worked in the coal mines owned yoyos, and were very good at showing off their prowess, performing tricks and challenging other miners to yoyo duels. The man who had the bed next to his walked by and Szymon asked him whether the company store sold them and how much they charged. He was told not to buy yoyos at the company store because he could get them for only ten cents each from someone who was selling them. Then the man asked Szymon if he'd like to see a yoyo tournament.

The next Sunday afternoon, a dozen men met the challenge by paying ten cents each to enter the contest to see who could perform the most tricks. Many were eliminated by the second round, and soon only two men remained. The match went on for another hour, until finally there was a winner. It seemed the man who won could do whatever he wanted with his yoyo. He performed all the usual tricks—like walking the dog, putting the yoyo to sleep, and more—but for his best trick he stood on his head and operated four yoyos at one time. He deserved the prize. The miner who organized the event ceremoniously presented the dollar and twenty cents prize while the other miners cheered and whooped. Jasz and Szymon walked together to the boarding house where Szymon gave his friend money for four yoyos for his sons.

The following day, he went to the company store

where he found a Christmas card for Barbara with a pretty winter scene on the front, along with a prayer card for his father from St. Mary's Church. Inside Barbara's card, he enclosed several Polish coins he had found in his pockets the day he landed in America. Perhaps, she could buy some ribbons for her hair. Then, he took the package to the post office.

Szymon told Jasz that he had to meet this guy for a wrestling match and invited him to meet him at the hall where wrestling matches were held. Szymon got the crap beaten out of him.

"Are you ok?"

Szymon could barely speak; his mouth was swollen and sore, and his lip cracked due to the pounding his head had taken during the match. It was fair game to put the opponent in an arm lock from behind and pound his head on the stations on which the rope was attached. But beating Szymon seemed to mellow the tough guy who became genuinely friendly with him after that day.

Chapter 23

On December 6, 1907 in Monongah, West Virginia, the worst coal mine disaster in American history killed three hundred and sixty-two men. Not only was it a great tragedy; but it also raised questions on ethics.

Thursday, December 19th, 1907 was a dismal, rainy day. It had been thirteen days since the Monongah mining accident. Word spread quickly that another two hundred and thirty-nine miners lost their lives in D'Arr, in Western Pennsylvania. Six hundred and one men and boys had perished in the two incidents. In addition to these deaths were thirty-five more that resulted from an explosion in the Naomi mine located near Jacob's Creek in Mount Pleasant, Pennsylvania earlier that month. That brought the total number of deaths in one small corner of coal country to 636 miners.

Szymon did not mention this in his letter to Roman. It was almost too much to bear. The men Szymon worked with were thunderstruck by the magnitude of the loss just before Christmas. Everyone

Szymon knew crowded into St. Mary's Greek Catholic Church. The Memorial service was somber. Grown men cried openly, unashamedly. Szymon was unable to sleep that night. He began to worry about how Barbara could possibly manage if he couldn't work. She wasn't young and pretty anymore. He wondered who would want to take on four growing boys as part of a marital arrangement. If something happened to him tomorrow, all the money he had saved amounted to less than one hundred and fifty dollars. Maybe he could save another hundred dollars. Szymon could not know that all the men working in Pennsylvania mines suffered similar nights, lying awake frightened about what the future might hold for them and their families.

He wanted to make more money, but his only chance would be when he received his accreditation as a certified miner and began receiving a miner's pay. Miner's helper pay was significantly less than that of an accredited miner. He went to talk to Llewellyn and was told it would take another year.

It was the beginning of his third year in America, 1908, and at last, he had become an accredited miner, having completed the two-year requirement and passed the oral test for accreditation. At last he was making miner's wages, but still he felt unsettled. He hated to admit it, but he was homesick; he wanted to see Barbara and his sons. Although he liked living in America, and could not fathom what life was like in Galicia now, Szymon decided to return. He went to the Barbarossa office on his first day off.

With his passport in hand, he talked to the representative about the details of traveling back to Galicia, and learned that he would require more money. Szymon calculated that he could save five dollars every two weeks, but that would only amount to one hundred and thirty dollars by year's end. His savings certainly didn't amount to much, but he was also contributing monthly to Barbara and his father. He realized that if he hoped to save more, he couldn't continue to patronize the taverns.

Back home in Galicia, Roman was experiencing increasing difficulty with heart palpitations, but despite his poor health Roman continued to work as a laborer on a dairy farm. He had started taking a new medication, but it wasn't doing much good. Since there really wasn't much that could be done to help people with heart conditions, usually home remedies for relief were exchanged.

Szymon spoke with a traveling, herbal medicine man in Pennsylvania. Chamomile tea was purported to be the latest cure-all in America, so Szymon bought two boxes; he sent one home to his father and the other box to Father Joe Korlaszcz. Of course, it didn't help.

For her part, Barbara kept up her responsibilities without complaint. At forty-one years old she didn't question the vagaries of life; she accepted what life dealt her. Jan, soon to be 14 years old, helped his mother and grandfather as much as he was able. He had completed four grades of schooling, despite missing out on so much learning during the years his family traveled from town to town while Szymon looked for work. When the family returned to Bukaczowce he picked up his studies where he had left off. He was a bright young man who caught up to grade level within one year. His mother encouraged him to go to school because she knew that life was uncertain and his education could be interrupted at any time by serious illness, his family's need for him to work, or even war. But Jan was eager to work because he was a mature, conscientious lad. He could read and write and often wrote a short letter to his father, tucking it into Roman's envelope before it was sealed. Now and then, Szymon would send back a short note to his son.

What most bothered the family was lack of money—not much was available for extras. Barbara had no money to buy new clothing for herself or her sons. Usually, she scoured the bins of used clothing at the Thursday fair. The boys were growing and although they were small in stature, every year they needed new jackets, shoes, boots and, at least, one new pair of pants and a shirt each. So, she continued to bake and sell her goods at the weekly fair. She began sewing again, although she had stopped sewing and embroidering altogether for the two years after returning to Bukaczowce, due to her ill health. Now that her youngest son, Michael, was five years old, it had been easier to take up her projects in earnest.

She found her bag with unfinished sewing projects, smiling to herself when she found her vyshevenka. She stared at it, pleased with herself. She had kept the white linen shirt that she wanted to cut down for a customer while she was living in Lwow. She would need a thread to embroider the collar and cuffs, determining she would search for it at the fair on Thursday. Suddenly, she felt a burst of optimism— maybe, just maybe, she could finish and sell it – tempered by the reality that people in Bukaczowce didn't have a lot of extra money to buy fancy clothing.

Her memories of life in Lwow surfaced now and then. Lwow was only sixty-five miles to the north, but it may as well have been on the moon. During the years they had lived in Lwow, while she was giving birth to her children, every apartment they rented had access to electricity, running water, and an indoor toilet. The same could not be said for dwellings in any direction within a few miles of Bukaczowce. Her life in Lwow was long ago.

Barbara stopped daydreaming and returned her thoughts to working on the vyshevenka. If she couldn't rework the white linen shirt, she would have to buy some linen material. She would also need a sewing machine. She wondered how she would be able to do that. She gathered the pieces of the garment and sat at the kitchen table. At that very moment, she heard a wagon turning off the road onto the property.

She went to the door, and opened it in time to see Max and Katarzyna climbing down from their wagon, calling out a cheery hello. She loved seeing them because they always seemed happy to see her. After pleasantries, Aunt Katarzyna asked her what she was doing. Barbara responded, "Daydreaming! I just found my sewing projects."

Katarzyna immediately liked what she saw. "Are you working on the shirt now?" Barbara explained that she hadn't accomplished anything during the past two years, but wanted to begin again. Katarzyna picked up the garment to examine it closely. "Oh, my, it's lovely! It's lovely! You do such beautiful work. Where is your sewing machine? Did you sell it?" Barbara laughed, explaining that she had never owned a sewing machine but wished she had. "Well then, dear, use mine." Barbara was speechless. Aunt Katarzyna's offer took her breath away. "Oh, don't be silly, of course you can use it. I haven't sewn in over a year."

Barbara began talking all in a rush. "I planned to look for embroidery thread at the fair this Thursday. I hoped to begin working on the shirt this coming week." She couldn't wait to share her good news. So, when Roman came home that evening, she was so happy that she babbled on and on.

Life had settled into a familiar and relatively comfortable routine for both Szymon living in America and Barbara and the boys in Galicia. Aside from money being in short supply, they were healthy.

Szymon, wanting to save as much money as he could in order to invest his savings in land back home, had stopped drinking. He realized he wasn't missing out on much: a lot of time and money were wasted on drink in taverns. He didn't hide from his decision to quit drinking, even though he was often teased by his co-workers. Szymon also considered having his family join him in America but didn't have a firm plan yet. He was satisfied living in Wilkes-Barre, but wasn't certain whether his family would like it. He had heard good things about the mines in Western Pennsylvania and wanted to travel out to see some of the coal mining towns before reaching a conclusion.

After mass one Sunday in February, Szymon joined Jacz at a tavern. The Polish tough guy was there and invited Szymon to wrestle after dinner. Wrestling didn't interest Szymon, but he didn't want to appear to be weak. "How about we wrestle next time?" Two other men stepped up and Szymon watched more carefully than he had done in the past. He resigned himself to a dual with the tough Pole. As Szymon walked back to the boarding house with Jasz, one or two other men kept up the harassment.

Szymon asked them to stop, but they continued, especially the Polish ones. Known bullies, they were always trying to prove their masculinity by egging someone on until he relented. Usually, the matter was settled in the boxing ring. Szymon wasn't particularly tall, but he was strong for his size. So, he believed he stood a better chance of making it to the end of a boxing match, than a wrestling match.

When Szymon had enough, he told his tormentor to meet him in the tavern and bring boxing gloves. For a couple of weeks Szymon had been mulling over whether he had a reasonable chance to beat him. Word spread that Szymon had challenged the big mouth. There were strict rules on how the match would commence. Szymon held his own, but he looked like hell after going the full fifteen rounds in the ring. When the fight was over, Szymon shook his opponent's outstretched, gloved hand. Szymon knew that he had fought a fair fight and given the guy a good thrashing. What is more, the harassment soon stopped. There was nothing better than to stand up to a bully and to win the respect of the Polish miners.

As spring approached, the Polish miners planned to roast a pig and invited Szymon. Back home, there were always reasons to have a party, and those men who had settled in the towns around the mines, carried on the traditional celebrations of their homelands. It took some time but, eventually each man met miners who had lived in his hometown or attended the same church he had, and Jasz knew many more people than Szymon did because he was Polish. So, on a beautiful, warm, spring, Sunday afternoon, a large group of men came together in the back of the Catholic Church for the pig roast. There were mugs of beer to wash down the pork sandwiches. One of the men baked a huge pot of beans and another prepared a potato salad. Everyone got drunk and staggered back to the boarding house, happily singing familiar Polish drinking songs.

Jasz invited Marty McDonnell, whom Szymon and Jasz had met in a local tavern, to the pig roast. Marty was related to the owners of several mines in and around Lucerne. He was a likable fellow, who didn't set himself above the immigrant miners. From time to time, Marty would invite a few of the miners to go for a ride in his Tin Lizzie to Wilkes-Barre on a Sunday morning. Szymon and Jasz were invited to ride along with Marty McDonnell to Wilkes-Barre the day of the pig roast.

A few months earlier, on November first, McDonnell had also invited Szymon and Jasz to ride along with him. The day was overcast but mild for the time of the year. Marty usually took the direct route to Wilkes-Barre, but on this occasion, he took a back road which was only five-and-one-half miles from the mine. It was a mistake. The road was rough and full of twists and curves, but the Tin Lizzie chugged along until they got to a steep hill. Marty seemed unconcerned until the vehicle slowed to less than five miles per hour, began sputtering and appeared about to stall. Marty remembered that he hadn't filled the gas tank and suspected that they wouldn't be able to drive forward up the hill because Ford hadn't developed a fuel pump for the Model T. Rather, gravity-fed gas to the carburetor. Marty stopped, laughing at Szymon and Jasz, he waved off their concerns.

"Don't worry, I'll back up the hill."

Jasz asked Marty if he had backed up a hill before. Marty tried to turn around, but his front wheel went off the road bed. He could move no further. They all got out of the vehicle. Jasz determined there wasn't enough room to make the turn. "Maybe we should push it." But Marty suggested they carry it. So, they lifted the car, turned it around, and placed it back in the middle of the road. Then, Marty tried to put the car in reverse, but that didn't work either. So, after another half hour of trying to get the car into reverse, Marty suggested they return to the tavern near the mine. After two beers, their plan was completely forgotten.

The next morning, Szymon had a headache. He could have kicked himself for one too many beers, but when he thought about the trip with Marty in his new Tin Lizzie, he began laughing. A five-mile trip took over two hours and, not only did they have to carry the car, but they had to find a farmer to tow the thing. Marty probably wouldn't appreciate it if he knew Szymon was spreading the story of and laughing about, their adventure, but Szymon couldn't resist writing about it to Roman and his family. Every time he thought about carrying the car and turning it in the opposite direction from where they were headed, he would laugh out loud all over again. It was the funniest and one of his fondest memories of living in America.

As the end of 1908 approached, Szymon missed his family terribly and wanted to see them. Although he liked living in America, he could neither imagine remaining there alone, nor what it would be like to return to life in Galicia. He would awaken at night thinking about this dilemma. Ultimately, he decided to go back home. He was contemplating the best time to leave, when, later that day, he stopped by the post office to find that letters had arrived from his father and Jan. Roman wrote that everyone was well, and everything was about the same as it had been for months, except for his grandson who would turn fourteen years old in May. Jan worked at the farm and was beginning to run around with some older boys who were teaching him bad habits. Roman reassured Szymon that Jan was a good boy, but didn't want him to get out of hand. He wanted him to be an obedient child.

Szymon was still satisfied to live in Wilkes-Barre but wasn't certain whether his family would like it. He had heard good things about the mines in Western Pennsylvania. So, as he was riding back to the boarding house with Marty McDonnel in his Tin Lizzie, he asked Marty if he had ever driven out to Western Pennsylvania. Marty said that it was a long ride – more than 300 miles—requiring several days of driving, and that there were steep hills between Wilkes-Barre and Western Pennsylvania. Marty also expressed concern that if the automobile broke down, it would be difficult to get it back to Wilkes-Barre. Szymon got the impression that he had lost interest in driving the automobile, and he couldn't quite believe that people would want to spend a lot of money on a car that wasn't a reliable vehicle. "I guess it is only good for taking rides around here," Szymon sarcastically responded. Recalling the incident later, he was embarrassed that he had put Marty on the spot. But Marty didn't appear to be offended by the remark, because he asked Szymon to ride out to Luzerne the next Sunday. Szymon told Marty that he had to meet this guy for a wrestling match and invited McDonnell to meet him at the hall where wrestling matches were held. Szymon was shocked: the tough guy didn't show up. His fellow miners slapped him on the back and sang the Polish equivalent of, 'For He's a Jolly Good Fellow'!

Around the middle of January Szymon got out his cardboard suitcase and packed his few articles of clothing. He didn't have much but would take everything he owned with him, including the good shoes he had bought. When he arrived in Galicia, it would be cold so, he would take his long coat, as well. That afternoon, he went to a barber and had his haircut. He was excited about leaving and going home, for he genuinely missed his family.

Szymon received a huge shock the next morning. He was at his locker, getting his work clothes, when Bowles called to him. He was standing by the bank of lockers. He asked Szymon to go to the office after he finished his shift that day.

"What is this about?"

"We are making some changes and we want to talk to you about moving to another location."

Szymon nodded slowly, wondering what this meant.

"But I have a contract."

"We know. Don't mention this to the others."

All that day, Szymon played different scenarios in his head. He felt that he had heard this line before, like the time that Bowles put him on the breaker, washing and sorting the big chunks of coal. He had learned not to trust anything that Bowles or anyone else in management said. "What the hell are they up to this time?"

That afternoon, he met Bowles and was told that he would be working in Scranton when he returned. "Do I have a say in the matter?" asked Szymon.

Bowles seemed disturbed by his remark. Szymon softened slightly. "I'll think about it. Let me think about it."

After supper, he took a walk. It was a cold evening, but he wanted to be alone so he could think. In the end, he decided to tell Bowles that he would not be returning. He offered no explanation and felt that he didn't owe the company anything. Bowles thought otherwise. "Look here, Szymon, we trained you and you have a certificate of accreditation."

Szymon stopped, and looked directly into Bowles' eyes. "I have been a good employee. I earned every penny that I got. I could have been killed in this god damned mine, you bastard!" He continued to stare at Bowles, who turned his head without responding, but Szymon wasn't done. "I didn't say anything to anybody about this, and I prefer that you do not discuss our conversation with the men before I leave." Bowles turned and walked away. "Take your job and shove it up your ass! Asshole!"

On the walk back to the boarding house, Szymon made another decision. He would not return to Wilkes-Barre, but would go out to Western Pennsylvania. Later that evening, Szymon checked his wallet and the calendar to see when he would leave from Bremen.

Meanwhile, in Bukaczowce, Barbara had found a sale on embroidery thread and bought enough to stitch several vyshevenka. She began by embroidering some lady's handkerchiefs and vests, and she had half a dozen of each ready to sell at the next fair. Katarzyna met her on Thursday, and was again impressed by her handiwork, as well as, her drive and perseverance. Aside from the handkerchiefs, there were several dozen coffee cakes and loaves of bread for sale. They were all gone within two hours of setting up her table. Roman was also impressed. Barbara was extremely pleased. "I want to save for coats for the boys, but since Szymon is coming home, I also want to prepare some of his favorite special meals. But I don't know whether I'll be able to do both. Money is always scarce, but at least, things are better."

She missed Szymon and would be happy to have him home. Sudden tears welled up into her eyes. Her harsh memories and the horror of the years they spent traveling from town-to-town, farm-to-farm, along with the deaths of her two daughters crashed down on her unexpectedly. "Why is this always so hard to bear?" But she couldn't cry. She knew in that moment, that the love she shared with Szymon would endure. They shared both good and bad memories and they would spend the rest of their lives together. "I want to be with Szymon. I know I wouldn't be happy without him." Her mind was made up and a feeling of peace washed over her. She had made her decision. Szymon is coming home! She looked up to see Anna standing at her table.

"Barbara, are you feeling alright? You've been crying."

"I know."

"Can I do anything to help? You have been through so much and you are such a dear, brave person. If I can ever help you, please let me know."

Barbara was oblivious to her surroundings. It was the first time that she had felt this strong bond with her sister-in-law. Barbara finally had a sister, someone to whom she truly could confide in, revealing her deepest secrets. Anna was true to her word and sought her out whenever she went to the Thursday fair. Sometimes, she came to inspect the latest embroidered scarf or handkerchief that Barbara had laid out for sale. Other times, the two sat on chairs Roman always provided for friends, neighbors or tired fair goers. She loved this special time they spent together. Now that Michael was going to school, Anna could sit and drink coffee or juice while the two gossiped. Whenever Barbara began to worry about her family or Roman, she would offer to take one of the boys with her on a shopping expedition or when Uncle Max sent her on errands.

Szymon's last letter stated that he would be arriving around the fifth of February, only two weeks prior to the start of Lent. "It seems so far away..." Barbara sighed wistfully, as her voice trailed off once again…